The Living Light

From Gods To Ashes

The Living Light

From Gods To Ashes

A Rogues of the Outlands Chronicle

By
Taliesin J. De Launey

Alucard Publications™

III of IX

I dedicate this volume to my dear Grandma, Carol Ann De Launey--aka "Nana"--to whom I owe the very faculty of my literacy. It was she who, on the northeastern coast of Australia, in the sweltering heat of Lismore nights (without air-conditioning), excited my imagination by reading me bedtime stories such as *Harry Potter*, *Nine Princes in Amber*, and *The Hobbit*.

I was a late reader and did not enjoy my early years at school, finding no interest in the subjects forced upon me. But once I got a taste for authors I liked, I worked Nana like a slave--with pleading words and persuasive entreaties to "recite just one more chapter!"-- before she was allowed to retire to her bedroom for the night.

However, on days when she refused--or when I had pushed her past the limits of reasonable business hours--and I desperately needed to know *what happened next*, I was forced to pick up the story with my own two hands and read. Eventually, I was reading on my own, devouring my favorite fictions, and Nana? Well, she was called in only for ceremonial occasions.

To my father, Matthew Dent, who has heavily supported my writing in recent years--being one of the first two test readers for this book, and helping me with editing.

To my dear mother, Tanietta De Launey who raised me as a single parent and has always championed my writing career--my first subscriber, and the first to buy every book.

Table of Contents

Prologue

These are the tales of the Old Earth, set in the year 1541 of the Skir Calendar—circa two and a half million years BCE, by current reckoning. The known world and its major powers exist in an age of contentment and complacency. Decadent cultures persist amid the fruits of their forebears' industry and genius.

The physical structures and technological remnants of a long-gone advanced civilization are everywhere. Yet those who might understand or operate such relics no longer exist. *The Ancients—* the greatest minds of that age—disappeared thousands of years ago, their societies undone by a strange and unknown event. Few who now inhabit their crumbling cities could replicate such works, nor even grasp the principles behind the crudest technologies they've inherited. The relics of the Ancients litter the avenues, gather dust and cobwebs in dark corners, or rust in heaps across plazas, patios, and rooftop terraces.

Prophecies of long-forgotten gods still rumble through the land —and, like whispers on an evil wind, weigh heavily on the minds of a largely uneducated, and thus deeply superstitious, race of men.

Who were the Ancients? Where did they go? What was the Cosmic Ruination they sought to avoid—and what brought about their own untimely end? This is a task for the brave and the willing to uncover. The answer lies not within the walled cities of man... but out there, in *the Outlands*.

Chapter 1
"An offense of Apple Portions ."

A sheer sandstone cliff, carved as if by the stroke of a gigantic blade, rose skyward against a backdrop of blasted earth and jagged, tangled crags.

Along a narrow ledge that clung precariously to the cliff face, a lone girl ran—swiftly, desperately, as fast as her legs would carry her. Her breath came in gasps as she leapt over boulders and scattered debris with the lithe agility of a trained athlete. Her chest heaved beneath a loose white blouse with cut-off sleeves, and her baggy, knee-length dark-red breeches billowed like pantaloons as she moved.

In the west, the sun spilled golden fire across the crags, painting the landscape in a hellish blood-orange. All around her, shadows stretched—like the fingers of some gigantic, malicious shade.

Leaping over a particularly large crevice, she raised her fist mid-air and shook it above her head.

"Take that, you *creeps!*"

Landing in a crouch, she flicked a quick glance behind her. Nothing.

No... *there.*

At the bend in the trail, an ungainly silhouette had lurched into sight.

"What the *hell* are those things?!" she hissed to herself, before dashing onward.

Her strong legs carried her quickly around three more bends—then she found herself staring down a gaping black tunnel that had appeared on her left, which continued into the murk without seeming end.

As she gazed, a hulking shadow separated from the inky darkness at the edge of her vision—something had been lying completely still against the tunnel's wall.

She turned.

To say that the girl screamed would do her hardened spirit injustice, but she did let out a grunt of surprise. Then a weighted net enveloped her, and she fell—struggling and cursing—to the tunnel floor.

A weighty object collided with her head, bringing an explosion of blinding white stars to her inner eye—and then, blackness.

Now all was quiet in the tunnel, save for the sound of a steady, regular dragging.

As of a burden tied to a rope.

Or a human body in a heavy, weighted net.

***

Three weeks later... west of the city of Revilis Ko'hur, *somewhere in the Outlands...*

Brand, a tall, lean youth of only nineteen winters, walked westward along a lonely trail that wound steadily through a landscape of sparsely forested hills and craggy outcrops. The view to the north was obscured by a steep rise covered in thick clumps of pine and oak.

To the south lay a green-and-brown canvas of plains and scattered woodland, occasionally carved by dark lakes and winding rivers. Far beyond this stretched the bright blue Trade Sea, resting in the bosom of an even brighter blue horizon.

The harsh rays of a blistering afternoon sun beat down from above, and the trail seemed to wind on endlessly ahead.

Brand was now desperately fatigued, and his normally jaunty, shoulder-length blond hair spiked out in gritty knots like some diseased sunflower. His clear green eyes were dulled into murky, poisonous pools, and his once-handsome, aristocratic features were set in a perpetual scowl.

Such hardship was unknown to Brand, for he had grown up in Drifts End, the outer city of Revilis Ko'hur, which Brand considered the "pinnacle of civilization" in this day and age. Like many youths from the poorer districts, he was unconsciously drawn toward glamour and conducted himself with an educated air—a paper-thin façade of false nobility. He had survived the streets by dint of his wit and cunning, *and* his agile feet, but none of this had prepared him for the uncanny trap set for him by his own king, Ezeret the Mad, who ruled over Revilis Ko'hur.

After making acquaintances with a particularly short-tempered outlander—who had helped him out of a sticky situation—Brand and his newfound companion had been lured into the king's tower with promises of a lucrative reward. However, instead of the stated task of rescuing a noble's sweetheart, the king coerced Brand and his outlander companion into a quest into the *Outlands*—something Brand would never have agreed to—to find an artifact he didn't even believe existed. In fact, he would have turned around at the first sight of foreign, possibly bandit-laden hills three weeks ago, had the Mad King not taken his mother hostage as collateral.

Bitter was Brand's luck. Gone were the days of fine clothes and easy dining. Now he wore a rumpled and tattered black coat, brown breeches, and scuffed black boots. At his side hung a simple shortsword, and an old brown pouch holding a map—left to him by Ezeret before sending him westward on his task.

All sources of water Brand and his companion had come upon in the last two days had been putrefied by some unknown agent. Now, dehydration had set in and Brand's mind had begun to wander in a disjointed fashion. He thought of better days—days spent carousing in *"Barthinol's Den,"* his friend's tavern back in *"Drift's End." Back home.*

Beside Brand stalked the *Outlander*—Berengar. Who too lacked his usual conviviality. His long blond hair, normally flowing and gleaming, now hung in matted, lank strands upon his broad shoulders. The sides of his head, once clean-shaven from temple to nape, were now sprouting untidy fuzz. His blue eyes were dimmed and bloodshot from fatigue.

His muscular, tanned chest heaved with rapid breaths, and around his generous lips lay a mask of dried mud and mineral dust, evidence of his recent attempts at drinking from muddy rainwater puddles. Berengar wore only a leather loincloth and carried no more than his great sword upon his back.

Berengar, cresting a rise, let out a hoarse exclamation.

"By *Mackmellah!*"

Brand, used to his large companion's over-enthusiasm, didn't bother to look up.

Berengar glared silently at the youth. Then, With one huge hand, he clasped Brand's head and forced him to look.

"*Ouch!* Damn you!" Brand grunted. But he looked.

Down in a secluded valley stood a small, ramshackle village, nestled against a broad river. The village's northern border was guarded by a looming cliff, its crest draped in trees and tangled shrubbery a hundred feet above.

"An *actual* settlement! *Out here?!*" He said in wonder—he had thought that no human life existed this far west.

The settlement was built atop a vast stone pattern laid into the ground—clearly the work of a far older and more magnificent craftsmanship than that of the crude village structures. As they drew closer, they saw that the pattern was formed of polished stone blocks—some green, some white—sunken deep into the earth so that only their top surfaces remained visible. At its southern edge, the stone pattern jutted out into the river, forming a promenade above the murky water.

As they approached the village, the contrast was even more striking—simple wooden sheds and log cabins, built from rough-hewn timber and tied loosely with coarse twine. Some had thatched roofs; others were topped with crude mud tiles. The windows gaped open, uncovered or screened with woolen rags dyed in earthy tones.

However, to our companions, the strangeness of this village lay not in its crude architecture, nor in its dilapidated and dirty condition, nor even in the ancient pattern beneath it. The true strangeness was that it was completely devoid of motion or life.

Berengar grumbled his suspicions to Brand, who half-heartedly dismissed them and began whistling loudly—much to Berengar's great discomfort.

"Shhh!" hissed Berengar. "I like not this place... There may even be... a *ghost*."

"*Pfah!* Besides, even if there *were* such a thing, if it meant us ill, it would have '*sucked our souls dry*' by now."

The remark, though clearly meant as a joke, did little to reassure Berengar—who, though he feared no man or beast, held a superstitious awe of magic and un-death. He muttered a prayer to Kulzibar, the god said to devour magic and paranormal anomalies, and drew his sword before moving onward.

Sheesh... He actually believes in ghosts? thought Brand.

They reached the center of the village—a kind of market square which, though empty of life, still held stalls and shops stacked with goods, seemingly ready for sale. Brand noticed that many had been left mid-operation, as if abandoned in haste.

Berengar grunted—an inhuman sound—and his stomach rumbled loudly. Brand followed the gaze of his massive companion and saw what had brought the giant to a sudden halt.

Berengar was staring at a wooden wagon overflowing with apples. Many had spilled out and lay strewn around the ground near its wheels. The apples, even at this distance, could be seen to be somewhat past their prime. Forgetting danger in his gigantic thirst, Berengar headed forth and reached the wagon in four long strides.

"Why does it have to be *apples?*" Brand complained, dashing to keep up with the Outlander.

Berengar sniffed the fruit and tasted it, checking for that unusually bitter tang of poison—but found nothing. Brand argued for further investigation, but Berengar ignored him, trusting in his own senses.

Berengar began pounding down rotten apples without discrimination. Further, Brand noticed that the golden-haired giant was eating core, seeds, and all. Sometimes the stem won free and fell to safety; more often it did not.

Brand spied a single worm wriggle-dive to safety and blanched, wondering how many *hadn't* escaped those strong, churning teeth.

Brand was more selective in his choices and managed to salvage four or five apples that were not too bad off. As they ate, their usual humor began to return. Berengar's eyes were less bloodshot and now glowed with a burning vitality. Brand laughed out loud and, as a ray of sun hit his green eyes, it could be seen that they once again glowed with humor and wit.

However, their levity was not meant to last. Brand and Berengar started in horror as the entire village suddenly burst into motion with a rush of clamor and activity.

Villagers carrying crude pickaxes, pitchforks, and rusty swords swarmed out from underneath upended carts, scuttled from inside darkened doorways, burst and slid from curtained windows, and crabbed out sideways from tall grasses. A number of hardy forest veterans appeared on rooftops with hunting bows.

Brand, in a detached manner, observed an old, turkey-necked man burst forth—black-faced—from a soot-filled chimney atop a high rooftop, wielding a dirty broom handle like a weapon. The old creep bared his gums at him grotesquely. Some part of Brand's mind wondered what the man intended to do with the broom handle, and he also felt vaguely affronted by the personal nature of the man's gaze—he was clearly targeting Brand in particular.

Berengar stood stock-still, ready—a deadly, musclebound golem. Brand laid his hand on his friend's shoulder, as a sign for the giant to settle down. There were at least fifty villagers arrayed against them, and a number of them held ranged weapons. Maybe they *could* fight them all and survive, but more likely not. Besides, where was the honor in killing fifty maniacal, starving villagers?

One stepped forth and, swelling with importance, began to lay a number of outlandish accusations at their feet.

"I accuse these two strangers of stealing *my* personal *apples*! Watchman! Give assistance, I have witnesses!"

A man in a crumpled gray uniform and iron breastplate parted his way through the crowd and leveled a dirty spear at Brand's chest.

Again, he was targeting Brand directly and didn't look at Berengar.

"Why pick on *me?*" Brand muttered to himself.

Brand noticed the guard was shaking slightly, and trying NOT to look at Berengar. Brand looked to the Outlander to see what all the fuss was about, and then understood.

Berengar stood with his shoulders hunched forward, massive hands spread wide, fingers clenching and unclenching in an exaggerated wrestler's stance. Muscles rippled visibly beneath the skin of his arms, chest, and even his jaw. His mouth and face were flecked with chunks of rotten apple, and more scraps clung to the hair on his upper chest. His head swayed left and right in great, aggressive sweeps, daring any man to approach. His eyes were wide—too wide—white rings shining around blazing pupils. Yes,

Brand and Berengar would surely die if it came to open conflict, but the villagers' losses would be considerable.

The guard squawked in a breaking voice, "You criminals *stole* from this innocent and peace-loving villager. You will have to be detained and face punishment in the water cage."

"*What?* Over a few rotten apples, and after such trickery?" said Brand with an expression of disbelief. "Berengar, would you *please* stop breathing so loudly? You're stifling my thoughts..."

The guard seemed to take courage from the disparity in numbers and called out, adding an imperious note to his voice, "We were simply on our noonday repose when you two viciously, and with malice aforethought, stole this good man's apples. No; you must face justice. *The water cage!*"

At this, the toothless cove on the rooftop let out a maniacal cackle, cut it short, and then glared directly at Brand with bulging eyes.

Brand found himself somewhat distracted by the nature of the sooty rogue's appearance. With an effort, he disengaged his attention from the old man and looked back at the guard. "Huh?—wait. Is there no other recourse for us?" he said. "*Water cage... what?*"

The militia edged forward, menacing the travelers with their assortment of arms, and Brand grew ever more tense, hoping Berengar could maintain self-restraint.

The guard paused and rubbed his chin for a moment, seeming to ponder a new thought. Then he said, "Well... there may be a small service you could do for the village as penance for your dire crimes..."

Brand looked up, his face creased with worry. Then he said, "I promise no definite action, but... go on. Perhaps you can describe the terms of this small service first, so that I may discuss it with my companion..."

The watchman beckoned them to follow and led the way toward the western part of town. The villagers moved as one, surrounding them with weapons drawn. The man who had accused them of stealing his apples walked beside the watchman at the front and soon began speaking, his back turned toward them.

"You see, apart from being an apple trader, I double as the village chieftain. If you could aid us in a small task, your transgression could be forgiven. Though my apples are my private trade, I am generous and willing to forgive your transgression—should you aid me in my civil duties of caring for this village. It's the least I can do for you." He looked back and gave them a sly wink. Then, not waiting for a reply, went on, "Some months ago, this village and its surrounding lands became afflicted with a strange curse. The water sources either dried up or became dark and putrid, spoiled and corrupt. Undrinkable. Even the large river yonder is murky and pestilent. The wildlife moved off or disappeared, and crops withered under the polluted water, refusing to grow. The villagers suffer now from famine. Brigands guard the passes in either direction, and relocation would have been a fatal endeavor. We have tried to find a solution and eke out an existence here, but alas, as you can see, we are now half-mad with malnutrition and dehydration. Flight to a new home at this stage is ever more unrealistic."

Brand wondered at the truth of these words. There was something funny about the man's eyes, and they had seen no bandits when he and Berengar had traveled through the eastern passes.

Presently, the party arrived at a point in the great stone pattern that had not been covered by huts or houses. The polished white and green slabs spread out in front of them. The village chieftain and the town watchman stepped to the side and indicated a gap in the pattern. The villagers pressed in on all sides with their weapons drawn, forcing Brand and Berengar to crowd close.

"This is 'The Jade Pit,'" said the chieftain, indicating the gap.

Brand cautiously edged forward and peered down. It was a structured shaft, three feet by three feet wide, and ran about twenty-five feet down. The walls were large slabs of polished green stone.

The floor was likewise green stone, and covered in detritus and ancient stains. A waft of compost, and a strange fishy smell rose from the shaft on a warm current. Brand reeled back in disgust and said, "The odor is somewhat disagreeable."

"Understandably," said the village chieftain with candor. "This is where we dispose of all the village wastes. It has been our practice since the beginning."

Brand pinched his nose. "Strange... I see no affluent pile accruing down there... Where does the waste go?"

The elder rubbed his chin and looked dubiously towards the clouds above. "We never thought to investigate further, and would never have, had I not found reason to believe that there is a connection between this tunnel and our current predicament. You see, only five days hence, I was exploring a dried-up pond on the northern side of yonder hill and, for the first time, encountered a cousin to this tunnel. It was exactly the same in make and structure, only it was clogged with waste and grit."

"Interesting... but is further investigation really necessary?" Brand croaked.

The elder smiled, "we require you to enter the Jade Pit, investigate what is down there, and return with a comprehensive report of the situation."

"Have you not sent any villagers?" inquired Brand hopefully.

"Indeed we have... Demarcus Myor, Angelica Borias, and old Twiskal of the bad knee," answered the chief. "Now we need you and your friend here," he nervously indicated Berengar with a curt nod and quickly looked back to Brand, "... to go, in your own turn, down the Pit."

"*Down the Jade Pit*!" echoed the villagers in a chorus.

"Wait! What happened to those that went before?" said Brand, his face becoming pale, and a rivulet of sweat starting on his temple.

The chieftain spoke in an odd lilting tone. "Best not to ask... No, never mind the past, we are in the 'Now,' my friend. I admonish you to be in the present! Yes, down the Jade Pit you must go."

"*The Jade Pit*!" echoed the villagers once more.

"I do not WISH to enter the Jade Pit!... On... several accounts!" cried Brand. He looked up to Berengar for support.

"Go on, *down the Jade Pit*," echoed Berengar, looking at him with a solemn, almost sympathetic expression.

Brand stared daggers at him, then took a deep breath. "Let me suggest a more profitable course of action. Berengar, you head down first, and, after a time, say ten minutes, you may call out to me and let me know that it is a good time to follow... This will allow you room to breathe, and prevent any accidents, such as me from landing on top of you."

Berengar's face took on a look of bovine obstinance, and he motioned for Brand to go first. "I'll be right here for you," he said.

The village chieftain stared off to the south distractedly. "Watchman, would you say the water cage is emptied of its... last occupants?"

"Yes, my chief, it was emptied just yesterday and is at the ready," replied the guard with froggy fervor.

"Okay! I go." said Brand with great foreboding, his shoulders slumped in resignation.

"Good. I am so glad we are of the same mind," said the chieftain jovially. He motioned for the villagers to handle the affair.

Two burly peasants with wild eyes brought over a winch and

sturdy line. They set it up at the mouth of the pit. Brand readied his weapon in his right hand, and clasped the line with his left. He swung his legs over the edge, and allowed himself to be lowered down into the gloom. His nostrils encountered a thick, piscine fetor, and he sucked in his last breath of clean air. He heard a rumbling chuckle from Berengar above. Brand swore he would return the favor one day.

Brand touched down on the stained stone floor and collected himself with speed. He then readied his sword and looked around. Directly ahead was another gap in the stones, opening into a long, dim tunnel of the same material. Far ahead, at perhaps the other end, seemed to be a dull yellow light. Brand heard a soft swish, and then felt Berengar's strong hand clasp his shoulder.

"Took you long enough, you great ox," Brand hissed.

"You're alive," Berengar noted, in a low boom, quiet but resounding, like distant thunder.

Brand shook his head and walked forward with back erect, not deigning a response. They moved forward on light feet, quiet as a breeze. Their rapid, stealthy strides ate up the distance quickly, and they closed in on the far end of the tunnel. As they approached it, the golden glow resolved into a doorway opening into a larger space. The space was filled with a dim, golden light and a thick profusion of steam, which obscured vision beyond ten paces. The smell was so foul and commanding here that their nostrils burned, and their breaths came in rapid gasps. Each made a sort of bandana out of cloth from their pouches and tied them around their mouths before moving on.

Checking for danger on either side, they emerged silently from the tunnel and moved out into the chamber. What they saw was no less bewildering than what they had seen thus far. The space felt large, but its exact dimensions were obscured by the mist. Light posts glowed dimly in the distance, spreading out to the east, west, and south, their end-points shrouded by the thick, acrid steam. Furthermore, the entire area was oppressed by a low ceiling of roughly seven feet, which lent a feeling of gravity to the dank air as it pressed heavily on their stifled senses. Dark shapes populated the room at regular intervals along with the lights that ran east to west. By looking at a nearby form, Brand could tell that they were support columns. Other strange shapes could be seen within the mist here and there, and Brand noticed a few curious devices embedded into the nearby floor—large circular devices of a strange material that, based on the scuff marks, seemed to be able to rotate.

Berengar moved over to inspect the wall near the tunnel they had just quit. Brand followed close behind, not wishing to be separated. Berengar was sweating profusely by now in the pungent, warm mist, and Brand felt the beginnings of a trickle down his own forehead.

There was a sort of workbench along the wall and Berengar had begun picking up and setting down various contrivances. Looking up, he said, "What do you think of this mummery, wolf? I... Ayaeeet tchkk!!!" He cut off with a yell, recoiling as a shadow rose from his left flank. Blue steel flashed in a crescent arc, and the shadow danced back with a yowl of its own.

"Peeeeeeeaaacccceee!" hissed a strange voice from the mist.

Brand stepped in close on Berengar's left, sword held low in front of him. The shadow resolved into a wiry, man-shaped creature with webbed fingers, slimy grey skin, and a spiny dorsal fin running down its back. Its hands were raised in pleading defense, and its mouth opened wide into a horrific grimace. Blubbery pink lips stretched taut over sharp, needle teeth bristling with saliva. There was a look of urgency in its fishy eyes, set too wide apart on its oval-shaped head. It looked strangely contrite. Brand wondered detachedly: *Was it attempting... a smile?* Then his mind rocked with the reality of what he beheld, and he stared frozen in wonder—a monster!

Berengar didn't. "Die, you filthy spawn of Dioflum!" he screamed as he lunged forward, sword swinging in wild arcs.

"Wait!" called Brand and jumped forward to restrain the giant. All that happened, however, was that Brand was pulled from his feet, and left hanging off Berengar's shoulders like a small child. Fortunately, the creature was fast enough to avoid a few more swings before Brand managed to force Berengar to a halt, by hanging off his head with both hands—one on the windpipe, and the other across the face, with fingers stuffed into his nose and mouth.

Presently, Berengar was panting and still agitated, but had thankfully stopped swinging. "Damnit, Ber, my hand smarts. I believe you bit a chunk out of me." Brand looked down and examined his swollen hand. "I better not contract anything... Hold your strokes; I believe this devilishly ugly creature is trying to parley."

"Have you seen anything as studiously disfigured?" panted Berengar. "The work of a deranged intellect, to be sure. By the devil Dioflum... or if a god made this child, it had an evil sense of humor."

"Must you be so blatantly disgusted? Such comments *smart*! Gwrgl..." said the creature. It had stepped forth from the mist and was now examining its slimy appendages with frank consternation. Its words came in thick gurgles, as if each word was painful to its inhuman throat, and had to bubble its way up through water deep within its chest. It came forward, raising its hands once more, and again attempted its toothy grimace—A mistake.

Brand frowned in disgust and jerked his head back. Berengar, on the other hand, started in shock, and then swung his sword at it, angrily driving it back. Once again, the creature jerked away in fright.   "Don't do... that... whatever that was," said Brand. "Trust me."

"Smile... No gwlgl...?" gurgled the creature.

Brand was now finding it easier to catch the words. "No, just... No," he answered wearily.

The creature looked up at them ingenuously. It was about five feet tall, standing with its feet shoulder-width apart, its hands open wide, and held at its sides like a mannequin. Its fishy eyes looked eager and expectant.

"Look at me like that again, and I will hammer your face into mush, you vile egg-sperm of Utakku!" Berengar said, then raised his blade again.

"Berengar, please!" Brand groaned.

"No threat, no threat." It raised its hands again.

Brand shouldered his way in front of Berengar, and addressed the creature. "What are you doing here? What... are you?"

"I is operator. Operatorrrrr." It still gurgled its words, but Brand could understand them now.

"Ah, operator of... this place? What do you do?"

"I operate the pathways, water, yes? Operate the devices left here in my trust. Passed down from operator to operator since the beginning of time." It gestured to the vague shapes in the mist— the various levers and cylindrical devices.

Brand was shocked at this revelation, but went on. "And... What are you? What's your name?"

"I am man!! No?" It said in agitation, its arms held curiously still, which Brand found uncomfortable.

"No," Brand replied. "No, you're not. Well, what's your name anyway?"

The creature looked down, inspecting its limbs again, obviously unsettled by this comment. Then looking up, it answered, "My name is Parsan the 2387th."

Brand blinked. "That's a long line." Brand could see Berengar in the corner of his eye, counting fingers. Brand gathered his wits. "There's many more questions I have, however I will start with this: What happened to the missing villagers? Demarcus Myor... Angelica Borias, and old... Twiskal?"

"I ate them," replied Parsan matter-of-factly.

This prompted another round of aggression from Berengar, which Brand eventually settled down.

Brand, now sweaty and exhausted, continued his questioning. "*Why* did you eat them? State the facts clearly, for this is a serious offense."

"They small, weak egg brothers... Sacrifices, no? No food scraps from village long time, I starving too. I must keep the waterways flowing for the good of all. When one egg brother needs to be eaten by the stronger egg brother, so that the stronger egg brother can grow, and survive the great pond barrier, the weaker does what he must. It's for the good of the nest after all. No?"

Brand considered this logic. "Your statement touches on an ancient ethical argument, so profound that I cannot contemplate all of its intricacies at this time... However, the following statement, as a practical expedient, must suffice: We do not *wish* to be eaten. If you attempt to eat us, we will *slay you*," he said.

Berengar simply glared in disgust at the creature, muscles tense, grip held tight on his sword hilt.

"Eat *you?!* Noooo!" The creature looked appalled, if that human term could at all be applied to its facial structure. "You are *strong* egg brothers, here to save the great pond! If you are hungry, you eat *me*... But wait... you cannot handle the equipment..." He pondered this new ethical problem, his principles seemingly in conflict. His fishy eyes strained even further apart before reaching their limit, and bouncing back into position as he reached a conclusion. "Well... take er... one arm. It will grow back over the span of about four months..." He held out his right arm expectantly.

Brand blanched, and could hear Berengar gag to his right. "No, we have eaten. I am quite satiated, thank you... Now about the waterways, Parsan. You have been operating them for some time. What has gone so wrong in recent weeks?" Brand continued.

Parsan became animated. "I do know what it isss exactly. I will show you, maybe you strong egg brothers will know... Yes, I'm sure you will know what to do!"

Parsan hunched forward, and powered off in a swift bow-legged gait, arms hanging stiffly by his sides.

Berengar and Brand followed along dubiously at a distance. Parsan's shadowy dorsal fin could be seen indistinctly in the mist ahead of them as he led them swiftly along the eastern wall, before turning into an offshoot tunnel. Parsan followed this for about one hundred paces, before coming to the lip of a circular shaft, projecting out of the wall on their right. It was positioned three feet from the floor and had an opening four feet in diameter. Parsan walked over to it and pointed.

Brand warily peeked into the shaft, and could see it ended in an obstruction about ten feet in. The obstruction was a confused jumble of debris, and an unidentifiable grey spongy substance that looked organic.

"Look, look!" said Parsan excitedly, as he bent down and picked up a long branch, which he must have placed there recently. He inserted the branch into the shaft, and began poking at the grey substance. It quivered eerily, and Brand withdrew in caution. Parsan laughed. "No danger, see..." and continued poking it. "I like to come and do this sometimes. It reminds me of the nest dayssss."

This raised a question Brand had been meaning to ask. "Where is the next Parsan? How do you, you know, come about?"

"I have laid the next sacred egg," he pointed to a side chamber they had passed, "and my successor shall grow under my close tutelage in the ways of the operator..." He finished in reverent tones.

"So you're capable of parthenogenesis?" Brand asked in wonder.

"Indeed, the Great Creator, Mother of the Pond has provided all for us..." Parsan's face took on a look of pure ecstasy.

"We do not make distinction in this regard," purred Parsan, with that same look of pleasure in his distended eyes. "Ah, holy is the continuation of the line..."

Brand felt a growing unease, and decided to interrupt Parsan's maundering. "So how does this blockage affect the water?"

Parsan came out of his reverie and said, "The lower central nexus lies in the chamber beyond. I cannot access it to truly find out. However, this strange blockage here leaves little room for conjecture."

Brand started pacing back and forth, considering a variety of courses of action. The moist, rancid-smelling air made it hard for him to think.

Parsan poked the stick into the tunnel again. Then, he suddenly gasped in surprise and looked down.

"Brand!?" hissed Berengar.

Brand immediately looked up, and saw that an elastic, grey tendril had snapped out of the shaft and attached itself to Parsan's left hip.

Brand and Berengar stumbled back in horror. The tendril jerked Parsan towards the shaft, while at the same time grey material burst out of it, elongating into a large set of grey, amorphous jaws. The substance snapped around Parsan, engulfing him. The horrible mass stretched and pulsed as Parsan struggled within. With a heroic effort, Parsan managed to tear a hole in the stuff, and re-emerge from the mass for a moment.

He called out, "A stronger egg brother takes me... Take the *sacred egg!* You must repair the water w—" His words were cut off as the jaws snapped shut once more. He did not re-emerge.

With sinister deliberation, the grey monstrosity turned its forward node in the direction of Brand and Berengar.

Brand instantly turned, and ran with all the frantic fury of a man activated by desperate, fear-ridden self-preservation. Despite this, Berengar overtook him and crashed past on his right, swearing profusely, before dashing into the side room Parsan had indicated.

"*Run!!*" Berengar bellowed, charging back out with a large, green-grey egg under his arm.

The sight of Berengar running away at a thunderous pace spurred Brand on to even greater efforts—*he didn't want to be left behind with that thing*! Despite his fear, he couldn't help but spare a glance backward as he ran.

The grey mass was enlarging as it spilled out into the corridor behind them. To Brand's horror, it transformed into the general shape of Parsan's head, gaping needle teeth and all—only giant, grey, and lacking emotion. He watched it as it continued to expand and then begin to form odd appendages. There was a lack of orderly design in its vacillating structure, and Brand watched in awe as limbs of all shapes and kinds formed to propel it forward, only to dissolve a moment later, then reform once more as was advantageous to motion. Taloned and webbed hands raked the floor, scaly legs kicked, whirling tentacles slithered, strange hammerhead proboscises battered at the walls to push it in his direction. On it came. A maelstrom of grey flesh and sucking, rending, mouths.

Brand dared look no longer, and charged on, following Berengar's echoing curses.

Within minutes he reached the narrow corridor to the world above and dashed down it. Berengar was waiting in the shaft, gripping the pull rope, the egg still cradled under his left arm.

Brand grabbed hold of the rope too and then called out, "Crank the winch! Raise the rope!"

There was no response.

Brand added, "We have repaired the waterways! *Raise the rope!* Make haste; the delicacies we found down here will be ruined by the rising tide!"

Brand heard movement, a click, and then the rope started to raise upward. Looking back down the dim passage, Brand saw a shadowy bulk black out the yellow square at the end of the tunnel, then his view was blocked by the green stone of the shaft as he was raised up.

Brand and Berengar clambered out of the shaft as soon as the edge was within reach. Each rapidly gained his footing and started edging away, whilst trying to feign calm in front of the villagers, who had been waiting for them with a bristling ring of spears and sword points. The village chieftain was close by, and a look of crafty suspicion washed over his ruddy face. He called out, "Ahoy there! Where are the viands you promised? What is that dreadful egg?—"

Brand cut the chieftain off artfully. "We stir up no trickery! The boxes of foodstuffs lie at the bottom of the shaft. Look for yourself! We need only to construct a pallet and raise them up. Quick!—*Before the tide ruins them!*" Then, with an air of officious importance, Brand led Berengar through the tangle of weapons, batting spear tips and swords aside as he went. The villagers looked on in uncertainty, so Brand called out in grandiose tones, "Help me! Where's the wood shop? Where are the stowage crates?" He pretended to scan around for a pallet, whilst getting them as far away from the shaft as possible. One or two villagers went into motion and headed off towards the huts to find pallets. The village chieftain went over to the shaft and looked down, greedily searching for the viands.

As Brand looked back, the chieftain seemed to blink in disbelief for a moment, then visibly sag, his knees buckling in terror. A split

second later, a grey amorphous maw engulfed him as the giant
Parsan head burst forth from the shaft.

For about five seconds, nothing changed in the village. Most
continued with what they had been doing without notice. Two or
three stood frozen, staring dumbfounded. The crumpled guard was
closest to the shaft. He let out a hoarse cry, and fell back on his
posterior. And then, he too was swallowed up. A scream of terror
from one of the watching women broke the stunned silence, and
the village went into complete chaos.

The grey head, disgorging itself from the shaft, had now
expanded to its full size. It was about fifteen feet high, ten feet
wide. It grew great, constantly shifting limbs and began thrashing,
snapping up stunned villagers left and right. Brand and Berengar
started sprinting westward. The golden giant pausing for only a
second to snatch a sheet of canvas from a windowsill. They dashed
through the dingy streets, spurred on by the growing calamity
behind them—the screams of villagers in utter terror following
closely on their heels.

Gaining a rise, Brand and Berengar looked back at the village
and beheld a horrific scene. Villagers ran left and right, or hid in
houses as the giant grey head chased them, sticky grey tendrils
darting out like elastic tongues, and sucking them up. Sometimes it
simply turned its great head and snapped them up as they ran past.
On occasion, the grey tendrils would shoot out from the back of it
instead, and, capturing an unprepared villager, drag them into its
rear end, where a new maw would form to engulf them.

From the rise, the scene looked to Brand and Berengar like that
of a great dismembered anteater's head, besieging a nest of ants. It
made Brand sick to watch, and Berengar nudged him to move on.

"Come, lad, nothing can be done for them now," he said gruffly
before deftly crafting the canvas sheet into a sort of baby cradle,
and mounting it on his broad back. The egg, the size of a small

melon, fit snugly within.

Some villagers, who had prudently discarded thoughts of hiding in their homes, could be seen reaching the eastern outskirts of the village. Now, they ran aimlessly towards the distant rise in stark terror. Another bunch were heading in their direction, and Brand and Berengar thought it best to move on, so as to avoid any awkward conversations.

They headed west at a brisk jog that easily ate up the miles. In the distance, they could still hear the screams of villagers, and the sound of wood structures being crushed to splinters under the blunt, heavy blows of monstrous limbs...

After they had outdistanced the fleeing villagers, Brand and Berengar slowed their pace to an easy walk. They travelled in silence for a spell, and then Brand, brows wrinkled with concern, spoke, "You know, Ber, I've been thinking..."

Berengar's big brows knotted, and his handsome, angular face flinched into a scowl. "Me too," he grumbled. "Parsan, right? I've been contemplating his last words: 'A stronger egg brother takes me.' He lived by and died by his principles. He *was* a man."

Brand scowled back at him, then said, "I can't believe you risked grabbing that egg. Besides, no! The village! You are more worried about the ethics of Parsan?!"

"In a word... Yes."

Brand stopped walking and looked incredulously at Berengar. "What about the villagers? In effect, we brought the monster to them. *Their blood is on our hands.*"

Berengar, came to a halt slightly ahead of Brand and looked back over his shoulder, shook his great mane in rejection, then started walking again. "No, they deserved what they got."

"How so?" exclaimed Brand.

"The evil within those villagers did not grow out of starvation," Berengar went on.

"Do tell me. Apparently, I've missed the obvious!" Brand snapped—he was in a state of nervous anxiety.

"Did you not see the stains at the bottom of the shaft? No food scraps could leave such stains. No, only the oily substance of heaped flesh and blood seeps into stone and stains it so. I saw no livestock, nor evidence of animals around the village. Of course, it was only a hunch. But then I scented human blood all over Parsan. Why do you think I attacked him? He reeked of the Reaper himself. But it was not his fault—I realize now—he knew no better. The villagers were feeding people to him. Another glance and sniff on the way back out of the tunnel verified my suspicions. I say, Brand, it was stained with human blood. The villagers were dead—or maimed—before Parsan got to them."

Brand became pale. "I see... And they dared not slay us, because they could see we were no pushovers?"

"Yes—and more likely, they had grown desperate. The sacrifices weren't working."

"Those damned degenerates!" scowled Brand.

Berengar continued, "I believe it goes deeper than these weeks of famine. Was it not odd that there were no young women or children in the village? I know not what these villagers have been doing up until now, but I have suspicions."

"By my daggers, what a backwater hellhole..." Brand interjected. "But, *what was that grey thing?*"

Berengar fixed Brand with an intense, sidelong stare as they paced along. "I've heard tales that true demons and ghosts are birthed from human cruelty. That grey thing was likely an evil spirit—a demon—or a ghost. Perhaps a trace of energy left behind by the *Children of the Light* gave it life and caused it to form into corporeal reality. But, I tell you, it was their vile acts that spawned its essence."

Brand furrowed in confusion, then asked, "*Children of the*

Light? Like in the old poems? A demon? An evil spirit? But such things do not truly exist. The scholars in Drifts End have proven this."

"Bah! Tell that to the villagers down there! Or better yet, have one of your scholars come down here, and tell it to yon grey monstrosity!" Berengar retorted, before letting out the derisive bark of a timber wolf. The big man adjusted the egg on his shoulder and walked on.

"I wish you'd told me some of this sooner," Brand complained.

"By Selefay! When did I have time for it?! Besides, how would you ever learn if I did? After all, this is an apprenticeship, young wolf—*an Outlands apprenticeship.*" He buffeted Brand with a shove of his oversized paw and laughed offensively.

"Apprenticeship?! You flatter yourself! How about when I talked the guards into letting you out of that noble's dungeon two weeks ago, after you had 'assaulted' his wife and broken into his wine cellar? You dirty old basement-badger!"

"Old?! I'm only a pup of thirty-four winters!" Berengar bristled. Then, "Ahh, the wife of... What was his name? Old Duke Tantermime? Young maids should never wed old men..." He then smirked thoughtfully, as if picturing an enjoyable memory.

Brand became serious again. "Yet, all those lives... The whole scenario in the village was like a strange dream. What if it all was just a figment of our imagination—you know, a nightmare?"

"Care to go back and test our blades on the beast and taste its fangs?" Berengar teased.

"No!" Brand rolled his eyes. "But, well... you know..."

Berengar directed a sardonic grin at Brand. And then, with that devil-may-care shrug that characterizes all Outlanders, shook his golden mane, and started singing a crude sea shanty, which carried them along the dusty trail.

Sometime later, as the golden rays of the late-afternoon sun glared down at them, Brand noticed something glistening high on the face of a nearby cliff. He stopped and stared through a gap in the trees, and saw a cascade of water trickling down the rocks. As he watched, it grew steadily in size, becoming a luscious, flowing waterfall. "Ber, *look!*"

"I see, lad... I guess something good came of this mess after all. Last one to reach the fall is a bush pig's lover!" And, with a lion's grin for Brand, he charged off into the brush, sacred egg and all.

Chapter 2

"Ator Periconias."

Entry 174—At last, I believe I've mastered the formula! The core syllables are mind-bending in their complexity by themselves, and when used in conjunction with the additional destabilizing effect of the dimensional modification unit, their potency is multiplied tenfold. If unprepared, one is quickly adrift in extra-dimensional currents.

It's a strange sensation, having fragments of yourself scattered light-years and eons away. Even the most brilliant minds struggle to return from that intact. Fortunately, my "Y, X, Z, Stabilized Helmet" has proven its worth on more than one occasion.

(A great example of how technology can magnify—or at least bring greater consistency to—the companion art of magic. True, both are sciences, yet only one is reliable and accessible...)

As for my formula: I've spent months refining the ratios and force equations. Today, I achieved the first successful trial. Using a miniature model of the city—complete with clay replicas of the surrounding terrain, and underlying rock strata—a success! Albeit on a small scale. Now, it's time to share this breakthrough with the collegium!

Entry 175—What a disappointment. Their lack of faith in my work is maddening. Dangerous? Uncontrolled? Do they not see the potential?! This discovery could provide *endless* water for the city!

The old methods are outdated and, to be blunt, cruel. No man would willingly toil in those sweltering aqua tunnels, so why should those poor engineered creatures? My solution eliminates the need for such barbarity, yet they fail to see my vision.

Entry 176—I've decided to move forward with my project, collegium approval or no. Once I demonstrate proof of concept, even the most skeptical minds will have no choice but to concede.

The city will gain a boundless supply of water—fresh springs on demand, wherever and whenever they're needed.

The results will speak for themselves.

The Diary of Amidad Catito
Amateur spell-write at the collegium of Varus'Dorae

***

The waterfall was short-lived. Without Parsan operating the waterways' devices, only an existing pocket of fluid had flowed out when the nexus freed up. Brand and Berengar, noticing the thinning flow of water, quickly snatched up their canteens and filled them before the silvery trickle stopped altogether. In dismay, they considered going back to the village; however, thought of the monster closed their minds to the possibility. They decided they must move quickly onward and rely on their luck to reach fertile land, or at least land with a natural system of water.

"Blasted Ancients tinkering with the natural way of things," complained Berengar. "In the northern frontier, we partake in no such deviltry, yet the water flows freely."

"Easy for you to complain, when water abounds freely in your lands," countered Brand. "Note that this valley stretching to the southern ocean is heavily forested, yet all around are only dry crags and dusty cliffs."

"Says the novice to the master. I've traveled more lands than you could count on one of your pebble devices... There's always a way to find water—but not in this damnable valley."

"What? You've traveled to nine billion, nine hundred and ninety-nine million, nine hundred and ninety-nine thousand, nine hundred and ninety-nine different lands?"

Berengar dismissed the notion with an airy gesture, indicating that all was one.

"Anyway," Brand continued, "I guess with Parsan gone, and no one operating the devices, this too will revert to desert..."

Berengar's face became fixed in a grim stare, "The products of man crumble into the sand when the minds that made them go to mush." And, with those oddly profound words, Berengar urged Brand onward.

The forests and heavy brush eventually fell away, and they found themselves entering an inhospitable badlands, carved up by great gorges and spiked aeolian ribs of stone, where sinister, shadowed defiles wound their way beneath empty, scorching plateaus high above. If the last landscape was the product of decaying ancient technology, this was that of a ghastly failed experiment.

Looking up at the jutting arches and rising crags ahead, they could see that the only possible route—no matter the lurking dangers—was to traverse one of the narrow defiles before them. Attempting to traverse the overhangs, and high plateaus would be impossible, and even if they did find navigable paths up there, the sun would claim their souls before long.

Berengar stopped and looked ahead with arms akimbo, inspecting the land with overt hostility, his blue eyes burning with a fierce fire. "We must travel through the low passes. I do not like it. A perfect place for an ambush—that is, if anything is able to live within this burning labyrinth of stone and wind."

"By my mother and the brothel she raised me in," said Brand, "it's even worse than the damnable corrupt forests behind us..." Unlike Berengar, who endured physical exertion with the stoicism of a wild animal, Brand moaned and complained regularly and consistently.

"The desert sands won't pity your cries, wolf cub. Save your saliva before it evaporates," Berengar admonished. He had spoken few words for many miles now, his survival instincts generating the super-conservational efficiency of a desert badger. Choosing a path that looked as good as any, Berengar led them onward into the blasted lands.

A day and a half later, spent winding and backtracking through shaded paths, eerie, dimly lit crevices, and covert underpasses, Brand stopped and drank the last mouthful of his water. Berengar had offered some of his, claiming he could walk for days in the desert before feeling discomfort, but Brand, believing this to be exaggerated braggadocio, had refused indignantly.

Presently, they were walking through a deep gallery, the sky a mere crack of light high above. Strange crystals grew out of the walls in clumped knots, occasionally catching the light and refracting it into a thousand tiny rainbows. Likely, the crystals had been exposed as part of the same erosion that had formed this walkway. The rock, superheated by the sun above, radiated warmth even at this low stratum, and the shade, without any fresh draft to back it up, did little to cool the air. Brand and Berengar were drenched in sweat, which made their clothes cling to them uncomfortably, and turned the dusty air to mud upon their skin. Brand had long since thrown away his coat and had more recently rolled up his shirt sleeves and breeches.

Berengar wore only a belted loincloth, which held a dagger at his waist, and his great broadsword on his back. Also, his high-strung sandals. The sacred egg was still slung across his back, and though dusty, seemed unchanged. Bedraggled and muddy as they were in these dusty crevices, they resembled a pair of primeval archaeologists.

Suddenly, Berengar froze and held up his right hand for stillness. His left hand blurred. A moment later, Berengar was retrieving his dagger from the head of a diamond-patterned snake which had been hidden behind a rock.

"Ha, luck!" Berengar exclaimed.

"Hey!" Brand said wearily, "You're left-handed."

"What of it?" snapped Berengar. "It shows the mark of genius and *artistry*!" He forced a smile, but Brand could tell the giant had been criticized for it in the past. It made sense—his people were a superstitious lot, after all.

Berengar got to work on the snake, and shortly, he had drained its blood. Brand refused any share, and Berengar, shrugging, skinned the creature, carefully keeping the skin intact. He tied it to his belt, and they moved on. As they walked, Berengar ate the snake meat like a long, raw sausage, occasionally offering some to Brand, who rejected it on principle alone.

"By Selefay and Makmellah, you'll let yourself die before lowering your princely tastes!" Berengar growled.

At that, he proceeded to relieve himself into the snakeskin, tying it off like a makeshift water sack. Brand swayed away, nauseated, and stumbled into a nest of spiked lizards. The lizards, greatly antagonized, formed into miniature, organized battle lines and, with beady glares and acidic hisses, assailed Brand and Berengar with such valor that the pair were forced to beat an ignoble retreat down the defile.

It was later that night, as Brand lay propped against the canyon wall, half-delirious from dehydration, and watching Berengar drinking his own urine from the mouth of the bloody snakeskin, that the young, civilized rogue began to question the choices that had brought him to this very moment. Then, passing into a semi-conscious reverie, he began getting disjointed flashes of the day he had met Berengar, the day he had been coerced from his home city of Revilis Ko'hur.

***

An agreement in a tavern. Drinking and a clasping of hands...

A fools errand...

A betrayal...

A circular chamber of white polished stone. There was Berengar, strapped to the wall on his right...

A gaunt face with thinning brown hair, pale-blue eyes burning with reptilian clarity, and the flame of lunacy. The face of a madman. The face of Ezeret, the Mad King.

The face spoke to Brand, "You two have nothing to fear from *me*, Brand. I need you to *perform* a task for me. Killing you would serve *no purpose at all*. The idea is merely *ludicrous!*" Then, the king's laughter. That horrible, maniacal cackle.

Blackness...

Large amber eyes. A fountain of scented black curls. A tanned countenance with a definite jawline. A face so perfect in its sensual masculinity that it seemed as if it were intentionally sculpted to represent the male virtues as an ideal. A terrible scar, carving up the right cheek, ruined the effect. The face of Lain Locke, his enemy and rival. They had both been members of the Wagglers. The amber eyes burned with a certain sick cruelty. The full lips parted in a smirk. The face spoke. "I have brought a present for you, Brand, for you and the King."
(Wagglers: A criminal syndicate in Drift's End, a city district built from salvage outside the walls of Revilis Ko'hur proper.)

The handsome face moved aside to reveal another face. Large hazel eyes. Auburn hair. A familiar face, with a round nose and delicate features. The face of his mother. A loving expression for Brand.

That's right, Lain had brought her to the Mad King as blackmail...

"Mother!" Brand cried.

Shifting colors...

The face of Ezeret. "You know *what to do*. Retrieve the artifact. Return within six months, and mother goes free."

Ezeret produced an intricate rod of copper and crystal. He began to laugh. He pointed the rod. Blue-white light splashed into Brand's mind. His world faded to black, to the accompaniment of that vile laughter, ringing incessantly in his ears.

Ringing, ringing, thudding, thudding. Thuda-thud-thud. Thuda-thud-thud.

***

Thuda-thud-thud. Thuda-thud-thud. Drums beating in the distance.

"Brand, *wake up!*"

Brand jolted awake at Berengar's whisper, the urgency in his friend's voice cutting like a knife through the haze of unconsciousness. Confused and bleary-eyed, Brand looked around. He was on a high, rocky outcrop which looked out over the maze of crags they had been traversing before he had passed out. Brand saw sets of posts on either side of the ledge. *Were they the support stakes of rope bridges?* He tried to move to get a better look but found he couldn't. Panic rose as he realized he was soundly tied from the tips of his toes to his neck. He could barely turn his head.

Berengar's voice came again, a hiss in the dark. "This damnable rope is as thick as a python!"

Brand could feel Berengar hacking away at the rope, the impacts jarring his aching head. A strange cry sounded out, followed by chanting, and a chorus of ludicrous giggling, high-pitched and warped, as if made by malformed vocal cords.

"I'll have to wait for the right time during their ritual. *I'll come back for you.*" Berengar hissed.

"Wait... *Ritual?!*" Brand snapped out of his haze. "Where do you think you're going, Ber?! Come back!"

But, swift as the wind, Berengar was gone.

Brand could only look ahead; he couldn't even turn his neck side to side. He waited with growing unease, feeling like a pig ready for the slaughter.

Straight ahead, he could see some kind of large basin, decorated with feathers, skins, and other tribal mummery. *Savages...* he thought. *What is this?* The wood stakes on his right started to shake, and Brand could hear the heavy, regular thud of ponderous steps. He did not like the sound of those steps. At the very corner of his vision, he saw a grotesque, lumbering hulk stagger awkwardly into view. He could not trust his eyes, and wondered if he were still delirious.

It was too large to be a man—it must be at least ten feet tall. Heavy, angular shoulders supported a fleshy, disfigured face crowned by a demented frock of lank black hair. A face so peculiarly still and stretched that it looked dead. The creature jolted and shuddered towards him, before edging intentionally into the blind spot to the right of his vision. Brand began to scream— loudly and clearly—hitting a perfect soprano. And for once, he felt no shame in the act.

A second later, Brand sensed movement behind him, felt the hot wind of breath upon his neck and began to strain frantically against the ropes that bound him. The pole to which he was tied jolted suddenly and then tilted backward, drawing another bout of shouts from his lips. The pole must have been mounted on some kind of crude rollers, for the creature began wheeling Brand towards the basin ahead.

A night lark cried out high above in the sky. A humid, hot breeze blew back the hair from Brand's eyes, and a sea of dancing yellow lights lit up the blackness of the canyon below. With horror, Brand realized the lights must be the campfires of the denizens who must inhabit the defiles. He raved and shouted all the way to the basin. Only to be silenced finally as the monster pitched the pole forward, dunking him face-first into the liquid-filled basin.

Coolness assailed Brand's skin, which had been scoured raw by the elements, and he gasped, involuntarily taking in mouthfuls of the liquid. Seconds later, he was drawn apart from the shimmering basin, coughing and sucking in air.

To his surprise, he found the concoction quite palatable. He decided it was a crude form of fruit punch, both hydrating and intoxicating. The next time he was dunked, he didn't fight it at all. Instead, he took in as many mouthfuls as he could before being raised up once more.

"Aeeehouuu," He cried, still quite delirious. "Put me back down, you thing of dream madness! I'll drain this basin dry yet!" The effects of the strong punch began to vie with his delirium. He gazed out across the blanket of darkness below, populated by tiny flames. It began to blur and shift beautifully, like a sea of fireflies burning up the night.

Suddenly, he was dashed sidelong to the ground.

Now, He lay there on his side, still tied to the pole, and observed an incredible scene unfolding before him. He saw Berengar strafe into view, sword held low. On the other side of the clearing lurched the lumbering horror, which had wheeled Brand to the sacrificial basin. Berengar's eyes were baleful slits, glinting in the moonlight, as he faced off against an uncanny foe in grim silence. The sounds of the creature's heavy breathing, and the crackle of smoldering torches filled Brand's ears.

The creature raised one massive arm, and a large blade shot forth from its steel gauntlet, sending a ring of steel across the night air. With a speed appalling for its size, the creature lunged forward —its dash like the unloading of a spring trap—and Berengar barely had time to flatten himself against the ground. The scythe-like sweep sundered the darkness above his head, leaving an afterimage of a wide blue arc. Brand knew that no man but Berengar could have escaped such a slash.

Brand's stomach sank. What grim chances had they against such a monster? But wait—Berengar had rolled to his feet and swiftly rounded the beast, outflanking it. The creature seemed to be having trouble turning, perhaps reloading the tension in its frame for another pounce. *Maybe it had never missed a foe before, and was not prepared for a swift follow-up?* Before it could regain its poise, Berengar leaped high in the air, and sent down a crushing two-handed, overhead stroke upon its misshapen head.

Oddly, the harsh sound of steel grating on steel assaulted Brand's ears, and Berengar's sword came to a stop, wedged five inches deep into the skull of the hulk. A strangely human cry rang out, and the creature stiffened, going wooden. The back of the creature's dirty canvas jerkin started undulating, and Brand stared on in confusion at what he was witnessing. *Was it the effects of the fruit punch on his, heat-exhausted, nutrition-starved body?* The jerkin peeled open in a large slit, and to Brand's dizzy gaze, it seemed a giant six-armed centipede tumbled out onto the sandy floor.

As Brand stared on in revulsion, the hallucination resolved itself —the centipede was in fact three small humanoids, sitting on each other's shoulders in a stack. Brand realized with wide-eyed perplexity, that he was seeing three four-foot-tall human dwarfs, now untangling themselves from each other. The first of these jumped up, squealing high-pitched invectives, and held his hands to his bald head, which now bore a thin slit along its peak. The other two jumped up and stood glaring at Berengar with balled fists.

The one with the slashed head seemed to be the leader, and demanded a handkerchief from one of the others, which he used to wipe the blood off his face and then wrapped it around his head in a sort of turban.

"What have you fools done!?" he growled in a cruel husky voice. "You have *ruined* everything!"

"I ruin nothing, these hands were made to *create!*" countered Berengar, his temper never long at the best of times. He dashed forward with sword raised high in a threatening manner. The three dwarves cringed back, hands held above their faces in fear, like three naughty children.

"You three, *stay!*" said Berengar, letting up and fixing them in position with a pointing finger. After this, he stalked over to Brand, still watching them sidelong, and began savagely hacking at the rope. Brand endured the pain of blood recirculating into his limbs with the stoicness of a drowning cat, moaning and complaining until Berengar directed a glare at him. Brand grinned back sheepishly and shut his mouth.

Brand, now free, climbed to his feet and swayed drunkenly, then searched for his weapons. His short sword, pouch, and belt had been taken, but they hadn't removed his hidden daggers. Flicking two into his hands, he staggered toward the short-folk, grinning like a wolf. His long arms and legs stretched out to their full length, creating what he hoped was a daunting silhouette against the moon behind him. He spun the daggers with agility as he approached the now contrite wee folk.

Stepping up next to Berengar, he stood over them, frowning them down. The leader dwarf had narrow brown eyes and heavy features. He had a broad, chiseled jaw covered in a growth of graying stubble. His nose was hooked. A large golden ring gleamed in one ear, and he had an athletic, well-proportioned, though miniature, body. The other two were mirror images but lacked the golden ring.

They must be triplets, thought Brand.

"Explain yourselves! Before you are rent asunder by this noble gallant," Brand said, indicating himself with a flourish, "and his royal squire!" He then indicated Berengar and did a jig, almost slipping over on the sandy ground before straightening. Berengar glared at Brand with a *you're-drunk-again-aren't-you* look on his face.

Brand leaned in close to the dead contraption, peeled back the canvas flap on its back, and looked in. There seemed to be a three-tiered seating arrangement with matching sets of wooden levers at each tier. Each station had a set of cycling pedals. Brand leaned back, even more bewildered than before, and turned to the dwarf questioningly.

"It's a mechanism? There are three sets of pedals? Were you operating this thing by your own manual labor?"

"Of course! The power cell died, and we had to improvise, alter the design," snapped the lead dwarf defensively.

Brand didn't understand what a power cell was, but couldn't help letting out a mad, drunken cackle at the idea of the three lumpy men packed in there, sweating and pedaling like mad, their crotches resting on each other's foreheads.

The three dwarves, divining his line of thought, bristled in indignation and scowled up at him.

Brand was certain that this ancient mechanism was originally designed for a single man and had been crudely altered.

"Well, that explains the heavy breathing," he said. "However, you breathed as one? That's quite some coordination."

The lead dwarf gave a small shrug. "We can speak as one too. It's a useful ability for voice amplification."

"What can *you* do to match such feats?!" squawked the second.

"We can do a lot of other things *too*!" said the third.

Brand pursed his lips and tilted his head, holding in another chuckle at the dwarves' earnestness. "Interesting," he said. Then Brand, knowing well the secret and connected society of the small fold, asked, "But tell me, do you know of a certain dwarf named Gizmo from Revilis Ko'hur?"

The three craggy faces stared back at him in blank confusion.

"Huh? *Are you stupid boy*?" Said the leader.

"Never mind," said Brand, hiding his disappointment. "Well, you better explain yourselves. *Why should we spare your lives?*"

"There is no time!" the leader replied sternly, his cheeks coloring with affront. He was also gaining courage from the obvious lack of malice in Brand and Berengar, despite their threatening words. He cocked his head and listened intently. "The pygmies are coming, and if they see their warlord slain, there will be no control over them."

The last vestiges of fear had fled the dwarves, and a sort of enthusiastic officiousness overtook the leader. He went into action as he spoke, investigating the now-still hulk they had recently quit.

"By Gangy—the god of second chances—its mechanism has been damaged by that last lunge," he said. He then began giving orders. "Two and Three, grab the arms." The other two dwarves rushed to obey. "Tall man," he pointed to Berengar, "wheel the pole your young friend was tied to, and wedge it under the torso of the hulk while we tilt it backward."

"Easy there, captain-cartilage," Berengar said, narrowing his eyes. "Don't think you can have one over us, I know you for the conniving little sack of walnuts that you are."

"It's *your* fault we're in this mess," countered the dwarf hotly and with arrogant gusto. "We must act quickly. If the pygmies riot, *we won't escape these murderous crags alive*. The pygmies believe this mechanism to be their leader. I was going to release your friend as soon as I got the chance, but you ruined the routine with your blundering. *Now quick*, all to work! Thin drunken boy, make yourself useful and *push!*"

Brand and Berengar stood still for a moment, both dubious as to the dwarves' honesty. Then, seeing rows of torches marching toward them along the darkened trails below, they saw he was right.

"Wait!" said Brand in sudden alarm. "Where is the sacred egg?!"

"Stashed in yon shadowed niche over there," said Berengar. "I will collect it after we help these rogues with their monster."

And so, with poor grace, they aided the dwarves in dragging the heavy mechanical construct to the back wall of the rock shelf and stood it upright there. They hastily covered the damaged scalp with a strip of canvas and shaped the arms into a pose of daunting command. The hulk itself was positioned in such a way as to leave a gap behind it where the others could hide out of sight. Berengar snatched up the egg from its hiding place and remounted it on his back.

All took to their positions, the dwarves once more within the construct, Brand and Berengar crouching out of sight behind it in the shadows. The pole-barrow was positioned in front of the mechanical monster as if it had never been moved, only now the ropes hung slashed and loose, bereft of their prisoner.

They waited. The torches sizzled in their sconces, the distant sounds of night creatures reached their ears. After a short time, the breeze died out, and the air became still. The hot, silent night now pressed in on them from all sides, and the chanting and drums grew louder and louder.

After about fifteen minutes, the rope bridge began to shake, and an aura of illumination, cast off by many torches, came into view, advancing ponderously across the bridge. As the bubble of light drew nearer, a line of grotesque silhouettes could be seen, stamping along to the rhythm of the chanting and the thud-a-thud-thud of the drum.

The shadowy shapes filed out into a wide semicircle on the rocky ledge, advancing toward Brand, Berengar, and their chance allies. As they came closer, the indistinct forms resolved into a line of small, heavily muscled, but miniature sub-men, each illuminated by their own torch. They had spindly yet tendinously strong legs, thin waists, and broad, heavily muscled shoulders. Their biceps bulged like small eggs on their arms. Their heads were disproportionately large and strangely square, with lank tufts of flat, straight hair hanging halfway down over enormous foreheads.

From his secret perch, Brand studied their twisted features. He recognized in them the blueprint for design of the mechanical monster's false face. The original, as displayed in the faces of these miniature savages, was somehow even more sinister. There was little humanity in those grim, angular faces, with their beady black eyes, pointed noses, and blank expressions.

Their bodies were pale, wild and fierce, and very likely boasted the animal strength of the chimpanzee—a primate of the southern continents Brand had read about. Unlike the rest of their body, which seemed strangely hairless aside from their heads, their hands were large and hairy, with long fingers ending in thick claw-like nails at their tips. The thought of wrestling with even one of those steel-trap anthropoids sobered Brand completely, clearing the last remnants of his temporary intoxication. He began to gasp and swoon as his mind struggled with the strange sights before him, but, quick as a flash of lightning, Berengar clapped a large hand over his mouth, stifling any sound and holding him still.

The pleasant, tipsy feeling he had had was now gone, replaced by the ache of thirst, hunger, and fatigue. His head spun in the darkness, the strange scene before him swimming and blurring into a shifting tapestry.

Berengar, noting Brand's wondering gaze, leaned in close and whispered, "They look to be a mixture of local natives, Sub-Boreal Ghoul and Southern Bog-Thumper."

This did little to relieve Brand's nerves.

Berengar gave him a little nudge, and grinned at him ghoulishly in the moonlight.

"Find these in the indexes of any of your scholarly books?" he teased.

Brand was about to retort, but now the drums and chanting stopped, and a shocked cry rang out from the platoon of pygmies — they had seen the empty, frayed ropes where their expected sacrifice should have been.

The torches trembled in their bearers' hands as violent emotion swept through the group. Hairy fists pounded pale chests, and bare feet stamped the earth in wrath. The din abated, and the shouts turned into a menacing, heavy breathing.

A scowl-faced pygmy swaggered forth to confront the mechanical terror.

"Great chief, *where* is the sacrificial flesh?" he growled in indolent tones, his large nose twitching in truculence.

To Brand's surprise, he had spoken in the common tongue, though with harsh, high-strung inflections. The pygmy in question wore colored bird feathers on his chest and waist, forming a bristling plumage. Now, he swaggered forward with each foot sweeping forth birdlike, one in front of the other. His large, dark eyes bulged and started from his square head. Any other man or creature would have seemed instantly ridiculous, but the words *ridiculous* or *frivolous* could never apply to the visage staring at them across the clearing.

In response, the dwarfs' voices rang out as one, in perfect unity, forming a larger voice than any one man could have mustered. Its reverberation inside the steel frame became strangely amplified:

"Where is the sacrificial flesh??!"

The sheer volume of the voice, the menace it contained, and the suddenness of its eruption stunned the pygmy, who took a step backward.

The pygmy attempted a sullen rebuttal.

"It was here moments ago, *right before you arrived*. Once again, it has *somehow* escaped..."

"You! You and your men lost the sacrificial flesh Pikar!" interrupted the voice from the metal shell with grating dominance. It then continued in quieter tones. "It was empty by the time I arrived for the ritual. You have been sorely remiss in your duties, Pikar."

"But you insisted that the flesh must be left alone, unguarded, to flavor its meat with fear, prior to the ritual..."

"Further," interrupted the steely voice again, "your swaggerous step and insinuating tone are insolent beyond acceptance. Are you ready to meet the silver slash and part your soul from body, Pikar?"

Pikar lowered his gaze to the ground sullenly, and made a sign with his hands, submitting to the dominance of his chieftain.

"Forgive me, Great Chief. I was greatly agitated by the loss of the sacrificial flesh, and I—forgot myself. I will spend three mornings in the horrid, blinding twilight, searching for new prey as amends."

"Go now! Go and find the sacrifice among the lower passes!" boomed the voice with great command.

The pygmies scattered, sliding over the edge of the ledge, down hidden ropes and trails, or dashing across the rope bridge on hairy feet. Pikar grimaced and spun on his heel, turning one secretive glare at his chieftain before marching off across the bridge.

Had the creature noticed something was off with its chief? wondered Brand. *They had only hastily covered the damage to the construct...*

Two minutes passed in silence, and then a great sigh of relief issued from the metal frame. A very sweaty dwarf leader crawled out of the frame and looked up at Brand, his face creased with worry.

"By Gangy, never have we had such a close call. Pikar must be dealt with before he incites a mad revolt! He is wily and suspicious, shrewd as a fox. You two almost got us all killed with that stunt you pulled! What did you think?—Wrecking the machine like that?"

"You attacked me..." growled Berengar ominously.

The dwarf gave a peculiar shrug and said in plaintive tones, "I cannot free everyone. If I did, they would become maddened and overthrow me, despite their fears... All I can do is mitigate the damage. By being here, I can save five or six out of ten victims. This is surely better in the long term, wouldn't you agree?"

"So you *would* have killed Brand? I see," said Berengar, danger lurking in his steel-blue eyes.

The leader spread his hands in an obsequious apology. "If I try to save all in the short term, they will forsake me as their chieftain, and then all men who travel these parts will die."

"Damnation..." said Brand, shaking his head and looking at the ground.

"What now?" said Berengar, grudgingly dismissing the moral dilemma from thought.

"We need my belongings," said Brand. "The map..."

Berengar grabbed the lead dwarf by the collar and squeezed. "Help us retrieve Brand's gear and show us a clear route of escape, *or I will cut off your head and throw it to Kulzibar, the Flying Death.*"

The other two went rigid and reached tentatively toward the wicked hooked knives at their belts—an act that did not escape the notice of Berengar. The Outlander lifted the leader off his feet and held him like a shield against the other two.

"Of course," croaked the lead dwarf, kicking his legs and signaling for the other two to back down. Berengar set him back on his feet.

The leader was congeniality itself. "I shall honor your demands. *This is a given!*"

"Good," said Berengar, wrapping an arm about the leader's throat and placing a dagger to his spine. "Now move! One false step *and my dagger shall carry your entrails out front for you to gaze upon.*"

They traveled in tense silence, all listening for any indications of approaching pygmies, their eyes straining against the night. Berengar tailed the leader closely, dagger held to his back, while Brand kept an eye on the other two, bringing up the rear of their haphazard convoy.

The leader guided them along his secret route, ducking through hidden back-passes, crawling through cramped crevices (which Berengar could barely fit through), and dashing across brief moonlit plateaus where they were most vulnerable to detection. Brand noticed that their circuitous route was taking them steadily upwards, to a higher part of the rocky cliffs, toward a sort of peak that dominated the broken landscape.

They passed many black tunnel entrances as they went, which led off eerily into unknown darkened places. Looking down into the shadowy depths of the canyons, Brand could see the trails of pygmy torches seemingly winding through solid rock, like lines of ants tunneling the earth. He suddenly realized that these cliffs must be pockmarked with innumerable passages. The idea of those black-eyed pygmies moving around in the darkness in secret pathways beneath the earth made his hackles rise.

After about an hour, Brand was beginning to swoon from exhaustion, the adrenaline from the encounter with the sub-men now waned, and he felt the full fatigue of his earlier heatstroke. His vision swam as he tried to focus on the dwarfs in front of him, the two lumpy backs multiplying to four, sometimes eight. Brand was also sweating feverishly. Looking beyond his charges at Berengar, he vaguely noticed with some irritation that the giant pressed on ahead without any indication of fatigue.

Presently, the dwarf leader paused—they seemed to have arrived at their destination, and not a moment too soon for Brand. They had stopped in a small moonlit clearing, hedged in by dark, rough stone on all sides. After a moment, he picked the trail he was after and, taking a turn to the right, led them through a natural arch in the rock.

As they followed him, the rocky walls gave way to a cliff-side pass with an amazing vista on one side. A complete panorama of the badlands, and the forested country beyond, could be seen from here—a view certainly worthy of a chieftain, thought Brand, who had positioned his own hut in Drifts End to much the same effect, though the order of magnitude was not comparable with this view. The sky was clear and dominated by a large, gleaming moon, which illuminated the landscape in silvery rays, lending a dream-like quality to the land.

Further up the trail was a cave, its entrance precariously close to the cliff's edge. The entrance was decorated with symbols, ornaments, and the general paraphernalia considered worthy of a savage tribal lord. A set of human and subhuman skulls were placed upon the arch above its entrance. Ragged spears, scythes, and other weapons were embedded butt-end into the sandstone or tied upright, beside the cave mouth. Bright feathers and fur scraps had been abundantly pinned to every article possible.

The display was everything that Brand would have expected of a savage culture, but its hard reality lent it a sinister weight and authority. Brand was impressed and more than a little shaken by the robust display—though some of this could be his fatigue. He was dead tired.

Berengar, of course, didn't pay it much heed. He was set on his task of watching the leader, and any glances he spared from his duty were directed longingly toward the smooth rock walls above, which looked boldly out across the beautiful moonlit panorama below. Brand, seeing his glances, took critical note. The inane fool was contemplating sculpting at a time like this? Of course he was. There he stood, looking upward like a bold statue of stone himself, the shifting silver rays outlining him like some ancient god effigy of days long gone.

His outline wavered in the moonlight, and Brand was confused for a moment. It looked as if the round shape on Berengar's back had jostled, but when Brand looked more closely, it was as still as before. He decided it must have been a trick of the moonlight.

They moved on, the leader going forth into the cave mouth. About five feet in, and quite incongruously with the tribal decor of the outer entrance, rested a large wooden door, painted dark red and mounted in an intricate framework of copper.

The lead dwarf stood still and looked back at Berengar, who was leering over his shoulder. The dwarf bristled and said, "Excuse me?" Berengar begrudgingly looked away, but pressed the dagger close. By some mechanism unknown to Brand, the door clicked open and swung smoothly ajar.

Brand was hit by a sudden wave of nausea but forced it down and followed the others through the door.

The door opened into a sandstone tunnel, well-lit by torches in little alcoves carved out of the rock on the right side of the tunnel.

The lead dwarf called out, "Brand, be a good lad and close the door behind you, would you?"

Brand shakily swung the door shut behind him and propped himself up on the wall. The room seemed to swim before his eyes.

The lead dwarf stomped off confidently down the tunnel. "Tall man, please calm yourself," he said. "Your incessant vigilance is taxing on the nerves. I can't relax with cold steel at my back. You are guests in our home—have no fear of betrayal here for the *Law of Host and Guest* applies. Besides, we cannot call the pygmies; we dare not show them this place. Thus, you two large men can easily overpower us—sho uld treachery be our game."

These words came to Brand slowly, as if through a foggy gulf. There was a rushing in his ears, and his vision began to close in on itself.

Berengar stubbornly sheathed his dagger, but then grinned. "Well, since you have named yourself as host, where is the wine? And a leg of goat would do no harm. By Mackmellah, I've eaten naught but venomous beasties and my own effluvia for two and a half days. I'm famished!"

These were the last words Brand heard before he tottered and fell headlong into a black, dreamless slumber.

***

Squeak... Squeak... Squeak...

The strange noise forced Brand to stir. Now waking, he noticed he was laying on a comfortable bed made of heavy Devirien rugs, tripled up to add thickness. He was now staring up at the rocky, vaulted ceiling that reached almost twenty feet up at its center. His head was clearer than it had been in days; it was like waking up refreshed in a clean pool of water after a hell-ride through a murky, bleary-eyed nightmare filled with pain and nausea.

In fact, he felt amazing. He hadn't realized how much he had needed a rest. It felt so good just lying there, he didn't want to move. However, a healthy and ravenous hunger began to assail him, goading him out of bed.

He sat up and looked around. He was in a large chamber of natural rock, about fifteen feet wide and thirty feet long. Shafts of sunlight projected into the room from apertures on the wall across from him, while torches in sconces were strategically placed to clear the shadows in areas where the sun could not reach. Again, Brand noticed a unique and repetitive tinkling sound reverberating through the chamber, though he could not immediately define its source. Also, a strange damp, nutty smell permeated the air.

"Ho, Brand! *You're up.* Host, *bring more wine!*" The familiar voice of Berengar called out as he came out of a passage to Brand's right, carrying a large slab of cheese.

"*Water please...* then food," croaked Brand, his throat too dry to talk properly.

"*Water?*" replied Berengar, a note of disapproval in his voice. "By Lyier, I've waited on you like a wet nurse, trickling water and honey nectar down your throat for nearly a day! Now's the time for *wine!*"

"*Nearly a day?!*" Brand cried in wonderment.

The lead dwarf came into view from behind Berengar, moving with a swift, bow-legged gait.

His high-pitched, kazoo-like voice, characteristic of diminutive peoples, echoed through the cavernous room, "Ay, he did at that, thin boy. You're lucky to have such a friend to preen over you so."

He was carrying a small barrel of wine in both arms as he ran. Brand noticed the little devil was as heavily muscled as Berengar, though in miniature. Almost a ferocious little pygmy himself, he thought.

"Not used to the Outlands, are you, Mr. Fancy?" squawked a cruel voice from Brand's left.

Turning, Brand saw one of the other dwarfs coming out of a tunnel that led somewhere north, carrying an empty pewter mug in one hand and an ancient silver plate in the other.

"Ease off, you rogues. Let the lad come to," said Berengar, as he stowed the slab of cheese under one muscled bicep, before cheerfully snatching the barrel of wine up from the dwarf and popping its stopper off with the butt of his dagger.

"Three!" called out the first dwarf over his shoulder. "Bring water and another plate from the pantry for Thin Boy." Then, looking to Berengar, "Tall Man, place it down—*save some for us, you rogue.*"

The solid table was positioned against the wall across from Brand, among the shafts of light. It was low to the ground, the legs having been sawn down, and had large cushions placed around it for sitting, in the Devirien fashion.

Brand zoned out to the banter of Berengar and the dwarfs, and inspected the chamber. The room was spacious, but filled with large crates and other oddities, piled against the walls or sprawling out across sections of the floor. Bundles of silk could be seen among the crates, and rolls of expensive rugs were bunched together or laid out copiously in places for sitting. There were ingots of various ores and metals, strange steel rods, and tools unfamiliar to Brand. An anvil and grindstones stood nearby. Upon the wall were mounted shelves, filled with various bottles of oil, tubes of unguents, and spices.

It was like a sort of pirate's treasure cavern, thought Brand. It was certainly worth a fortune, but it wasn't exactly a pirate's treasure trove—it was more of a stock of trader's stores, or the loot taken from plundered merchants.

And it was certainly overcrowded, but there were at least cleared spaces for dining and walkways that allowed egress to the other chambers. There was one tunnel to the north—the cave's entrance. One to the east—the pantry room. And another to the south—unknown.

Another thing that caught Brand's attention was how cool it was in the chamber. *Where was that sweltering heat that had destroyed me?* he wondered.

The third dwarf now came out of the pantry tunnel and proffered him a large mug of cool water. Brand sucked it up in a trice. Never before had water tasted so good. It soothed his dry lips and throat, and he felt half a man again.

"Thanks, err... 'Three'?" he said, giving the dwarf the mug back. "Could I have one more?"

"Sure," said Three, and walked back towards the pantry.

Feeling suddenly foolish sitting in bed while others moved around him, he decided to get up. He got up fast and, to his credit, wobbled only slightly before finding his balance. He wandered over to the table where the others were piling up a hearty feast of hard cheese, coarse meal, wine, and some sort of rotisserie kebabs on blackened spits.

"May I join you?" he asked, and then with a critical glance at the kebabs, "What meat is that?"

"Of course! Here, take a seat by Tall Man there," said the lead dwarf. Then he grinned. "That's giant desert hamster, roasted to perfection with Two's cooking skills."

"Thanks," said Brand, eyeing the kebabs askance. He took a seat on a large filigreed cushion. "Cheese and meal for me please. By the way, what are your names? And what is this 'Two' and 'Three' business I've been hearing?"

The lead dwarf grinned broadly, his angular, stubbled jaw flexing as he did so. The grin of a grisly desert hound.

"Tell him, Berengar!"

"Oh no, not a chance. I want to see your ridiculous little dance again," Berengar said with a derisive laugh.

The leader scowled at Berengar, but jumped to his feet. His bearing altered slightly; he seemed now a performer rather than the barbarous hermit Brand knew him as. The other two dwarfs instantly stopped what they were doing and joined their leader, walking backward to stand as three, shoulder to shoulder.

The leader with the golden earring raised his hand in a precise and complicated salute.

"I am 'One,' see my ring?" The one on his right made a rude gyrating gesture with his hips. "I am 'Two,' see my blue neck tattoo?" He pointed to it. The one to the left juggled the cutlery he was holding, then caught it in a crazy pose, with a fork balancing on his nose. "And I am 'Three,' see my missing finger?"

"*And we*," they all shouted as one, "*... are Ator Periconias!*" As if this meant something. Then they proceeded to do a brief, eccentric hornpipe in time with clapping cutlery.

Berengar rolled off his chair laughing and almost choked on a mouthful of hamster kebab.

One scowled and went back to his meal in good humor. Two threw his cutlery at Berengar before returning to his cushion. Three stood for a moment, looking expectantly at Brand. Brand raised his glass in return. This seemed to please Three, who then nodded to himself, as if in confirmation of some inner conviction, and went back to his seat.

Brand dug into the cheese and coarse meal with gusto, making up for many days of travail and hardship. He was eventually bullied into trying some of the desert hamster meat, which he found disturbingly palatable. Presently, the banter of Berengar and Ator Periconias faded into the background, and as he sat there filling his gullet, he mused on his recent adventures.

He decided he would never enter a badlands again by personal volition—this much he was certain of.

The Mad King had outdone himself this time. Oh, how he deserved retribution. And don't forget Lain. Most certainly, they would pay. Brand would return someday to collect. With these succulent thoughts of revenge comforting him, Brand into his food once more.

Chapter 3
"Cil."

Journal Entry No. 25 — Three's handwriting: "I think I have figured out how to rewire the Z6-8000 so that it can be operated by kinetic-energy. I will just need to remove some of the padding and luxury components in order to fit a circular wheel and three sets of foot cranks. This will be a real boon, seeing that it's been out of commission since the power cell died."

Journal Entry No. 26 — Two's handwriting: "Three's got a tiny pee pee."

Journal Entry No. 27 — A series of advanced calculations and engineering equations in Three's handwriting.

Journal Entry No. 28 — Three's handwriting: "Having the Z6-8000 back up has solved a lot of problems for us, but I don't feel like One or Two really appreciate the work I do for them. Well, I guess they can't help being self-absorbed, if that's how they are naturally. I guess I'm just built different."

Journal Entry No. 29 — An incomplete lexicon attempting to translate the symbols of the ancients into the common tongue, followed by a dissertation on energy storage systems and electronics in Three's handwriting.

Journal Entry No. 30 — One's handwriting: "The recent expeditions into the tunnels below, as guided by *my* expert planning, have been a complete success. More blueprints for Three to monkey around with. Sure, he does a good job, but without *my* planning, he would just monkey around. Without *my* clear direction where would he be? Soon we will have the local pygmies completely under our control. Another great product of *my* leadership. Damn, I'm good."

Journal Entry No. 31 — Three's handwriting: "One's been bragging again about how his plans allowed us to conquer the local tribe of sub-men. Sure, *he* guided the operation, but we never would have been able to do it without *my* 'tinkering,' as he calls it. Also, doesn't he realize that I can read all of his entries? We only have one notebook available."

Journal Entry No. 32 — Two's handwriting: "Yah yah yah! Who's the bigger man? Why don't you two just cut this short, drop your pants, and measure who's got the bigger (___)?"

Journal Entry No. 33 — Three's handwriting: "Two can be really crass sometimes. I'm going to just start skipping his logs from now on. I haven't seen anything from One recently. I wonder if he even reads this thing anymore? Probably not — he's probably too busy with his 'new project.'"

Journal Entry No. 34 — A series of advanced calculations in the symbols of the ancients, followed by mechanical drawings of various bird-like machines in Three's handwriting.

Journal Entry No. 35 — A crude sketch depicting a large phallus with an arrow pointing to it, and notation saying *Mine,* in Two's handwriting.

— *The Notebook of Ator Periconias*
Found by Alucard in the mountains of Varus'Dorae.

***

The next day, Brand found himself once again ravenous upon waking. Rousing himself and finding the others at breakfast, he wandered over to the table. It had been piled high once more with food and beverages. He ate the rations of four or five men, and drank three large mugs of water before slowing down. After this, he was once again rational, and he looked around to his next order of business.

"So, One, this place, it seems a veritable merchant's stockroom. I mean no offense, and each man out here is beyond the regular conventions, of course, but well... I can see you have no scruples in *stealing from the dead*." He gestured to the plundered goods.

One glared back at him sardonically. "*Scruples?* Who should we have learned these off, me and my brothers? Who were raised in a circus like confections, and were the first to be left behind when rations ran short on the trail? Nay, let us not even *go there*. Suffice it to say, that these spoils would have gone to waste had we not collected them. The pygmies don't care for any of these man-goods. They raid the Trade Road to the north for man meat, then leave the stores to molder in the sun. Wherever they kill, there are wasted goods, and whereof we... manage to eke out a modest existence. I have *already* stated that we try to curb the killing of men where possible, and so... *shove off!*" He made a vulgar gesture towards Brand and then continued digging into his giant-hamster kabab.

"I see," said Brand, not deigning a rebuttal. "And how did you come to live in this—*what is that irksome squeaking?*"

Three piped in, "That's my invention, *mine!*" He became animated and jumped up, pointing to a number of small alcoves in the chamber's western wall. They were about five feet above head height. Brand stared at one of them and thought to observe some kind of circular cage — and was that some sort of critter in it?

Three grabbed Brand by the shoulder and pulled him along, his steely grip hurting as it dug into Brand's flesh. The little man was strong! Three pulled over a step ladder he had stowed nearby, and motioned for Brand to climb up. Brand then mounted the ladder and inspected Three's handiwork with sheer fascination.

Never before had he seen a contraption to match this. A sort of window, or short drift, had been tunneled from the chamber to the outside, similar to the light shafts that lit the room. However, this had a shaft excavated at ninety degrees to the horizontal drift, crossing through it at an intersection. In this shaft, there was a trickle of water, which fell from an unknown source above and continued downwards and out of sight.

Positioned outside the curtain of water was a metal three-bladed fan, mounted on a bracket that allowed its smooth rotation at the turning of a steel rod. The rod ran through the curtain of water, and was in turn connected to a wheel made out of steel wire, mounted within a cage. On this wheel was a giant hamster, running to its little heart's content. This was the source of the strange squeaking.

The rotation of the hamster wheel was causing the fan to spin, thereby drawing fresh air into the drift from the outside and blowing it through the curtain of water and into the chamber — an action which cooled the air considerably. Brand enjoyed the cool breeze for a moment while the giant hamster stared at him nervously as it ran with a wild, side-eyed glare.

"Ho Brand, what do you think?" called Berengar from his cushion. "Have you ever seen the like?"

"Certainly not," replied Brand, impressed.

One, Two, and Three all seemed pleased and were grinning.

"Ingenious, isn't it? Three has a way with mechanisms. See, near the entrance is another set; they are the exhaust fans. 'Fans' are those three-bladed devices you can see *there,* behind the water," One called out between bites of his hamster kabab. "He tunneled all these drifts and shafts with long steel-bladed burrowing rods, found water springs, and even made a system which ensures the water isn't wasted and re-circulates back into the water source. The smell of the hamsters is less than one might wish for, but the benefits outweigh the disadvantages ten to one—do they not?"

The damp nutty smell was most intense in Brand's current position, and he held his nose with thumb and forefinger as he replied. "The advantages speak for themselves and are... manifold."

The three dwarfs nodded their heads vigorously in agreement.

"Amazing..." Murmured Brand, eyeing the contraption once more—and in doing so, he noticed that certain of the hamsters had begun to breathe heavily and slacken their pace, their little breasts heaving with exhaustion."

Three noticed as well and, asking Brand for the ladder, began taking them out of their cages one by one, and carrying them off into the southern tunnel, only to return each time with a replacement which he replaced into each of the cages. The replacements began running happily with fresh vigor.

Brand looked curiously towards the tunnel Three had gotten the replacement hamsters from. "What's in there—"

One quickly interrupted, his voice taking on an obsequious tone with metallic undercurrents. "Yes, that's our cage room for the animals, and it is also our mechanical workshop. We ask you as our worthy guests to not ever go in there—for fear of disturbing the hamsters, and... to be entirely candid... we do not wish to let you know our engineering secrets..."

Two and Three nodded vigorously. One grinned broadly at Brand, but his smile did not reach his eyes. His attitude had subtly changed, and he was not so cheerful as before. Two stopped eating and became tense.

"Suspicious lot you are," Brand said dryly.

Three hunched his shoulders as if slightly ashamed.

Brand shrugged and let it go. "As you wish, you are the hosts. I shall inquire no further."

Brand walked back to his bed of rugs and stretched out on them, intending to doze for a spell. Then, remembering his missing gear, he sat up and said, "speaking of prerogatives, where are my belongings, good sirs?"

Berengar gestured to a small crate to Brand's right. There was his pouch, short sword, and scabbard, set in a tidy bundle. He immediately opened his pouch and checked for the map and mechanical drawing of the artifact. There it was. He unfolded the thick canvas and gazed upon it for a time. They must travel west beyond something called the *Darkwood Runs*, and to a line of cliffs that marked the border between the *Western Foothills* and the Sunken Tundra. There were brief sketches of the lands in between that they must traverse. It seemed they were currently in an unrecorded badlands; in fact, per the map, the city Varus'Dorae should be located right at their current coordinates. Strange.

"What's that?" called out One from the table.

A streak of churlishness came over Brand. "Ahh, you have *your* mechanical secrets, these are *mine*."

One frowned and spat into a clay pot, then shrugged and went back to his food.

Brand grinned, "No, I'll tell you One—It's a map. Say, it says the city of Varus'Dorae should be located right at our current coordinates."

"Yeah, it is. Only about two hundred feet down." One growled back.

"Huh?"

"You heard me, Thin Boy. It seems the ancients went too far with their experiments this time. The city has sunk entirely beneath the earth, and the rocks and sand were pushed up above it, creating this blasted badlands."

Brand licked his lips. "*By my mother*... what sort of meddling could cause such destruction? And how do you know it's down there?"

"When we were abandoned on the Trade Road north of here, flagging from hunger and dehydration, we passed out beneath an old wagon. Imagine our consternation when we awoke in a livestock holding pen, deep beneath the earth. It turned out a race of subhumans—whom you now know—had burrowed into the sunken city and taken up residence in its abandoned structures and the surrounding passages. We escaped the pen and set off in a random direction, wandering the dimly lit tunnels for a time, not even knowing which way was up.

"It is very fortunate that the subhumans, being of an imperfect, mongrel stock of man, beast, and demon, still needed torches to see in the pitch dark. Such torches were irregularly placed throughout the subterranean network—just enough so that we could make our way, squinting and crawling. Without such, we would never have escaped those black tunnels." He shuddered and then scowled.

"As was to be expected, a pack of pygmies eventually picked up our scent and gave tongue in the tunnels behind us. We ran in blind panic through those corridors, pursued by an unseen enemy— sometimes in complete darkness. We held hands so as not to be separated, feeling along the stone walls to find our way, while gasping, hairy shadows—reeking of rank game—followed close behind. By this point, we had abandoned all considerations of deportment and were fleeing wildly, gripped by a certain kind of madness—a madness that was, paradoxically, both sane and appropriate for the circumstances. We imagined we could see in the dark, and for a moment, it seemed we almost could—" He shook his head, uncertain.

"By a stroke of luck, we stumbled upon that machine you damaged. We hid inside it in the pitch dark while sub-men rushed around us on all sides, trying to sniff us out. Luckily for us, the smell of the machine's degrading power cell hid our scent. Ahhh, a power cell is like a metal thing that holds small amounts of... 'lightning' inside it and can be used to work the ancients' devices."

Brand listened on in wide-eyed wonder. *Stored lightning?*

One continued, "Anyhow, we hid and slept in that machine— and it seems the gods were with us, for there was an operation manual and a blueprint stored in one of its inner compartments. We couldn't read the ancient symbols, but through experimentation, and by studying the diagrams, we managed to start the machine and use it to traverse the tunnels. Some pygmies fled at the sight of the metal hulk, but many more dropped to their knees in prayer, offering themselves to it as if it were an ancient god. We eventually made our way back to the surface—and the rest is history. That was five years ago now."

"By Makmellah! *Five years!* What a tale!" bellowed Berengar from his cushion, looking the triplets up and down with open admiration. "True *Outlanders* you are! It takes horror and hardship to weed out the weak and put fire in a man's belly! I shall sing of you around the campfire, and within the taverns *among the buxom maids!*"

Brand had to admit that such a feat would not have been easy to endure. But what of its effect on the mind? He had noticed that a strange light burned in One's eyes at times of agitation. He thought it better to change the subject.

"And how goes your study of the old tongue now?" he asked.

"We've since made further inroads into the sunken city, and using the first blueprint—in combination with other writings found during our expeditions—we managed to decipher some of the ancients' symbols. Then, by a process of elimination, we translated many more. Say, I believe there's more to that chart than just a crude map... I can see from here that there's a blueprint as well— on the other side."

Brand cursed. He had been so enthralled by the story that he, like an indiscreet player at cards, had let the blueprint side tilt forward. He quickly pulled it back, blocking further observation.

It in fact detailed a strange metallic cylinder, its cross-section revealing an inner array of intricate, glowing cables and nodes. A hundred lines stretched from each component, ending in what appeared to be labeled tags. Brand, of course, could only guess— that's what he assumed they were, as neither he nor Berengar could understand any of the symbols.

I'm not a man who tells all he knows," he said to One, frowning at the dwarf's prying gaze.

One became suddenly cheery. "I will strike you a deal you cannot refuse—but all in good time. Why haggle when we barely know each other? I've told you our story—so, what of yours?"

"Yes!" Chimed in Three excitedly. "What of *you*? And of you too, Tall Man?"

"Brand's story is much more exciting than mine, I'll wager," chuckled Berengar. "He's seen more beauties than you three or I could ever dream of."

One sat up, a lewd smile curling his heavy lips. "Oh, and how is this?"

"What kind of beauties?" said Two, for the first time showing interest in the conversation.

Brand stared daggers at Berengar, who was now hiding behind his kebab. "It's nothing that exciting. I was raised in a house of ill repute, in *Drift's End*—the outer district of *Revilis Ko'hur*. My mother was the mistress of the house, and, well... my father, I never—"

"Raised in a cathouse! Tell us of the *girls!*" broke in One impatiently.

"The *girls!*" echoed Two.

Brand pursed his lips. "That's all you dirty dogs will get from me. I shall not speak ill of my sisters."

An all-round riot broke out. Mugs slammed against sturdy oak, and curses flew as the two dwarfs shouted their outrage at being denied. Then, they turned away from Brand in disgust, and went back to their meals.

Brand went to finish, "Well, after that—"

One raised a hand, cutting him off. "We have heard all we care to hear. Tall Man, tell us something *interesting*."

Brand made a sign of contempt, glaring angrily at One.

"Well," said Berengar thoughtfully, "I recall my travels started when I was no more than fourteen winters of age. It was after a village festival, and I found myself in the hayloft of my father's barn—half-straddled by a buxom redhead on one side, and a sleek blonde on the other."

"*That's better!*" declared One. "*And then*?"

Brand rolled his eyes. Then, seeing that no civilized conversation was possible with such ingrates, he drifted off into thought while Berengar told one outrageous tale after another.

And so passed three days of halcyon ease. Brand and Berengar ate and dozed away the mornings on hammocks rigged among the sun shafts, while One, Two, and Three slept in their southern chamber.

The afternoons were full of much large talk and drinking, Ator Periconias then heading off each night to handle their affairs as chieftains of the subhuman pygmies, only to return at an ungodly hour in the morning, and then once again sleep until well after noon each day.

Brand checked daily on the sacred egg, which Berengar slept with, huddling it in his arms like some great golden hen guarding its chick. Brand thought he had seen it move that night, but it had been still ever since. He decided that it was probably just a hallucination from his heat-stroke.

And so it went, Brand passing his days without concern, apart from the subhumans' howls that woke him up at times in the night. And the strange muffled cry, which came infrequently, and which caused him to pause and strain his senses, wondering as to its nature and source.

One would tell him each time that the shafts and caves work in strange ways, and that sounds had a way of echoing up from deep beneath the earth, somehow seeming closer than they really were.

This made sense to Brand, as far as the chirping, high-pitched caterwauls that hollered out in the night, but this strange muffled cry was disturbingly different. It sounded much closer.

It came at odd hours of the day, and Brand had considered the pygmies as primarily a nocturnal race. So then why did this muffled cry, echo through the shafts at high noon? Brand found himself pondering it more and more as the days went by.

It was now the fourth day of Brand and Berengar's stay in the cavern, and the three dwarfs and Berengar sat around the table on the cushions, as was their habit, drinking and trading boisterous talk.

Brand had recovered and now was restless, and ready to move on with their journey—his mother's life relied on the whimsy of the Mad King's caprice. However, they had not figured out how to escape the badlands yet.

One watched Brand as he paced back and forth, and judging the youth's anxiety with the practiced eye of a trained haggler, he took this moment to offer a trade.

"*Ho, Thin Boy*! You look about ready to jump out of your skin."

Brand was, at this precise moment, inspecting the group of hamster wheels on the southern end of the chamber for the hundredth time.

"And if so, *what then*?" replied Brand hotly. "We can't stay here and swill away the days forever. If I'm to see my mother again, we must complete our task. Berengar, I find you far too casual."

Berengar's large face took on a look of bovine innocence. "How now, Brand! You do me wrong. We needed rest, and we took it. Now we need a means of egress and"—he paused to take a swig of ale—"no doubt something will fall into our laps shortly..." He gave Brand his most reassuring grin.

Brand glared at him darkly for a moment, before turning back to the hamster wheels.

One, with a crafty glint in his eye, called out once more.

"Brand, we too have pondered upon a way to escape these lands. But I see you're in greater need than we, and so... I'll make you a *deal*. Let me study that chart you carry, and in exchange, I'll give you a means of escape—along with six days' provisions. You can't ask for a better deal than that, boy."

Brand grew suddenly suspicious and cast a sideways glance at One. At that moment, the hamster directly in front of Brand sneezed loudly, and a waft of spittle blew across his face. Leaning back and wiping his mouth angrily, he said, "And why is this chart so important to you? You won't be coming with us."

"True... Well, I'll be straight with you, as I always am—and always have been, if the truth be told." One's voice took on that familiar obsequious tone. "You see, we only dare go so far into the caverns, and we've only been able to gather so much knowledge of the ancients. But now that we can somewhat read the writing, any written material is of great value to us. Think of it as simply sharing a bit of knowledge with your good friends—friends who might one day owe their lives to it. Is that too much to ask, considering the hospitality we've shown you these past few days? Not to mention *the deal*."

"I don't trust you when you talk like that, One. You've got the crafty expression of a toddler pilfering the cookie jar."

"Why, you little—" One climbed off his pillow with clear intent to scold Brand physically, but Berengar rested a large hand on his shoulder and laughed—so loudly that all paused to look at him.

"Brand, *take the deal*. So what if One is shrewd and crafty? It's all he knows. You must learn that people come in all shapes and sizes out here in the Outlands—no one person is perfect. *Except me, of course*." At that, he laughed all the harder. "Besides, what harm could come of it?"

Brand thought Berengar far too lenient, and knew a rogue when he saw one—as he should, he was raised in *Drift's End!* But, he could think of no obvious harm in showing One the chart...

"OK, One, I'll show you the chart—on two conditions." The hamster to his left squeaked loudly, giving him a side-eyed look as it ran, as if asking for food. "First, tell me what method of escape you have for us. Then, tell me what the chart says."

"Why, my boy—" One began.

"*What is that strange cry?*" interrupted Brand. The odd haunting call had occurred again.

It was louder this time, and Berengar had heard it too, his uncanny hearing catching it from where he sat across the room. Brand was certain it had sounded out from behind him, and he turned to stare over his left shoulder towards the southern passage.

One, Two, and Three went silent. Berengar sat up and looked quizzically across the room with his head cocked to one side, listening like a hound. Nothing. The sound had ceased.

Brand looked slowly back towards the others and met One's sinister yellow-eyed glare.

"Forget it, Brand. Come sit with us and show me your chart," he said, without a drop of warmth to his voice. He sat extremely still. A palpable tension filled the room between them, and Brand felt compelled to walk over and sit down as he was bid—*to do anything to ease that tension.*

"A deal's a deal... Okay, d*one*," said Brand.

"*Done,*" intoned One. "Now come, sit back down like a good lad..."

An eerie feeling built inside Brand, and it told him not to let this slide. He had to know what had made that noise. Berengar, had he been inside Brand's head, would have mocked him, calling it his *womanly* intuition. Well, so what if he had grown up with only girls to look up to? There was the sound again, and suddenly the faint muffled cries of three days reverberated in Brand's mind. And at once, the recollected sounds resolved into clarity.

It had been a girl's voice.

Brand dashed into the southern passage, ignoring the calls from One.

Brand's lean, long legs carried him rapidly through the dimly lit tunnel. It angled to the left, and then opened up into another broad chamber, like the one he had become so familiar with.

Against the left wall of the chamber was a large table, clearly a workbench, boasting all the necessary tools and devices for wood and metalwork. It held clamps, hammers and saws, hand-cranked drills, bits and scraps of steel and wood. A number of incomplete projects were littered on the bench and around *it* on the floor.

Directly ahead was a large stack of wooden crates, filling that quarter of the chamber.

The right wall was stacked high with many giant hamster cages, most housing a healthy, large rodent, but some empty—obviously the homes of those hamsters currently on duty in the main room—or of those who had been yesterday's lunch.

Brand ran through the chamber, banging cages as he went, and calling out, "Hello! Is anyone there?! Hello?!" He paused to listen with the practiced ear of a Waggler. He heard footsteps in the tunnel behind him. Three pairs of rapid steps. One pair of long strides. Nothing else.

Brand reached the wooden crates and moved among them, rapping on their tops, continuing his broadcast. He paused. A faint muffled call? Yes, there it was again. Definitely a girl's voice. And it came from... behind the crates.

He waded through the crates as fast as he could, and, reaching the far corner, dragged the last crate aside to reveal a circular trapdoor of wood, like the lid of a great clay pot fitted snugly into the stone floor.

One flew into the room with Two and Three on either side, his face a horrible mask of wrath. His hazel eyes glinted yellow with hatred in the dim light—the eyes of a hunting wolf. His compact body bulged with rounded muscles, a living walnut-beetle of a man. Two and Three spread out at his sides, flanking him, spitting images of One, but not angry—only tense and determined. All three drew their serrated eight-inch knives.

"Keep your prying hands out of our business, you ungrateful brat!" One bellowed as they advanced.

Brand turned to meet them, then, looking down glumly at his belt, realized he carried no weapons. He knew he wouldn't survive sixty seconds with those three brutes among the tightly packed sea of crates.

"Easy there, friends. I don't like spilling the blood of mine host —but touch the lad, and you won't have any further need for secrets, *at least on this side of hell.*"

The sheer menace in a voice normally easy and calm gave them pause. All three looked back to see the looming silhouette of Berengar, as he disgorged himself from the tight tunnel and straightened, extending to his full six feet four inches. His face was indistinct in the dim light, but his white teeth glinted in a lion's grin, and blue steel flashed in his hands—he had not forgotten his weapon.

One froze in indecision, fuming, his bald head red with wrath. He knew the odds as well as Berengar, and his devious mind searched frantically for a route to victory. Two and Three stopped also, waiting for One's command. Two looked only petulant; Three, however, looked ashamed.

Brand took this moment to tear loose the wooden plug in the floor. He found himself staring down into another dimly lit natural cavern, similar to the main room and the one he now stood in. Only it was empty of clutter, aside from a neat stack of used dishes and a basket with the remains of food in it.

In the center of the room, staring up at Brand with wide, angry eyes, was a beautiful girl, short but well-formed. She wore oversized, dark-red breeches, tied off at the knees, revealing tanned calves. Her feet were planted shoulder-width apart in ridiculously large, brown shoes with big, gray-colored, rounded toes. She wore a baggy white shirt with the sleeves cut off, revealing tanned and strong—but not unwomanly—arms. A brown silk sash was tied tightly around her waist into a complicated knot on her left hip, leaving a long tassel hanging at her side.

She appeared roughly the same age as Brand. Her face was symmetrical with a perfect straight nose. Her eyes were large, green, and spaced evenly apart. She had a wild jagged fringe of straight, dark-red hair, the rest of which was piled high, and tied off with a long white ribbon, ending in a tuft which fluffed out like a timber wolf's tail. She had small ears set above a strong but delicate jaw, which ended in a triangular chin. She had thick rosy lips, which were, at this moment, curled in an angry snarl, showing strong white teeth. She was beautiful.

"What are you looking at, you gawking sunflower?! *Get me outta here!*" she said, shaking her fist in anger and making crude gestures at Brand.

Brand looked away from her, and grimaced. "*Perhaps I was mistaken, she's a damned wolverine,*" he muttered under his breath.

"What was that?? *Why you!* Don't you leave me down here!" Came the girl's voice from the hole.

Brand directed an icy stare at One. "What is the meaning of this, One? You conniving, beastly little—"

"Oh, enough!" cut in One with a dismissive gesture as he paced side to side in the center of the room. "Be damned to you, Brand. I've treated her well and all, fed her, allowed her to keep herself clean, never forced myself upon her yet." He spoke with angry gesticulations, waving his hands wildly about his head as he paced.

"Like I'd believe you after *this*," said Brand, indicating the hole. "And since it is quite obvious that you keep her captive for some use, why *are* you keeping her?"

"*Damnit, Brand*! It gets lonely out here in the hills. I crave human companionship... She is to be... And don't you *dare* laugh! She is to be my lawful and wedded wife."

Brand didn't laugh. Instead, he scowled bleakly and shook his head.

"*Wife, hey?*! I'll show you *wife!* You misbegotten spawn of an ill-bred..." Brand put the plug over the hole temporarily to facilitate further communication.

"Well, as you can see, she doesn't *want* to be your wife, good Ator Periconias." Brand paused, considering that very statement— Ator Periconias—was a three-man show and... He wondered if all three intended to... well... never mind, it was not to be thought of.

The girl had ceased her tirade and Brand once again removed the plug off the hole.

"In time, I planned to gain her affection," One growled back at Brand, refusing to make eye contact.

"We have been good to her!" spoke up Three earnestly.

"And you planned to, somehow, 'win her over'? By keeping her pent in a hole in the floor? I can see you have a way with women," said Brand angrily.

"*Be damned!* She's mine! Alright? Mine! I found her fair and square. Now be off with you two—take your leave from these parts! We struck a bargain; stick to it."

"I propose a different agenda. The girl comes with us," said Brand, an edge of danger to his voice.

"What? Would you spill my blood? Break the Law of Host and Guest?" sneered One.

"I ain't going with *none* of you!" cried the girl from below.

Brand directed a pained glance down at her. "I'm *trying* to help you."

"Words! Nothing but words!" she said with a sneer.

Brand didn't deign a response. Instead, controlling his annoyance, he reached down and held out his hand.

A small, strong hand clasped his own, and he pulled the girl up through the mouth of the hole. As soon as she could gain purchase, she clambered to her feet and awkwardly released her grip on his hand. She stood there tense, ready to pounce in any direction—a cornered she-panther.

Seeing the girl for the first time, Berengar looked her over with a sudden sparkle in his blue eyes, as if an idea had just come to him. "Nay, Brand, we shall not break the Law of Host and Guest. Would you draw Kulzibar down on us?"

"So you're going to just let them keep her here?" Brand asked, shocked.

"*Over my dead body!*" raged the girl, shaking her fist at one and all.

"Nay also to that, good Brand," replied Berengar, ignoring the girl's comment, but sizing her up and down admiringly. He nodded decisively and spoke with a smirk upon his lips.

"One, you wish to force her to be your wife? Well then, show us you are man enough to do so."

"What are you saying, you great oaf?" said One, squinting blackly up at the golden giant.

"I am saying, you damnable devil of a half-man"—Berengar's voice took on a steely edge—"either you win her fairly, or we'll defend her—*trial by combat*. Go on. *Win her love.*" He waved his sword at One, shooing him forward, a grim smile on his thick lips.

Brand was staggered by this barbarous proposal—man against woman? He spoke out indignantly. "You can't be serious... that is not a *fair* fight—"

A swift buffet interrupted his sentence, and he found himself cupping a ringing ear with one hand. *That smarted like the devil!* he thought. Had he been clouted with a wooden paddle? But turning to his left, he saw the girl grinning, her open, calloused palm still raised.

"Not a *fair* fight, hey?" she said to Brand, flashing her teeth. "And this one's for interrupting my comments with that horrid plug!" She struck again. But this time, Brand dodged deftly between the crates.

"I'm in a mood to whip all of you today!" she went on. "Trial by combat it is! *I* am the challenger, and the challenged may choose his preference—armed or unarmed—it matters not to me."

"Like helping a wounded animal," Brand muttered under his breath as he leaned back—intentionally out of her reach.

"*What was that?*" the girl said, advancing on him ominously.

"I said, 'she must be as hungry as a cannibal.'"

"Oh... Well, yes. But, I shall do my killing *first* and eat afterward." She returned her menacing gaze to One.

Berengar laughed in savage enjoyment at the prospective conflict. He called in a great, booming voice, "One against the girl, trial by combat! The stakes: this fair maiden's hand in marriage!"

"This '*girl*,' this '*fair maiden*,' has a name. And that name is *Cil*!" replied the girl, gritting her teeth. "And, *I'll show you marriage!*"

"*Cil?*" replied Berengar, unfazed. "A good name. A steadfast name." He chuckled with grim humor. "So be it! *One against Cil!*"

One, somewhat disconcerted by the girl's dynamic energy, stood nonplussed for a moment, sizing her up. Then prideful wrath overtook him once again, and he roared, "Why, I shall put you in your place, you ungrateful hussy! Feed you for weeks with no thanks, will I? Slave over a hot fire for you—gifts of silk and— *weapons it is!* For me... and the lads!"

All three advanced on her with their serrated knives, grinning like evil little children.

"Alas, One, you intended her as *your* wife. I'm sure you had no intention of sharing."

"What? *No sharing?*" cried out Two in plaintive tones. "I was told at least once a month."

"*Ey, what?!*" cried out Berengar, for the first time taken aback. "Why, *you naughty gnomes!* It is to be one-on-one, and that's final! *No more of this 'Ator Periconias' deviltry!* And where is Cil's weapon?"

One had now worked himself into a sort of quiet rage. His lips were grim and downturned in a gremlin's frown. His eyes flickered with the light of insanity—an insanity perhaps birthed in those dark tunnels five years before. He motioned silently to the far wall without taking his eyes off Cil.

Cil grinned wickedly and jumped into the air, skipping lightly over the crates to Brand's right. Alighting once more on the ground, she picked up a dark steel rod about a yard long. She held it with arms apart, one hand gripped close to each end, and her body turned sideways to make a smaller striking target. She then began advancing with the footwork of a trained fighter, pushing off the rear foot and never crossing her legs. Brand still could not condone the affair, but he had to admit that she at least *looked* like she knew what she was doing. Without realizing it, he was gaping. *Never before had he seen such a girl.*

Berengar, observing Brand's gaze, laughed. "What? Never met an *Outlander* girl? Why, Brand, I believe you to be smitten."

Brand glowered but said nothing. The fight had his attention.

One hunched his shoulders and stalked toward Cil with knees bent—a tense ball of springy thews, his deadly knife wavering back and forth in distracting patterns.

Brand realized that despite Cil's gusto, she had a hell of a fight ahead of her. Looking back to Berengar, Brand could see that the giant knew it too—but he had faith in the girl. And, refusing to break the Law of Guest and Host, he had likely seen no other way.

Brand was more practical. If the rogue began harming the girl, he would jump in without a second thought. He caught himself—*why was he thinking such thoughts? Where was his suave, level-headed self?*

Berengar held up a hand, signaling for the fight to begin.

One circled swiftly to Cil's left, aiming to move away from her power arm. However, she flicked a quick blow toward his head from her left. He ducked and slashed at her exposed thigh. She raised her leg high above the cut with an athletic suppleness that was a joy to behold. Then, turning in mid-air before her left foot returned to the ground, her right leg swung high in a vicious roundhouse kick aimed at One's left temple. He grinned wickedly, leaned back, and reversed his knife to slash across her incoming foot—but instead of the rending of leather and flesh, the dazzling clash of steel on steel rang out. Sparks flew, and a rending clang reverberated through the chamber. One was momentarily taken aback. The toes of her shoes were steel-capped!

Taking advantage of his surprise, Cil followed through on the kick, allowing herself to spin a full turn. Then, letting the rod slide into a batting grip, she delivered a devastating two-handed blow to One's head. Crack! The sound of steel on bone rang out.

It should have knocked him clean unconscious—and would have —had he not leaned inward, going with the blow and letting it slide off the top of his sweaty scalp. He roared in pain and anger. He dashed in close, feinted low, then froze, and made to throw the dagger at her chest. Cil fell for the feint, leaned back to avoid the toss, and at the same time raised her rod to guard her midsection. One instead turned the throw into a backhanded slash, aiming for Cil's right thigh. She realized her mistake and attempted to launch herself backward—too late. The slash caught her across the thigh. A deadly blow. She gasped and went pale as she staggered to regain her balance.

This was bad—a terrible mistake. She would be losing blood now, and with it, her strength. Soon the muscles in her thigh would begin to seize up, leaving her flat-footed and vulnerable. She would need to end it quickly. She dashed in, feinting with a wild low swing toward One's left knee. He bridged awkwardly, unprepared for the blinding speed of the attack, and leaned forward, throwing his legs backward—a terrible move. She took full advantage of it, turning the feint into a thrust, launching the rod toward his chin like a bullet.

She would have had him there. However, by a stroke of fate, he tripped and stumbled to his right. The deadly thrust slid harmlessly past his cheek. He grinned and slashed out at her unprotected forearm. She was ready. She leaned back with the speed of a leopard, reversed the short rod in a rapid, spring-like movement, and smashed the knife from his hand with its opposite end. He grunted in pain as the knife flew from his punished hand.

But instead of pausing or glancing after his lost knife as Cil expected, he instantly stepped in close and grabbed onto her rod with two strong hands, pulling her in and aiming a brutal head-butt at her. She ducked it, but he took advantage of her awkward footing at that moment to wrench violently on the rod. She clung on tight and was lifted off the ground. He swung her around and slammed her against the wall behind him. Then, he pinned her with her own rod, preventing any more fancy footwork or steel-toed kicks. She was a skilled fighter, but he was stronger. His steely, wild muscles had been honed by five years in the desert, fighting for survival among hostile sub-men.

Cil had gone pale from loss of blood, and her right leg was stiff and locked up. One himself seemed worse for wear and tottered drunkenly, using only his blind strength to keep her pinned, as unsteady fighters often do. Perhaps that blow to his head had been worse than it looked. Whatever the case, concussion or no, One had the advantage. He now began pressing Cil down, crushing her into the corner where wall meets floor, giving her no room to move, her own weapon being used against her.

Brand stood on the edge of the imaginary ring, hands clenched, face pale, and gnawing his lower lip in frustration. One now mounted Cil and sat on top of her belly, pinning her down with the rod across her neck, choking her. With his free hand, he began raining down blow after blow upon her face and torso. One! Two! Three!

Brand couldn't take it anymore and hoisted a crate to dash across One's back. But Berengar raised his sword, blocking him off, and shook his head solemnly. His serious, steel-blue eyes spoke volumes: *No, we mustn't interfere*, they said.

Whack! Another blow. Cil was now dazed, bruised, and bloody —and put well in her place as far as One was concerned.

Brand was done with codes and rules. He was about to backstab this treacherous woman-beater.

One paused for a moment, taking his eyes off Cil to say something to Two... Cil's hand reached out and closed upon a steel ingot, which had fallen from the nearby workbench. Her hand flashed toward One in a wild arc. One turned back to Cil, and met the wild blow. Crunch! One was completely turned about. His eyes looked wide and perplexed as he toppled from Cil, like those of a dead fish, the light of awareness blown into the wind.

Three ran over to One, sobbing, and Two looked of a mind to commit murder on Cil. He advanced toward the panting girl with knife held high, for he believed she had just killed his brother.

But before Two could get close, Three exclaimed, "By Mackmellah, he's alive! Still, never have I seen such a knockout— would you look at that! His eyes are wide open!"

Hearing that his brother lived, Two put away his knife and

helped Three position One in such a way as to avoid further damage or suffocation.

"It is true, that was a fell blow!" Boomed Berengar. "Brand, don't stand there like a great eel—help out the lass!"

Cil chuckled weakly. "Gotcha," she said. Then continued to mutter in a quiet, disjointed fashion, as Brand and Berengar carried her into the main room. They laid her gently on Brand's rug bed, and Berengar dressed her wounds with a piece of stoic cloth, while Two and Three saw to One's needs.

Shortly thereafter, she propped herself up and looked around the room with quiet interest. "So this is what the rest of this place looks like?" She said, speaking distractedly to the world at large. "I passed out in the canyons to the north three weeks ago, only to wake a day later in *that hole*. And I've been in there ever since."

Her whole demeanor had changed; gone was the vicious spitfire. Regaining her freedom and being left alone, she had become peaceful and unassuming, simply enjoying her own space for the time. "Well, at least it's cooler in this room..." she went on.

"You're welcome," said Brand.

Cil paid him no more attention than a slight curling of her lip. Besides, she was busy looking at the hamsters above. "Such cute, hardworking things," she said, her green eyes bright.

Three and Two dragged One past them and toward the pantry. Brand rose and followed behind the struggling dwarfs at a leisurely pace, intending to observe their doings.

The pantry was a small, tall chamber with walls stacked high on two sides with food stores and cooking implements. Sacks of grain were on the floor, and the improvised shelving was stocked high with stores. On the left side of the chamber was a sort of cramped kitchen, with cooking benches, and an ingenious wood-fire oven molded into the wall with a clay chimney. Beside this, a natural rock basin supplied fresh water from a hidden spring. There was an ingenious drainage system around the basin so that, as it constantly overflowed, the water was caught in a moat and carried away into an exit hole at the corner of the room.

Two and Three laid One gently on his side near the basin, and began dabbing his head and face with a damp cloth. This went on for some time, and Brand, growing bored, wandered back into the main room.

Cil seemed at peace, relaxing on Brand's bed and gazing around the room like an inquisitive cat. Berengar had returned to his favorite cushion and was shuffling a rough pack of cards he had found amongst the crates.

"Care for a game, Brand?" he said, as Brand took a cushion opposite him.

"Sure, nothing to do until that scoundrel One is back among the living. He better have a good exit plan for us..."

"Will you play *Sharks* or *Clavilet*?"

"*Sharks—Clavilet* is an evening game," replied Brand suavely.

"Here, have a drink," Berengar offered, pouring Brand a goblet from a great skin of wine. He kept the skin for himself, drinking directly from it, and began to deal out cards.

A couple of hours passed by, with Two and Three coming and going—checking on their brother, joining in on a hand or two, and then wandering off again to tinker on some affair or another. Brand grew impatient. "Berengar, let us go and check on One."

"Aye, why not," replied Berengar, happy to get away from another losing hand. Three nodded too and rose with them. The group made their way into the pantry together, and found Two pressing a damp cloth on One's forehead.

"I see you're still trying that gimmick," teased Berengar.

Two scowled up at him, muttering under his breath.

"Well," continued Berengar, now standing with arms akimbo, "at least his eyes have closed. A more natural slumber, to be sure."

"Aye, that was quite uncanny, with eyes wide open and all, was it not?" replied Two with a grim chuckle.

Berengar bent down and examined One with an officious air—feeling his pulse, sniffing his breath, and performing various other unaccountable actions. Then he nodded firmly. "It's as I suspected. He needs *professional treatment.*"

"Really?" said Two, concerned. "Where will we get one of those?..."

"*Allow me,*" said Berengar, stepping close. With one great hand, he picked One up by his leather jerkin and pitched him headlong into the basin of icy-cold water.

Chapter 4
"Alucard."

Wind blows through the canyons, o'er yon desert deeps, when wild it rises atop sweltering heat

We delve through the night; by day do we sleep, with pygmies below, black shadows that leap

When the gliders bear us, we'll pray for Godspeed and soar through the canyons from mountain's high peak=

Though lowly in station, still freedom we seek—lonely the tale of One, Two, and Three...
—Song of Ator Periconias

***

One glided into the water like a stiff board, face presented upwards, arms by his sides. Nothing. A twitch of the muscles. His eyes flicked open. A silent scream bubbled out of his mouth. Then, with a convulsive start, he thrashed upright, the end of a strangled cry becoming audible as his face emerged from the water.

"*Yeaarrkk!*" He looked around in surprise, then snapped, "How did *you* get in here?" he said, staring at Brand and Berengar. Then, remembering they were his guests he grimaced and gathered himself, "Where's Pikar?... Wait, what time is it? *Give me ten more minutes...*" he muttered and, closing his eyes, he lay back in the pool, floating with arms folded behind his head. He rested his eyes for a moment before speaking again. "Two and Three, prepare breakfast, would you? I have just had a terrible dream..."

Two and Three became animated. *Their brother was okay!* "Sure thing, One!" they replied in unison, then got to it.

One cracked open a sly, little eye and peeked sidelong at Brand and Berengar. "*Vile wretches!* So it wasn't a dream. *Just my luck...*"

He looked more petulant and surly than ever. "*What?!* Can't a man bathe in peace? *Off with you!*"

Brand and Berengar turned their backs and swaggered slowly from the room.

Noting their unhurried gait, One took further offense. "Know you no speed? Begone, I say! *Go!*" he raged at their backs, shaking his fist and splashing cold water in their direction.

Brand replied stubbornly, "*I'm going,* but I shall not rush helter-skelter through this cramped and disorderly burrow."

One shouted more invectives. But they faded out as Brand returned to the main chamber.

Brand and Berengar went back to playing cards for a time. Occasionally, Brand watched Cil from the corner of his eye, observing this anomaly of a girl with great curiosity. She seemed entirely content, entertaining herself by gazing around the room or working the areas around her wounded thigh with her strong hands. Occasionally, she would get up and stretch like a cat, then hobble around to ensure her leg didn't freeze up completely.

"It's quite cool in here, though the smell could be improved," she said, to no one in particular.

Brand looked over from his cushion and ventured a casual comment. "Yeah, it's nice, isn't it?"

Cil looked at Brand as if he were an unwelcome insect. "Who asked you, *ugly?*" Then she scowled and stuck out her tongue in childish fashion.

Brand frowned with displeasure and looked away.

Cil flashed her teeth, then turned her attention back to the hamster in front of her, making little squeaking noises and scratching its ear with one finger through the cage.

Shortly after this, Two and Three came out, cleared the table, and laid out the evening's repast.

One appeared with a large mug of wine, and it was clear he had been drinking—his cheeks were flushed, and his eyes were slightly glazed.

"This damnable headache is only just leaving me. Ah, the sweet embrace of wine," he mumbled, trying to sound cheery. However, it was impossible to hide the surly glower on his face at the sight of Cil.

Brand grabbed his chart and brought it to the table, sitting across from One.

"Okay, One, we made a deal. Here is the chart, but first, tell me the escape plan as we agreed."

"*What?* After you meddled in my affairs? The deal is off. Find your own damned way out!"

"What!? *Oathbreaker!*" Berengar ejaculated, jumping to his feet.

"We did not shake on it!" persisted One stubbornly.

"Nay," Three spoke out, "you said '*done*.'"

"Break your word on a struck deal," Berengar grinned icily, "and *The People's Law of the Outlands* no longer applies to you, as you well know."

"Meaning...?" replied One stonily, pausing mid-drink and giving Berengar a glassy-eyed leer over his shoulder.

"Meaning," replied Berengar, his eyes pieces of steely flint, "all other rights of yours are null..." One brawny hand shot up and clasped the hilt of his sword.

One stared at Berengar for a long time, his pride vying with what little reason remained in his befuddled mind. Then, swallowing his pride, he answered, "Forgive me. It was the wine, and this damn clout to the head..."

Berengar nodded, accepting One's apology.

One took another swig of wine, and then told them the plan.

"It takes two days and a night to clear the pygmies' territory. The first night, they would sniff you out and come upon you in unguessed numbers." He paused and looked shrewdly at Berengar.

"I know not how you eluded them the night Brand was captured."

Berengar vouchsafed nothing.

One continued, "Our situation is precarious, to say the least. So, we wanted a sure-fire route of escape should things turn sour. Three here, being the genius that he is, constructed three contraptions of wood and canvas—like large birds. He said he got the idea from some old sketches. He calls them 'gliders.' He made three of them for us, and said that if it ever became unsafe here, all we'd need to do is grab them and charge off the large outcrop higher up the mountain... that they'd carry us, swift as an eagle, and out of the badlands."

Brand looked at him for a long moment. "And you have tested them?"

"No. We never became desperate enough to attempt it." One shrugged and scratched his bald head.

Brand narrowed his eyes. "*This was your great plan?*"

"Well, what I'm getting from your chart is as great an unknown."

Berengar's eyes became wide and wild. He turned slowly to face One. "I have been waiting for this moment for a *long time*."

Brand gave an anxious grimace of reluctant hesitation. But Three broke in. "They *will* work as designed! I swear it! And I shall show you how to operate them! I would have tested them myself—if One had let me..."

"Great—" Brand said, with exaggerated sarcasm.

"*Well said, Three!*" cut in Berengar, sprinting to his feet in excitement. "I like a man confident in his craft!" He turned to Brand, his great arms raised above his head, "Brand, I've always thought it would be *grand* to fly like a hawk—*high* in the sky, *wind* in my hair, *master* of the lands below. Would you deny me this?"

Brand still hesitated. "But what of Cil?" he said, gesturing toward the girl, who had just taken an interest in the conversation.

"*What of Cil?*" she mocked. "Don't you *dare* think of leaving me behind. I will fly with Berengar, *if you're too cowardly to try it.*"

Brand drew back in disbelief. "Are all *Outlanders* mad? But what of your leg?"

"My leg is as sound as my mind. Besides, flying is better than walking for me right now, *stupid!*" She rolled her eyes.

"Then, we fly!" said Berengar, his eyes faraway and wistful. He was completely enraptured. "Three, begin the training..."

Crack.

"I'll master the contraption before the day is out..."

Crack.

"We shall fly like... What in *Makmellah's* name?"

Crack! The sound of a hard, crisp substance snapping apart tinkled through the chamber. Everyone went silent. All heads turned toward Berengar's hammock, where the noise had emanated from. Brand jumped to his feet, calling, "*The sacred egg!*"

The men dashed over to observe, and Cil, unable to contain her interest, limped over to join the rest. The group crowded around the hammock, and Berengar reached inside, gently lifting the large egg out. A section had been pushed outward and fallen loose, leaving a shadowy crevice on one side. Berengar carefully placed the egg down on the floor and waved everyone back.

"Don't stifle the thing!" he bellowed.

"What in *Gangy's* name is it?" asked One grimly. "Is it a bird?"

"No, it's surely a dragon!" called out Three excitedly.

"You think so?" asked Two, showing some interest.

All watched the hatching unfold with bated breath. Another piece broke off and fell clear. Then another. And another. Suddenly the remaining structure crumpled to the floor, forming a small mound. At its center was a small man-shaped creature, the size of a human hand. It had blue-green skin and delicate webbed hands and feet. Large, pale, blind-looking eyes stared uncertainly about the room. Its mouth opened in a vacuous gape, showing two rows of pink gums. The overall impression was that of a misbegotten frog walking upright, covered in a thick layer of grayish slime.

One, Two, and Three all let out strangled cries of dismay, fell backward onto their haunches, and scuttled away across the floor.

Berengar frowned and said, "Don't act toward baby parsan like that!"

Brand knelt on one knee and spoke soothingly to the creature. "There, there, it's okay."

Cil instantly became enamored with the thing and lowered herself to the floor beside Brand, saying, "Oh, it's so cuuuuuute! Come here, my little baby-frog—*mummy is here.*"

Berengar knelt nearby as well, spreading his arms wide. "Don't listen to these miscreants, Baby Parsan. You know who your daddy is, don't you? You recognize the one who labored over your egg for days and kept you warm through the nights, don't you?"

The creature tottered on unsteady, bowed legs and began to wander about blindly, first in one direction and then the other. Presently it moved toward the cries of Berengar and then, uncertain, changed its mind and staggered weakly toward the sounds of Cil. Almost reaching her, it turned aside suddenly and tottered up to Brand with arms wide.

Suddenly the gray film of slime caught on the floor and peeled off like a cloak. Its blind eyes blinked, shedding their temporary shells, and revealed glowing-blue eyes, bright as the summer sky.

It stared up at Brand with eyes full of love. "*Mama!*" it cried in a soft gargle.

The fact that it could speak immediately might have surprised the others, but Brand and Berengar knew it was a genetically programmed creature—and thus, they expected the unusual. Brand smiled with affection, scooped it up, and held it against his shoulder.

"Nooooo!" Cil cried out in despair, beating her small fists on the floor. "That is simply not fair! How could you choose that ugly boy over me? He's not even a *girl!* How could he be your mother? Brand, won't you let me hold him? *Please?* I'll be nice!"

Berengar turned away. Then stood up and gazed out one of the light shafts, a single tear sparkling on his sun-browned cheek.

Was the great oaf sulking? Brand wondered in disbelief.

"So be it," Berengar mumbled beneath his breath.

The man's like a great child sometimes, thought Brand. "Will you two stop it? Don't be so ridiculous. Here, Cil, if it will cease your cries, have a hold of him."

Cil grinned and took hold of the creature, who immediately began letting out a plaintive gurgle, and attempted to paddle its way back to Brand.

With a frown of dismay, Cil handed the creature back to him, where it cuddled peacefully against his shoulder.

Eventually, One, Two, and Three got over their shock and came to inspect the creature.

"Ey, it's not so ugly now, is it?" said Three.

Cil gave him a withering look.

One asked, "What in the devil is it?"

Brand directed a meaningful look at Berengar, who simply shrugged. Then Brand decided to tell them: "It's a genetically engineered creature—a construct of the ancients, left behind. Its forbearer died in a calamity in a mountain village. We salvaged the egg as we escaped."

"It's like a fish-frog-man," said One crudely.

"Don't be insulting, it's so much more than that," said Berengar defensively.

"One's words at least have the merit of brevity," admitted Brand.

"*Amazing.* Who knew that such things still remained?" said Cil, fascinated.

"*Back off!*" said Brand, suddenly agitated by their closeness. "You're stifling him."

"Ah, his motherly instincts are kicking in!" barked Berengar with an offensive laugh, slapping his knee.

Brand rolled his eyes while the others laughed.

"Well," said Berengar finally, "the plan hasn't changed. Three, teach us the ways of the *sky!*"

And so, Three instructed Brand, Berengar, and Cil on his machines and the basics of aerodynamics, in the presence One's hateful gaze. The hours went by, and the shafts of afternoon sun eventually faded, to be replaced by the silvery shimmers of moonlight. Three was at this moment explaining what an updraft was and sketching their locations within the canyons on the map when baby Parsan awoke from his nap and began a plaintive gurgle. Brand attempted to soothe him, but this time nothing worked.

"I believe he's hungry," said Cil, with that motherly insight inherent in all women.

"Ah, okay... but, *what does he eat?*" replied Brand in a huff.

"What does a frog eat?" said Three.

Brand and Cil glared at him, but then Berengar broke in. "He may be right. Frogs need no milk and eat insects and small fleshy things... and he does be *like* a frog after all... Three, hand me that desert-hamster kabab."

Three handed him the kabab, and Berengar broke off a piece of meat the size of a fingernail. He proffered it delicately on one large finger to baby Parsan.

The creature ceased its plaintive noises and turned its eyes upon the meat, sniffing it. It then began to suckle on the meat and fingertip, delicately.

"Ah, that tickles," laughed Berengar. "Oh, his gums feel hard, like a lizard's beak."

Suddenly, its jaw stretched wide like a pelican's and engulfed most of Berengar's large finger.

"Ouch," he cried in surprise, laughing all the harder as he quickly tugged his finger away. "*He nipped me!*"

"Did you see how his jaw expanded?" said Brand, aghast.

"Let's see what he can do with something larger!" said Berengar, his voice full of barbaric curiosity. He tore off a full leg—about the size of a chicken drumstick—and offered it to the creature. Its jaw opened, and its elastic lips stretched wide to engulf the entire leg, which was nearly as tall as the creature itself.

Its eyes bulged as its small head ballooned around the meat and bone. Its flexible body molded to the shape of its meal in an unbelievable fashion. All watched, gaping in stunned silence, as it overcame the drumstick lengthwise. Then it looked up at Brand with affection in its blue eyes. Its body now appeared strangely shaped, lopsided and hunchbacked, due to the stiff drumstick within. It leaned against Brand's chest and promptly fell back asleep.

"It's a damned monster!" said One in surly tones. "Imagine what it could do if full grown!"

Brand swallowed nervously. Then said, "We'll bring him up right. Also, I believe a name has just come to me."

"Yeah?" said Cil.

"Yes. *Alucard.*"

"*Alucard?* What kind of name is that?" Berengar said, scratching his chin.

"I don't know. It just came to me, and—well, it seems right."

Berengar looked crestfallen. "I was thinking it could be called something grand, like *Sky-Eater the Blue* or *Drak the Insatiable.*"

"I like it! It's a handsome name," said Cil.

"Whatever you say... it chose you, after all," said Berengar sadly.

Two smiled maliciously and said, "Let's try giving it a whole live hamster!"

"Moving on," said Brand. "Let us review the gliders again."

"Now, what about your side of the bargain?" cried One. "*Let me see that chart!*"

"By all means," replied Brand with aplomb. "Here." He placed it on the table before the the eager dwarf.

At once, he snatched it up and greedily surveyed it with narrowed eyes. "Two, Three, *look at this!*"

Two and Three eagerly joined One at the table.

Brand pretended to peruse the crates littering the room while surreptitiously watching their faces. Their body language and flashing eyes told him much: the chart was clearly of great importance. Three took copious notes on a piece of paper as One whispered to him, pointing eagerly at certain symbols. This continued until One seemed satisfied with their findings.

"I see it was a good bargain for you, indeed," said Brand.

"Well... it gives us hope," said One, slumping slightly, feigning dejection in an attempt to conceal his excitement. "It's rough out here in the Badlands for three small folk such as ourselves." He shook his head with exaggerated sorrow.

Brand felt the dwarf was minimizing their gain out of sheer bargaining habit. "Well, I'm glad we could help," he said flatly. "Now, *I'll take back my chart, thank you.*" He rolled it up, then asked, "Can you tell me what it does?"

"Aye, but there's a price... let the girl stay, and I'll tell you."

At this, Cil, who had been playing a dice game in the corner with Berengar, looked up and swore. "How many times do I—"

"Peace, Cil," said Brand, raising his hand. "One, you know I cannot do that. She has her own say, and she does not want to remain here."

"Yeah!" Interjected Berengar cheerfully. "Can't you take rejection on the chin like a man, One?"

One's face went red. He became sullen and quiet, then stalked out of the room into the southern chamber. There they heard him wrathfully vent his emotions to a terrified audience of giant hamsters.

Once total darkness fell, One, Two, and Three left the hideout in their mechanical monster. Brand and Berengar planned for a smooth escape, deciding One could not be trusted, and set watches for their final night. Berengar offered to take the first watch while Cil slept on Brand's bed, and Brand took one of the hammocks. After this, Brand took his shift, and Cil took the final, shortest shift before sunrise.

Brand awoke to the pristine shafts of dawn-light, and gathering his things, he found Alucard had grown larger, and was now oddly shaped. He wondered with concern what Alucard had eaten during the night, and had an eerie feeling that it was one of the giant hamsters.

Berengar and Cil were already up, packing their few belongings. Brand got dressed in the fresh set of clothes One had given him, then gathered his weapons. After this, he strapped Alucard to his chest in the canvas pouch Berengar originally used for his egg.

He looked to Berengar and Cil and asked, "Where are One and the others?"

"They are waiting outside, by the entrance. They have come and gone a couple of times in the past hour, and more recently, checked in to tell me all was ready," replied Berengar.

"Fantastic. They've come to see us off on our lovely flight," said Brand, his voice heavy with sarcasm.

"Yes! Let's go!" said Berengar, rushing for the exit with Cil half-draped over his shoulder, her injured leg dragging.

Three opened the large circular door for them as they approached, and let them pass before locking it again. There stood One and Two, by the entrance, staring sullenly at their departing guests. The morning air had a slight chill, and all three of the dawrfs sported oversized coats of coarse leather, which dragged at their feet. Brand thought they looked ridiculous, but made no comment.

"What's in the coats?" said Berengar suspiciously.

"Instruments!" said One, opening his coat to reveal a strange, oval-shaped clay wind instrument with many holes. At the same time, Two produced a percussion device: a wooden circle strung with rattling beads, while Three revealed a flat drum and a double-sided stick. "We wished to send you off with a song, as was the custom among our circus folk."

"A large-hearted gesture. And one of which I greatly approve!" said Berengar happily, his suspicions lulled.

One gave his best smile, but his bloodshot eyes somewhat ruined the effect. Brand could tell he hadn't slept at all.

One let out an impatient grunt, finding Brand's close inspection somewhat offensive, and moved off, beckoning them to follow. With Two and Three at his side, One led the party through a series of sloping crevice pathways, always upward, winding round and round the mountain as they went. They clambered over low rocky ledges and up steep, crumbling walls. Berengar was forced to lift Cil bodily and carry her over such obstacles, much to her disgust. But, seeing no other way, she sullenly acquiesced.

One, Two, and Three seemed on edge, their gnarled faces pale and tense. Brand also noticed Berengar stop a few times to sniff the wind, before searching the nearby crags and crevices with his piercing gaze.

After forty minutes, the party arrived at their destination: a flat-topped outcrop guarded by a hidden pass. It had an overhang that jutted out into space, seemingly defying gravity. They were now at an elevation of over one thousand feet—far below, the canyons smoldered.

One, Two, and Three were grimacing and sweating copiously in their long leather coats, adding to the ridiculousness of their aspect. Brand looked away, covering his smirk with a cough.

The outcrop faced west and was bathed in shadow, cast by the rising sun behind the mountain's peak at their backs. The three gliding contraptions were prepared out on the runway—small, precarious things nestled atop the great outcrop.

Beyond the gliders, spread a wide vista, where the tangled crags of the badlands fell away to a blanket-dark forest, which stretched clean to the western horizon. The dark forest was wreathed in morning mist, rising from the moist flora in response to the sun's first heat of the day.

Between them and the forest's edge was an obstacle course caused by the upheaval of Varus'Dorae—a series of smaller peaks, a maze of spiking outcrops, broken up by frequent canyons and crevices. This they would have to navigate in the gliders, using the wind patterns Three had calculated for them.

"*Beautiful,*" murmured Cil.

"The stuff of life! Ah, *this is why I am a traveling sculptor!*" Berengar's eyes gleamed as he spoke.

Brand agreed too, but said nothing, enjoying the sight with silent admiration.

"Aye, this is our favorite lookout," grumbled One. "Well, I guess this is goodbye. We'll play you a song of safe flight once you're in the air." He waved them away awkwardly, and Three took them over to their gliders. One and Two did not follow, but instead stood there watching them glumly, their backs to a shadowy pass behind them.

Berengar and Brand waved their thanks to the small trio.

"One, I will carve a great face for you three—Ator Periconias—so that people shall know your lonely station here, out among the crags," said Berengar, his fist to his chest.

"Thank you. All I had to offer you was the chart. I hope this helped," said Brand, slightly embarrassed at his previous mistrust for One.

Alucard let out a large burp, snuggled closer to Brand's chest, and began snoring.

Cil simply turned her head away—an act which caused One to scowl blackly at the ground before his feet.

Three went to move back to One and Two, then paused awkwardly, as if stuck in indecision.

Now, an uneasy feeling prickled at the back Brand's neck. It reminded him of the uncanny sense he had—that gut pull that let him know when *Drift's End* city guards were closing in on him, ready to spring their trap.

Three looked ashamed for a second and then said, "Sorry, I... I forgot something." He rushed back to One and Three.

"*What the devil is going on?*" ejaculated Berengar, now too sensing something amiss.

One, Two, and Three each pulled a loaded crossbow from somewhere in the folds of their heavy coats — it seemed musical instruments were not the only things they had been hiding. They pointed the three deadly devices at Berengar. Fast though the golden giant was, he couldn't dodge crossbow bolts.

One stared at them, his grim expression betraying the plotting brain of a demented leprechaun. "The girl stays, or Berengar dies. And then you, thin boy..."

Berengar's neck muscles tensed into steely cables, veins pulsing across his forehead and chest. The savage growl of a timber wolf rumbled deep within his throat. *"Treacherous gnomes!"* he roared.

Ignoring Berengar, One said, "Boy, Tall Man, take your gliders and go." He spoke in slow, deliberate tones.

Brand blanched, sweat breaking out on his forehead. "Easy, One.

Let's talk this out. You know this isn't how you wanted things to be..."

"No more *talking!*" One roared, his short temper flaring. He steadied his crossbow sights on Berengar's chest. Then, with an evil grin, he went on, "Take the gliders, and go. What's the girl to you anyway? She's more trouble than she's worth."

"You're right," said Brand, trying to match One's emotion. "Exactly right. I'm trying to save *you* any more trouble." Then, feeling he had some momentum, he kept going. "She hasn't done anything for you but waste your resources." And then, getting overexcited at his own genius, he added, "I mean, she's basically just dead weight, right?"

"Hey!" said Cil, taking offense.

"All true, but—*she's mine*. No more wheedling. She comes now or I'm firing. Five... four... three..."

Brand froze, his hand surreptitiously sliding to a throwing knife, though little good it would do.

"Two..."

In the corner of his eye, Brand saw Berengar begin to tense, preparing to spring.

But One never finished his countdown. A monstrous, broad black shape—a misshapen silhouette—appeared behind him, looming over his small figure. Out of the shadows, Pikar leapt onto One's back. His vicious claws clamped onto handfuls of flesh, his filed teeth snapped into One's right ear with a sickening crunch of tearing cartilage.

One bellowed in pain and surprise, accidentally firing off his crossbow. The bolt flew into the sky and disappeared. Blood now streamed down his face, and he dropped the crossbow, attempting to draw his deadly, serrated blade. Two and Three yelped in surprise and turned in shock. They lowered their crossbows, fearing to hit One. After a split second of indecision, both drew their knives and dove at the muscle-bound sub-human.

The combined weight of their charge toppled Pikar backward, and the pygmy fell into the shadowy crevice with the three dwarfs clinging to him like a litter of suckling puppies. As they rolled out of sight, their knives began to rise and fall like butchers' cleavers, the inhuman vitality of the pygmy withstanding damage that would have killed five men. Now only howls and savage breaths could be heard echoing from the crevice. Brand was glad he could see no more of that terrible struggle.

"Quick! Now's our chance—*to the gliders!*" said Berengar in a harsh whisper. He scooped up Cil and hooked her into the glider. Then, lifting both her and the glider onto his great back, he charged down the runway. After thirty paces, the sails caught the wind, and Cil was lifted like a feather out of Berengar's grip. Then, dashing back toward his own glider, he bellowed, "*Go, Brand! Get going!*"

Brand snapped out of his trance and dashed toward his glider. In the corner of his eye, he saw One climb bedraggled out of the crevice. His thick leather coat was torn into bloody shreds, and his right ear was gone. His face was a mask of gore, with blood streaming down his bared, hairy chest. Two and Three followed, also ragged and torn, but not as badly as One, who had clearly borne the brunt of Pikar's wrath.

Brand reached his glider and picked it up. He started running. Looking back, he saw that One was only twenty paces behind him, bearing either Two's or Three's loaded crossbow. Brand tried to lift off, but he didn't have enough speed yet. He glanced back again. Now, One aimed the crossbow right at his back. Brand clenched his teeth, his abs, and then his butthole, ready to receive the killing blow.

It didn't come.

One gazed after Cil, already gliding off over the ledge, far out of his reach. He swore and slung the crossbow onto his shoulder.

"The damn girl's already gone. No point in killing the boy," he muttered. Then he let out a bitter laugh—full of grim irony at his own fate. It caught the wind and echoed through the canyons below.

Berengar was far ahead when Brand's sails finally caught an updraft. He was lifted into the air above the overhang, then he plunged down over its edge like a swooping eagle.

One walked glumly to the brink and sat down, his feet dangling over the edge. Two and Three came and sat beside him. They could see Brand, Berengar, and Cil gliding away below, following the hot air routes through the canyons, as Three had instructed.

One smiled sadly, pulled out his clay wind instrument, and blew a few notes. Two and Three looked at him inquiringly.

"Aye, lads," One said, "it is the song of the wind today. No good in wishing them ill luck."

"You're a good man, big brother," said Three affectionately. One played on.

"Rats," said Two bitterly. Then he took up his improvised shaker and joined in.

Three followed with his drum, and all three began to sing to the tune.

Wind blows through the canyons, o'er yon desert deeps; when wild it rises atop sweltering heat.
We delve through the night; by day do we sleep; with pygmies below, black shadows that leap...

The song continued, but the rest of the words were lost to Brand. For as soon as he had passed over the edge, all other thoughts had left his mind. His entire mental capacity was now focused on staying aloft. He had thought it terrifying when a gust first carried him into the air above the overhang—but when a swift downdraft shot him over the rim of the ledge in a dive, he had nearly blacked out entirely. Now, he clung to the handrail of the glider with

sweaty palms, praying his grip wouldn't slip, and that the leather
tether keeping him attached to the frame would hold firm.

His wide eyes rolled side to side, unwilling to look down at the
tiny specks of shrubbery and thin outlines of trails far below.
Frantically now, he glanced around for Berengar and Cil.

"*Hazzaaarrr!*" came Cil's voice from up and to Brand's left.

Brand caught a glimpse of Cil's triangular face and dark red hair
as she glided by. Her green eyes sparkled with confidence, and her
full lips were spread in a tiger's snarl of defiance. Despite her
injured leg, her glider flew straight and steady. "This beats
walking!" She called as she shot ahead of him.

Brand found her casual attitude both galling and offensive. Then
he scowled and tried to gain control of himself — it wasn't a good
look to be a coward in front of a lady. Rallying his courage, he
assayed to change the direction of his glider by pulling back on the
control cables. His glider angled. And, perspiring heavily, he
started gaining on the red-haired girl.

He turned his head, searching for Berengar on his right. But
couldn't see him. Instead, he heard a barbaric exclamation from
above:

"*Ackanshai aralaman sharalaman!!!!*" A second later, Berengar
spiraled downward, into a canyon below.

Brand shook his head in horror—his friend was surely a goner.
"Berengar!" he cried out.

But the wild man pulled out of the dive, hitting a hot air current
at the lip of the canyon he'd dropped into. Seconds later it sent him
soaring up through the air on Brand's right.

Presently, Berengar reappeared. This time, on Brand's left,
attempting a loop-the-loop. He failed halfway through and began
plummeting backward, falling against his glider and tangling in its
sails. Letting out a strangled, hoarse cry, he fell out of sight behind
a crag, jerking amongst the cables of his glider.

Brand, his stomach sinking, tried to trace Berengar's fall.

That would have been the end of Berengar, had not an extremely strong buffet of hot air from a heat trap caught his sails, flipping him upright and launching him skyward once more. A now shaky and perspiring Berengar reappeared on Brand's right, laughing grimly.

"By Makmellah! *Brand, did you see that?*!" he roared, looking thoroughly pleased with himself. "Why, that's the closest to death I've *ever been* hah!!"

"You damned fool!" cried Brand in a hot rage. "Did not Three show us that, due to the design, such maneuvers would be impossible?"

Berengar managed to pull off a casual shrug, despite hanging off a jerry-rigged glider two thousand feet above a deserted wasteland ruled by demonic sub-human pygmies. "Had to try it..." he said with a grin.

Brand wiped his forehead with a shaky hand.

"Don't be such a spoilsport," called Cil, her harsh laugh ringing out from his left. "You take things too seriously. Why don't you try taking a dive? Have some fun for once!"

"*I have a baby on board!*" Brand stormed, his face red with fear and frustration.

"Oh... you're right!" Cil crooned, finally cutting Brand some slack.

Brand looked stonily forward, a picture of dignified resentment. Then, he glanced down at the pouch strapped to his chest. Poking out of it was Alucard's little froggy head. His bright blue eyes scanned the terrain far below with wonder and interest.

While Brand was checking on Alucard, Berengar and Cil glided on either side of him, enjoying the thrill of the flight. It was at this moment that the music from the Ator Periconias trio caught up with them.

First came the sounds from One's wind instrument, as if carried on a cool breeze right to their ears. The notes were light and free, speaking of the falcon and the great eagle, the fabled air barges of the ancients, the grandeur of the trumpet and the horn, and the gusty laughter of the freeman. All that the wind brings and embodies, that tune told. It lifted Brand's spirit, melted away his tension. The shaker of Two arrived, adding spirit to the tune and keeping the tempo of the flight. Then the drum came, *dada da, dada da*, lending a depth and breathing courage into the soul.

Brand now felt strangely at ease in the glider, a surge of exhilaration filling him. With wind in his wavy blond hair, he glanced around at the broad vistas on all sides. Small, shining emerald birds began appearing in the air, swarming about the three companions, eventually forming a great, swirling cloud.

A feeling of magic was in the air, as if reality bordered on a dream.

Cil laughed, this time a pretty tinkling sound that Brand found attractive, and Berengar's booming bark echoed comfortingly to his right.

Alucard gurgled in delight at the flashing green creatures. "Be-au-ti-ful," came the word in his strange, halting voice.

Never had Brand moved this fast, nor felt so free. Down below, a trail winding among the deep burning canyons rushed by rapidly —they were certainly making good ground. But best of all, the sweltering heat was not felt—not here, not while traveling among the people of the wind.

And so, focusing their minds on staying aloft, the three companions navigated the cliffs and canyons of the blasted lands. At times they precariously swerved between two peaks or, by necessity, dived under a great underpass of rock, as rough-hewn walls sped close by on either side. They glided around the edge of a great rounded crag, always riding the heat waves higher when their altitude dropped too low. Their emerald bird friends, like fleeting, animated gems, kept them company, guiding them as they went, giving advance notice of sudden perils. And always, they were followed by the Song of Ator Periconias. The song found echo in the bellies of the canyons below and reverberated throughout the tortured land, lending courage to their hearts and wind to their wings.

Though they had been gliding for an hour and a half, it had gone by in a rush that felt like only minutes. Ahead lay the dark fringe of the forest, now seemingly cold and gloomy in comparison to the bright, high places of the wind and the sky.

"We should slow our gliders, as Three taught us. There's a good, flat runway before the forest's edge. Remember, landing is the most dangerous part, and it's important that—"

"Nonsense! Don't be such a coward," mocked Cil.

"Bah, I've tamed a Tundra giant's daughter," cried Berengar. "*I* at least don't fear a rugged desert landing!" Then so saying, Berengar soared onward, angling upward once more to make another circle.

Brand shook his head. "*Outlanders,*" he said with a sigh.

Easing off on the speed by tilting the sails backward, Brand lined up a flat runway and smoothly cruised down. Moments later, he leaned back and touched down lightly. Once. Twice. And then, he leaned backwards heavily, coming to a sliding stop on his feet. The lightweight glider, losing its air suction, gently tilted off to the side. He let it down and then checked on Alucard.

The small creature's eyes were bright, but its face was squirming in a grimace of discomfort. Suddenly, it vomited a large, slimy blob onto Brand's chest.

"Unsavory. An unsavory business *indeed.*" Brand said. He had heard of such behavior and guessed that it was bound to have happened eventually—but that didn't make it any less unpleasant.

Leaning forward, he let the heavy gray glob fall to the ground, and then began wiping clear the remaining goo. As the blob hit the ground, a hard, angular corner was revealed inside it. Grabbing a nearby stick, dried and bleached by the sun, Brand proceeded to scrape the goo off the object.

"Why!" he exclaimed. "It's the notebook of Ator Periconias! Oh, I can only imagine One's face right now..." A malicious chuckle escaped him as he scooped it up and added it to his pouch.

"Mine, mine!" cried Alucard, his little froggy, four-fingered hands reaching for it.

"So this is what you ate last night, you little devil?" Brand replied. "You can have it later, okay?"

"Okay," replied Alucard forlornly, with such conversational skill and dignified restraint that Brand was forced to look twice in awe at the small creature.

"This is how you do a landing, Brand!" Cil called out as she sped dangerously close, clipping him on the ear with a small, strong hand.

"*Villainous hellcat!*" he called out, holding his head and wincing. Alucard poked his head further out of the pouch and growled protectively, glaring at Cil through narrow eyes.

Cil's laughter rang out as she dived to the ground—still traveling, Brand noted, at quite a fast speed. He saw a look of realization cross her delicate features as she pulled back suddenly, one hand fumbling anxiously for the release catch of her harness. She touched down hard with a squeal of pain. Bounced once, and then again, before digging her feet into the loose, sandy earth. Leaning on her good leg, she skidded along the ground before toppling forward and sliding for twenty paces on her back, tangled up in her crumpled glider.

Brand chuckled with satisfaction.

Cil disentangled herself from the glider. Then, with further grunts of pain, she lurched upright and glared at Brand. She looked ragged and dusty, and now blood had begun to seep through the bandages on her wounded leg.

Brand gave a subtle shrug, somehow communicating both innocence and disinterest—*he wanted no more whacks to the head.*

"Aaaaaeeeehhh! By Thorkar, Rinbar, and Gangy!" Berengar boomed, then let out a strangled exclamation.

Cil and Brand turned their heads and saw Berengar, fifty paces ahead, go down hard into a sandbank near the forest's edge. He hit at such a speed that when his feet made contact with earth, he cartwheeled rapidly—still attached to his glider—and ended up in a dense thicket by the tree line. A strange, high-pitched chirp rang out from the shrubbery, followed by a strangled cry of alarm on the part of Berengar.

A tall, wavering black figure dashed on long, shaky legs from the thicket. It was holding a tiny black cub in its arms. The creature was about ten feet tall, but so thin and flexible that it looked like the strokes of a paintbrush, shimmering and wavering in living motion. Its limbs, body, and head were all of uniform shape and width, and the top of its head was bent backward at its tip, giving the impression of a sagging gnome's hood. Below this was a single white circle, resembling a painted-on eye, with a black dot at its center. The creature glared frantically backward at the thicket and then danced away with its cub—to disappear among the misty reaches of the forest.

A few seconds later, Berengar's tousled head emerged from the bushes, gazing after it.

Brand and Cil, gaping like smitten children at the strange apparition, were so taken aback they forgot to laugh at Berengar's plight. Berengar fought his way out of the bushes and jogged over to them, his hair a tangled wreck full of twigs; his face, arms, and chest scratched to hell. He was grinning like a lion. "By Makmellah! Brand, did you see that?!" he roared, looking

thoroughly pleased with himself. "I almost *died*!!"
Brand just gawped then shook his head with incredulity.

"Oh, Ber, half your skin is torn to death," Cil exclaimed.

"I'm half a mind to go back through that damnable desert so I can do it again!" he said in return, gazing forlornly up at the distant peak. "Mackmellah, what a ride that was. Never have I experienced such *freedom.*"

"I think I actually agree with you for once, Ber," Brand said, letting out a light chuckle.

"Aw, brotherly love," sneered Cil, with the face of a green-eyed pixy child. "Now, someone help me re-dress my leg! Can't you see there is a lady in waiting!?"

They took a moment to drink and repair Cil's bandage. Then Berengar and Cil dusted themselves off as best they could. Brand, of course, had gotten a new set of clothing from Ator Periconias and now stood clean and unscathed due to his cautious landing.

Standing erect in polished black boots, tight dark trousers, a ruffled white shirt, and a fashionable black coat, he looked the part of a swashbuckler, a swaggering duelist, or even a young prince at play. His golden, shoulder-length hair was clean and bright, sparkling in the sun. His green eyes caught the light too, reflecting a kind intelligence.

Berengar had refused any clothing from Ator Periconias' crates, insisting it restricted his movement. Thus, he wore only his loincloth and high-strung sandals. His great sword was slung high on his back, tied to a single thick leather harness across his chest. He stood tall and perfect, his golden hair tied back above his shaved temples, his full lips, proud jaw, and bold chin defying all and sundry. Only the raw, red scratches from his abrupt landing marred his statue-like appearance.

Cil stood as proudly as she could, given her injured thigh, straining upwards as if to match the statue of the two tall men. Her white, oversized tunic—with its torn-off sleeves—was now marred by dirt. Her gorgeous dark-red hair, in its high-tied coiffure, was ragged and fluffy after the flight. Her wide dark-red breeches were tattered, giving her the look of a pirate—even more so with the bandage tied around one leg. Yet her beautiful green eyes gave her presence enough on their own.

Brand noticed her inspecting him, and looked at her. She turned her proud, triangular chin upward, crossed her arms, and looked away.

"*What?*" said Brand. "You were looking at me first!"

"I was looking at Alucard," she replied with dignity.

Brand looked down and saw that Alucard had fallen asleep again, now snoring with eyes closed. "Ah, the little feller had a lot of excitement today. Time for a nap."

"Can I hold him?" Cil asked, putting her hands together pleadingly, her eyes bright and yearning.

"*No,* I don't want to wake him up right now," said Brand.

"*Fine,*" said Cil, turning her back—the very image of cold anger.

Brand inspected the map and began to curse. In their excitement, they had drifted south during their flight. Now they were more than a day and a half's march from the Trade Road. "So Ber, we drifted far south. What now?"

Berengar's humor vanished and he scowled. "*Damnation.* Well, we dare not remain so close to the border of the pygmies. Nay, we must venture into the woods, and then cut north. Let me see that map." The giant then inspected the map and began to spit profanities. "Yonder lies the *Darkwood Runs.*" He indicated the forest. "A dire place. I was a fool to let myself get carried away amid the flight."

Brand grimaced, then said hopefully, "surely there is naught but the occasional forest beast?"

Berengar looked at him askance. "Do you *truly* believe that?"

Brand frowned, becoming uncertain. He looked toward the misty forest, heavy with undergrowth, and began to wonder what might lurk within. A cool breeze blew from the woods that chilled the air around them and he felt suddenly cold.

"Damnit, Ber, why tell us now? You could have guided us northward instead of fooling around in the air."

Berengar's steel-blue eyes scanned the tall trees. "I know it, damnit."

Brand sighed. "We all make mistakes."

Berengar nodded, coming to a decision, then said, "We will go quietly and quickly. We will travel westward for a day or two, then head due north to meet up with the Trade Route."

"But surely there are settlements and such? A tavern or two?"

"It's not impossible..." said Berengar, scratching his stubble thoughtfully, "Let us hope so. For I like not the rank smells this forest holds."

Chapter 5
"Zanon and the Zanonnites."

And, as the imbalanced ones played God with the woof and warp of nature, so did they bring about a dissonance.

In sightless sin against the primeval equilibrium, did they craft their demons and devils.

Such are the unholy offspring of man, left behind in the wake of his imitating the gods.

So say the words of Zanon—blessed be his equilibrium.
—Zanon's Tranquil Almanac: Verse 15.

***

The snap of every twig echoed out across the still, primeval forest, as Brand and his companions made furtive progress through its shadowed glades. Each sound seemed glaringly loud, and was answered only by a deeper silence which presaged the presence of a stalking predator.

It had been two days since any of the companions had smiled, or laughed with cheer. The stress of constant tension, the straining of their senses, and the necessity for creeping, cautious progress, weighed heavily upon them. They kept strict watches each night, sleeping in small glades guarded by thick bushes or within tightly woven thickets of an unknown species. Once, Berengar deemed it necessary to have them sleep high up in a crooked black tree of massive girth, tying themselves with their belts to its branches.

Despite the overriding feeling of menace nothing had harmed them, and to the contrary, they had seen many unique and wondrous things: towering grandsires of trees, seemingly standing since the beginning of time, majestic in their height and maturity; glowing trails of poisonous fungus; and innocuous furry critters of various kinds, including a small flat-faced, white bear that clung to a tree, and squinted truculently at them through puffy red eyes, likely inebriated from the ingestion of some toxic fruit.

But there was likely much they had missed, for Brand and Cil had slept little in the past few nights, and their minds were mazed with an extreme fatigue that dulled their awareness. They mechanically followed the guide of Berengar, who showed no signs of weariness. The stamina of a wildcat was his, and he led them onward through thick, low, damp gulches; across stone shelves, and sunlit clearings. He left no footprints, teaching them how to step without leaving a trail, and how to avoid brushing their scent onto branches or tree trunks. At times, he paused to stand motionless in the forest's silence, straining his ears, or sniffing the wind like a timber-wolf. Each time Brand or Cil suggested a deviation from his set path, Berengar patiently shook his head and whispered his reasoning, "Nay, that path leads to the cave-nest of a Marmoreal Gobbler. Can't you smell the decomposing flesh of its catches?"

Or: "Halt! This way. The vulture-owls hunt in such open glades as that one, where the grass is short."

Or again: "No, friends, take not that trail. See the scores on the trees? The Furred Neander-Ursa hunts that territory."

Inexorably, he led them northwest, toward the trade road, his path guided by the sun and the wind, never faltering, never flagging. He avoided dangers untold, unnoticed, and unguessed at by his more naive companions. Had he not been there, their journey would have likely been more eventful, and much shorter.

Presently, it was late afternoon, and Berengar seemed eager to find reliable shelter before nightfall. Brand could tell something had been troubling the bronze giant for hours, though Berengar had kept silent, likely to avoid alarming Cil and Brand.

The Outlander's behavior, however, betrayed him. He paused frequently, straining his ears, and shooting piercing glances over his shoulder into the forest's shadows. The urgent look to the giant's normally cheerful face, combined with the tense readiness of his movements, made the hair on Brand's neck rise.

Cil, usually spirited and outspoken, had also felt the danger, and now kept silent. Even Alucard seemed to understand the gravity of the moment. The small creature no longer cried aloud, but sulked in silence, his wide blue eyes darting fearfully at every movement in the undergrowth.

Alucard had been growing quicker than Brand had expected, and he was now the size of a shoe, rather than that of a small hand. More so, his intelligence was uncanny. The fact he could talk from birth was incredible in itself, but in addition to this, his speech improved at a speed unheard of in human children—Brand had been quietly tutoring him each evening, and Alucard could now use a variety of basic words.

"Feels bad. Feels danger," he gurgled to Brand, who patted his smooth head reassuringly.

"*Shhhh!*" Berengar hissed with fierce intent and glared wrathfully at them, wide-eyed, his finger to his lips. Then, without a sound, he picked up his pace and beckoned them to follow.

The companions pressed on, tension rising with the fading light. Berengar quickened his speed, forcing Cil and Brand to struggle to keep up. Despite the haste, Berengar maintained an uncanny silence, his movements tense and precise—like a tiger stalking its prey—ever poised to pounce. His steel-blue eyes burned in the fading light as he glanced back once more.

"*Run!*" he commanded abruptly. Then, scooping up Cil in his arms as if she were a child, he took off at a speed Brand struggled to match, despite the larger man's encumbrance.

Against his better judgment, Brand looked back. Nothing. Or, was that a large shadow, flitting from tree to tree some distance back? Perhaps it was just the beams of fading light, shifting angles among the trees. And then, something else. This he didn't see with his eyes. But, he felt it—a burning hunger. A tangible malevolence, reaching out to him from the gloom. It was a presence that wanted more than just his body, it hunted his mind and soul as well.

Brand ran, fear lending him a desperate speed that allowed him to keep pace with Berengar. He ran like a frantic, gangly gazelle in flight, his long legs prancing alongside Berengar's powerful strides. Together, they charged forward, in a blind rush. They kept it up for fifteen agonizing minutes, the tension at their backs building to an unbearable crescendo.

Berengar was about to throw Cil to the ground, and draw his sword, when a clear, merry tune rang out through the forest.

The music shattered the oppressive silence like a beam of light, falling upon a frozen landscape. It invigorated the anxious companions, and lent strength to their weary legs. They sprinted toward the sound, leaping over fallen logs and small creeks, ducking under low-hanging branches, and diving through thick underbrush. Glances over their shoulders revealed only the blot of darkness, dancing through the glades behind them.

Suddenly, the forest was gone, and they were on a broad road, clean and well kept.

"The Trade Road!" gasped Brand.

Berengar didn't slow. *"Keep going!"* he shot back at Brand.

Brand kept going.

They dashed across the road, burst through another screen of leaves, and found themselves back among the thick underbrush, ducking and dodging branches. The music was just ahead now. They dived beneath a final wall of shrubbery and tumbled out into an open glade, devoid of underbrush. The ground was carpeted with soft, velvety grass and dotted with tall, well-spaced pines. A narrow stream ran down the small slope at the center of the clearing, dividing it into two halves.

At the base of the slope, by the stream, a troop of travelers had made camp. They were thirteen in number and accompanied by two traveling carriages, each pulled by strange, furry four-legged beasts unfamiliar to Brand. Half of the travelers were brightly dressed in a variety of colors, adorned with extravagant hats and billowing pantaloons. The other half wore dull gray pants and sober gray coats, their heads topped with respectable gray hunting caps.

Brand took all this in at a glance, as they dashed toward the camp, still sensing the ominous presence behind them. Yet, as they drew closer to the lively group, Brand felt the oppressive shadow recede, beaten back by the vitality of this bright, noisy, and joyful group. They skidded to a halt twenty paces from the camp, panting and slick with sweat. Berengar roughly threw Cil down, and spun to face the forest, his sword drawn, his eyes narrowed into steely slits.

"It's gone," Berengar growled at last, rivulets of sweat streaming down his face, his golden hair matted and dark with exertion, his shaved temples pounding.

"What... was it?" Brand asked, still gasping for breath.

"Something not good," Cil answered with a shiver.

Alucard peeked out from Brand's shirt, his wide blue eyes filled with fear. "Feels... bad," he said in his halting speech.

At that moment, a commanding voice rang out from the camp. "*Ho now!* What's the meaning of this? Why do you three travelers approach the camp of the Zanonnites with such unseemly haste?"

The companions remained frozen, still catching their breath and staring warily at the forest. But Brand, ever the negotiator, turned to the speaker. Between labored breaths, he answered, "A black shadow came for us—a malignant intelligence from the murk. I—I know not what it was..."

The speaker rubbed his chin thoughtfully. "Hmm, perhaps a Banderwhul... or maybe a Knel?" He glanced toward the shadowy tree line. "It seems the levity of our song has driven it back for now. Zanonnite protects us, of course. But what of you? Be ye righteous followers of the true faith?"

Brand stared blankly at the man, unsure how to respond. He was an elderly gentleman, of striking appearance, one of the brightly garbed members of the troop.

He wore a pink-and-purple striped top hat, beneath this, erupted long gray sideburns that connected to a frosty, gray beard. His upper lip was invisible under heavy whiskers, and his bright blue eyes twinkled with a paradoxical mix of kindness and sternness. His great bushy brows furrowed in an inquisitive frown, and his thin lips were pursed in perturbation. His vest was bright-blue, worn over a voluminous, flounced white blouse, complemented with billowing blue pantaloons. His plain brown leather shoes seemed comically banal beneath the rest of his striking outfit.

The old man's authority was clear, for now the other members of the troop ceased playing their instruments, and cautiously lined up behind him in a neat row. Brand also noted, with some unease, that many of the troop had exchanged their instruments for loaded crossbows, now held at the ready.

"Huh?" Cil broke in impatiently, her arms crossed as she glared at the old man.

Brand licked his lips, then spoke hurriedly, adopting a gracious tone. "We are indeed."

The old man's face darkened. "Do you *mock us*? You say you are true followers, yet you forwent the customary greeting of equalizing praise, and your dress is imbalanced." He shook his head gravely. "Do not think we Zanonnites are so naive."

Whispers broke out among the crowd.

Brand scowled. "I'm sorry... You're right—but, you startled me, old man."

The old man grimaced, then turned to his troop. "Let you not be called busy-bodies, for such a practice destroys the harmony of living relations—*so says the teachings*."

The crowd of Zanonnites turned away, many with a momentary expression of guilty shame on their faces, and returned to their festivities. The musicians resumed their merry tune, and most of the others got busy around the camp, though a few younger girls cast curious, sidelong glances at Brand, and a particularly handsome young man watched Cil with more than casual interest.

The old man turned his attention back to Brand and his companions. "That's better, my son. Honesty is a powerful weapon.

So, what brings you nonbelievers to these parts? Oh, forgive my rudeness in my old age—I am Gilfingle, Grand Corrective of this pilgrimage."

Brand blinked, somewhat confused. "Well... I am Brand, this is Cil, and this giant is Berengar. I see... a number of your companions cracking a keg of ale yonder. Should we perhaps... join them and finish our chat over a tankard or two?"

"*Companions?* No, not companions..." he said, gesturing to the troop with a long, bandy arm. "This is my parish of loyal and worthy *Zanonnites*—followers dedicated to learning the ways of Equipoise, as taught by Zanon. I, as Grand Corrective, ensure equilibrium in all our actions. Sometimes, a young Zanon might stray..." He wagged a long, chiding finger. "And it is my sacred duty to bring them right and restore the balance."

"I know nothing of these things..." said Brand glumly.

"Let me show you. Observe our troop," Gilfingle said, gesturing. "Note that half wear gray, and half wear splendid colors. Naturally, some incline toward the grays, while others are drawn to brightnesses. So, I consciously balance the troop—equal numbers of each disposition. In this way, harmony is preserved, and all are content. Zanon did not wish for his followers to be constrained." He smiled with compassion.

Brand swept the group with a calculating gaze. "But I see you are thirteen in number. Six wear color, and seven wear gray. That is uneven..."

"*Shhhh! Have a care!*" Gilfingle hissed, his voice hoarse with alarm. He glanced over his shoulder to ensure his followers hadn't overheard the blasphemous remark. Then, with a weary slump of his shoulders, he confessed, "You're right. It is my greatest failure at present."

He moistened his lips—a flicker of pink tongue darting through
the gray of his whiskers—before continuing. "We began as sixteen,
departing from Culcep, far to the east. How perfectly balanced I
thought our troop to be! But alas, I was mistaken. Poor Kethrik
perished to the sting of a Red-Nosed Sand Flapper on the fourth
day. Then, just last week, Janica wandered into the woods to
answer nature's call... and vanished without a trace. Young Gelbrid,
despite my well-balanced advice to the contrary, insisted on
continuing the search alone, long into the night. He was never seen
again."

Gilfingle sighed deeply. "Ah, but Zanon tests us in strange ways,
does he not?"

"Precisely so," agreed Brand. "You said you came from the east?
Should we not combine parties then, since we both head in the
same direction?"

Gilfingle made an apologetic gesture. "I would dearly love to,
but..." He shook his head sadly. "You know nothing of our ways.
Your discordant actions may bring us all to ruin."

Brand scanned through his conversation with Gilfingle thus far,
then said, "Good Gilfingle, did you not say that only recently you
had lost three of your members?"

Gilfingle stopped. "Yes."

"And is the troop not now unbalanced?"

"Yes, why bring up such nasty matters? *Have you no shame?*"
he said, a sad frown darkening his face.

"I mean no insult. Simply this: you recently lost three of your
members. Today, you find *three* new companions..."

Gilfingle looked taken aback by this. "Are you inferring that this
could be the work of *Zanon himself?*"

Brand smiled, and shrugged his shoulders.

A gleam of excitement began to build in Gilfingle's eyes. "Yes, but the teachings require that you know our ways..."

"Indeed—it will be a challenge for you to teach us. But did you not also say that Zanon tests us in strange ways? And could not the introduction of three fledgling Zanonnites in the middle of an ongoing pilgrimage be one of the greatest trials a Grand Corrective might face?"

Gilfingle looked up quickly and pierced Brand with a crafty glare. "Are you sure you have not studied *Zanon's Tranquil Almanac?* You appear unusually versed in the ways of the teachings..."

"No, indeed, I haven't. But meeting you here, in this glade, has already changed something in me... In fact... *I think I can feel Zanon's presence now."*

He looked upward slowly and gazed majestically into a ray of sunshine that had fortuitously fallen across his face that very second, illuminating his blond hair so that he stood out like a beacon in the shaded glade.

Gilfingle was put in a state of awe. "In—indeed!" he said quickly. "Yes, quite so! I see it now."

"Oh he's so full of himself," Cil muttered, watching Brand's performance.

Berengar smiled, and whispered back, "A finicky lot, but kind and harmless all the same."

Gilfingle called out, *"Zanonnites, attend!* Gather round, I have an announcement! You there, playing on the wing-tailed banta-flute—*cease!*"

The festivities came to a halt, and the twelve pilgrims came over to stand in a half-circle before Brand and his companions.

Gilfingle waved a hand. "I will make introductions. These are our new fellows, Brand, Cil, and Berengar!" he said.

The crowd murmured in hushed tones.

And then, "All wish to learn the ways of Zanon!"

The crowd let out a raucous cheer.

"I ask that you treat all three of them with kindness, tolerance, and patience. Remember, you are all well-versed in the ways of harmony; they are new to them. They will make errors. Correct them with helpful instruction and positive guidance—these things go further than carping criticism and harsh punishment."

The crowd chorused, *"Blessed be his equilibrium!"*

"Now, step forth as I call your names, Zanonnites." Gilfingle started moving through the semi-circle from left to right.

"Twithik!"

A young, rug-headed man, short and muscular to the point of appearing blockish, stepped forth. His hands were unnaturally large and calloused. His face was clean-shaven, and so commonplace that it escaped notice. He wore the somber gray, in odd contrast to his wild hair. He bowed and smiled at the three.

"Do not let his placid expression and simple countenance fool you. He is a hardy companion, and cares for the wagons and beasts with a practiced hand. Now, Salome Desseu!"

A lithe, brown-skinned girl wearing a bright orange sarong, which barely concealed her pleasing contours, stepped forth. She was likely a year younger than Brand, and had the look of one from far Devirien'Su. She had a long, straight nose and large almond eyes of a deep violet color. She curtsied politely and batted her long lashes at Brand, who didn't fail to notice the gesture.

Cil also noticed and quirked an eyebrow, before crossing her arms in distaste.

"And now your younger sister, Dimi Desseu!"

A spitting image of the first girl, but perhaps one or two years her junior, in a flowing blue robe, stepped forth and bowed. She gave Brand a saucy sidelong look, as if to say, *"I can compete with my older sister in many ways."*

"Enough moon-eying the boy, Dimi. Back to position," chided Gilfingle crossly.

"Now, next up is our young gallivant, Jamus Malovar."

It was the overly-handsome man that had eyed Cil before. He was perhaps a few years older than Brand. He stepped forth from his possessive position next to the two sisters. He was tall and well-made, with an athletic frame. His shoulders were broad, his waist was thin. He wore no shirt, only a bright blue and purple fur-lined vest, left casually open to display his firm and defined abs, and an assortment of attractive, dangling necklaces. He wore loose-fitting white silk pants after the desert fashion, cropped close and high at the ankles. Upon his lean, delicate feet were padded silk shoes, which turned up at the toes. His skin was white but tanned from the sun, and his hair was long, auburn, and spiky—a veritable lion's mane—and was filled with a myriad of brightly colored beads and semi-precious stones. There was a reckless ease about the man that was instantly annoying to Brand. He seemed to own the immediate environment, and the world at large, like a great relaxed cat yawning lazily over its pride.

He stepped forward gracefully, bowing with one leg bent in front of Cil. Taking a large purple flower from his vest, he placed it in her hair whilst staring fixedly into her eyes.

"The flower cannot compare to your beauty, but it was lonely and needed a companion," he said. His voice was rich, deep, and slightly complacent.

Cil looked blankly at this display of gentility. Then she blushed and glanced down at her feet.

Jamus spoke again, this time to Brand. "Relax, young sunflower, be at ease with me. For I am at ease with you." With a bow, and a lingering look at Cil, he stepped back into place.

Brand frowned and muttered under his breath to Berengar, "Look at this popinjay. Have you ever seen the like?"

"He has the body of a fighting man. You might find him a heartier opponent than his demeanor at first suggests."

"Unlikely," grumbled Brand.

Berengar shrugged, and chuckled to himself as if at some private joke.

Gilfingle continued, "Here is Pathar Harvim. Quiet-spoken, but staunch and loyal."

A small, vulture-headed man in solemn gray stepped forth. He had a notable limp and was slightly hunchbacked. He bowed silently, and then stepped back in line.

"On to Balin and Fonicia Coonse, experienced Zanonnites to the core who set an all-round stellar example, whether it be in obscure subjects such as iridescent insect categorizing, or those more mundane tasks such as marital duties and husbandry."

Balin was a tall, rangy man who had the look of a plantation farmer. He was garbed in a gray vest and gray knee-length breeches. He stepped forth and was joined by his wife, Fonicia, a short, buxom, plain-featured woman. She likewise wore gray—a homely, loose-fitting dress that did little to complement her already banal features. She followed Balin forward with polite decorum, then stopped to hang affectionately off his elbow.

Fonicia spoke first. "We have a lot to teach, and are willing."

She smiled benignly, then looked up to her husband, fixing him with a loving stare.

"That's right indeed," answered the taller man, aiming a sentimental smile down at his wife—a gesture Brand found a trifle overdone. "Pleased to make your acquaintance. I trust this relationship will bring fortune to both sides."

And so it went with the remaining members of the troop: a pair of gangly brothers in their late teens named Thron—dressed in a bright green and turquoise doublet—and Muls—wearing a gray version of the same. Both boys stared constantly and awkwardly at Salome and Dimi, and now added Cil to their rotations; Blakcab Moor, a heavily muscled walnut of a man, brown-skinned and black-haired, with a beard and an aggressive, windswept mane. He looked perpetually agitated. He wore gray leather armor with solemnity and was the Guardian of the pilgrimage; an elderly woman named Martinae, with a pinched nose and half-moon glasses, who looked around at one and all—especially the youths —as rambunctious effronteries to proper decorum; and finally Ms. Taloulie, a heavyset battleship of a woman with dark brown hair and rosy red cheeks. She wore the outfit of a washwoman, but in bright yellow—a color that only accentuated her prodigious size.

Gilfingle announced that she worked as the troop's chef, and that there was no better cook out there. It was instantly apparent she was more than a little infatuated with Berengar.

Gilfingle continued, "Ladies and gentlemen, children of Zanon all. Let us get our new companions settled in. Basic instruction will begin on the morrow." With that dismissive remark, the crowd dispersed.

"Come this way," Gilfingle said, leading the new guests over to the wagons. "You may store your belongings in this side cabinet here. Have you sleeping effects? No? Well, we will get to that. The first thing that must be decided, however, is your dress. You must choose: colors, or the gray. *We must maintain the equilibrium of the troop.* Currently, six are brightly adorned, and seven wear the gray. Thus, two of you may choose colors, and one must wear the gray. So what shall it be?" He looked at them inquiringly, his blue eyes bright.

"I shall wear this outfit. It is already colorless." Brand said, indicating his apparel.

"You wear black and white. This must be adjusted to... the gray."

"Black and white are both shades of gray, good Gilfingle," replied Brand flippantly.

Gilfingle bristled and responded to Brand with mild reproach saying, "Already, I see you shall require intensive tutelage..." Then, taking a deep breath: "*The world shan't be balanced in a day.*" He looked over Berengar and Cil. "What of you two? Cil, you are somewhat colorful already. However, those pants are cut and stained with... what looks to be... *your blood.*" He shook his head disapprovingly. "I shall give you a pair of the same, but in bright red. What say you to that, hmm?"

"That would be grand, thank you!" Cil said sweetly.

Brand eyed her suspiciously.

Gilfingle looked to Berengar. "And you? You seem to be, in fact... *wearing no clothes at all.*"

"I find the rasp of woven linen, *suffocating.*" Berengar grumbled stubbornly.

"Well, this does technically fit with one of Zanon's wise provisos, and I quote: '*When equilibrium cannot be conveniently achieved by action, the most pious answer is to leave things as they are. Nature, of course, is the best balancer.'"*

Seeing the blank looks on their faces, he went on, "I see I have skipped some levels of indoctrination here. Well... in short, no clothes is indeed a natural state. But something needs to be done about that brown loincloth—if it truly *be* brown. I cannot tell what its original color was, but it seems clotted with dust, sweat, and... *other unknown substances.*

"We were in a tunnel of vile steam, then crossed a sweltering desert," grumbled Berengar. "I care not to wear the colored sandals of a dandy, but a purple silken loincloth could do no harm."

"I'll have Mrs. Coonse sew one up for you immediately," replied Gilfingle with an elaborate bow.

The soothing twinkle of a wind instrument broke out nearby, and was carried pleasingly to them on the cool evening breeze. The notes were those of a lonely poet, speaking of amorous adventures, and seemed specifically designed to pluck the heartstrings of any young potential sweetheart. The three companions turned to see the source of the tune and saw Jamus, mounted on top of a large moss-strewn boulder by the stream, playing an exotically carved Ney flute. He had strained his features into a sadly noble look, and had positioned himself so that the dim rays of the twilight sun fell about him.

Salome and Dimi sat with their legs crossed on the soft grass at the foot of the boulder, listening with little interest and sending glances toward Brand. Jamus, noticing the attention of Brand and Cil, turned the full force of his dreamy eyes upon Cil, before tilting his head forward, letting his luxurious mane fall across his face, and playing a poignant trill on his flute.

"Come on," said Brand, tugging at Cil. "Let us get settled in and have a good night's rest. Also, I am famished. Gilfingle, what is the usual arrangement for sustenance?"

"Do not fret. During your Zanonnite discipleship, you need only share in the general tasks of the troop. In exchange, you may eat and travel with us free of charge. Of course, one day, we expect you to start your own Zanonnite parish and forward the act to the next generation—and so the cycle of furtherance repeats."

Brand hesitated and asked, "Would you define this... expectation as a... *contractual* arrangement?"

"More of a... *holy covenant*."

"And... the potential *repercussions* of contractual negligence?"

"Who can say? That is between you and Zanon. I myself never wish to find out."

"Yes, we agree," said Cil shortly. She was hungry, angry, and tired of it all.

"I'm sure you shall do what's right," said Gilfingle, an indulgent smile on his face.

Brand shrugged dubiously, and nodded his head.

Berengar's eyes showed a touch of nervousness. He looked around and up at the sky. "Brand, one day we must carry out a pilgrimage as he said. Breaking oath with a god is an unhealthy practice."

"By all means," said Brand somewhat absently—he was eager to get on with the meal.

Gilfingle was satisfied and settled them in, feeding them and organizing their sleeping arrangements.

After this, Brand, Berengar, and Cil positioned their bedrolls at the base of a large tree next to the wagons.

Cil yawned and stretched like a cat before speaking. "Ah, this might be the first restful night I've had in days."

"Let it be so," said Berengar, gloomily eyeing the shadowy wall of foliage at the edge of the glade.

"What?" said Brand. "Do you think that thing will come back?"

"Who can say," grumbled Berengar. "Let us stay up for a while and see what their watch routine is."

And so they sat, well-fed, relaxing upon their bedrolls beneath the stretching branches of the giant oak, which blocked out the stars above them. As far as the rest of the troop was concerned, the night continued on with much music and revelry—Jamus playing merrily on his Ney flute, Ms. Taloulie singing along in an operatic baritone, Pathar playing harmonies on a small, high-pitched piccolo, and Blakcab, incongruously to his gruff demeanor, accompanying the trio with gentle chords on a decorative sitar-like instrument.

Brand and Berengar listened to this with warm hearts while Cil snored on by their side.

A feeling of unreality overcame Brand. Strange it was to be with such a people. He did not believe in their god, and their ways were tiresome. Yet, they were kind, and had treated him far better than any others had since leaving Drift's End.

This got him thinking of his trusty den, Bartha, and his mother. How far away they all were now—they too seemed as a dream. He decided not to think too deeply on it.

As the night drew to a close, the company packed up their affairs and made for their own beds. Brand and Berengar rose stiffly from their bedrolls and sought out Gilfingle. They found him discussing the night's watch with Blakcab.

"Ah, gentle children," said Gilfingle, spying them as they approached. "I am surprised you are not in the land of the nod?" He eyed them with blue, inquisitive eyes.

Blakcab stared on in grim silence.

"We never sleep without a watch. We wished to survey your arrangements before settling in," said Brand.

Blakcab took offense at this. "I ought to spank you, boy! Think you not that *I* can do my duty well?"

"Peace, peace, Blakcab," interjected Gilfingle graciously.

"Strange that you only have one watchman in such a large group, and in such dangerous parts—how do you keep safe from the demons and night beasts?" said Berengar with the candor of a woodsman.

"Ahhh, much of the ways of the Zanonnites confuse the layman," replied Gilfingle with a knowing smile. "But here, Zanon does indeed protect his children.

"Blakcab, it's time to bring out *the Artifact*. Please instruct Brand and Berengar on its use. I expect you to share the watch three ways from now on. More sleep should do wonders for your temper—*and your complexion*." Gilfingle said, then strolled off without waiting for an answer.

Blakcab growled assent and stalked toward the larger wagon of the two, leaving Brand and Berengar to follow awkwardly behind.

Blakcab began unloading a great fence of many folds from the back of the wagon. It was strong, flexible, and of a material unknown to both Brand and Berengar. Once extended, it was able to fully encircle the entire camp, including the wagons. It connected to itself to form a smooth, latticed wall about ten feet high. A long cable ran from the part where its ends met, and Blakcab plugged it into a cylindrical metal device, which looked disconcertingly similar to the image on Brand's chart.

"Do not touch the fence. It is dangerous," said Blakcab shortly, before walking back to the wagons.

Alucard poked his pale blue-green head out of the pouch at Brand's chest and inspected the fence with avid interest. He pointed to the metal cylinder. "Pow-er Cell," he gurgled, then at the fence, "E-lec-tricit-y." It seemed that the Ancients' DNA programming was fast at work. Either that, or he had been spending too much time reading the notebook of Ator Periconias.

Brand and Berengar didn't understand the words, and looked at each other nonplussed, then followed along after Blakcab.

Blakcab instructed them on the new watch schedule and showed them the various weapons the Zanonnites had brought along, which mainly consisted of enough crossbows for fifteen people to use, and sixteen short swords. However, he said most of the company could not wield them, relying heavily on the more convenient crossbows.

There was also one small hand crossbow—more of an assassin's tool than a war weapon. A weapon which Brand found to his liking.

"May I use this, Sir Blakcab?" asked Brand.

"As you like," replied Blakcab.

"Not my idea of a manly weapon," said Berengar, before turning to eye the weapon cache critically. "It is a paltry collection. It seems you must rely primarily on this *'Artifact'* for protection... if it were to fail..."

Blakcab frowned darkly at Berengar and said, "*I know it, damnit!* Well, what then?"

Berengar made a face and shook his head. "I'll start training the troop to use these swords. That's the best we can do, for now."

Blakcab nodded. "Well, the fence is up, and holds strong at present. Go. I'll wake you in three hours."

Berengar nodded, and he and Brand headed off to bed.

Chapter 6

"Dinner in the woods."

The night passed without event, and Brand rose from his bedroll amid a milky morning glow, the dawn light filtering softly through the trees above.

Berengar had been shaking his arm, and now, seeing him awake, said, "Patrol the perimeter of the campsite and watch the tree line. Don't touch the fence—I saw it cook two toads and an owl last night."

Brand wandered the campsite in a sleepy haze, negligently inspecting the forest through bleary eyes. After an hour, Twithik roused himself and began tinkering about the wagons.

Brand moseyed over to see what the man was doing. He was handling the beasts. Strange creatures they were—hairy and four-legged, with long ears and heads like sideways watermelons. They had wide, flat mouths filled with short, conical teeth, and great oval, black eyes.

Twithik scratched and combed them, rubbing them down with soothing oils, then fed them from large feeding sacks.

Twithik nodded politely as Brand approached, but then remained silent as he went about his work.

After watching in silence for a time, Brand asked, "What are these beasts? They seem docile enough, but I do not know them."

"In my hometown of Culcep, we call them 'Gers.' In other places, they may be known under other names."

Twithik offered no further conversation and Brand, eventually getting bored, wandered off to further explore the camp.

The Zanonnites, for the present, still slept in their places around the camp—little gray or multi-colored cocoons in their sleeping rolls. All was quiet apart from the sounds of crickets and the occasional song of the morning lark.

Brand wandered over to a section of the stream that had been contained within the guard fence and drank deeply. The water was crystal clear, fresh, and tasted like nectar. He decided he would wash in it later—once the camp was roused.

He heard splashing a little way upstream. The noise was coming from behind a triangle of three large boulders. Deciding he should investigate, he walked up the slope and rounded the boulders.

He stared in confusion for a moment at the image of a naked girl, up to her knees in the stream, rivulets of water running down the smooth, brown contours of her body. The realization of what he was looking at began to unravel upon his befuddled mind, but before he had time to look away, the girl turned and gave him a bold, indignant glare from over her shoulder.

She then spun with the fierce cry of a desert woman and threw a container of cold water at him, drenching him thoroughly. He gasped and stumbled back, wiping his face.

"I'm sorry, I—"

"I'm telling Gilfingle!" she cried.

"*Wait!* Why would you do that? It was clearly an accident," he replied, covering his eyes.

"You may uncover your eyes now, Brand," she said. Her tone subtly changed.

He opened his eyes to find her wrapped in an exotically patterned sarong, tied tightly around her breasts and hanging down to her ankles. It did little to hide her figure.

She grinned with a certain wicked perversity and said, "If you want to keep this a secret, then you owe me a favor—you will have to do whatever *I* want. Otherwise, I'll tell the *whole* troop I found you *perving* on me."

"Bah!" Brand answered. With a contemptuous gesture, he turned on his heel and strode off.

Salome flushed with shame, and the look she directed at Brand's back, had he seen it, would have made him think twice about spurning her another time. But—*he didn't see it.*

An hour or so later, Gilfingle mustered the troop.

"The night went well and without mishap. Please, show thanks to our faithful Guardians, Blakcab, Berengar and Brand."

A lackluster cheer went up as people wiped the sleep from tired, red eyes.

"We will continue our routine of daily instruction, and for the benefit of certain newcomers, we shall retread certain, fundamental basics."

A sullen silence followed, then Mr. and Mrs. Coonse both clapped with enthusiasm, their faces cracking in broad smiles. The display irked Brand for some reason. He looked across to Cil to see what she thought, but to his disgust, found her smiling at Jamus, who was, at that instant, *handing her a fruity morning refreshment.*

Gilfingle cleared his throat and continued, "Now, from the *Tranquil Almanac*, I quote:

'In the beginning, there was a primeval equilibrium, a stark tranquility of space and matter.'"

"Wrong!" a voice gargled from Brand's chest.

Brand looked down in surprise to see Alucard poking his head out of his pouch, propping himself up with his tiny arms, and showing his small chest in an attitude of defiance.

"In the beginning, there was a thought. Then, *a vibration*," the small creature said.

Gilfingle's face turned red with irritation. Then, noticing Alucard for the first time, he stared—nonplussed—for a moment, and said, *"What is that creature you hold as though it were a babe at your chest?"*

"Ah—long story, Grand Corrective, but it's my charge, and I am duty bound to raise it as my own."

Gilfingle looked perplexed, and more than a little disturbed. "*Well,*" he said, recovering himself, "bring order to your charge, Brand."

"It—true," Alucard grumbled quietly to Brand. "The book—"

"It's okay, I believe you," Brand whispered back. "But let him speak—it's rude to interrupt others." Then, to Gilfingle, "He has been soundly chastised. Please, Grand Corrective, continue."

"In the beginning, there was a primeval equilibrium—a stark tranquility of space and matter. Then came a disruptive force, disturbing this virgin placidity. This force was *Man*.
Thus, it is incumbent upon us, as Zanonnites, to restore equality by following the teachings of Zanon—*blessed be his equilibrium*.

On this premise, follow the unequivocal truths as given in Zanon's words:

"'*Balance your daily activities. A period of rest should be preceded by a stint of exhaustive activity. Conversely, a period of harsh action should be followed by a period of relative ease.*'"

Brand could agree with that.

"'*Balance your consumption and diet. Should you eat meat one day, vegetables must follow the next day, and vice versa. Alternatively, you may eat a balance of vegetables and meat each day if this is possible.*'"

Brand scowled—he had never taken to vegetables...

"However, I am not unyielding; if you despise either meat or vegetables, you need not eat what you despise. Zanon does not wish for his followers to be unhappy. Instead, you must simply twin yourself with a buddy of opposite inclinations. This way, you will eat the meat while they eat the vegetables, or vice versa.'"

"Ok. Which one of these guys eats only vegetables?—likely no use twinning with Berengar." Brand thought to himself.

Gilfingle continued: "When picking flowers, if there are three, take only one. If there are nine, take five should you wish. However, if there are only two, desist. Nature has its own way of balancing, unseen to the eyes of man. If you cannot ensure your own actions leave behind an equilibrium, you may not act at all."

And so on it went, in similar fashion, covering topics such as having children, dressing oneself, and that of warfare. And, as Gilfingle spoke, some of the strange actions of the Zanonnites became clearer to Brand.

He learned that today was the off day for music, and that they must travel in silence, engaging in small, quiet conversations only until tomorrow.

As soon as Brand had a moment alone, he spoke to Alucard. "*Hey!* Since when did you learn to form whole sentences?"

"*Speak?*" Alucard looked up at him, blue eyes full of confusion.

"You know, you said that whole thing about 'thought is the blah blah blah.'"

"In the beginning, there was thought. Then, a *vibration,*" Alucard echoed his earlier proclamation.

"Yeah! That."

Alucard fought his way out of Brand's shirt, hopped to the

ground, and ran over to dig at Brand's pouch.

Brand assisted him, and together they retrieved the notebook of Ator Periconias. Alucard fought for control of the pages, and flipped to a page thick with blocks of ancient symbols. It meant nothing to Brand. Alucard ran his finger over the first paragraph of glyphs, and read it in a strange tongue. Then he said, "In the beginning, there was a thought," in the common tongue.

Brand was astonished. "Why, *you little parrot!* You can read the stuff already, but you don't know what it means!"

Alucard looked up at his father, embarrassed. (Brand had grooved him in to think of him as his dad instead of his mama—as Alucard had originally called him.)

"It's okay, don't be too down. You've done an amazing thing. But now I'm going to teach you the basics of speech."

Alucard looked confused, but nodded brightly.

"Come along then," said Brand, heading toward the front of the caravan where he would hold lookout. He strode through the camp which had by now come to life with members moving purposefully about, busily packing things down and securing their belongings. Alucard ran along behind him like a tiny blue toddler—trotting along on bandy legs.

"Ahh, they grow up so fast," Brand muttered to himself sadly. He recalled how it was only days ago that he was regularly cleaning up baby vomit off his shirt. *Who would have thought he'd miss those moments?* Yet, in a normal child, these phases would go on for some months or even years. For Alucard, the engineered creature, they had passed in a matter of days. Four days ago he was the size of Brand's hand. *Now he was about a foot tall—and was speaking.*

Brand met with Blakcab at the front of the caravan and manned his station. In short order, all were in position, and the troop headed off, following an ancient wagon trail on a north-westerly tack, despite the Trade Road being just south of their position. Brand tried to argue the benefits of traveling on the Trade Road instead, but Gilfingle would have none of it.

"Much of what we do confuses the nonbelievers," he said, with obvious pride. "We follow a map, as laid upon my mind by Zanon himself. You see, all I need do is follow his latest revelation."

Brand was doubtful but said nothing.

On they traveled through the dark, silent forest, talking little but seeing much of the shady woods around them—thick with brush, towering pines, oaks, and spruces, with the occasional chestnut or other ancient, gnarled species unknown to man, all heavy with moss-beards and nesting critters.

The day passed without event, and the troop settled in a large clearing for the night. The sun cut an orange glare across the western horizon, and the twilight began to darken the woods around them. The evening brought a chill to the air, and all but Berengar covered themselves in their coats or cloaks.

Once more, Berengar, Brand, and Blakcab brought out the Artifact and enclosed the camp with it.

After Brand finished his work, he returned to the wagons to find Cil sitting by a campfire with Salome and Dimi. The three girls were listening to Jamus, with what appeared to be dumb adoration, as he told them stories and served them hot tea of a mixed-fruit variety.

"Better make a move there, Brand, if you don't want him to

swipe your girl," Berengar teased as he walked past, nudging him.

"My girl? Disgusting," Brand replied, stuffing his hands into his pockets and walking off. He didn't need Cil! *He would go do Alucard's lessons.*

"Hey," called Berengar, "you might be good with a knife throw, or that womanly hand crossbow, but if you want to survive in the Outlands, you'll need more than that. Tomorrow, I'll start training you—and Cil too, once she can walk again. Out here, you need to be able to slay a foe with a single thrust—before it gouges out your innards..."

"I get the point, Ber. Whatever you say," replied Brand distractedly—*Jamus was really annoying him.*

Brand found Alucard by his bedroll, once again tinkering with the notebook.

"What do you get out of that thing?" he asked.

Alucard looked up and opened the book, displaying a set of intricate hieroglyphs, as if that answered the question.

Brand shook his head. "Put that away now. We are going to learn normal stuff. We can't have you becoming a highly educated inhuman freak."

Brand paused and thought, *Well, that's exactly what Alucard was* —but he resolved to do his parenting duties to the best of his ability.

Sitting down, he scratched his head, thinking. Then, decided to begin with body parts.

"Hand." He raised his hand in front of Alucard and made him repeat it.

Alucard raised his own and echoed, "hand."

This went on with various body parts, and then Alucard pointed at Brand's wavy blond hair.

"Nice," he said.

"Oh, that's hair."

Alucard repeated the word, "hair." Then he swiped a webbed hand over his smooth scalp. A sad look came over his small piscine face.

"Why—no hair?" he asked, looking up at Brand.

"Oh yeah, right. Sorry. I don't think your kind grows hair. But maybe we can get you a hat."

"Hat?"

"Something you wear on your head—like hair."

Alucard gave a positive nod and seemed pleased with this.

"Now, let's continue..." Brand said.

The sun set, and darkness fell like a blanket across the camp, alleviated only by a bright, waxing moon and Jamus's campfire.

Presently, Gilfingle called the camp together for dinner.

Balin and Fonicia set up a long collapsible table, and enough chairs to seat the troop. Muls and Thron assisted with the heavy lifting and laid out the cutlery and other utensils. Pathar, Gilfingle's secretary and assistant, placed large candles on the table and arranged Brand, Berengar, and Cil's seating assignments. Alucard was allowed a small "child-seat" next to Brand's chair.

Brand found himself sitting before more varieties of knives and forks than he could shake a stick at—as well as goblets, mugs, and glasses of various sizes. All laid out for purposes unknown to him.

"What a collection—what's the use of so many utensils and cups?" Brand whispered cautiously to Berengar.

Berengar shrugged. "Beats me. Any container could serve as a mug—the bigger the better—and what good is a plate and knives anyway, when a beef bone takes two hands to hold?"

"I think it might be a good experience for you two to learn some sophistication," said Cil, who was on Brand's left.

"Like you know any better—growing up in a lowly fishing village!" Brand retorted.

Cil scowled and dug his ribs with her elbow.

It was quite surreal, sitting there, experiencing fine dining in the middle of the nighted woods—the table, fine spread, and guests all illuminated like a bastion against the gloom, while darkness gathered all around: a thin covering, seething with unknown life beyond the safety of their guard fence.

Brand heard a strange gasping hoot and squinted out into the murk. *Nothing.*

Alucard drew Brand's attention back to the table. The small creature was barking in glee as he looked at all the wonderful things spread before him.

Gilfingle called for everyone's attention. "Etiquette is a fundamental building block of tranquility. This applies also to the dining table. As such, all Zanonnites are tutored impeccably in the ways of dining etiquette—as they are in all forms of etiquette."

"Hear, hear!" cried Fonicia and Balin.

"Thank you. Now, for those of you who are new, one of the first rules of dining etiquette is to not begin eating until the host has been seated. Thus, while Ms. Taloulie finishes preparing the meal, let us take this chance to get to know our new companions better. Let us start with Brand."

Gilfingle looked expectantly at Brand.

Up and down the length of the table, heads turned, and some leaned forward to get a clearer view of him.

"Well... I grew up in the outer district of *Revilis Ko'hur*, known as *Drifts End,* in a humble household. My father was never there, though I am told he was of noble blood and carriage. My mother, she worked in a service house—where she raised me."

"What kind of service?" asked Salome sweetly, perhaps sensing Brand's discomfort.

"Oh, you know, she, ahh, was a professional at relaxing men—during stressful times—to help them forget the—troubles of the day."

"She was a *masseuse!?*" ejaculated Gilfingle enthusiastically.

"Something like that..." Brand replied, glancing down.

"Well, speak up, man. We like to know the past of our fellows *in detail*—so as to understand them all the better," said Gilfingle bluffly.

"She just..." Brand stumbled, his face turning red.

"*She was a prostitute!*" interrupted Blakcab with a knowing grin.

Brand went silent and shrugged.

Salome and Dimi giggled. Certain others, including Jamus and Ms. Martinae, gasped and shook their heads sympathetically. To Brand, this was worse than the giggling.

"What! Raised in a brothel?" cried Gilfingle. "But how can this be? You have an educated air!"

"Well, there was a library in Drifts End—I read what scholarly works I could get my hands on. Though Berengar tells me I'm quite lacking in knowledge of the Outlands."

"How so?" said Gilfingle. "I have never spent time in any of the major cities, and therefore do not know what knowledge of us they have—or don't have."

"Well, much of what is out here is unknown in the cities—mere myths to us. Since being out here... I—I hardly know what to make of it myself. It's like... *another world*. How did such strange things come to be?" Brand looked up, embarrassed at his own frankness.

He caught Cil looking at him with a strange light in her eye, but she quickly looked away when she noticed his gaze.

In the background, Salome and Dimi began to pout.

Gilfingle made a series of sharp clicking noises with his tongue. "My, my... I see we have been remiss in spreading the faith. As to your confusions—perhaps the works of Zanon can shed some light on the subject? Humph... I recall an old fragment:

"'And as the imbalanced ones played God with the woof and warp of nature, so did they bring about a dissonance.'

"Humph... Perhaps it's disrelated. I struggle to recall it in full. But I believe this refers to *the Ancients.* Playing God. Bringing things from other places—creatures that do not belong in our world, or perhaps altering and mixing things that *do* belong here..."

His eyes flicked toward Alucard, then he said, "Another segment comes to mind, *'Such are the unholy offspring of man, left behind in the wake of his imitating the gods.'"*

The table was silent for a moment, and Brand considered Gilfingle's words. *In the wake of his imitating the gods?* Indeed, the words left him with more questions than answers. Still, he was thankful that Gilfingle had changed the topic of conversation.

"Well," said Gilfingle brightly, attempting to lighten the mood, "Berengar, what of you?"

Berengar spread his arms negligently. "I was raised on the northern frontier, beyond the Sunken Tundra. Where it meets the endless fields of ice—*The Borderlands.*"

A small hush went out from the crowd.

Berengar shrugged. "My village was large—the greatest in the Borderlands. I fought, I lusted, I rambled. They said I was meant for war... But I called them fools. I yearned for something greater than war. Yet... perhaps I'm the fool..."

And that sad look Brand had noticed before once again crossed the Outlander's rugged features.

"Indeed. Well, it seems your past conduct was not entirely balanced," Gilfingle noted with a disapproving frown. "But I can see you are making an effort at a new start... So then, how did you and Brand cross paths?"

"Ah, now that's a tale!" said Berengar, brightening. "I helped you out of a scrape. Didn't I, wolf?" He smiled down at Brand.

"And got me into another! I knew that job was a bum gig."

Berengar chuckled. "And it was too."

He then recounted the day they first met—how he had been drinking at a tavern in *Drifts End,* and Brand had gotten into an altercation with a fellow Waggler, Lain Locke. Seeing the lad was outnumbered, Berengar had stepped in.

How they'd been beguiled into helping a cloaked stranger, claiming to be in dire need—only to discover it was all a strange game orchestrated by the Mad King himself. How the king took Brand's mother as ransom and sent them on this quest.

Gilfingle and the others listened with great interest, silently taking in the story. When Berengar had finished, Gilfingle said, "*You never said your mother was in dire need!?* It is important that you finish your task! We shall help you in whatever way we can... *won't we?*" He looked around the table.

The other Zanonnites nodded their heads earnestly.

"Thank you." Said Brand, somewhat taken aback.

Then, turning to Cil, Gilfingle said, "And you, young miss? Where do you hail from, how do you fit into this picture? And what of your leg?"

"I grew up in a port town to the southwest, where the weather is warm and time flows placidly by. The clothing is as colorful as what half of you people wear. The village itself is small and not well known—but we call it Clankerage."

"Never heard of it!" exclaimed Gilfingle.

Cil rolled her eyes. "Indeed... as I said, it is a little-known village, but it does get some trade from adventurers traveling between Revilis Ko'hur and Keel. Life was good. Life was peaceful.

"That is, until the Bikhal Dukes raided our town."

"I was only thirteen when they kidnapped me and a handful of others from the village. They raised us to be acrobats and show fighters—to be sold as performers or used in gambling dens."

"*Oh how dreadful!* You poor thing!" cried Fonicia Coonse.

Cil bristled, disliking such sympathy, then shrugged. "They didn't maim or harm us—beyond the rigors of the severe training. I graduated a few months ago, at the age of seventeen. A convoy took me east, hoping to sell me. We were waylaid in the night on the Trade Road, where it runs north of the Blasted Lands. As to how I came to fall in with these two lug-heads, and how I received this leg injury—" Her face flushed red. "I'd rather not say."

"Fair enough," said Gilfingle graciously. A man with a strange and sometimes surprising mixture of naivety and wisdom, thought Brand idly.

Gilfingle then said, "Why don't you go next, Twithik?"

Twithik—a reticent man—stood up, bowed politely, and said, "I am Twithik. I care for the beasts." Then he sat back down.

"Thank you, Twithik," said Gilfingle, clearing his throat. "Perhaps I'll go next..."

The autobiographical announcements continued around the table —each carried out in turn to Gilfingle's satisfaction.

Finally, Ms. Taloulie brought out the feast.

The first course was a salad of mixed greens, figs, and nuts. This was followed by large platters filled with cheese and bits of hard dried goat-meat.

The meal progressed, and Brand found himself eating under the tyrannical gaze of Gilfingle, who corrected him instantly on every breach of etiquette.

Brand learned which was the salad fork and which was the water goblet—it was not the red-wine glass, nor the white-wine glass. Just when he thought he had things under culinary control, Gilfingle cried out in alarm, "Brand! Control your beast!"

Heads turned. Brand looked around in confusion, wondering what all the fuss was. It seemed that Alucard had taken an empty teapot and placed it on his head, attempting to wear it like a helmet. It hung precariously over the front of his face as he gripped an oversized knife in one hand and an oversized fork in the other— apparently preparing to blindly brave the cheese.

He looked up to Brand, tilting the teapot backward with a flick of his head to make eye contact. He indicated the teapot with a glance and said, "Hair."

Gilfingle was fussing about in Brand's peripheral, but Brand ignored him and spoke tactfully to Alucard. "Good job! That is some lovely hair you've got, but that pot is needed for something special at the table. All of these items are," he said, indicating the various utensils. "I will find you some great hair later, okay?"

Alucard looked sad but nodded, and let Brand take the teapot and place it back on the table.

"It needs more training," said Gilfingle, his upper lip becoming a stiff slash between beard and mustache.

"'It has a name, and it's 'Alucard,'" replied Brand, confronting Gilfingle with a level glare.

Gilfingle took slight at this and straightened indignantly. "That's Grand Corrective to you." Then he softened. "Well, is it a boy or a girl?"

Brand stared blankly for a moment, recalling that Alucard was capable of parthenogenesis. "Good question," he said. "Hmmm, let me ask."

"Alucard, are you a boy or a girl?"

Alucard frowned and looked at Brand. "Are you a boy or a... girl?" he asked in his gurgling voice.

Brand waited for the laughter to die down along the table. "I am a boy, Alucard!"

Alucard stared blankly at Brand, then said, "I... want to be like you. So... I am a *boy*."

Brand turned back to Gilfingle. "There you go."

"Humph... it seems he now wears one of my prized Devirien napkins as a robe."

"He shall be corrected at once—if not sooner."

"Indeed. Well," he repeated a favored saying, "*balance isn't achieved in a single day.*"

After this, Gilfingle noticed Blakcab stabbing a piece of sour pudding with his meat knife and thundered off in the Guardian's direction.

Brand sighed with relief. But his respite was short.

"Brand, would you pass me the wine?" said Salome.

Brand passed her the wine, then went back to eating.

"Brand, the bread plate, please."

"Sure."

"Brand?"

"Get it yourself! I'm eating."

"Humph, you sure don't know how to treat a lady. You should be more like Jamus."

Jamus puffed up and took on a didactic demeanor. "Brand, it is the duty of the man to place the woman first in all matters—other than that of danger, of course." At this, he winked at Cil.

"Thank you," Brand replied.

"Brand, can you pass me the water?" Dimi said, imitating her sister.

"Not you too," Brand sighed.

This continued for a time until Brand was ready to burst, and the three girls, Cil included, began giggling in spiteful glee.

Meanwhile, Berengar had his own hands full with an effusive and fawning Ms. Taloulie, who began to wait on him to the exclusion of all others. She brought him special dish after special dish and kept his wine goblet always full—an activity which Berengar could not find fault with, that is, until she began to try to wipe and dab at his mouth with a washcloth. This last action encroached on his personal space to the point where he sent her scurrying off with a deafening shout of wrath.

Thron and Muls stared stupidly at Cil, Salome, and Dimi throughout the entire dinner, only to be repeatedly reprimanded by Mrs. Martinae.

The meal ran its course.

Brand left the table stressed and irritated, and stalked off to take a walk around the camp with Alucard.

Sometime later, Brand happened to pass by Salome, Cil, and Dimi as they sat chit-chatting by Jamus's fire. Ignoring their withering glances, Brand rounded the wagons and found Berengar lounging on his bedroll.

He laid down next to the golden giant and posed a question. "Ber, I've been meaning to ask you something."

"Yes? What's the matter?"

"Nothing's wrong, Ber. It's just... each time you talk of your past, sorrow crosses your face. Why is that?"

Berengar stared up at the tree branches for a long while, then said, "I have a shameful past, Brand."

"How so?"

"I guess you've told me your embarrassing past... so," after a final grimace, he began his tale. "Raanor, my father, was a great chief of the Borderlands in his day—and our village earned great renown due to his battle prowess, his military strength, and tactful cunning.

"This incited much jealousy from other clans, and how the snow ran red with their blood!" He allowed a grim smile to grace his lips. "Raanor maintained supremacy over his adversaries with an iron fist. But like all things in this world, it didn't last forever—his body aged. His strength and vigor declined. It was around this time that I came of age. I was the oldest son, and was to be clan chief, but I refused. A constant struggle over barren lands, the management of a clan, confined to one location—this was not the path of my heart. I disobeyed my father's wish and left.

"For some years, I traveled widely, mingling and gallivanting within the bastions of humanity—and also among more uncivilized circles. I carved great stone pieces in the high places, and even on the frozen cliffs of the northern shores—beyond the Endless Fields of Ice. Eventually, I decided it was time to return home."

When I got there, all that was left of my village were the blackened husks of huts—and the frozen, splintered, and gnawed bones of my kinsmen.

"I believe I must have gone mad for a time—I screamed my bloody rage at the heavens and beat the ground until my knuckles were bloody travesties. I desperately ransacked the ruined shelters for any sign of my father or brothers. I could find nothing. I could not even do the burial rites. Though…" again that grim humor washed across his face, "I guess they must have burned in the cairns of their own homes."

"To make amends, I traveled to the cliffs nearest the village and carved out a prodigious monument. Thereupon I carved the names of my fallen kinsmen. The project took me two whole years and left me with the strength you now see."

"Since finishing the monument, I have not returned to the Borderlands. But in recent months, I've been thinking it was time."

Brand frowned. "I'm sorry, Ber—it wasn't your fault."

"I know that, lad—but at least I would have died an honorable death, alongside my kinsfolk."

Brand looked at the giant for a long moment. Then said, "Well, I'm glad you didn't, Ber—it's good to have you around." Brand felt suddenly awkward and looked away.

Berengar grinned, a twinkle coming back into his eye. "Thanks, Wolf."

Brand looked back again. "But wait—don't you wish to return to the Borderlands?"

"It's been years, Brand. The Borderlands can wait—your mother cannot."

"True... thanks, Ber. I couldn't do it without you."

Berengar clapped a hand on Brand's shoulder.

Somewhere on Brand's right, Alucard growled—then, sticking his head out and recognizing Brand, relaxed and retreated into the little hemp sack he slept in.

Brand rolled over on his side, then said over his shoulder, "Thanks for telling me your story, Ber. Good night."

"Thanks for pulling it out of me."

Brand faded off into darkness.

The next morning, as they were taking down the fence, they found a group of horned creatures—cousins to the deer—grazing nearby. Jamus swaggered over to them confidently, making affectionate clicking noises and gathering handfuls of grass.

Within minutes, the herd had accepted him and were eating out of his hand. He looked at the girls slyly to see if they were watching, then began to lounge luxuriously against a big buck, as if it were his pet pony. Pretending to just notice the girls' interest, he called them over and helped them to pet the creatures—an activity which brought much delight to the three young girls.

"The man is intolerable," Brand said to Berengar.

"You must admit, he has a way with the beasts—*and the ladies,*" replied Berengar, a tinge of admiration in his booming voice.

"He tries too hard," said Brand.

Berengar laughed.

Presently, Cil had finished petting her buck, and Jamus said, "Are you thirsty?"

Cil shot a glance at Brand, then nodded.

"Come then, and I will teach you the ways of my mind—as we sip sweet nectar tea and eat lily blossoms." He put his arm around

Cil's elbow and guided her off toward the wagons.

Salome finished up with the buck she was feeding and walked over to Brand. She looked up at him and touched the back of his hand. "Well?"

Brand, still looking at Cil's retreating back, was already in a huff and spoke perhaps a little more harshly than he had intended. "Well what?!"

Salome snatched her hand away and, with a venomous glare at Brand, swayed off. Dimi came by, paused, gave Brand a girlish sneer—copying her sister—and ran off after her.

A few minutes later, Thron and Muls came by, nodded awkwardly at Brand, and hobbled after the girls.

Brand could only stare in disbelief.

Berengar patted him on the shoulder. "You little dunderhead, Salome probably just wanted you to walk with her."

Brand frowned, still looking in their direction. "That's obvious. What I don't understand is how Cil is falling for the clichés Jamus keeps throwing out. She even let him touch her!"

"Oh, *so you're jealous?*"

"Jealous? Over that little imp? You are dreaming, Ber. I just... didn't think she was like that."

Berengar laughed, then said, "And you say you're not jealous?!"

"Well... no! But..."

Berengar held up a hand. His face became more serious. "Listen, there are some tracks I noticed around the fence this morning that I want to inspect more closely." So saying, he swaggered off— leaving Brand to brood.

Once the troop members had finished their daily recitations and stowed their gear, the caravan moved off to the northwest. Brand was forced to walk at the front of the caravan with Gilfingle and listen to the old man's rants, while behind them came Twithik, managing the Gers as they stoically pulled the wagons. Berengar brought up the rear guard, and the other troop members walked beside the wagons—all except Cil, who was allowed to ride atop the lead wagon due to her injury; and Jamus, who had somehow convinced Gilfingle that he needed to be up there as well, in order to "best project the notes of his flute for the benefit of all."

The convoy continued north, and since it was a day for music, all members who could play took full advantage. Jamus played a beautiful, rhythmic riff in B major that echoed across the forest, blending harmoniously with the natural sounds of the woods. Pathar joined in with his piccolo, and Blakcab accompanied them on his sitar.

The music was enlivening and seemed to lift Brand's weariness —like a cool breeze that freshens the face of a tired traveler—and, with it, the miles seemed to roll by effortlessly beneath his feet. He had to admit, Jamus was damnably good on that flute.

In the late afternoon, the caravan paused to rest the Gers, and Berengar carried out Brand's first training lesson—an activity in which no holds were barred. Cil and the other girls laughed at Brand and goaded him from the sidelines as he gasped in pain and fought to survive against Berengar's "instruction."

Jamus, watching from the sidelines and twitching with jealousy, attempted to gain the girls' attention. Removing his blue vest, he began performing a variety of acrobatic feats, while calling out advice. "Brand, you should do more stretching—like so..." or, "Some strength training would improve your swordplay— something like this..." And so on.

Five days passed in much the same manner, during which Gilfingle schooled Brand on the ways of the Zanonnites, and Berengar continued his grueling combat training. Brand continued to teach Alucard as much as he could, and Cil's leg healed more and more each day.

On the sixth day, around noon, Brand stood at his customary

station at the front of the convoy. When, glancing to his right, he spotted a trail of filmy, glimmering stuff floating over the treetops from the north. He called a halt, and the convoy stopped. As the rainbow-like thing drew closer, it became clear that it was a flock of transparent, iridescent ray-like creatures with wide, flapping wings and long flimsy tails.

The creatures glided placidly across the trail in front of the caravan, showing no interest in the troop. Brand thought it a magical sight, reminiscent of the schools of jellyfish he had occasionally seen in the clear bays of Revilis Ko'hur.

These creatures, however, either defied gravity or were made of such flimsy material that they drifted on the wind like flower petals.

Jamus cried out in childish wonder, leaped from the wagon, and bustled past Brand toward the creatures, making sing-song noises in the back of his flexible throat.

Brand shook his head. "Can't we just let them be?"

"Nay!" said Jamus over his shoulder. "Have you ever seen such beauty? I shall take this moment to immerse myself within it, and thereby combine with these placid creatures in mind and soul! This, my friend, is my calling."

With that, he ran and leaped lithely onto a high boulder in the path of the creatures. Soon, he was illuminated by a sea of refracting lights as the creatures floated around him, their substance fracturing the sunlight into rainbows. The dazzling colors gave him a magical aspect.

Seeing the girls were now riveted, he arched his back, flinging his arms wide in an attitude of wild abandon.

The sudden motion irritated one of the rays. Its tail turned bright red and curled downward to sting Jamus on the arm. Jamus cried out shrilly and toppled from the boulder. He rolled to his feet and began frantically rubbing mud into the wound, attempting to soothe it. Then, giving this up, he fell to the ground and began to thrash. His movements faltered. A spasm racked his body, twisting his limbs awkwardly. He went still. His arm turned black.

A light breeze carried the creatures majestically over the treetops to the south—and at the same time, wafted the stench of decomposing flesh over to the stunned troop.

Chapter 7

"Women, and Sleepless nights."

A small ceremony was carried out on behalf of Jamus, and his belongings were divided among the troop members—Brand receiving the Ney flute as his portion.

After this, once the troop members were re-settled from the shocking event, Gilfingle set the caravan back into motion.

Another week passed without incident, and the heavily foliaged woods gradually gave way to a chilly pine forest—the trees spaced far apart and standing upon a thick bed of needles. Tall trees obscured the surrounding lands, but a great range of mountains loomed far off to the west.

Cil was now back on her feet and immediately insisted on being added to the watch crew and training daily with Brand and Berengar. This was not to Gilfingle's liking, as he thought these activities "unwomanly." However, she won out in the end and was added to the daily rotation of both.

Alucard had now advanced in his development to the comparable level of a teenage human, though he had definite oddities—he was exceedingly advanced in understanding technical subjects, numbers, and the symbols of the ancients—but on the other hand, he couldn't perceive whether someone was displeased by the look on their face. It seemed he had also stopped growing physically at a height of about two feet.

Brand thought this strange, as Parsan had been about five feet tall, and he wondered if it was due to something Alucard missed in his rearing or diet. This was likely the first time such a creature had been raised outside the environment of "The Waterways," as Parsan had called it.

Presently, the troop traveled along an ancient, dusty road that wound its way up a gentle, forested incline. Looming pines stood like sentinels on either side of the path, and the forest around them seemed ominously quiet. Their progress was slow, lit only by the dim twilight rays of the setting sun.

Gilfingle stoically drove the caravan on, searching for a suitable campsite for the night.

Berengar approached from the rear and joined Brand at the lead. "I do not like this place. Not a sound from a single forest bird or critter."

Brand grimaced. "Well, what then?"

"Just be on your guard, that's all." With that, the giant stalked back to the rear of the caravan.

Brand hunched his shoulders against a sudden chill and looked intently from side to side, attempting to pierce the shadowy vastness of the woods. However, he saw nothing untoward, and he began to wonder if it was just the Outlander's superstitious nature getting the better of him.

Half an hour later, Gilfingle spied a pine-covered clearing by the side of the road suitable for the nightly camp, and the troop carried out their routines.

Brand took a moment to approach Cil. "Hey, you don't seem too upset about Jamus?"

She gave him a sardonic smile. "What? Should I be fawning and sniveling like a woman should?"

"No, but... I thought—well."

"You thought I had fallen head over heels at his amorous approaches?"

"Well... yes."

"No. I just enjoyed seeing how annoyed you got. You lug-head." She grinned wickedly.

"*Damn*... but he didn't deserve what he got."

Cil became sober. "That's true... but this is *the Outlands*. This is how it goes." Then a gloomy expression took her, and she turned and walked away.

Salome had watched their interaction from behind the wagons, though she couldn't hear what they had said. And now her eyes glowed like the twin sapphires of a jealous snake.

As the night drew to a close, Brand secured himself in his bedroll and curled up next to Alucard, exhausted.

Almost instantly, blackness took him. However, after what seemed only a few seconds, he was shaken awake by Berengar. He instantly sensed something was amiss—the night was at its darkest point. No sign of pre-twilight glow.

Brand struggled out of his bedroll and clambered to his feet. "What's the matter, Ber?"

"Come, let us wake Cil! *The fence has failed.*" Berengar's voice was tense. *"Come."*

Brand stumbled after him, tripping over roots in the dark and wiping his sleep-clogged eyes.

They reached Cil's bedroll, and Berengar said, "Wake her."

Brand looked at Cil's sleeping form askance, then said, "I feel it is best that *you* wake her."

"Come now, Brand. You wake her daily after your watch; she is more used to *your* voice."

Brand hesitated a moment, then said, "Fine, but if she's angry, it was your idea."

Berengar waited for Brand to get close, then moved a little distance away.

Brand—not noticing Berengar depart—began cautiously twitching at Cil's blanket. Then said, *"Cil, Cil, wake up!"*

He smiled bleakly and touched her shoulder.

She came awake with a gasp and hit Brand with a solid cross on the jaw. Brand reeled backward, his head spinning.

Cil looked around in confusion, then recognized him. "Why did you wake me so soon…" She stifled a yawn, *"idiot?"*

"Ouch, *you're* the idiot," he said, massaging his jaw. "Come on, Berengar tells me it's an emergency."

Cil leaped out of bed. She was fully dressed and only needed to retrieve her weapon.

Berengar, having waited at some distance, led them across the camp.

At the opposite edge of the fence, they found Blakcab pacing back and forth, swearing profusely. He held a torch in one hand and glared at them as they approached, the torchlight casting shadows across his brooding face and accentuating his sunken eyes. He wore only a white nightshirt and breeches, and an explosion of curly black chest hair made itself known at his collar. His image was grim indeed, like that of a wife-beating alcoholic peasant.

"Why so dour, Blakcab?" asked Brand.

Blakcab growled and thrust the torch toward a shadowed section of the fence.

Brand and Cil gasped. It wasn't a "shadowed" section at all.

Across the fence sagged an unnameable horror, crushing part of it under its massive bulk. The beast—monster—whatever it was, was the size of a wagon and covered in a slick, black, leathery skin-like substance. Its shape was indistinct but loosely resembled a large cylinder—rounded at both ends.

From the smooth cylindrical body sprouted ten thin black legs, each ending in a flexible foot with two sets of opposing hooks. It lacked anything resembling a head; instead, it boasted only a gaping circular maw at the forward end of its strange body. The maw sagged wide, displaying an inward spiral—rows upon rows— of needle-sharp teeth. It lay completely still in its messily sprawled position atop the fence, radiating the smell of burnt insect.

With a cold trickle of horror crawling along his spine, Brand realized he was looking at the very thing from a folklore book his mother had given him when he was quite young. What else had he seen in that book?

"The damnable thing ruined the fence," spat Blakcab in disgust. "I reckon it won't work after this, and I don't know how to fix it."

"At least it's dead," said Brand, eyeing the creature askance and forcing down a growing nausea. The more he looked at it, the paler he got. His mind began to reel and he staggered back. Dizzy.

"A devil of a foe that would have been to encounter in a dark forest," said Berengar stonily.

Cil also looked pale and dizzy and staggered back to where Brand was.

"Bah! What good is it now? We are as good as dead without the guard fence!" Said Blakcab, black rage overtaking him.

"We are not dead yet," replied Berengar, his face inscrutable in the torchlight.

Blakcab thrust the torch handle at Berengar and stalked off, kicking tree roots as he went.

Brand looked over the monstrosity. "I guess whatever the fence's power is... it burnt it?"

"Yes, like the owl and the toads," grunted Berengar.

"What... is it?" Cil asked, her voice filled with horror.

"There are many unnamed things out here," replied Berengar.

Suddenly Berengar hissed and danced back. The loose folds of the creature's mouth had twitched. All three drew their weapons and stood tense, ready. A faint, high-pitched grumbling came from behind the many rows of sharp teeth. Then, a small figure crawled into view, delicately picking its way through the deadly maze of prongs. The three companions leaned back, aghast.

The small figure reached the lips successfully, but then slipped and tumbled out onto the bed of pine needles below. It stood up and eyed them with a critical, sulking glare. It looked like a small gray man, with a round, balding head—bordered by tufts of gray hair above the ears. Its body was naked and had no genitals, but otherwise resembled a human. The face was smooth, the nose long and pointed; the eyes dark, black pits of hate.

"You have killed me! You have slain my outer shell, and hence —me! You have taken my one life and now, I die! *I curse you! You shall suffer an unexpected end in this world!"* Its words ended in a dreadful, waning scream that echoed out across the dim forest. With that, it toppled backward and lay still beside the smoking, black hulk.

The three companions quickly distanced themselves from the creature—each hoping to avoid becoming the target of its dying curse.

Once far away, they stopped and discussed the rearrangement of the night schedule, deciding that all four of them must remain awake in case there were more of those things.

Morning light came, and with it the rest of the troop rose.

Gilfingle looked anxiously at the four when he noticed that all were awake. "What has happened?" he asked.

Blakcab grunted sheepishly and nodded toward the fence. The black corpse stood out like a blot of hate in the now well-lit glade.

Gilfingle let out a sucking gasp. "*The Artifact has fallen!*" He walked over to the hulking shape and stared in horror, "By Zanon, I believe it has slain a demon this night."

"You are probably right," agreed Berengar.

Gilfingle's old face creased with concern. He looked to Blakcab. "I trust you have a backup plan for the troop's safety, good Blakcab?"

"Yes, Grand Corrective. We must arm the troop with crossbows and increase the watch."

Gilfingle frowned sadly. "If Zanonnites must kill to survive, then they must. Though such acts bring me sorrow."

The camp was roused, and Gilfingle began readying it for travel.

Certain members of the troop stared anxiously at the black corpse. However, their doubts were put to rest by a proclamation from Gilfingle:

"Though you see our Artifact is broken, fear not. For it has served its purpose and ended a great evil in these lands. Perhaps the visions led us here for this very purpose? Who can say... Further, fear not for yourselves, since your safety is in the able hands of your Guardian, Blakcab, and our hearty new companions."

Brand smiled bleakly. "Thanks, Gilfingle. No pressure," he muttered.

"Yeah!" said Cil, and then seemed annoyed that she had agreed with him so readily.

Berengar shrugged. "We can only do our best."

Salome and Dimi approached, and Salome addressed Brand. "You will protect us, *right, Brand?*"

Brand scratched the back of his head and smiled nervously. "Yeah... I'll protect you."

"Thank you, *Brand,*" Salome crooned, and gave him a kiss on the cheek before swaying off to the rear wagon. Dimi smiled cheekily at him and followed her sister away.

"Yeah, *I'll protect you!*" mocked Cil as she shouldered past him.

Brand cursed. "What was I supposed to say? 'No, you're dead meat'?"

Presently, the convoy were ready to move on. However the fence, now pinned down, blocked their exit and, despite Berengar's and Blakcab's best efforts, the monstrous carcass could not be raised. So, they were forced to flatten another section and roll the wagons back onto the dirt trail, leaving the Artifact behind.

As the sun crossed past noon, Gilfingle called a halt for a break by an icy brook that trickled into a shallow pool beside the road. Balin, Fonicia, and Twithik braved the cold water, enjoying a brief swim, while others merely sponged themselves with damp cloths. Twithik watered the Gers and refilled the large barrels on the wagons while Ms. Taloulie prepared the afternoon meal.

Berengar decided it was a good time to train while the meal was being prepared, and took Brand and Cil off to a nearby flat area.

Today, however, Salome insisted on being trained with them, saying, "Why can't I train too? I could be as good as Cil." She stood in a haughty posture, her hands resting on her shapely hips.

"Now then," replied Berengar, "I'm happy to train you, but separately. This is a three-man formation I am practicing for the night-watch crew."

"Humph. Yet you let Cil train and be part of the watch, even though she is a girl. Why can't I too?" Salome retorted, not moving.

"Come now, Salome. Cil is one of the watch members because she has had real combat experience and—" began Brand.

"So you think she is tougher than me? That I can't keep up to *your* standards?" Salome hissed. Then her expression twisted into one of spiteful malice. "I am of noble blood! I could best that peasant hussy at any task!"

"*Peasant hussy?*" said Cil, her face becoming dangerously still.

Salome straightened to her full five-foot-ten inches and swayed threateningly over to Cil. "You are speaking to royal blood, and you best keep a civil tongue in your head." She leaned close, towering over her by at least half a foot.

"That's it! Give it to her, Salome!" called out Blakcab in poor taste.

Brand went to intercede, but Berengar stopped him. "Let nature run its course. Things will resolve more quickly that way."

Salome's confidence grew at Cil's silence, mistaking it for fear. She said, "That's what I thought." Raising her hand, she poked Cil in the chest. "Oh my, now I know why they let you train with the men."

That did it. Cil's right hand swung up in a lightning-fast arc, delivering a thunderous open-palmed blow, which connected with Salome's unprotected jaw. Salome went down like a felled sapling —landing hard. Tears instantly sprung from her eyes, and she cupped her face, which now bore a red handprint. Dimi rushed over and put an arm around her, comforting her older sister.

"A great right from Cil!" cheered Blakcab. "Salome goes down for the count. Get up! Give her one back, Salome!"

Brand glared at Blakcab. "Will you cut it out?"

Salome wept quietly for a moment, then steadied herself and climbed back to her feet. "You... *dare*—" she said. Then, with tears still streaming down her cheeks, she directed a gaze at Brand that made his stomach turn cold, before swaying off toward the wagons.

"That one may be trouble," said Cil, glaring after the girl.

Brand also stared after her, wondering how he could have handled the situation better. The look on her face was still fresh in his mind—her beautiful dark face a mask of scowling hatred, her violet eyes blazing like hellfires. *If looks could kill...*

After the afternoon break was over, Gilfingle called for the caravan to move, and the troop tramped onward. The convoy wound its way, ever onward, and the forested hills flattened into a dank, misty lowland—filled with pale, thin trees, horribly twisted and grotesque in aspect.

As the final rays of the afternoon sun faded to gray, Gilfingle called out to find a campsite for the night.

Brand spotted a tight copse of trees five hundred feet north of the road that seemed perfect for a defensible campsite. There was a shady clearing within, and the outer trees were closely packed together, bar a single wide gap, which a wagon could fill. A rocky mound guarded the west side, preventing entrance from that direction.

Here they made their camp, placing one wagon in the center of the clearing and filling the gap in the trees with the other as best they could. The females of the troop placed their beds on one side of the central wagon, and the men on the other.

They set up a smaller and less stately dining arrangement and ate their evening repast.

During dinner, Gilfingle reprimanded Brand, saying, "Brand, I am a patient man, and I search for the good in all things. But playing the flirt, and stoking discontent among the young girls simply will not be tolerated."

"But wait, I—" Brand interjected.

Brooking no argument, Gilfingle refused to listen. "Nay, you shall not wriggle out of this one, my young gallivant. Some abstinence shall be good for you—no dessert today."

Brand looked toward Salome and Dimi. Both avoided his gaze.

Gilfingle continued, "Furthermore, you shall stay hungry until everyone else has finished. Use this time to think upon your mischief and repent."

Brand went to complain, but looking into Gilfingle's stubborn blue eyes, he knew no good would come of it. "Yes, Grand Corrective," he said with a grimace.

"Good. There may be some hope for you as a Zanonnite yet." Gilfingle let out a pleased sigh and tucked into his own copious serving of the meal.

After dinner, Brand went to take a nap before his watch began, but found that Alucard was missing. Becoming concerned at once, he leaped to his feet and began searching the perimeter. At first, he couldn't find the creature anywhere. However, as he doubled back to the men's side of the clearing, he saw Alucard rush out from under the central wagon—like a tiny turquoise chimpanzee, his short, bowed legs powering him along at great speed.

He had a guilty air about him, and so Brand decided to investigate at once. "What were you doing?" he said.

"Nothing, father, I was..." Alucard's blue eyes rolled wildly side to side as he searched for an answer. "I... was just answering the call of nature." He held his hands behind his back and smiled.

"Humph. I see you're wearing a pair of Cil's underwear for a bonnet. Does she approve of this?"

"It is such lovely hair! One day I will find some golden hair just like yours!"

Brand tore the underwear off Alucard's head and was just about to reprimand him soundly when Cil rounded the wagon on her watch routine. The first thing she saw was Brand, grasping her choice underwear in one hand and waving it in the air for all to see.

Half an hour later, Brand sat down stiffly on his bed, dabbing at his various bruises and contusions with a damp cloth. His injuries were mostly superficial, and none of a disfiguring sort. However, he felt that Cil's reaction was... excessive, to say the least.

"See what you've gotten me into!" he growled at Alucard, who sat nearby reading his book, completely ignorant of Brand's plight.

"I do not understand?" Alucard piped in a high-pitched voice. "What does you being injured have to do with *me?*"

"Oh, really?" said Brand hotly.

"Precisely so. What does *me* finding hair for myself have to do with the completely unrelated incident of Cil defeating *you* in a contest of manly virtue—thereby establishing her dominance in the pack?"

"The answer is simple in the extreme: One, *you* stole her underwear—an article of clothing girls can be quite touchy about. Two, *I* try to take it off *you* to correct the situation. Three, Cil sees *me,* thinks *I* stole her underwear, and unleashes all ten tons of her instinctive female wrath upon *me.*"

"There is somewhere an error in your logic. Even if what you say is true, the condemning error was in your action of taking the underwear off my head. This, in your own words, is what brought Cil's wrath upon you. This only reinforces my original viewpoint that the underwear should not have been removed from my head in the first place. Thus, if you had listened to me, the entire episode could have been avoided."

"Bah!" said Brand, giving up.

Fifteen minutes passed, and Brand began to drift off to sleep. A shadow loomed over him, blocking out the starlight. His eyelids fluttered open. A black shape. The fragrance of lilac. He started upright in alarm, only to be met by the smarting slap of a smooth feminine palm.

Brand reeled back in confusion. "Cil?! I thought we were past —"

"No, it is *not Cil!*"

This too was a mistake.

"*Always Cil!*" came Salome's voice from silhouette above him.

"Salome? What the devil?" Brand stood up, raising his arms defensively, and struck a match. Salome was illuminated in most ghastly fashion, the shadows flickering across her beautiful features accentuating the malice of her scowl. She peered at him like a hateful witch from hell. He noticed something further, which added to her fearful aspect—her once-beautiful hair was now messily hacked and slashed off, leaving it short and unruly.

"*This! This!*" she screeched, indicating her slashed hair. "This, Brand? Did dessert mean that much to you?"

Brand stammered in confusion.

Gilfingle and Dimi came over, along with other witnesses.

"Well, Brand, what do you have to say for yourself?" said Gilfingle, a look of stern reproach on his wrinkled face.

"I swear, I did not do it. I was here the whole evening—apart from setting up the security with Blakcab."

"Humph... you have a witness, then?"

Blakcab and Berengar strolled over, having heard the commotion. Blakcab spoke. "Aye, as much as I enjoy seeing this twerp get thrashed about by the girls, he was with me and Berengar all evening."

"Most peculiar..." stated Gilfingle. "Well, Brand, it seems I owe you an apology." Then to Salome, "My dear, someone else must have done it. Perhaps Dimi was jealous?" He looked critically at her younger sister.

"Of course I didn't!" Dimi cried indignantly.

"Hmmm. This is indeed a mystery. If anyone has any information on the situation, or even a theory, please share it with me. I would be very interested to hear it. Until we resolve this, Salome, please go back to bed."

Salome looked at Brand. "I know it was you—or perhaps that little monster you're raising—regardless of what you say. Be warned, Brand, I am of noble birth, and can only put up with so much." She shook her fist, gave him a parting banshee-glare, and then swept off forcefully to the women's side of the camp.

Finally, Brand was able to go to sleep uninterrupted.

However, like the previous evening, it seemed only seconds had passed when he was violently shaken awake.

Berengar's voice was tight with alarm. "Wake up! Something is wrong. I sent Cil to rouse the others."

So this was life without the Artifact.

Brand leapt out of bed, not understanding what was going on. Luckily, he had slept in his clothes. He grabbed his daggers and short sword, and loaded his hand crossbow.

"Alucard! Come along." He grabbed Alucard and pulled him out of bed before following Berengar.

The full moon hung high in the center of the sky, lighting the copse and outer forest in a silvery, fey light—making it seem a nightmare realm.

Cil's shouts rang out within the camp as she woke the others.

Berengar beckoned for Brand to follow, and he stumbled after the giant toward the edge of the copse. Cil, Gilfingle, Balin, and Ms. Taloulie were the first to join them, and all present strode out beyond the wall of trees and into the broadly spaced pine forest. The crunch of pine needles was all that could be heard in that silent place.

A thick mist had developed and spread like a blanket across the forest floor. Visibility reached about fifteen paces; beyond this, the mist hung like a cottony white wall, obscuring all to sight. A slight breeze caused it to flow and swirl in filmy tendrils around the bases of the trees, lending it the aspect of some great octopus grasping at things within its range.

"What has happened?" whispered Gilfingle in alarm. "I see no danger."

"Blakcab has not come back from the perimeter scan. It's been twenty minutes. It's best to be prepared. Ready your weapons while we wait," said Berengar, with a stony expression that chilled Brand in its intensity.

Shortly, Fonicia, Ms. Martinae, and the others arrived, looking anxious and disheveled. Each shakily held a crossbow, with a short sword belted at their side.

Berengar inspected their bearing and swore. "A farce. Stay here and guard the gap. Put your backs against the wagons and have your crossbows ready. I don't know what's out here. Brand, Cil, and Gilfingle—follow me."

Brand detached Alucard and placed him on the wagon. "Sit tight. Hide in the wagon if you need to."

Berengar spoke again. "If Blakcab has wandered far, he's lost. We cannot walk into this mist. Come." He began to circle the perimeter of the copse, his great sword held low, glinting in the moonlight. "Brand, Cil—watch to the right. Gilfingle—watch our backs."

They did not have to go far. They had made it about a quarter of the way around the copse when a shadowy mound appeared in the mist before them. Was it Blakcab? Strange—it looked too tall.

At first, part of the mound resolved into Blakcab's pale face. He had the most peaceful expression Brand had ever seen on him, and his skin was white as snow. A second later, the rest of the tall mound resolved into a great corpse-white creature, its bony arms holding Blakcab from behind in a tender embrace. A face of nightmare and lunacy peeked over Blakcab's left shoulder. The face of a man, but horribly emaciated, with pale-blue eyes bulging from sunken sockets, and a large white head that showed too much skull. Its mouth gaped in a hideously foolish grin, showing clean white human teeth. It looked at them for a moment with calm, curious interest, then the pale-blue eyes flitted down to look lovingly at Blakcab, who hung like a toddler in its gangly pale arms. It looked as if the creature were cradling a babe. If not for the strange circumstances—and the odd posture of his body— Blakcab could have been sleeping, held there upright, oddly slumped, in that creature's embrace.

"Ahh, so warm. So, so warm," said the creature affectionately.

A chain of hushed comments echoed from the trees around them, almost as one, creating a strange, pattering reverberation of voices.

"Cold." "So cold." "Delicious warmth." "Cold." "Luck." "Yes, luck! Just our luck." "I'm coming." "I'm coming." "Wait. Wait." "Wait."

Berengar grunted in alarm and glared around, attempting to penetrate the mist by the sheer intensity of his gaze.

A pair of lambent blue eyes appeared in the mist. Then another. Then another. Soon a veritable sea of glowing specks spread throughout the forest. A sudden chill wind dispersed some of the fog, revealing a host of tall white shapes—some peeking out from behind trees as if bashful, displaying only their faces and the tips of long white fingers; others tottering into view on unstable legs, like ten-foot-tall lackwits.

"Heat Sloths!" cried Berengar. "Their touch is death. *Quick!*" He signaled a retreat.

A reverberation of gasps rang out from the creatures:

"Wait for us!" *"Wait."* *"Oh, terrible! Wait."* *"So cold. Wait!"* *"Marcus, stop them!"* *"Don't let the warmth escape!"*

Some mouthed silently, their thin white lips forming empty black circles in the dim light—haunting, ghostly visages. Then, as if responding to some unseen cue, the still figures suddenly geared into motion as one. So sudden and uniform was their shift, it created the illusion that Brand was being drawn toward them—the forest itself sliding under their stride.

On they came, with an inexorable slowness that was somehow more fearsome than incredible speed would have been. Brand's senses reeled. He felt giddy. Gilfingle shook like a wind chime caught in a gale. Cil, to her credit, blanched but held firm. Berengar was as active as ever, though sweat ran in great rivulets down his shoulders and back.

The sloth that had been holding Blakcab released him and straightened. Blakcab's body fell to the earth, and bits of him snapped off and shattered on contact. The creature looked down, as if sorrowful to part with him, then slowly turned its head up to grin at the newcomers.

It now stood well over eight feet tall, its pale skin smooth and completely devoid of hair. It wore only a ragged animal-skin loincloth around its waist. Its arms were unnaturally elongated. Though it stood erect, they hung to the ground. Its feet were manlike but flexible and elongated, ending in pointed toe hooks. Its hands were similarly stretched, with clawed, probing fingers which now tested the air—sensing the warmth.

"I feel... *amazing,*" it said, smiling at the party with a rapacious excitement that chilled Brand's blood. "I shall stop the heat from escaping." It flexed its shoulders grotesquely, emitting a sound like gristle tearing. Its face became slightly flushed—the only coloring Brand had seen on any of them yet.

"Capture the heat, Marcus!" the whispering voices echoed from all sides as they came on in painful slowness.

The creature—Marcus—lurched with surprising speed toward Berengar, who was in the lead.

Berengar was faster. He slashed out wildly and brought his great blade down. The creature raised a bony forearm in alarm. Berengar's blow bounced back, jarring him. As he tottered backward, his foot caught on a root, and he fell prone.

Marcus looked at his forearm with interest. It was unharmed. He giggled—a dry rattle of laughter. "That tickled. Hmm... some warmth. But I sense more!" He smiled and lurched downward, arms outstretched, his face a ghastly mask of exaltation.

Cil and Gilfingle fired their crossbows at once. The bolts bounced harmlessly off its bone-like exterior. It came down, mere inches from Berengar as he scuttled backward, slipping on the pine needles. It almost had him. Just an inch more.

Brand's hand shot up like lightning. He fired his hand crossbow at point-blank range. His accuracy was unmatched. The bolt pierced the only soft part that existed—the creature's eye. It carried through, burying itself deep in Marcus's brain. The creature lurched backward with a hideous sigh and fell twitching a few feet away. Berengar snatched up his sword and scrambled to his feet.

Brand managed a pale-faced grin. "A woman's weapon."

"Aye, you got me there, Wolf," replied Berengar, his face ashen. "It was like hitting a solid stone wall—only it froze my blade! If not for the leather binding, my skin would've welded to the steel. Even now it hurts to hold the hilt."

A series of shocked gasps rang out from the sloths, then a cacophony of whining complaints:

"Oh!"   "Oh!"   "Marcus! Oh no!"   "Marcus, get up!"   "Terrible."   "So uncivilized!"   "Ghastly!"   "Poor Marcus

"So dangerous!"   "Poor manners!"

An army of bony figures began closing in from the forest on all sides. They were slow as turtles and moved with painful rigidity. Though, as they drew closer to the warm bodies of Brand and his companions, they appeared to gain speed—faster and faster, as if feeding on proximity to the heat alone.

"Run!" Berengar cried.

The small group took to their heels in a wild scramble and quickly reached the rest of the troop at the gap in the copse.

"Grab your pouches and follow me. No time to pack the wagons!" said Berengar in a rush.

The others hadn't seen Blakcab's fate, and Salome attempted a derisive comment. "Berengar, I thought you were meant to—"

"Go!!!" he roared, cutting her off. The sheer volume of his voice nearly knocked her over. She went. So did the others.

Brand located Alucard—he was not sitting on the wagon where he was supposed to be. Instead, he was beside the second wagon, rummaging through one of its compartments. Brand moved to reprimand him, but the small creature held up Brand's basic belongings, along with his own pouch—which contained only One's notebook.

Brand stopped and said, "You did good. Let's go help the others." Alucard grinned and jumped onto Brand's back.

The campsite was complete chaos—men and women flying about, snatching up their prized possessions. Brand saw Berengar bolt past to grab his pouch, then caught a fleeting glimpse of

Gilfingle carrying a volume of *Zanon's Tranquil Almanac* high above his head.

"What of the Gers?" cried Twithik in dismay. "I will not leave them!"

"Do what you can to set them loose—but be quick!" Pathar called back, grabbing a pile of blankets for the troop.

Brand dashed around to the females' side of the clearing and found Ms. Taloulie stuffing a sack full of vital provisions—two sacks of water already slung over her broad shoulders. Brand fell to work assisting her with the foodstuffs, while the others fumbled around him on all sides.

Seconds later he heard Salome scream and looked up to see the grinning, skeletal faces of six heat sloths peeking through the copse's tightly packed trees.

"The faces are here," said Alucard, his voice calm. But Brand knew the small creature felt the fear.

"Time's up!" Berengar bellowed.

Brand aided Ms. Taloulie with the stores, catching up to the others as they ran toward a small gap on the southern side of the copse.

The heat sloths cried out in alarm:

"Wait!"   "Please don't go!"   "So cold! Let us join you!"

A second later they were through the wall of trees and out.

Berengar did a quick head count—Twithik was missing.

"Brand?" he said. "On me. The rest of you, return to the trail and run westward! Stick to the road!"

"I'm coming!" said Cil stubbornly, though she looked pale and shaken.

Berengar grunted in reply and started back towards the copse.

Brand passed the supplies to Muls and Thron and told Alucard to climb onto Ms. Taloulie's back, then followed Berengar and Cil back into the copse.

They reached the inner clearing and found Twithik struggling amid a pack of crooning Gers. The animals were panicking and pulling in all directions, tangling Twithik in their leads.

Brand cocked his hand crossbow expertly and aimed at the sloth nearest to Twithik.

"Cease! Desist! Control your lust for warmth, or die!"

"I cannot," it said bleakly, shaking its head.

"Remember Marcus? I'll make you still like Marcus. Tell your brothers to retreat. *Now.*"

The sloth's lambent eyes blinked once. It regarded Brand with a heavy-lidded gaze, then shook its head with a whimsical smile. "I cannot control my own lust for heat, let alone theirs." It lurched toward Twithik in a sudden convulsive movement.

Brand fired. The bolt pierced the creature's brain, blotting out one of its glowing eyes. It fell back. Dead.

The other sloths gasped in dismay—but they did not cease their advance. They surrounded Twithik, closing in. Others grabbed some of the tangled Gers. The animals whinnied and made hoarse barking noises as the sloths encircled their flanks with great pasty arms. Upon contact, the Gers went still, as if suddenly asleep. Their skin and fur went pale, rimmed with frost.

Berengar dashed in among the Gers, slashing at their heavy leads. It was useless. Seconds later, he fell back with a grimace of dismay. Twithik was entangled in a maze of straps. And now ten sloths surrounded the sturdy animal handler.

Twithik cried out once, as the nearest sloths embraced him with their long hooked hands—then he slowed to a stop, becoming a vacant statue.

They had sucked him dry of warmth in an instant, snuffing out his life like a candle. For a moment, they stood like a clutch of white spiders feeding on a caterpillar. Then, one by one, their grinning faces turned toward Berengar.

"So warm. So good. More!" came the whispering voices from multiple gaping mouths.

The ones who had touched Twithik turned slightly pink—their faces flushed as if drunk on liquor. Then they galloped forward on all fours with sudden speed, charging Berengar, Brand and Cil—who darted from the copse in fear-fueled flight.

They sprinted through open glades for thirty seconds, not daring to glance behind.

The sloths' speed burst didn't last long, and the companions soon found it easy to outdistance them once out in the open. They made it back to the wagon trail and caught up with the rest of the troop, who were already a ways down the trail. They paused briefly to see if the sloths were still following.

A few minutes passed. The sloths appeared on the trail—a horde of pale, hairless, elongated spiders.

Ms. Taloulie gasped, her thick lips hanging open in a vacuous gape.

"They won't stop!" Salome cried, her eyes sunken, frantic with fear. Her younger sister Dimi simply hugged her and whimpered.

"No," Berengar replied solemnly, "keep going."

"I can't run all night. I must rest," complained Ms. Martinae.

"If you wish to join Twithik, then stay still," Berengar replied, with the callousness of the Outlanders.

"Oh, Twithik!" cried Gilfingle, "not another one. Oh Zanon protect you, my son!" The old man's eyes grew dim and filled with tears of grief.

"Save your prayers for the living!" said Berengar. "The Heat Sloths come—but we can outdistance them. *Move!*"

Berengar's voice cut through the troop's confusion like a whip, and their fear-stricken minds obeyed, shifting into action at once, heading west on the trail.

Alucard climbed down from Ms. Taloulie's shoulders and

returned to Brand.

Their march continued, accompanied by the grumbling and sulking of the weaker troop members.

Behind, the sloths followed patiently, without flagging. Without pause—skeletal faces grinning in the gloom...

Chapter 8

"The Wizard."

Spells are awful capricious things. Yes, the Lantern Lights can guide you to the precise and exact syllables and stresses. But it is *you* who must master control over them. They worm and squirm hither and thither. They try to break free from your control, for such vibrations are the antithesis to the natural laws of this world.

And just when you think you've got your elocution exactly perfect, your cadence precise—they go and change the rhythm on you! And if you get one syllable wrong... This is probably why many forgo "The Art" for the less fantastic, though more consistent calling of traditional science.

Regarding magic, I guess you kind of have to learn to *"ride the wave,"* so to speak, and "feel it out" as you go. You'll get the hang of it eventually. That is, if your mind is still intact, and your physical makeup is still such that you can yet form syllables... and if you remain in a universe that is compatible with the laws of magic you know... So yes, in this particular aspect, one could say that magic is more of an art than a science—but it is, in its intrinsic nature, still a science. *Never forget that.*

To succeed, you must ensure your delivery remains minimally within an error margin of 0.00001—as far as allowable percentage of deviation. A deviation percentage of 0.00002 is most likely innocuous—but it is best to avoid even this much, as there will always be some unknown and unwanted complication.

Play it safe and stick to the 0.00001 rule.

—A Brief Talk on Your Spell Delivery by Fingalad the Ineffable

***

The companions trudged on through the murk.

After an hour or so, the dirt road rounded a bend, and the companions saw an offshoot of the main trail ahead. As they reached the intersection, they saw that it was a paved pathway, leading through a section of landscaped forest.

There were fewer trees on this patch of land, and the shrubbery had been either removed or cultivated into tasteful clumps and rows. The trees seemed deliberately placed, and through the gaps in their twisted branches, the companions could see the eccentric towers of a large manse silhouetted blackly against the night sky. Within it, golden squares of light indicated warmth and occupation —safety.

The older companions were huffing and puffing, lathered in sweat despite the cool night air. Berengar had even carried Ms. Martinae for a time.

"A dwelling!" said Brand.

"Out here?" Berengar frowned. "Seems strange to me."

"Have we much choice?" cried Ms. Martinae, ready to faint from exertion.

Berengar chewed his lip and grumbled something indefinable.

"Ber, some members of the troop won't last the night if we don't find shelter."

"Better some than all."

"Perhaps we can scout it first—spy through the windows?"

Berengar scowled but relented. "Let us go then. The sloths draw near."

He led the way up the drive toward the manse. Five minutes later, they stood in a well-kept yard of pleasing aspect. The path was clean, bordered by neat hedges. The entrance was grand—a beautiful portico with a balustrade staircase leading up to it. The manse itself was large, with many gabled roofs and high steeples of strange geometric design. The architecture was foreign to Brand, but expertly crafted—though undeniably eccentric.

"The house of a sorcerer," said Berengar with a hiss.

"Sor-cer-or," intoned Alucard from Brand's shoulder. "Great!" The small creature buzzed with excitement.

Brand frowned at him—*What the hell are you talking about?*—then turned to Berengar. "Too late to go back now." Then, making a broad gesture, he said, "Besides, does such landscaping truly speak of depravity? Order is the occupation of reason—and never have I seen a more pleasant yard."

"Note the eerie tilt of some of those towers," said Berengar, pointing upward with his keen eyes.

"I agree. The architecture is somewhat eccentric. But the sloths are imminent."

"Don't blame me if we're all turned into toads," said Berengar with a final shrug of disgust.

"Let us see what is to be seen," said Brand, dancing lightly up the stairs. The prospect of a clean bed, away from the perils of the forest, had made him reckless.

The beleaguered troop followed close behind, crowding nervously up the stairs—anxious to get inside. Many cast glances back down the shaded path, where thin white shapes began to show through the trees.

Brand crept to one of the glowing windows and peered in. He saw a cozy salon with a brick fireplace at its center, a reading desk, and several comfortable couches. It was empty. He felt Berengar's hard-muscled shoulder press against him as the giant fought for a glance.

"Black magic," he said.

"How so? I see nothing but a salon—clearly made welcoming for passing guests."

"Exactly. Why would there *be* passing guests?"

Brand said nothing. He grasped the ornate knocker that hung

from the door and knocked twice. Silence followed the echoing blows. He glanced over his shoulder at the shapes in the trees, and knocked again.

A reedy voice called from within. *"I'm coming, I'm coming. I'm not as young as I used to be, you know."*

Everyone sighed with relief. Berengar growled and drew his dagger.

Brand looked back once more. The sloths had reached the edge of the yard. Their leering grins peeked from behind trees, over hedges. Their faces strained with worry—their prey so close to safety. A chorus of sulking whispers spilled from their mouths.

Just as Brand was about to kick in the door, it flung open to reveal a kindly old man with a masterful gray beard, a long black silk robe, and keen, scintillating eyes.

"Ah, why... it is unusual to receive guests at this hour... But, it just so happens I have a hot meal cooking." He then fumbled for something within his robe.

Berengar cursed and lunged with his dagger—quick as a wildcat. He clutched the old man by the beard with his left hand and drove the blade over and over into the frail frame until it was riddled with slits. The old man, as surprised as everyone else, had no time to react. Berengar drove him to the floor with deadly blows. The old man let out a single pitiful sob, then went still.

Berengar didn't stop. He jerked the man's head up by the beard and savagely sawed at the neck until it came free. Then, raising it in one hand, he hurled it high into the air above the dark forest.

A shadow passed across the moon. The flap of great leathery wings echoed through the night as a large figure flew into view. Its form was obscured by a billowing black robe, but it appeared humanoid. It reached out a clawed appendage and snatched the head from the air—then flitted off over the treetops to the west.

A harsh, grating voice rang out in its wake, carrying back to the stunned troop. "Ah, a gift! Tonight I shall dine on exquisite tartar."

Brand gaped in dumb amazement. Then made the mistake of looking down at the pitiful red ruin that had been the old man.

Similar reactions broke out among the Zanonnites, and Muls toppled backward into Thron, sending them both tumbling down the stairs.

Berengar stared thoughtfully at the sky, "Kulzibar really *does* exist..."

Gilfingle stared at Berengar, horror-stricken. "Berengar! Why... You... You are no Zanonnite! I name thee demon, devil! Begone! Go hence and leave us in peace!" He leaned against the balustrade and dry retched.

"Berengar—what...?" Brand finally gasped.

Muls and Thron clambered back up the stairs, squealing, "The monsters—the monsters are in the yard!"

Berengar shook his head stubbornly. "I thought he was pulling a wand on us. Besides, he had an aura of dread."

"What if you were wrong?"

Berengar shoved the door open and stepped inside, scowling.

"We shall not enter with that demon in there!" Gilfingle cried.

Brand gave the Zanonnites one weary, pleading look—then stepped inside. Cil, pale-faced, followed behind.

Gilfingle hesitated, then looked over his shoulder.

He let out a small wail of terror—the sloths had made it to the foot of the steps.

The Zanonnites stampeded over the wizard's remains—cramming through the doorway in a panicked dog-pile.

As soon as the last person was inside, Berengar slammed the door and barred it with a wooden broom resting nearby.

Brand sat down on a couch, catching his breath, ignoring the bumbling, terrified crowd for a moment. He needed to collect his thoughts.

The salon was just as he'd seen through the windows, though now he noticed the warm glow of numerous large candles. To the right of the wide room, a large open archway led into another seating or dining chamber. To the left of the arch, a spiral staircase wound out of sight to unknown upper levels. Beside the couch where Brand sat, the brick fireplace crackled, a sturdy log burning lazily within—its warmth spreading through the room.

Opposite the archway, on the left side of the room, stood a chair and an oak reading desk cluttered with books and odd curios. The windows Brand had used to inspect the room from the porch looked out beyond it.

The place was quiet—strangely soothing, especially in contrast to the constant hardship. The closest thing to a house he'd slept in since leaving Revilis Ko'hur had been the cavern of Ator Periconias.

Berengar, ignoring the ill will he had caused, stretched like a great cat and lay before the fire on the hearth, facing the entrance. His expressive face betrayed the internal struggle he tried to conceal.

Gilfingle and the rest of the troop huddled near the archway, as far from Berengar as possible.

Gilfingle stared broodingly at him, gesturing once or twice, but for a time said nothing. Eventually, duty overtook fear. "Berengar, I'll... I'll not tolerate a murderer in our midst," he said, voice shaking.

Berengar glared at the fire in silence.

Gilfingle's face was pale, but he stood between Berengar and the rest of the troop, as if preparing to defend them.

Brand sighed and shook his head. Something had to be done. He rose from the couch. "Cil, let's inspect the corpse—see if anything there explains this mess."

"Okay," she said, following him.

Brand eyed the bloody wreck dubiously. "Check his hands, Cil."

Cil glanced at him sideways. "*You* check his hands. You're the man."

"She's right, Brand," Berengar called out.

"Damn you, Ber—I'm clearing your name!" Brand grumbled, crouching beside the corpse.

He heard the pitter-patter of tiny webbed feet behind him.

"I'll search the wizard," said Alucard. "Maybe he has something I can read—I mean—use for some fine hair?"

Brand thrust out a protective arm. "Stay back! No, Alucard—go sit by the fire. You're too young to be seeing this."

Alucard grumbled like a sullen teen, but shuffled over to Berengar. He leaned against the big man with his arms folded behind his head, as if Berengar were a small hill to lounge on, and watched with a bland, unreadable expression.

Brand tugged tentatively at the robe's pockets. Then, with growing courage, he reached in. From one he withdrew a large wooden soup spoon—harmless. From the other, a small glass cylinder.

He held it up to the candlelight. Inside were tiny green, rolled-up insects. Their type was unknown to Brand.

"What is it?" Gilfingle called from across the room.

"See for yourself," said Brand, extending the vial.

Gilfingle took one look and recoiled. "Wyre Worms!"

"Wyre worms?" Brand echoed.

"They climb into your skin, then eat your brain to mush." Said Berengar from the hearth.

Brand dropped the vial in fright, caught it mid air, then carefully placed it on the floor.

"And how many are there?" Berengar asked, a gleam rising in his eyes.

Brand knelt and counted. "One... two... three..." He stopped.

Looked around the room. The hairs on his neck stood up. "Fourteen."

Gilfingle counted the people present. His face paled. "You don't think... do you?"

"I don't *think*," said Berengar bluffly. But the grim curve of his mouth betrayed relief—*he was clearly glad he had not been wrong.*

"Indeed," said Brand. He shivered and began pacing the room. "But how could he have known our exact number?"

"Probably saw us from afar with his magic," growled Berengar. Then added, "Stay in this room, and don't touch anything. This place is likely riddled with his tricks."

"But what of the sloths?" asked Salome, suddenly snapping from her stupor into renewed panic.

"Don't worry," said Brand, stepping to the windowsill. He flicked his coat back, revealing his hand crossbow. Resting a hand on the weapon, he added, "I will protect you."

Just as he reached the climax of his display, he felt a tingle—a twitch of instinct. He looked over his shoulder.

A heat sloth grinned at him from the other side of the glass.

Brand screamed.

The sloth banged on the window with a great hooked hand. The whole wall rocked, but the window held.

Brand leapt away, landing on long, unsteady legs.

The face vanished into darkness.

Everyone stood frozen as the door handle began to rattle— gently at first, then violently. Frost bloomed across the metal as the sloths' plaintive voices rose outside:

"An impasse."   "Oh no!"   "Calamity."   "A terrible disaster." "So cold!" "Calamity!"   "Let us in!"

The cries echoed across the manse, but the door held.

They waited in silence, but the creatures' strange strength and cold made no mark. The manse resisted them.

"It must be the wizard's magic," said Berengar.

With that certainty, the companions relaxed. They lay down to sleep.

Brand pulled out Jamus's Ney flute and attempted a cheerful tune—something to lift the troop's spirits, as Jamus once had.

However, his jarring piping only startled the girls. Sunken faces frowned back at him in anxious silence. Brand scowled, tossed the flute down, and gave up. He lay next to Berengar, near the fire.

The rest of the troop gradually settled in around them. After a time, a heat sloth's face appeared at the window, gazing hungrily at Brand. Others joined it, but could only moan and mouth silently through the glass. The last thing Brand saw as he drifted into uneasy sleep were their grinning visages—watching.

He awoke in the gray hours of pre-twilight, startled once again by those same leering faces. He sat bolt upright—then remembered: they couldn't get in.

He considered drawing the curtains, but the thought of the sloths creeping in behind them unnoticed made his skin crawl. In the end, he left them open. Eventually, exhaustion overtook him again, and he fell back asleep.

Brand awoke bleary-eyed and fogged. He forced himself upright and ran a shaky hand through his wavy blond hair—the night had been anything but restful. Everyone else was still asleep, little bodies curled in cocoons of the salvaged blankets Pathar had snatched from the wagons.

He dared a glance at the window. Empty. A cheerful morning sun peeked through the glass, high in a blue sky. Golden light streamed across the reading desk.

He thought of Alucard and scanned the room. There he was— curled behind Berengar, leaning against the northerner's broad back like it was a couch, a large red leather book in his hands. His webbed feet were crossed near the glowing coals of the fire. Berengar slept on in complete comfort, unaware. The big oaf likely hadn't slept in days. Even when it hadn't been his watch, Brand was sure he'd stayed awake—just in case. That habit had saved their lives.

He called out to the little blue creature, "Alucard! What are you reading?"

Cil grumbled nearby, still half-asleep. "Shut up, beanstalk. I'm trying to sleep."

"A book," Alucard replied without turning.

He hunched his shoulders slightly.

Stubborn defiance? Brand frowned. "Look at me when I'm talking to you!" he snapped.

With a dramatic sigh, Alucard laid the book on his lap and, with great care, turned his head a full one hundred and sixty degrees to face him. "Yes, father?"

Brand flinched. "I didn't know you could do that. You're—ah—quite flexible."

"A simple matter," Alucard said.

"Please give me warning next time," Brand muttered, then squinted at him. "Humph—what's that on your head?"

"Oh, just some mere brummagem I found on the table."

"It looks to be a purple felt tea cozy—and what are you reading?"

"Just some ancient symbols. Would you care to hear?"

Brand eyed the frog-dwarf warily. "Show me first."

"Fine," Alucard sighed with mock theatricality. He slid off Berengar's back and waddled over, the book nearly as tall as he was. "Here."

Brand peered at an elaborately inked page of fantastic glyphs. The paper looked thick. Old. Possibly skin. Some of the symbols quivered or shifted on the page—as if resenting their captivity. Just looking at them made his head spin.

He reeled back. "It looks eerie. How long have you been reading this morning anyway?"

"Since you fell asleep."

"Alucard! That's way past—in fact—completely *missing* your bedtime!"

Alucard shrugged. "I don't need as much sleep as you."

"And how can you *read* this stuff, anyway?"

"It uses the same symbols I learned from my notebook's lexicon —as compiled by Ator Periconias."

"Hmph. And where are you up to?"

"This line here," Alucard said, pointing to a paragraph of writhing script.

"What does it say?"

"It's hard to explain. When I try to speak it, the syllables dance out of my mind before I can hold them. It's taken me all night to *envision* the enunciation of just this one passage."

"Odd."

"Not really. Will you let me read it to you?"

Brand hesitated. Then shrugged. "Okay."

Alucard looked directly at him and began uttering a string of syllables so precise, so resonant, that the air itself warped. A pressure settled over Brand like a shifting tide. The syllables cracked and sizzled—the air between them thickened, charged.

Something twisted in Brand's gut.

Gilfingle sat bolt upright, alarmed. "Brand, that sounds like— like *magic*!"

"A wha—" Brand's reply was cut off by a jolt of energy that pulsed through him. His blond hair lifted. Instinctively, he braced himself, though he didn't know why.

Nothing happened.

Blinking, he looked around. "What was *that*?"

Berengar sat up fast, his eyes scanning the room before landing on Brand and Alucard.

"Alucard? What did you *do* to me?" Brand demanded.

Cil sat up, blinking groggily.

Alucard looked hurt. "All that rehearsal... and I got it wrong. I had it right in my head, but the syllables shifted at the last second! It was nearly perfect..." He hung his head.

"What was *meant* to happen?" Brand asked, voice rising.

"It was supposed to make you *fly*! I thought it a great gift, for all you've done for me. I must've been a fraction of a rhythm off." He scratched his rubbery chin. "Can I try again?"

Berengar jumped to his feet and roared, "You let him use *magic* on you?!"

Brand spun to face him, shouting back, "He studied the book *on top of you* all night long!"

"How is *that* my fault? I was asleep!" Berengar bellowed.

"Aren't you supposed to nap like a tiger and all that? Besides, I'm sure it'll be fine. Because, you see, there's no such thing as magi—whoa!!..."

Brand's words became a gasp of dismay as he abruptly floated upward, toward the ceiling.

Berengar seized handfuls of his own hair and unleashed a stream of barbaric curses.

Cil looked up, her green eyes full of wonder.

Alucard jumped up and down in glee. "It worked! It worked!"

Brand felt himself grow giddy. The unreality of the moment overwhelmed his senses. He thought, this could not be happening. This simply could *not* be happening. *This could no—*

He bumped into the ceiling. The jolt of contact snapped him from his thoughts. Looking down at his friends, he grew suddenly cross.

"What have you *done*?!" he shouted.

"Um... I could try to remove it... let me see..." Alucard fumbled with his little blue thumbs, flipping through the spellbook.

"No! You've done enough. You are forbidden from reading *another line*!" Brand called down from the ceiling.

But as his initial fear wore off, he realized he sort of liked it—apparently, he'd grown somewhat inured to otherworldly shocks. "Despite the inconvenience, one must admit it's a *thrilling* experience," he added thoughtfully.

"You could have been turned into a toad," said Berengar, still clutching his hair. "Or exploded into a million motes, or launched into another dimension, or turned into a man-eating monster!"

"Why, Brand, I believe you've raised a little magician," Cil said, apparently the only one not panicking. "Can't say it turned out all bad. This way, I don't have to see your annoying face at eye level."

"You never had to, *shorty!*" Brand retorted.

By this time, the commotion had roused the others. A wave of confused gasps rolled through the Zanonnites.

"What is the meaning of this?" said Gilfingle, rising from his bed like an angry old owl. His eyes narrowed when he spotted Alucard holding the spellbook. "You meddle in the wicked ways of the Ancients! There is no greater disruption to the natural cosmic order than *magic*!"

Alucard gave a small shrug—as much as one could say he did. With him, it was always hard to tell.

"Ey? What's that?" Gilfingle snapped, apparently divining something of the shrug's meaning. "Look what you've done to your father. How's he supposed to go outside like that? We can't have him floating off into the sun now, can we?" His face creased into a thunderous frown.

"We'll have to tie him down," said Berengar sullenly. "Anyone bring rope?"

"I did," said Balin, his voice subdued from the mounting

absurdity. He approached, handed Berengar the rope, and retreated.

"Good man," said Berengar. Then to Brand, "Come down here."

"I can't," Brand replied.

"Let me grab a chair," Berengar muttered, turning away.

A sharp yelp and a *thud* echoed through the room.

Berengar turned to find Brand facedown on the floor. "How'd you even manage to land like that, Wolf? That takes *effort*."

"Yeeoow!" Brand sat up, rubbing his face. "Shut *up*, Ber! That *hurt*."

"You really have a talent for falling out of the sky," Berengar said, a grim note of humor returning to his voice.

Cil chuckled, releasing some of the tension of the last few days.

Not so the Zanonnites, who stared on in silence, pale and tight-lipped.

Brand didn't respond. He rose with as much dignity as he could muster and brushed off his coat.

"Come here," Berengar said, moving in with the rope and tying it roughly around Brand's arm.

"Ouch—that's too tight!" Brand winced.

"Didn't I teach you not to complain? Besides, you don't want to float off again, do you?"

"I *don't* think it's going to happen again. The spell likely wore off."

"Alucard?" Berengar barked.

"Yes, Uncle Ber?" came the innocent reply.

"How long does this last?"

Alucard flipped open the page, running a blue-green thumb along the glowing script. "Well... if cast correctly—yes."

"How long?"

"An hour or so."

"And if *not* cast correctly?"

Alucard shrugged and raised his hands.

Berengar grumbled, then tied the other end of the rope to his purple loincloth.

Brand eyed the knot. "Are you *sure* that's secure? That loincloth looks... remarkably flimsy."

Berengar's face split into an eerie grin. "Trust me. If it's strong enough to contain *all this man,* it's—"

"Stop! Say no more!" Brand and Cil shouted together.

Ms. Martinae gasped, covering her mouth.

Ms. Taloulie swayed and muttered a prayer.

Alucard stared up at Berengar deadpan, blinking with amphibian innocence—wholly unacquainted with human innuendo.

Gilfingle cleared his throat loudly. "We have suffered a terrible loss. Three loyal Zanonnites have fallen in only the last couple of weeks! I believe this is a punishment. Clearly, we have not been faithful in our rituals and routines. That ends *now*." His voice sharpened. He glared around, daring any challenge. Then, licking his dry lips, he continued. "Now, second order of business— despite the *barbarity* of Berengar's act, it seems it was necessary for our preservation. Thus, it was a holy and pious deed." He paused. "I propose a cheer for Berengar!"

Everyone clapped—half-hearted but sincere.

"Next," Gilfingle went on, "we must restore balance in our *dress*. We have seen what befalls us when we lack *equilibrium*. Five wear the gray. Seven wear the color. Brand... you still wear *neither*. And who can say what chaos your fashion has summoned?"

"But I have nothing else—" Brand began.

"Uh uh uh—let me finish," Gilfingle said, holding up a hand. "In my wisdom, I salvaged *this* fine pair of fluted, pink-and-purple-striped corduroys from the wagon." He held them up with theatrical flourish. "They may even exude an *anti-magical aura*. Rumor says they're the fabled trousers of Xang Xil the Fabian—

flamboyant, fond of hunting violators of inter-spatial travel."

"Not in a million lifetimes would I be caught dead in those," said Brand, turning away.

"I think it's a good idea," Cil grinned.

"Don't you even..." Brand said, staring daggers at the red-haired girl.

"Hold him down," Gilfingle said ominously.

"*Wait! Noooo! Nooooooo!*" Brand kicked and flailed as Berengar pinned him down with those brawny arms—with Cil's eager assistance. Even Alucard joined in. Apparently, *everyone* was against him.

Five minutes later, Brand climbed stiffly to his feet. His stylish black coat was still intact, but beneath it, the purple-pink striped corduroys made themselves known to all—clinging tightly about his hips, flaring out at the ankles like two great bells.

"There, that's better. I feel the balance returning already," said Gilfingle cheerfully. "Now, since we are thirteen in number, we remain unbalanced. However, I see Alucard is now of age to represent himself—thus, he shall be admitted officially into the troop. This leaves the matter of dress once more. Fortunately, I had prepared for this very occasion. Just yesterday, I had Ms. Martinae tailor these two fine cloaks to Alucard's size. One, a dashing light blue. The other, a sober gray. But since Brand has eagerly taken to the color—" He raised his voice. "Berengar, please hold Brand still and keep him quiet—the noise is irksome and interrupts my speech. Thank you. Now, where was I? Ah yes. Here, Alucard, is your first article of clothing: the somber gray cloak."

Alucard ran forward in great excitement, his short arms outstretched. "Thank you, Grand Corrective," he said.

Gilfingle nodded in approval, then looked back at Brand. "See that? You should follow his example and use my proper title." He puffed out his chest, seeming to grow taller.

Brand mumbled a string of incomprehensible profanities into Berengar's gagging hand.

Once Brand was... neutralized, Gilfingle launched into their morning indoctrination.

Clearing his throat, he began, "One Zanonnite may boast and speak stridently about their equilibrium. Another may say not a word, but display a certain restraint of living, which is pleasing and fine to behold. How may you judge who is true and who is false?

"You may know them by the aesthetic harmony of their dress, by the grace of their movements, and most importantly, by the wise equilibrium of their actions... Brand, are you paying attention? You seem distracted..."

"Yes, Grand Corrective," Brand mumbled.

"Good," said Gilfingle.

He finished the lesson and moved briskly to business. "Now. We lack provisions, and the situation with the creatures outside remains uncertain." His face clouded, then brightened as a new idea took him, "Berengar, I hereby assign you as Chief Guardian of the troop and defer to your discretion on such matters."

Berengar scratched his stubbled chin thoughtfully. "Well. Let's see what's happening outside." He walked to the window near the reading desk and peered out. Then turned. "The sloths lie like crocodiles basking on a riverbank."

"Excellent progress report, Chief Guardian. Tell me, then—what now?" Gilfingle prompted.

Berengar shrugged. "Maybe they're still dangerous to the touch, maybe not. They look glutted. Swollen."

"As Chief Guardian, I hereby charge you to go outside and discover the truth of the matter," said Gilfingle with priestly fervor.

"Thank you," Berengar replied, allowing just a whisper of sarcasm. He hefted his great sword and strolled to the door.

"Brand, Cil—cover my flanks," he said.

Brand, for the fact he was tethered to Berengar's loin strap, realized he had little choice in the matter and reluctantly made haste. Both Brand and Cil grabbed their weapons and followed Berengar, leaving Alucard at the fire with strict orders to read no more of the spellbook.

Berengar carefully unbarred the door, cracked it open, and peeked out. His blond brows furrowed in confusion. His large canines showed in a scowl.

"They're sprawled out in torpor—stupefied, as from drink," he said.

He opened the door wider. A sloth lay directly before the threshold. The skull no longer showed beneath its skin, and the body was bloated, tinged pink. Its massive head flopped sideways, lips and tongue lolling from its slack face. Its eyes were misty with ecstasy.

Berengar hissed in disgust and swung his sword in a gleaming arc. It sliced through the sloth's flesh as a hot knife through jelly and rang against the stone beneath. The blow jarred him badly, sending him stumbling backward into the room. The head fell away from the bloated body, sagging like overripe fruit, trailing thick black-red blood.

He leapt to his feet and pushed past Brand and Cil, scanning the portico. The other sloths remained where they were. A few turned to look, their faces dreamy with detached joy. Some giggled. None moved to rise.

Brand blanched, covering his mouth. A strong, musty, nutty odor drifted in—like the python he'd once handled at a fair in Drift's End, but *so much worse*. Heat radiated off their swollen bodies, mixing with the stench.

Cil coughed and staggered backward into the room.

"They are *Sun-drunk,*" said Berengar, a grim smile twisting his lips. "I'll do the honors." He detached Brand's safety rope and passed it to Cil.

Berengar went to work. One by one, he began decapitating the sloths, dispatching them with brutal efficiency. None resisted. None even stirred. Brand soon felt queasy and retreated.

Alucard, undisturbed, wandered out and perched on the balustrade.

Brand laid down by the fire, his head spinning from the miasma. There had to be at least a hundred of the things out there.

Alucard, casting a glance back to confirm no one was watching, quietly pulled the spellbook from his pouch and resumed reading on the portico while Berengar continued his grim task.

The sound of wet slicing and that godawful stench drifted through the door. Brand had left it ajar, not wanting to bar Berengar from reentry... but now he regretted it.

Eventually, it became unbearable. With the windows sealed shut, they had no choice but to escape through the archway into the adjoining room. Berengar might've objected, but he was too absorbed in his slaughter to notice.

Brand was the last to slip through the arch. He paused, eyeing the new space. It seemed innocuous—a drawing room, maybe. Four large cushioned chairs and a wide couch surrounded a serving table. All rested on a thick, lush long-weave rug, the kind Brand had only seen once in a caravan from Devirien'Su.

The eastern wall opened onto what looked like a kitchen. The southern wall, like the last room, had windows overlooking the porch.

But the northern wall caught his eye. Behind the couch hung a fine display of ancient sabers, every one of them high quality. Beneath the blades stretched a row of low shelves, filled with oddities: leather-bound books, a small stone pillar with a ball rotating atop it, flasks and vials of colored liquids—some ordinary browns and blues, others in hues Brand couldn't name. And there, at the far end, a polished slab of obsidian... reflecting the room in a shimmering, warped distortion.

"It seems the place is not as disastrous as the barbarian made it out to be," said Ms. Martinae in a well-modulated voice, dripping with haughty disdain.

"Now, now, Ms. Martinae, he is the Chief Guardian of the troop. It is characteristic of such to be suspicious and cautious where the safety of the troop is concerned," chided Gilfingle.

"Oh, pish-posh," she countered. "What of *my* comfort? I marched all night, skipped dinner *and* breakfast, and slept on a hard floor—and for what? There was a perfectly innocuous lounge here, and a kitchen right over there." She pointed.

"Now, now, Ms. Martinae," said Fonicia, "this is the Grand Corrective you're talking to."

"I agree with Ms. Martinae," said Salome with a stony grin. "I feel Brand and Berengar and Cil—but *particularly* Brand—have neglected our health in handling the troop's security. What good is all this caution if we die from exhaustion and starvation?"

Cil clicked her tongue. A single red eyebrow lifted, sharp with annoyance.

"Exactly my point," said Ms. Martinae. "The girl's got a good head on her!"

Salome grinned at Brand, as if to say, *I won this one.*

Brand yawned and scratched his head with lazy indifference— an act which only further antagonized her.

Gilfingle relented. "Well, I'm sure the Chief Guardian would not wish us to starve. Ms. Taloulie, if you're willing to risk the kitchen, would you inspect the wizard's stores and see if there's anything usable?"

"Yes, Grand Corrective," she said with a red-faced, tremulous grin. She wiped her brow with a heavy forearm and waddled into the kitchen. At first, she moved with exaggerated caution, but after a few minutes and no immediate catastrophe, she eased into a more casual rhythm and disappeared deeper into the shadows.

"Brand? Don't you think we should put a stop to this until Berengar returns?" Cil said.

Brand waved a hand. "Since when did you care about others?"

Cil blinked. "What gave you *that* idea, beanstalk?!" Her delicate face tightened in a frown. "Besides, it's my job to protect these people right now."

"You're right," Brand sighed. "Everyone, I suggest you return to the main room. Don't touch anything." He folded his arms and frowned with authority. No one moved. His frown deepened.

Across the room, Muls and Dimi were already rifling through the curiosities on the shelves. They stopped before the smooth square of obsidian.

"How pretty and mysterious," said Dimi, excitedly. "Come, Muls, let's look."

"I wouldn't do that..." Brand warned.

"Let us rest and relax for a moment," Salome cut in, glaring. "Why are you so tense? Are you afraid?"

"No. Of course not. But well—"

Dimi and Muls stepped closer. Their faces lit in the warped sheen of the slab.

"So beautiful," Dimi murmured. "The reflections... they're *moving*, like gentle waves. And... oh, I can see myself inside there."

"Strange, that," said Muls, voice wavering.

"Step away from the slab. Now!" Cil barked.

"Just a few more seconds..." Dimi began—then gasped.

Brand looked up.

Their outlines wavered. And then, slowly, grotesquely, their bodies stretched and warped like smoke—becoming flowing ribbons of themselves, sucked toward the slab.

Salome screamed.

The room froze. No one could move, though everybody twitched as if to flee. Eyes locked on the obsidian.

Berengar burst through the arch, blade ready—must've heard the scream—and without hesitation hurled his dagger. The blade shattered the stone. Fragments rained to the carpet below.

The tension snapped. Everyone moved again, as if breaking free from a spell—and indeed they had upon the shattering of the stone.

Dimi and Muls turned toward the others—and what had been two delicate, youthful faces were now shriveled, sunken horrors. Oily yellow eyes rolled in purple sockets. Their mouths sagged with rot, lips curled back from blackened gums.

Salome screamed. The others gasped.

Cil moaned beside Brand.

Dimi and Muls looked at the others in the room and, seeing their horrified expressions, clutched at their faces in alarm. Then, catching their reflections in a sideboard's glass windows, they froze in horror!

"What happened to me?" Dimi sobbed, her grotesque features twisting with panic.

Berengar's eyes narrowed, hard and cold.

Salome shrieked again, and the rest of the Zanonnites bolted—fleeing through the salon, out onto the portico. Gasps of fear and disgust could be heard as they encountered the weeping corpses of the heat sloths. The shouting continued, eventually growing faint as the Zanonnites made their way down the drive.

Seconds later, Ms. Taloulie appeared from the kitchen, arms cradling a pile of potatoes. She froze at the sight.

"Ohh ohh! What's happened?"

"*Put down those potatoes!*" Berengar barked, voice like a cracking whip.

She gasped. "Oh—oh, sorry, what?"

"Now!"

She shrieked and flung the potatoes over her head.

"What else did you touch?" Berengar demanded.

"N-nothing, but—but there were... fourteen bowls of barley. Set on the table. Like for guests."

"More proof of the wizard's treachery," Berengar growled.

"What's happened to us?" Dimi and Muls cried.

Berengar studied their ruined faces, then said simply, "Come."

He led them into the other room, tore up spare blankets, and fashioned desert-style scarves. Their faces vanished beneath wrappings, save for the eyes.

He turned to Brand and Cil. "We leave. *Now.*"

They started for the door, but before they could cross the threshold—Brand began floating upwards...

"Not again..." he muttered, rising off the floor.

That was it. Thron, Dimi and Ms. Taloulie bolted, shrieking from the manse.

Berengar cursed, grabbed Brand's rope, and with Alucard and Cil in tow, followed. They passed the bloated corpses of heat sloths, and continued down the path, Brand bobbing overhead like a human balloon in their wake.

They found the Zanonnites a little way up the trail—hollow-eyed, shaken, and hungry. Muls and Dimi hovered at the edge of the group, wrapped in their makeshift veils.

Even Gilfingle looked diminished, leaning on Pathar like a wilted reed. Ms. Martinae cursed between ragged breaths. Salome was trembling. Fonicia stood beside her husband, red-eyed and silent. Thron looked close to tears. Ms. Taloulie's face pinched in worry, eyes scanning the others like a mother hen counting lost chicks.

Alucard, oblivious, perched cheerfully on Berengar's shoulder.

Cil looked up at Brand and they exchanged a look of shared

weariness and pity.

Gilfingle's gaze sharpened. A suspicious glint entered his eye as he studied Brand and the others.

"Perhaps... it is due to adding unbalanced members to my faithful troop. For ever since taking you on—"

"Please, Grand Corrective," Brand interrupted as smoothly as he could whilst hovering in ungainly fashion. "Let's not leap to conclusions. Had we not been here, your entire troop would've been consumed by the heat sloths. And was it not the Chief Guardian who *forbade* entering the other room?" He paused, then added, "Could *that* be the imbalance that caused this recent dismay?" He gestured.

All eyes turned to Muls and Dimi. They flinched.

Gilfingle's face twisted in shame. Then his shoulders slumped. "Forgive me, my children. You are right. A Grand Corrective mustn't lay blame at the feet of his charges. The trauma of recent events has clearly affected my sensibility."

He sighed and placed his hands on his hips.

"Well. Let us take stock of our provisions."

And so they did—and the sum was grim. A few personal pouches. A single waterskin per person—except Salome, who had prioritized a makeup bag. Enough rations for two days, salvaged by Ms. Taloulie. And a single copy of *Zanon's Tranquil Almanac*.

Once the items were arranged, Gilfingle spoke again. "This is a paltry cache." He shook his head sadly, then added, "We have a good ten hours of daylight left. I had hoped to get us as far away as possible from these dire woods before nightfall, but now I fear we may have to either go back to the wizard's manse... or back to the wagons for supplies."

Berengar shook his head. "There could be another herd of sloths in these parts. Once night comes, they'll pick up the heat in our spoor."

Tension spiked in the group. A murmur rose, turning swiftly into a heated argument as the fear-stricken Zanonnites began to panic.

"Perhaps..." Brand began, trying to defuse the situation, but his voice faltered. He blinked, distracted.

A bird had joined the circle. Not just any bird—a beautiful, bright blue creature with pale feathers and a striking elegance. It swooped down, impossibly calm amid the chaos, and alighted on Gilfingle's outstretched hand.

The old man stilled.

The bird stared up at him, unblinking. Its eyes locked with his in unnatural focus—a wordless conversation held in the silence of that moment.

The arguing quieted.

Gilfingle's voice trailed off. His posture sagged. His eyes became distant and clouded…

Chapter 9
"Zanon's Paradise."

The effect of religion on the collective thought patterns and resultant behavior of a people is an age-old topic of study. More practical—and to me, more intriguing—is the potential modification of a people's *abilities*, due to their belief system and the characteristics of the god(s) they worship.

Take, for instance, the Bromoli Cultists of 890, whose god was a plentiful acre of grass, and who worshipped the art of herding cattle. The quality of their meat and dairy was fabled—a fact which might be reasonably expected. More curious, however, were their renowned beards: healthy, robust, and glossy, with a sheen that glinted green under certain lights.

Or the Ascetic Anarachs of the *Darkwood Runs,* who worshipped Glipgol the Great Spider. They operated wholly in twilight and the silence of night, spinning thread from glowworm farms and weaving webs large enough to support human weight. Their sole source of protein came from captured insects. Over time, their eyes grew keen in dim light, taking on a strange luminescence. Their limbs, chalky and gray from lack of sun, became unnaturally flexible. Their silks and satins drew merchants from as far as Devirien'Su.

And who could forget the Berserker-Monk Legion of Rang-Mang Tog, devotees of Baerah, God of Combat and Fate—who ignited the Great War of Religions in 1032? They revered the art of war, and all who stood before them fell to their mastery. The men of Rang-Mang Tog were preternaturally athletic, surpassing all common warriors in development. Each held to an unshakable conviction in their "fighting fate"—a belief that they could foresee an enemy's movements before they happened. Based on eyewitness accounts, their combat reflexes were so uncanny, the claim seems almost believable.

A people bound by such a specialized doctrine could—and did —conquer their competitors in a contest of arms. During the Great War, the Legion of Rang-Mang Tog devastated great swaths of territory, from the Western Foothills to the edge of Varus'Dorae, wiping out fifteen other sects and killing tens of thousands— believers and non-believers alike. The other sects, being generally peaceful in belief and inclination (as most religions tend to be), were unable to resist the onslaught.

Eventually, an "antibody" formed to combat the scourge of doctrine-run-wild: a new nation, forged from a mix of neutral non-believers and survivors of the conquered fifteen. They called themselves the United Army of Ethical Non-believers. Believing that a strict code of military mores was the only way to offset the combat prowess of Rang-Mang Tog, they established a system of unrelenting wartime discipline—without holy days, rites, or pious rituals to dull their edge.

For a time, the war between the two groups was evenly matched. The United Army excelled in planning and coordination. Rang-Mang Tog still dominated in hand-to-hand combat. But eventually, the Ethical Non-believers found a weakness—a religious holiday: the winter equinox, believed by the Legion to be the one day each man's Fighting Fate paused in stasis.

When the U.A.E.N. struck the Legion's camps on that day, the warriors of Rang-Mang Tog appeared to go inexplicably blind. They were slaughtered to a child. Their books were burned. Their knowledge vanished into ash.

After serving its purpose—and lacking long-term principles for peace or governance—the U.A.E.N. degenerated into what now inhabits the decimated citadel of Shie'Naru. A society without direction, clinging to ruins now known as the "Holy City"... due to the steady stream of religious pilgrims inexplicably drawn to the site.

It is a shame that such brilliant examples of belief-driven human potential are now lost forever. I would give my life to study such societies firsthand.

That religion affects its believers' unique abilities is certain. Whether this results from the supernatural influence of actual gods, or is merely the unlocking of the mind's latent potential through indoctrination, I cannot say.

—The Effects of Religious Indoctrination on a People An essay by the Philosopher Anghan Apoficus

***

Gilfingle gasped and snapped back to the present.

Gone was his dismay—in its place, the very image of pious fervor. He began pacing in manic strides, making wild, looping gestures with his arms, elucidating the magnitude of his exaltation. "Ahh, a vision! A *vision!* In our greatest moment of need, Zanon does not disappoint!"

Brand stared, dumbfounded. He turned to Berengar to share a biting comment—but the giant was glancing nervously to the east, then west, then up into the sky, clearly bracing for divine intervention

Brand frowned and muttered to Cil, "There he goes again with his superstitions."

Cil didn't scoff as he'd hoped. "He *has* been known to be right on his gut feelings..." Then, more pointedly, "Unlike you, Ugly— you wouldn't even know how to pick the right girl."

"Childish." Brand started, then blinked. "Wait—what?"

"Never mind," said Cil, her face shifting into a smug, satisfied grin. "Besides, was it not strange that the bird landed on him like that?"

Brand had to admit—it was strange. Still... a vision? *What had Cil just said? Picking the right girl?*

"My children, Zanon has spoken to me once again!" Gilfingle cried out in a great, throaty baritone. At this point he had to pause briefly as Brand plummeted to the ground once more, screaming—an unwarranted interruption to the equilibrium.

Despite the disturbance, the Zanonnites, brightening with hope, shuffled toward their leader.

Gilfingle puffed up his chest, resembling an old bird mid-mating display.

"Zanon—blessed be his equilibrium—has revealed the final destination of our pilgrimage! And joy upon joy, it is the fabled Holy City itself! A place I have long yearned to see. I saw it in my vision—a city carved from pristine white crystal, rising like a cloud citadel above the lowlands of frozen waste. A glowing city. Joyous. Radiant. Zanon's *paradise!*"

Murmurs of hope spread through the group like a thaw.

"I just *knew* the time was near!" sobbed Fonicia, clinging to Balin's arm. He patted her head gently, smiling down at her.

"It's about time," muttered Ms. Martinae.

Ms. Taloulie grinned wide, unconsciously squeezing the ration sacks she carried with meaty fingers.

"How far is it?" asked Pathar, with a tremulous smile.

Gilfingle's voice went shrill with fervor. "This is the most glorious part of all! Our course through these dreary woods now makes perfect sense. Based on yonder cliffs to the north, I believe it to be only a day's march northwest!"

A cheer rose from the troop, giddy and unrestrained.

Even Salome brightened—laughing a little too easily, a little too loud.

Cil watched her closely, frowning she muttered, "Her happiness feels more forced than real."

"What was that?" Brand asked.

"No one spoke to you, beanstalk," Cil said, flashing clean, white teeth.

"Yes, my Zanonnites!" Gilfingle cried. "Let us march! We shall reach paradise before nightfall!"

He took off at a spirited trot.

The old man had recovered fast—but Brand, for once, was glad.

He was just beginning to think the day might not be *so* bad after all when—whoosh!—he shot skyward again, rope taut, screaming like a firework. The spell failed mid-arc. Brand plummeted, clipped Berengar's shoulder on the way down, flipped once, and landed on his neck and shoulders in the dirt.

Berengar glanced over and flashed his canines. "Oh. It's you."

Brand staggered upright, red-faced. "Next time, *catch me!*"

Berengar shrugged. "Nay, its good training for you."

Brand shook a fist in his face, then brushed off his coat.

Cil smirked, but her grin twisted into a scowl when Salome skipped over, all pouts and perfume.

"Oh dear! Brand, are you all right?" she cooed, offering a scented handkerchief.

Brand blinked, disoriented, but pleasantly surprised. "Why... yes. Thank you, Salome." Then dabbed at his face.

"You're welcome," she said sweetly, then drifted back toward Balin.

"Good lass," said Fonicia, beaming.

Cil scowled. "That girl will be trouble."

"Humph. Wish someone would pamper *me*," grumbled Ms. Martinae.

"My throat's as dry as a Devirien desert, and no one cares. If age meant anything to this generation—well! I'd outrank the lot of you..."

She kept going. No one stopped her. Everyone else simply let her voice dissolve into background noise.

After a time, Gilfingle forced a discordant chanting hymn out of the troop as they marched, which occupied their thoughts and helped eat up the weary miles.

With all the excitement involved in leaving the manse, Brand had failed to notice the bulging pouch at Alucard's side, which now held not one book of ancient symbols but two: the notebook of Ator Periconias, and the wizard's grimoire. Alucard carried it always on the side opposite Brand, and would casually drape a little blue arm over it whenever Brand looked his way.

They marched through stark gray hills with little foliage. Copses of dry, bedraggled trees became more and more scarce, and eventually, they found themselves alternating between bare, stony passes—flanked by grim cliffs—and wide open plateaus of stone, devoid of all life.

Occasionally, Berengar stooped to turn over a rock and grab a handful of sickly-looking, white crystalline creatures, which squirmed and chattered all the way into his gullet. He crunched them down cheerily, while everyone else refused his generous offerings—even Ms. Taloulie, who adored him, and would usually do anything to please him.

Nothing disturbed the convoy on this final leg of the journey, and the steady marching helped to drive recent horrors from their minds. The only thing that continued to bother Brand throughout the day was the haunted, wistful look Salome occasionally cast in his direction. She no longer even tried to hide it when he caught her. *Was the girl entirely well?* he wondered.

Presently, their path wound through a gloomy granite pass, which obscured all vision—the fading light of day a single orange slash far above. On they trekked through the dim passage, stumbling on loose rocks and scraping their limbs on the granite walls. Finally, just when all had begun to doubt the vision's promise, the pass opened up into a sudden, majestic panorama.

To the north lay a vast precipice that ran from east to west as far as the eye could see. Beyond it, frozen lowlands stretched out endlessly, dissolving into the distant northern horizon—the Sunken Tundra.

The view was broken only by a solitary granite bluff that jutted from the frozen basin like a sentinel. Upon it stood the ruins of an ancient city, its crumbling towers catching the sun's last rays like pale bones in the dying light. The circular bluff was ringed on all sides by sheer cliffs that dropped away to the Tundra far below— perhaps a thousand feet or more—and was connected to the mainland by a precarious natural arch of stone.

All was bathed in the blood-orange glow of the setting sun.

Even from their current position, they could see the lights of occupation flickering among the stone ruins atop the bluff like so many fireflies. This must be the "*Holy City*" Gilfingle had seen in his visions.

As they approached the natural arch, Brand noted that it connected to a road which ran south. The road looked broader, more well-traveled than the haphazard trail they had followed. Perhaps this was the usual route to the Holy City?

"Wow, what a work of art this place must have been originally," said Berengar in awe, his inner sculptor reignited by the lofty cliffs that filled one's vision in every direction.

"I must admit it is impressive," said Brand, without enthusiasm, eyeing the natural arch they would soon have to cross.

"You never get excited about the right stuff, ugly," said Cil with a leer. "This view is *breathtaking*."

Brand assumed a show of courage. "Yes. Quite so. And I normally enjoy traversing such precipices as that... when I'm not on an important journey to rescue my mother, of course. So perhaps we should just—"

"I want to cross the bridge!" said Alucard, lacking any and all concern.

"Zanon's paradise is before us! *Look,* honest Zanonnites, your struggles have not been in vain!" cried Gilfingle with all the fervor of a preacher, his voice taking on that characteristic deep and resounding tone his kind always seemed able to muster. "We complete the pilgrimage. Onward!" He lowered his arm like a general dropping a lance, and started across the natural arch.

The troop revived, and charged toward the precarious stone bridge with reckless abandon. Berengar insisted on caution, but even his massive frame could not restrain the electrified zealots. Seeing that they weren't slowing, he stepped aside before they bowled him over the precipice. Turning, he watched with a frown as they ran along the thin strip of rock toward the bluff.

Brand, Berengar, and Cil waited a while before crossing. But no sudden crack sounded out to spell their doom, and no swarm of half-human harpies swooped down to carry off the lithe figures as they dashed across the fragile strip, with only the blue sky above and thin mountain air below.

Eventually, Berengar was convinced it was safe. The four of them started across. The arch was no wider than five feet. Brand made the mistake of looking down. That strange effect that comes when gazing from great heights took hold of him—the empty space below seemed to expand, reaching up. He felt himself drawn toward it and tottered dangerously. A firm tug on the safety line from Berengar kept him from plunging over the edge.

"Easy there, young wolf," Berengar grumbled.

"By my daggers... thanks, Ber," Brand replied, pale-faced and embarrassed.

"Scaredy-cat," Cil scorned, though her face had gone a shade paler.

Brand tried to recover some dignity, directing what he hoped was a charismatic smile in her direction. He achieved only a sickly, gray-faced leer.

"Ew," said Cil.

"Huh?" Said Brand.

Alucard laughed uproariously, holding his small blue pot-belly. "That was a good one Cil."

"What was?" said Brand, irritated.

"You wouldn't understand," Cil said archly, taking the opportunity to rinse him.

"Yeah, you wouldn't understand," Alucard echoed, still laughing.

"Oh?" said Brand, turning to Alucard. "So what did it mean?"

"I don't know," said the little creature, then laughed again—the way children laugh, without understanding why, just because adults are laughing. But with Alucard, the gulf of understanding was even greater—not merely between child and adult, but between entirely different species.

Brand had just regained his equilibrium and was preparing to chastise Alucard soundly when the floaty thing happened...

This time, Brand found himself not just leaning over the edge, but floating above it—nothing between him and the lowlands but thin air.

He screamed, then fainted.

He hung like a limp kite above Berengar for the rest of the crossing, and only woke once Berengar was jerking his rope insistently, after they'd reached solid ground.

The plateau was filled with the ruins of an ancient city, once sculpted from golden-white marble and adorned with bands of silver and gold. Its grandeur must have been majestic in its prime. Now, only a few spires remained, towering above a maze of short, square structures. Some bore great colonnades, but the columns were chipped, many missing altogether.

Wide avenues had been cleared through the rubble to form inner streets, while the edges of the bluff were piled with shattered marble and debris. There was no gate or formal entrance—just the beginning of a grand avenue cleared from ruin, down which distant figures walked to and fro.

At the head of this avenue, the Zanonnites waited, waving with exultant expressions.

The spell broke, and Brand thudded to the ground with a grunt. He spat dirt from his mouth and glared at Alucard, then stood and dusted himself off for the fifth time in two days.

Gathering what dignity remained, he waved back at the Zanonnites and headed toward them with Cil and Berengar.

Salome ran to meet him halfway. "Oh! Isn't this wonderful, Brand?" She grabbed his hand and pulled him to the others.

Cil rolled her eyes, and now it was Berengar's turn to chuckle and jibe at the red-headed spitfire.

Brand, still confused by Salome's behavior, tried to make sense of it. She *had* been through a lot... and he *had* saved her life. He smiled smugly to himself.

"Hail Brand, Berengar, and Cil! Our Troop Guardians who brought us here safely!" cried Gilfingle in exuberant tones.

"Here we are. We began as sixteen in Culcep. Sadly, six of our original party are gone. However, near the Darkwood Runs, we made new friends—who aided us well—and so, once again, we are fourteen."

"*My beloved friends,* I invite you all to join me in *Zanon's Paradise!*"

A cheer went up from the crowd.

"What of drink and food?" asked Brand, suddenly realizing he had no bullions—*money had been the last thing on his mind in recent times.* Gold and silver meant little in the wilds, but here... he was back in the realm of civilization, at least *partial* civilization. The lack of coin gnawed at him. "Did anyone think to bring any bullions?" he asked the group.

Blank faces stared back.

Gilfingle frowned, looking slightly irritated at such talk during their holy moment. He waved a dismissive hand. "I'm sure the righteous people of this holy place will provide."

He arched a bushy brow at Brand, daring him to argue.

Brand shrugged off his irritation, inclined his head, and motioned for Gilfingle to lead the party forward.

Presently, the party walked down the main avenue toward the center of town, the ancient structures rising on all sides, the golden veins in their marble catching the setting sun's light in dazzling coruscations.

A number of the buildings bore weathered wooden signs labeling them: dressmakers, herbalists, accessories and gift shops, supply stores, and more.

The people wandering the avenue and slipping in and out of shops glanced at the new travelers without much curiosity, going about their business unconcerned. It was obvious that visitors from strange and varied lands were nothing new here. They saw wild, hairy men of the northeastern woodlands, swarthy, cursing seamen from the southern coasts, sleek silk-robed merchants from Devirien'Su, and even a few rangy, dark-skinned folk from the southern continent.

But it was the locals who began to stand out. They wore a sort of quasi-uniform: blue and white tabards with no insignia, often worn to rags. Their faces were sullen, their skin unwashed, their hair matted and unkempt, their overall aspect slovenly.

Soon, a central square came into view. Reaching it, they observed several notable features. To the west stood a broad structure that must have been a tavern. A sagging sign above its entrance read *The High-Rise Keep*, and as they looked, a clutch of inebriated patrons stumbled out, collapsing into the plaza in a heap.

More storefronts flanked either side, and several crooked market stands clustered around the edges of the square.

To the east rose a tall, colonnaded building with a cracked sign over the entrance: *Town-Master's Hall*. Straight ahead stood a strange, angular structure with many facets, at the very center of the square, a fountain carved of blue and red marble glistened in the dying light.

"Look at this marble," said Berengar, pointing to a nearby spire. "Have you ever seen such luster? Pristine white with gold veins, gleaming in joyous reply to the sun's rays?"

Brand nodded distractedly. He was eyeing a group near the fountain—pilgrims, by the look of them—milling about with barely contained excitement. Something sparkled atop the still water of the basin.

"Humph," said Gilfingle, unimpressed. "Where is our welcoming party? It seems the locals are somewhat... out of practice in their etiquette. We must work to correct this slackness."

Looking back at Gilfingle, Brand said, "Slackness on all accounts." He offered the Grand Corrective a solemn frown.

Gilfingle nodded in approval. "*Well*, let us make ourselves known to the town-master. Surely Zanon's inner sanctum will make up for any lacks in the town's outward appearance."

The party moved toward the building marked *Town-Master's Hall*. Inside was a cold, rectangular atrium, sparse and lifeless. The marble walls and tiled floors were cracked and dust-ridden. A crust of crystalized filth obscured the skylight overhead.

To the right, a low stone bench sagged under heaps of clutter. Behind it sat a short, greasy man, slouched in an old wooden chair, listlessly picking the legs off a dead fly.

Gilfingle cleared his throat, loud and imperious. The man looked up with drowsy disdain and yawned.

Gilfingle spoke sharply. "Your reception lacks grace, your dress is drab, and, if I'm not mistaken, this place has not been cleaned in *hundreds* of years. Why are you so remiss in your sacred duty of guarding Zanon's Paradise? Are you not an honorable Zanonnite?"

"Zanonnites?" The man's face bunched in piggish confusion, his pale eyes watery and dull. "That sounds like some blasted religious talk."

Gilfingle clicked his tongue and shook his head sadly. "I should not have asked. *Clearly you are not.*"

The man barked an offensive laugh. "Indeed, and by no means! Keep that talk away from me."

"So... which god do you serve, then?" said Gilfingle, incredulous. "For this is the *Holy City*, is it not?"

"This town is run by the glorious United Army of Ethical Nonbelievers. Ain't it obvious? We wear plain tabards, no gaudy symbols or signets, do no rituals, *and mind our own business!*"

Gilfingle frowned. "The United Army of Ethical Nonbelievers... I've read of such. But what of your fabled discipline? I mean no offense, of course, and a Zanonnite cannot expect balance from the uninitiated at all times.... But... Your people seem to... lack all standards of cleanliness and deportment."

The grubby man's tone turned defensive. "What's *that* supposed to mean? You want me to call the constable for rabble-rousing? See how our 'discipline' is then!"

Gilfingle bowed slightly. "Forgive me. I will return balance to my words. But I cannot help but find it strange that Zanon's most sacred place is guarded by nonbelievers."

"*Guarded?*" the man scoffed. "We post ourselves here *in protest* of the pilgrims. It's a dire task... but we're dedicated." He grinned, revealing a row of rotten teeth, and plucked another leg from the fly.

"Pilgrims?! So there *are* others who've come to the call?"

"Zanonnites, Birulians, Vogues, Whateveryacall'ems—

hundreds, year after year."

Gilfingle leaned forward, blue eyes bright. "And where do they go? How do they access Zanon's inner sanctum?"

"Who knows. They say they enter the shiny palace out in the fountain, but that's just hogwash. For all I know, they strip down and jump off the cliffs in some kind of fanatic abandon."

"Humph," said Gilfingle, his brows narrowing. "What of this shining palace?"

"It's out there." The man pointed a stubby, greasy finger toward the square. "In the fountain. Don't make me get up. It ain't my turn to do the rounds."

Gilfingle squinted into the plaza, bathed in red glare and the long shadows of crumbling spires.

"So... what are the usual formalities for entering this palace?"

A sly look crept over the man's face. "Usually, folks leave their valuables here as a donation." He gestured to the wooden stalls built along the wall. "What use are bullions if you're jumping into paradise? Might as well leave 'em behind—more useful here."

"I like not the gleam in his wretched eye," said Berengar, hand on his hilt.

"Peace, Chief Guardian," said Gilfingle, lifting a hand. "It makes sense indeed. For does Zanon not say, '*Forgo your worldly struggles and accomplishments. Instead, aim for spiritual balance and tranquility, and you shall be rewarded ten-thousand bullions in equivalence*'?"

Berengar scratched his head.

"Yes, well. We carry no bullions," Gilfingle continued pleasantly, "but we will gladly donate the soiled clothes on our backs and these empty waterskins—unneeded things in paradise, surely."

The greasy man looked disappointed.

"*So*, we leave our belongings in the stalls. And then what?"

The man shrugged, clearly bored now. "Put your stuff there. After that? I don't know. Pilgrims talk about touching the palace or something. But since I refute the existence of gods, magic, and all other hocus-pocus, I say you'd do better getting a drink in the tavern... or the bordello yonder. There—I've done my bit and made my protest. Now I've got better things to do." He dropped his gaze and went back to his desk.

Gilfingle looked awkwardly at the stalls, then out at the square.

"Should we get some water, or something to eat before entering Paradise?" asked Ms. Taloulie, her throaty voice nearly drowned by the rumbling of her stomach.

"Nonsense! Paradise will provide," snapped Gilfingle, now tense from the abounding lack of equilibrium. "Besides, we have no food and no coin to purchase it... what is there to wait for?"

"I guess you're right, Grand Corrective," said Ms. Taloulie, eyeing the tavern longingly.

"Brand, you four are initiates now. You have an open invitation to paradise—which I assume you will accept gladly!" Gilfingle said, looking intently at Brand with his bright blue eyes.

"Certainly, just after we grab a bite to eat. Who knows, after all, how long the journey into paradise may take us and—"

"It shall be *instantaneous*, so my mental impressions have led me to believe."

"Yes, well, I would like one last tankard before taking our holy vows and—"

Gilfingle frowned at Brand and seemed disappointed. "Do you *truly* feel this way, Brand? Even after all I have taught you, you *still* doubt? Has my tutelage been so *poor?*"

"By no means." said Brand. "Never that. I have learned much good from you... and the words of Zanon—"

"Ah, Brand, I see it in your eyes. You do not wish to join us. This saddens me, but I will not force you—it is not the Zanon way."

Brand shuffled uncomfortably on his feet.

"You, Cil? *No?* How about you, Berengar?" Gilfingle asked.

"I dare not touch that which I don't understand," Berengar answered, tossing his mane nervously.

"Well," Gilfingle said with a sigh, "we ready ourselves for paradise. Decide as you like. We will be entering within the hour, and hope to see you on the other side. Your companionship has been wonderful, and I hope the reverse is the case."

"You are a good man, Gilfingle," said Brand. He tried to think of something meaningful to say. "Yes... it has indeed been valuable. Regardless of each other's beliefs—we have shared some... moments, learned much from each other, and—saved each other's lives." He then bowed politely.

"Now that you've blown smoke up each other's asses, can we wrap up this touching moment? *Y'all are crowding my lobby,*" piped in the grimy man from his desk.

Gilfingle turned to the grubby man. "Are you the town-master?"

"Ha! Thank my mother, no. He's drunk and asleep in the fifth stall. Don't wake him; he has a terrible temper until after dark."

Gilfingle shrugged, and didn't bother inquiring further. *The man's name and position were clearly unimportant.*

"Let's go grab a tankard of ale," said Cil.

"I agree!" said Berengar.

"I concur, though we may have to act a comedy trio in the tavern to earn our board as we have no bullions," said Brand wryly.

"What's ale?" said Alucard.

"Let Uncle Ber show you," said Berengar with a wink.

"Hey! He's too young for that!" said Brand.

The three walked toward the exit—but before Brand made it across the threshold—he heard soft footsteps behind him. A delicate hand grabbed him by the wrist. He turned and looked into the sad, beautiful eyes of Salome.

"Wait, Brand," she said. "Will you not join us in paradise?"

"Ah, about that. I am still thinking it over. It's a big commitment, you know?"

"Oh, please, Brand, will you please consider it?" she said, with a bright, but pleading look in her eyes. "This world has not been kind to me in recent months—poor Dimi I would love to have you there with me. A familiar face, you know—to make it fun."

Her sweet breath hypnotized him, and he nodded dumbly.

"Just think about it. Please," she said and squeezed his hand warmly, smiling up at him all the while.

Brand looked into those eyes, like pristine sheets of violet glass, reflecting both the beauty and the evil of the world. Yet, even now... what did they hide behind that bright external reflection? Was there a tinge of something darker there? Even if there was—it made sense, thought Brand—she has been through hell.

"Okay," he said earnestly. "I will come look at it with you." *What could go wrong?* He agreed with the man at the desk—*it was not real anyway.*

"Ugly? Hurry up!" Cil's voice called from outside, breaking Salome's spell on Brand. He glanced toward the door before looking back at Salome.

A flicker of jealous panic tinted the girl's eyes for a second.

"Don't worry, I'll come back and check it out with you before you go." Brand said, disentangling himself from the girl and jogging out the door.

He caught up with the others out in the square and called, "Let's hit the tavern! I'm *starving, and thirsty.*"

They headed across the square toward the High-Rise Keep, and as they crossed the central, deserted area near the fountain, Brand noticed a great golden glow which, as he looked further, seemed to shift between many colors. He went to move closer to get a better look, but Berengar's strong tug on the rope holding them together restrained him.

"*Don't,*" he said. "More vile magic. You can't trust it."

"Berengar, please—"

"Even after the spell Alucard wrought on you? Also, did they not say people disappeared?"

"Perhaps they really did toss themselves over the cliff?"

"I doubt it," said Berengar with a growl.

After wandering in and out of shady establishments for forty minutes, they gave up finding a family-friendly tavern for Alucard and began browsing the haphazard market stalls for something to eat.

"Here," said Brand, indicating a market stall with roasting kebabs. "Let's get something to fill our stomachs at least."

As they arrived, Brand found himself regretting his choice of vendor. He eyed the corpulent belly of the stall's owner and the trickle of grease running down the front of his dirty tabard. Then, looking up, he beheld a pair of cynical brown eyes resting above a dirty mustache, and an even dirtier grin.

Brand placed an order without enthusiasm. "Ah, three of these kebabs. May I ask—what meat?"

"Roasted pigeon sausage. Mostly bone-free," the man replied, unabashed.

"Great," Brand replied with a quiet sarcasm.

"Gotta eat," said Berengar with a shrug.

The man thrust out his hand for payment.

"Oh," said Brand, suddenly recalling he didn't have any bullions. He froze for an embarrassed instant and looked at Cil and Berengar, who both shook their heads.

Alucard stepped forward and raised a hand, as if to say: *Step back. I got this.* Smiling, his eyes mere slits of smug satisfaction, he drew a silver bullion from his crowded pouch and handed it over.

The man looked surprised and stepped back, just now seeing Alucard's face peeking from the hood of his gray cloak. After a moment, he relaxed and grumbled, "Nice costume, kid." He took the silver and eyed it suspiciously before tucking it into a grimy pocket. He handed over three pigeon sausages, then seemed to forget their presence and began fumbling noisily with something under his bench, as if they had never existed.

"Wait," Brand said. "Where can we get water?"

The shop owner sighed heavily, and with an effort that seemed beyond him, lifted an arm and pointed vaguely in the direction of the Town-Master's Hall.

The man refused further questioning, and Brand was forced to stare intensely for a time before finally spotting a well behind the Town-Master's Hall.

They headed in that direction, but before they could make it across the square, Salome appeared from the hall and intercepted them, running over and grabbing Brand by the hand.

She smiled up at him warmly. "Isn't this fantastic?"

"Oh... the..." Brand was distracted by her large eyes and that intoxicating perfume she wore.

"The *Paradise!* Yes! The others have already made their transition."

"I don't trust this girl," Cil grumbled in the background.

Brand was too distracted to notice. Salome caused him to feel terribly uneasy, enraptured and nauseous at the same time.

Alucard began to growl.

"Here, let me show you—just a look, like you promised," she said, turning and dragging Brand over towards the fountain.

"Wait!" said Berengar, tugging on Brand's safety rope.

"Oh, Berengar, he doesn't have to go in—just look at it. The others all went in already, and it doesn't take you from afar, like that damned obsidian sheet that stole my Dimi's looks."

Her mood dropped at the remembrance, but she quickly put on a cheery face again. She dragged Brand toward the shiny object. As they got closer, the glowing golden shape began to take on form and solidity.

"Wow!" said Brand. "It looks like a small... well, *palace,* floating on the water of the pond."

"That's what it is!" said Salome exuberantly.

"It really is beautiful," Cil admitted, staring at the shifting lights and colors. It was not just a stagnant model of a city—*it was alive!*

Brand leaned in close. He thought he could hear subtle sounds coming from the thing: tinkles of laughter, wisps of alluring music, ale cups clinking together. Berengar's grumbling warnings quickly became distant. As Brand looked on, he could see tiny partygoers walking down lantern-lit promenades, the shadows of laughing, drinking revelers behind the rice-paper walls of many-tiered taverns built in a beautiful but unfamiliar style.

"The people in there are real and alive!" said Brand in sudden awe. It was beyond any stretch of his imagination. *Maybe there was something to this 'Paradise' business after all,* he thought.

"And how does one enter the place?" he mused idly.

"Like... *this,*" said Salome with an evil smirk that wiped away Brand's levity. Her free hand shot out like a striking serpent. Using herself as a conduit, she connected Brand to the glowing golden palace.

Berengar, Cil, and Alucard watched agape as Brand and Salome's forms faded into translucent shadows of golden light, then vanished. All of their worldly possessions were left hanging in midair—Brand's knives and crossbow, his black coat, his belt, his boots, and his pouch containing their map; Salome's beautiful orange sarong, her green and turquoise beads, her ankle and wrist bracelets, and golden bangle earrings; all fell to the ground with a crash.

Before they had recovered from their shock, the fat man from the Town Master's Hall waddled over like a hungry badger and went to collect the dropped articles.

"Just a minute!" raged Cil, balling up one of her tiny but powerful fists and swinging at the man, causing him to tumble backward. The fat man recovered from his shock and became irate. He stood up, puffed out his chest. Cil took two steps forward—the man realized his mistake and wobbled back to the Town Master's Hall in a huff.

"And stay there!" she called out, shaking her fist. Then she turned back to Berengar. "Oh, *damnit Ber!* What are we going to do now? Brand, you idiot! You stupid beanstalk! What have you gotten yourself into?!"

Berengar, had he not been distraught about Brand's plight, would have chuckled at the concern in Cil's voice over Brand. Instead, he let off a stream of unknown barbaric curses and roared, "I told him! Damnit, *I told him! Damn magic, witches, devils and Gods!*"

He paced back and forth for a time, and then paused, pale-faced and sweating, and said, "I'm going in to get him out. You stay here and guard our belongings. The lad's like a child, and won't last a day without me."

"Where are the purple-pink striped corduroys?" said Alucard, scratching his chin. He was wearing a piece of wrapping paper from one of the market stalls as a conical hat.

"I agree, but how will you get out?" said Cil, ignoring Alucard's comment.

"I don't know, *damnit.*"

Cil bent down and looked through the dropped items. "It looks like everything that wasn't part of their body was left behind. You'll have no weapons."

Berengar had been pacing and now paused, grinning maniacally, his emotions making him wild. "There's nothing these hands cannot crush. In this world *or another*." He seemed to say it more to reassure himself than Cil.

"*Where are the corduroy pants?*" said Alucard again.

"Glad to hear it, Berengar, but—how will you get out—"

Cil stopped and looked down at Alucard, who was waving his hands up at them like a child.

"Oh, Alucard, what is it?" she said.

"Take me with you, Berengar. This book will follow us." He held up the wizard's spell book.

Berengar looked confused and darkly suspicious.

"How will you get—" Cil began. Then Alucard's words came back to her. "Oh, the pants! You're right! Brand's pants aren't here —Gilfingle mentioned they may resist magic."

"Gilfingle was wrong. They are not *anti-magical*. They are merely *magical*," said Alucard, his face impassive.

"I see... but so what—oh. You think that book will go with you because it's magical too?"

"Yes," he said again.

"How will you get out?"

"I shall look. I shall search. Something inside the book *must* help us."

Cil stood up, placed her hands on her hips, and said, "It's as good a plan as any, Berengar."

Berengar vibrated with his fear for magic, "*Damnable Seventy-Five Hells*!" He bent over and picked up Alucard.

Then, with a nod to Cil, he stepped forward and—with a hand shaking from terror—reached out and touched the floating palace.

Like before, their bodies faded into a golden afterimage and then vanished. All of their items clattered to the floor except, Cil noted with relief, the wizard's spell book.

Cil looked down at the growing pile of belongings Brand and

the others had left. Seeing Salome's earrings and bracelets, she grinned wickedly.

"I'll take those, thank you," she said, and slipped them into her pouch.

Then, with sudden insight and a smile of malicious satisfaction, she took Salome's beautiful orange sarong and used it as a makeshift sack to wrap up the rest of the items. She tied it to her steel staff and dragged it across the dirty ground of the market square.

"Those two idiots. They better not leave me waiting here forever." She said, feigning anger, but the tightness at the corner of her lips showed the concern she felt for her friends—especially Brand. Then, suddenly recalling that Alucard's pouch had bullions in it, she brightened. "If they are going to make me wait out here, I'm at least going to get something good to eat!"

Chapter 10

"Hell Hath No Wrath..."

Queen: "This food tastes awful. Servant, bring me something with some flavor. I cannot eat such piffle. It's like blended wood chips, soapstone, or perhaps soap itself. Chalky garbage.

I'll only say this once: I will not tolerate any distractions on the day of my coronation!"

Chief Steward of the Castle: "Yes, Your Majesty. I shall have the cook prepare an entirely new feast, and this time, I shall oversee the preparations myself."

—Dispatch to Chief Steward of the Castle, dated Saturday, Day 1, Year 1. The Queen's Calendar

Found on the boudoir table in the chamber of the High Queen

***

Brand awoke in a dark place, curled up on a cold stone slab. He was naked, except for the purple-pink striped corduroys.
He looked around, his head spinning, trying to make sense of the unfamiliar environment. What little light there was seemed to operate on a different set of wavelengths—shifting through poisonous greens, drab maroons, and dark reds. The colors disturbed him and made his eyes ache with an innate sort of rebellion to the strange spectrum.

The air was cold and carried a faintly fetid odor. Brand shivered and, for the first time since he'd been forced to wear them, felt thankful for the purple-pink striped corduroys.

"Whatever your bad points, Gilfingle, I am thankful for these stout trousers," he muttered as he sat up.

He stumbled weakly to his feet, wincing as they touched the

cold stone floor. A wave of foreboding overcame him as he took in the stark room. The walls were made of dull, gray stone and stood bare.

A large crack in one caught his attention, and he recoiled in disgust as an enormous cockroach crawled lithely out of it and fluttered its wings. Its two, long antennae twitched in his direction. *It was the size of a dog.*

"What in the...!" he cried, stamping the ground as hard as he could.

Then, "Ouch!"—he had forgotten he was barefoot, and the floor was unyielding.

"At least it decided to look for easier prey," he muttered, as the creature backed off into its hidden den.

Turning around, Brand saw something else in the room: a large wooden writing desk and chair in one corner. Slumped in the chair was a shadowy form, a gray-fleshed hand on a long, bandy arm hanging limply at its side, still clutching a rusty knife clotted with dried, red-black blood.

The man was clearly dead. That alone was distasteful, but Brand had seen dead bodies before. What really made his hackles rise and knees wobble was the fact that the man—and the desk, and everything in the room—was far, far too big.

He stumbled toward the figure to confirm it wasn't just an illusion caused by the strange light, but the closer he got, the larger it seemed.

With a sudden shock of terror, like ice water pouring down his spine, he realized: the dead man wasn't big; Brand himself was *small.*"

Flashbacks of being a small child—no, a baby—hit him forcefully." His brain reeled with the unreality of it all, and he fell into a stupor, landing heavily on his haunches. The cold stone under his hands snapped him out of it slightly, and he sat there for a time, waiting for his head to stop spinning.

This was all wrong. Where was the revelry? The lights? The mead? The pretty girls? Something had gone awfully and terribly wrong with paradise.

After a time, the initial shock of the environment and the warped spatial dimensions wore off, replaced by a feeling of terrible cold—and a sort of desperate curiosity. These two factors were enough to drive him to his feet and goad him to investigate further. He stalked over to the giant corpse at the desk, moving on tiptoes, as if this eccentric gait would somehow make him less noticeable.

Looking up, Brand was confronted by a great, leering face. The giant man's forehead rested on the edge of the table, his glassy gaze forever turned downward. Shivering now, Brand noted the man's great yellow teeth, his graying gums, and the jagged gash of black-red gore stretching from ear to ear. With a prickle of horror at the base of his neck, Brand realized the man must have slashed his own throat. Why?

It was strange. The man seemed to have been here a long time; his skin was cold and gray, the blood black and ancient—yet no decomposition had set in. Brand forced down a wave of nausea and struggled to keep down the remains of the pigeon sausage he had just eaten moments ago.

Then he suddenly became confused... Had it only been moments ago? How long had he been here? It already felt like an eternity—perhaps another side effect of the strange light?

Looking up once more, he judged he was perhaps one-fifth his usual size—so about a foot tall by normal-world standards. As he tried to come to grips with this, a further discomfort stirred. The room began to slowly slant, tilting to the side, and the whole world creaked with a deep, tortured groan, like that of a wooden ship adjusting to the surf—but magnified a hundredfold. Then, in the distance, a great horn rang out, shaking the world with its thunderous cry. The sound only added to Brand's growing sense of dread.

Looking to the other end of the chamber, he saw a large, open doorway with more of that strange light streaming in. He darted over to it on shaky legs, and as he approached it, it seemed more gigantic than ever. He crept forward like a frightened toddler having woken from a nightmare.

What he saw was in no way reassuring.

The doorway led into a corridor of the same spartan, dilapidated condition. A brighter, more wholesome light poured in from a vent high in the ceiling. Brand hoped it was moonlight, but suspected he was too deep within this structure—or whatever it was—for that to be true.

The illuminated section of the corridor showed only an empty wall-mounted cabinet, with what looked to be the remains of a medical supply cache. Empty wooden cases lay strewn about, and a strip of gauze hung from the lip of the cabinet, almost touching the floor.

There was an old stool—giant to Brand—knocked over beneath the cabinet. To the left and right, the corridor extended into darkness. To the right, a trail of spilled papers littered the floor and vanished into the gloom. Straight ahead was another doorway leading into a darkened hall. But here too, a pool of light glimmered—a haunting glow, but still better than endless dark.

On the wall above Brand and to his right, a long wooden flotation device hung from a hook. He wondered what that was for, but fear stopped further speculation, and he edged into the hallway on trembling legs.

Once again, the ground groaned deeply, and the whole place tilted in the opposite direction from before. In the distance, the great horn rang out.

Brand continued down the corridor toward the next patch of

light, his mind conjuring unknown creatures in the blackness. Reaching the glow with a sigh of relief, he found himself at another crossroads. Two directions led into eternal dark; one held another faint light. He chose the light again, with the eerie sensation that he was being guided—like a rat in a miniature maze. Even so, he didn't stray. The light was better than a labyrinth of black.

This didn't last long. As he neared the next glow, he saw it wasn't a crossroads but a doorway into a well-lit room. Brand hurried forward, spirits rising ever so slightly, and found it led into a long gallery, bright with silvery-blue light.

He stepped across the threshold.

BANG!

Brand nearly jumped out of his skin. It was the first sound he'd heard—aside from the horn and creaking floor—since arriving in this silent nightmare. He whipped around and saw that a great door had slammed shut behind him, cutting him off from the corridor maze.

Was that really a loss? he wondered, grimly. More importantly— how had it closed by itself?

The gallery stretched far ahead, made all the more vast by his miniature stature. On the right wall ran a series of gigantic maps pinned to cork boards. The landscapes depicted were wholly foreign. The left wall was floor-to-ceiling glass or crystal, warped and wavy, blurring out whatever lay beyond. This was the source of the silvery light, which threw stretching shadows across the maps opposite.

Brand thought he could see great objects behind the rippling glass, but nothing was clear. Standing there, he felt a sudden, unnerving certainty—he was being put on display.

He shivered and walked straight ahead. It was as good a direction as any—there was nowhere else to go. He walked a long time. On and on the gallery stretched, and soon it began to feel like a never-ending tunnel, looping through time and space.

A flicker at the edge of his vision. He jerked his head left—nothing. Stillness. Silence. He hunched his shoulders and kept walking.

Another flicker. He spun.

This time, he was met with a giant, staring face.

The face of a giant lackwit youth, with sandy blond hair and wide, glassy blue eyes. The eyes were locked on Brand. Below them, a slack mouth hung open, lower lip sagging. Two enormous hands pressed against the glass on either side of the face.

The boy lurched forward unexpectedly, pressing his face against the glass in a silent pucker.

Brand screamed and fell over, almost passing out from the shock.

His scream seemed to frighten the boy because, as soon as it rang out from his quivering lips, the great figure spun away from the glass, vanishing into the indistinct blur beyond.

Picking himself up, Brand began sprinting in utter terror down the gallery. He looked like some eccentric party-goer who'd taken an extremely bad trip—completely naked apart from his purple-pink striped corduroy flares.

For a time, he ran undisturbed, sprinting in silence, his terror too deep for thought, staring straight ahead.

Bang! BANG!

He let out a wail and leapt to the right in a great, gazelle-like bound, slamming into the wall on his right.

The face and hands were back—this time slammed hard against the glass. The giant boy let out a moan of frustration and grasped for Brand, swiping impotently at the barrier.

Now Brand screamed at full blast and didn't let up. He kept it going as he ran, until it became part of his breathing. In out, in out, screaming each time on the *out*.

The screams and motion seemed to trigger the boy. As Brand ran, the giant face kept pace beside him—like a great fish in a tank following a tracing finger. Only this time, Brand *was* the finger, inside the glass. The massive hands began slamming and battering the pane, causing it to ripple and shake.

Tearing his gaze from those idiotic blue eyes, Brand checked ahead for escape. The end of the gallery was in sight—but not the kind he wanted. Twenty paces ahead, his desperate stare was met by a blank wall. Still, he ran on.

He slowed before the wall, eyes darting around in a panic. To his left, the boy redoubled his efforts to break the glass. The sounds of the blows reached a crescendo.

It was working.

Large cracks spread through the barrier. The boy banged and smashed with abandon, ignoring the damage to his now-bloody knuckles.

Frantic now, Brand scanned the room for any exit. Then he saw it—low on the wall behind him. A duct. He dove, yanked open the flap, and launched himself headfirst into it, just as the glass shattered.

A great, dumb bellow rang out, deafening his ears. As he wormed into the cramped tunnel, he felt the tickle of searching fingers on his bare feet. Just beyond reach. The bellows of dismay that followed shook the foundations and turned the contents of Brand's bowels to water, nearly adding a shade of brown to his rainbow pantaloons.

But he didn't look back.

He crawled and slid, wriggled and paddled on his belly, trying to get far, far away from that thing. Anywhere—*anything*—was better than that thing. And of course, he was still screaming.

In his haste and terror, he failed to notice the vent's downward tilt. It steepened fast, and soon Brand was sliding headfirst, unable to slow his momentum. He plunged deeper into the bowels of this unknown hell.

Luckily, the vent didn't end in a hard corner. It smoothed at the bottom, like a chute, and shot him out into a dark room beyond. His bare heels caught the floor, and in the space of a second he went from sliding on his back to sprinting upright. Brand ran through the dark for a time, unaware of his surroundings. Then, with no pursuit behind him, he collapsed. His chest heaved, heart pounding. The cool stone beneath him was oddly refreshing. It grounded him. For a moment.

The now-familiar tilt began again, accompanied by groaning creaks—louder, closer. Brand felt deeper within the cyclopean structure than ever. He thought he could hear the faint sloshing of massive waves below, and somehow, more intuition than perception, he sensed a gulf of black water churning endlessly beneath him.

Thumps echoed faintly from below. In his mind, vast creatures stirred in the blackness, brushing against the hull of this floating palace. A wave of nausea surged through him.

It was all too much—too big, too sinister. He felt crushingly small. The millions of tons of stone and steel above seemed to press down on him, while the abyss below pulled, threatening to swallow him whole.

Finally, the nausea won. He vomited up the remains of the pigeon sausage. The physical relief did little for his nerves. He swore he'd never doubt Berengar again. He swore he now hated magic, gods, and devils just as much as the Outlander did—but none of it shook him free from the nightmare.

A sound caught his attention—a soft chain rustle, then silence.

Brand froze. The noise yanked him out of his thoughts. The room was stark, unadorned, dimly lit by that same sickly spectrum. But a warmer glow radiated from a nearby doorway.

He tottered toward it. The golden light filled his center vision. The red-green haze lingered at the edges and blended with the dark. The next room was wooden-walled, a lantern swaying overhead. Old sacks, worn barrels, and clay pots lined the walls. It was all dry, ancient, unused—not a hint of anything fresh.

The next room had no lantern, but backlit silhouettes of barrels and shelves marked another chamber beyond. From this darker storeroom, the chain rustled again. Close now.

Brand held his breath. On long legs, he tiptoed to the doorframe, clutching it with both hands, and leaned around.

To the left, a large shelving unit covered the wall. From a black shadow between two crates came the faint rustle of chains—and the glint of steel catching lantern light behind him.

Brand edged inside and pressed himself flat against a giant crate. Peeking around, he saw another doorway leading into a long, dark corridor. It was cluttered with crates, ropes and metal hardware. At its far end, glowed a patch of golden light from which echoed the chaotic clanging of pots and pans.

He stood still, letting his eyes adjust. Then he peeked—and froze.

A lithe young woman, about his age, was chained to a metal stake in the stone floor. She looked up and gaped at him silently. Her dark, purple-brown hair framed a face that would've been attractive if it weren't so dirty and wan. She wore only a tattered white smock. Her face, hands, and feet were streaked with soot.

Summoning a sliver of gallantry, Brand raised a hand and whispered, "It's ok! I'm not going to hurt you."

The kitchen noises stopped. The girl's eyes went wide, and she raised a finger to her lips.

At the far end of the hall, heavy footsteps sounded. A massive black shadow blotted out the light. The girl pointed frantically behind her—to the crates.

Brand scurried over, squeezing into a tight crevice behind the deepest crate. The footsteps grew thunderous.

They stopped. Now—ragged, rasping breath.

A foul heat wafted over the crates and reached Brand where he hid.

A violent jolt—the crate slammed against the wall, nearly crushing him. Outer crates shifted recklessly. Grunts of confusion followed.

The steps resumed, dwindling this time, retreating.

Silence.

Brand began to edge out—but the girl's wide-eyed look froze him. A sudden thump thump thump—then more crashing. Closer. A massive, greasy hand appeared. It reached past the girl and groped behind the crates. Several times, the huge fingers brushed inches from Brand.

A grunt of irritation. The steps began again, retreating down the corridor. Soon, the chaotic clanging resumed in the kitchen beyond.

Brand exhaled shakily. He motioned to the girl, miming an attempt to undo her chain.

She stared at him, eyes haunted and mistrustful. Then, after a moment, she signaled—describing a key—and pointed toward the kitchen.

Brand blanched, his stomach turning at the thought. Fear gripped his spine, but he forced a nod to maintain at least a shred of manly composure. Mustering a show of courage he didn't truly feel, he made a careless frown and nodded again, this time more firmly, before stalking off down the hall.

Each furtive step of that journey was a silent hell, and his heart began to pound so heavily that he was certain it would give him away at any second. It didn't, however, and soon the patch of golden light resolved into a gigantic doorway.

As he approached, he began to make out a large pile of enormous dishes beside a great cooking bench, which ran along the left wall before turning at a right angle and continuing out of sight. The booming footsteps of the giant creature echoed loudly through the doorway as it banged around somewhere in the unseen part of the kitchen.

Brand peeked in from behind the frame. The place was a mess. The counter was cluttered with filthy utensils, knife racks, cooking tools, a pile of rags, and stacks of unwashed dishes crusted with grime, dripping with a stench so potent it felt *visible*. The floor, slick with filth, gleamed with an oily sheen that was daunting in Brand's current diminutive state. He ducked back and took a few deep breaths.

Steeling himself, he held his breath and risked another glance— this time to the right.

What he saw froze him with terror.

A hulking figure stood with its back to him—a grotesque mountain of flesh wearing a soiled apron. It was tied so tightly that fat mounds bulged grotesquely across its shoulders and back like wild, runaway love handles. The exposed skin on its neck and arms was pink, mottled with red sores and patches of peeling eczema. A crumpled mockery of a white chef's hat perched atop its greasy curls. Dandruff rained in chunky flakes with every jerky motion.

Brand considered himself lucky that he'd first seen the creature's back. He wasn't sure how he'd have reacted if he'd faced it from the start.

The thing began to mumble in a disturbingly high-pitched, vicious voice that shocked Brand with its suddenness.

"Must cook. Must cook for the queen. The queen, the damned bloody queen! Hungry! *So hungry,* but no, the queen must get the best. Must get the best, or she makes the flesh *burn.*"

The voice was a sickening blend of malice and groveling—made more deranged by its lilting quality than any deep, bellowing timbre would have.

Brand's ears caught another sound, faint and intermittent—muffled screams.

He strained to hear over the creature's muttering and the clattering pots, but couldn't locate the source. Edging forward like a wary rat, he peeked around the doorframe again.

In the center of the kitchen, a massive table overflowed with filthy pots, maggots, and piles of rotting meat of unknown origin.

Beyond the mess, the creature moved deliberately, muttering ceaselessly—its grotesque monologue blending with the kitchen's clatter and stink.

At the far right end of the back wall's counter stood a cast-iron stove, its grate open, a small fire flickering inside. The faint screams seemed to be coming from near the stove.

Seizing the moment, Brand dashed silently to the base of the left-hand counter. He climbed onto a wooden stool, and using it for leverage, scrambled onto the counter.

The muttering stopped.

Brand's blood turned to ice. Without looking back, he dove behind a spice container the size of a wagon and landed in a tight crouch.

For a tense moment, the kitchen fell silent. Brand held his breath. His heart hammered in his ears.

Then—the muttering resumed. He dared to breathe again.

Peeking out from behind his cover, he scanned the kitchen from his new vantage point. The view did nothing to ease his nerves. Heaps of dirty dishes. Piles of gray, unidentifiable meat crawling with walnut-sized maggots. The looming bulk of the giant chef as it jerked this way and that.

And then he saw it. There, on the bench—to the left of where the creature worked—lay a key.

A frantic game of freeze ensued. Brand tiptoed across the bench in fits and starts, diving behind stacks of rotting dishes, ducking behind ladles or towers of filth. At every twitch of the creature's head, he froze.

It took time. By the time he reached a steel cup full of wooden spoons, he was sweating and trembling. The creature's stench—stale sweat and unwashed flesh—clung thick in the air.

Peeking out again, he caught the thing in profile: the dangling jowls, apron-covered gut, rolls of fat hanging off sagging arms. Then it turned fully into the light.

His breath caught.

Its face glistened with sweat. The flesh was pink and peeling. The eyes—sunken and black—were the worst. Pits of madness. Not just insane, but *wrong*—a soul driven beyond death and *then* into a state of gruesome animation. Only his instinct for survival kept him from screaming aloud.

The thing's demeanor changed. It became brisk. It scooped up two rolls of pastry from the countertop—that was what it had been preparing.

"*So hungry,*" it crooned, opening its cupped hands and gazing longingly at the pastries.

The screaming started again—louder now, frantic. Brand recognized the voices.

Balin. Fonicia Coonse.

Horrified, he stared at the pastries. Their *heads* stuck out of the ends closest to him.

The creature shook its head, sorrowful, and with shocking speed, shoved the pastries into the oven. Slammed the door shut.

Brand reached out in vain. *"No!"* he mouthed. But it was too late. The screams rose to a piercing pitch—then faded to the sizzle and crack of firewood.

Brand retched silently into a sugar bowl the size of a bathtub.

"So hungry. *So hungry it hurts!*" the creature muttered in its manic falsetto. "But no, I shouldn't. The High Queen will burn the flesh. Can't stand it. Can't stand to watch the fresh meat cook. *Clean* meat. But... '*Clean meat is the Queen's meat.*'"

Shaking, it reached for the oven—then smacked its own hand away. "*Bad hand.* Bad hand will get Kurlyle burnt."

It bustled out in a rush, fleeing the scent of food it didn't trust itself not to devour.

Brand exhaled and crept to the key. After one final glance, he snatched it and dashed back to his cover, holding it like a short sword.

He retraced his steps across the bench, weaving through pots and pans, darting under utensils. He imagined that hot breath on his neck the entire way.

Back near the doorway, he hopped onto the stool—and slipped.

He hit the floor with a muffled clatter and froze.

Heart thudding. Eyes wide. Waiting.

Nothing.

He bolted down the dark corridor.

Halfway through, the footsteps returned. Slow at first—then rapid. A grotesque roar, a crash of dishes hurled to the ground.

Then came the chase.

Brand ran as if in a nightmare—the kind where you can't run fast enough. Behind him, the roaring drew closer, focused now.

Just as he thought he was done for, he reached the storeroom.

Without stopping to look back, he dashed under the shelf and stuck the key into its home with a deft accuracy that surprised even himself, given the circumstances. The steel ankle band clicked open and fell to the floor. Brand dragged the girl to her feet and darted between the two giant crates behind her, already feeling the grasp of giant hands at his back—and judging by the wide-eyed glances the girl kept throwing over her shoulder, his instincts weren't wrong.

A great calamity erupted behind them—strangled cries of wrath, the thunderous smashing of crates—deafening. Brand pressed forward, deeper into the stack beneath the shelves, hauling the girl behind him. But soon they reached an impasse: A blank wall of stone bordering the furthest recess under the shelf.

The wall before him was suddenly bathed in golden light as the final pair of crates were ripped loose and dashed against the far side of the chamber. Turning in helpless horror, Brand saw the growing shadow that reached for them.

"This way!" the girl cried, dragging Brand toward a vent he hadn't noticed—half-hidden in a shadowy corner behind the crates. They dove in at a dead run and shimmied forward on hands and knees.

A high-pitched roar of anguish blasted hot air into the vent behind them, and a great fist pounded at the entrance, buckling the metal. But Brand and the girl were already beyond reach. The jarring blows continued for a long time—longer than reason would dictate—offering another hint at the mental state of the creature behind them.

They crawled on in silence through the black tunnel, the mad clanging growing fainter.

With the immediate danger behind them, Brand's thoughts darkened again. The sound of sloshing water returned, louder than before, threatening to drag him under and drown him among unseen horrors below. His mind strained at the edge of madness.

In that moment of need, he thought of Berengar and clung to the memory of the bluff giant.

I am not ruggedly built, he thought, *not like Berengar. What would Berengar do?*

Then it struck him: Berengar wouldn't *think* at all. He would act.

So Brand stopped thinking. He focused on the tunnel ahead, the pressure of the girl's hand in his, the itch of the corduroys chafing his groin.

He smiled grimly, suddenly aware of how ridiculous he must have looked, creeping through a nightmarish labyrinth in colorful striped pants. A low rumble of laughter escaped his throat—probably sounding like madness to the frightened girl at his side.

A pale gray light appeared ahead—the exit of this particular vent.

The girl stopped, turning to look at him, her face close to his in the narrow tunnel. They were face to face now, features lit in Rembrandt fashion by the silvery glow. Her eyes were wide with alarm, and strangely beautiful—in a haggard, pitiful way. Her breath smelled faintly of roses.

"Why are you laughing?" she asked, her clean-cut features strained with concern.

"Oh, nothing. Just these pants." He gestured downward.

She studied them thoughtfully. "They are pretty. I like them." She hesitated. "Why did you help me?"

"Who wouldn't help a stranded fellow human? And one so pretty?" said Brand, attempting a gallantry.

She looked down, embarrassed. "You think I'm *pretty?*"

"Sure."

"Many people—" She stopped, eyes on the floor.

"Many people what?" he asked.

"Many people wouldn't have helped me. Many people have come here over the years. No one has helped me."

Years? Brand shivered. "How did you come to be here?"

She shook her head.

"Okay. How long have you been here, then?"

"Many years. Many, many years."

"What are these giant things that want to eat us?"

"They are *men.*"

A creeping disgust slid down Brand's spine and seemed to pull his stomach toward his backbone. "*Truly?* How can that be?"

"It's this. This place. It's what it *does* to you. The food here... the *food.*"

"What of the food?"

"Any food made here is lifeless and dull. It's like eating clay and wax. Worse—if you eat it, *you* become like clay and wax. Eventually, you become desperate and turn to... *other food...*"

"Other food?... *Oh.*"

"*Yes.*"

"So that's what happened to those things that tried to eat us?"

"Yes... Well, sort of."

"What do you mean?"

"The High Queen. She controls this world. She chooses some men to be her servants, changes them. Makes them big—so they can hunt well for her."

"So these giants are her servants?"

"Yes. They catch and cook the fresh food for her—or do other things. I don't care to say what some of them do to new arrivals."

Brand tried to collect his thoughts. The horror of what she'd said cluttered his thinking.

"But—if she's so powerful, why doesn't she just materialize a feast? A great banquet? Or a roast pig, for example?"

"Oh, she does. And the servants are forced to eat it. It sustains— but not the way you'd want. *More like embalming.* Didn't you notice the gray flesh?"

Brand nodded, eyes wide.

She went on. "Yes. The gray flesh comes. You eat and eat, but the hunger never leaves. The food is chalk. Chalk and wax. Slowly, you too *become* chalk and wax. An animated travesty of life."

Brand's head snapped up. He eyed the girl with sudden suspicion. "You talk like you've lived it."

She laughed—a bitter, tinkling sound. "Oh no. Look at me. Is my skin gray and swollen? Am I giant and deformed?"

"Well, no, but..."

"I've *seen* it happen. To people I loved. And then to many, many more." Her voice grew distant, her eyes unfocused. She stared down the tunnel, lost in something bleak.

"Sorry... I didn't mean to stir up bad memories. But tell me, then —*how do you survive?*"

The girl shook her head.

"You're being suspicious now."

"*What?* Tell you so that you can take it away *for yourself?* Leave me to die? *Never!*" She was shaking her head, small tears coursing down her dirty cheeks.

Brand felt bad, and so he let it drop—for now.

"Well, what then? You can't stay here forever."

"One day a prince will come to rescue me from this place. I know it, *I just know it!*" she whimpered, wiping the tears from her face.

Brand patted her back gently, suddenly sorry he had pried so much. "Well, let us get going then. There's a small chance my friends will come to rescue me, but we need to find them."

She looked up, suddenly interested. "Friends?"

"Yeah. Good people. People who *always* figure out a way."

"Do you think they will help me too?"

"Yes! *I'm sure of it!*"

The girl nodded, as if pleased. "Okay. Let us go then. I will show you the safe passages I have found over the years."

"Good! By the way, my name is Brand. What's yours?"

"Charlotte."

"Nice to meet you, Charlotte. Let's go."

They continued down the last stretch of the tunnel and soon reached its end, a new excitement building in both of them—there was hope.

As Brand pulled himself to the edge of the vent, he heard a faint sound—the whimpering of a frightened girl or child. Charlotte's hand tensed in his, and he gave it a reassuring squeeze before peeking into the dark room, straining his eyes. There, in the corner —a girl. It was Salome. He recognized her at once and moved to call her name—but Charlotte motioned sharply for silence.

"The Queen's servants have impeccable hearing," she whispered.

Brand nodded, and they climbed from the vent as quietly as possible.

The room was small and square, leading into another dark corridor. Brand paced silently to its edge and peered out. Long. Stark. Empty. He listened—no footsteps, no sounds. He walked back to Charlotte, who stood in the center of the room, watching the sulking girl.

Salome was curled in the corner, face down. She had wrapped a ragged cloth around herself—probably torn from one of the corridor sacks. Other than that, she was "naked as the day."

"Corridor looks clear," Brand whispered.

Charlotte nodded, then pointed toward Salome.

Brand approached slowly, careful not to startle her—she looked even worse than he felt.

"Salome!" he whispered.

She froze, going still.

"It's me. Brand!"

Salome gasped and turned, eyes wide. "*Oh, Brand,*" she sobbed, and launched herself into his arms. Her body trembled with sobs against his shoulder, clinging to him for support. Her bare breasts pressed tightly to his chest, and he strained to keep his thoughts holy.

After a moment, he said, "It's okay, Salome. We'll get out of here." He gently disentangled himself and gestured toward his companion. "This is Charlotte. Charlotte, this is Salome."

The two bedraggled girls stared at each other like wary cats, silent and tense. Then—as if reaching a private agreement—they both nodded.

"Well..." Brand said, slightly confused. "Which way do we go, Charlotte?"

"There's a vent shaft at the far end of the hall," she said, pointing. "It leads to the sewer system. It has connections all over the palace. That's where I stay."

"Okay then. Let's go," said Brand, doing his best to sound confident.

The three of them moved cautiously down the corridor. But this time, nothing came for them. Charlotte led the way to the vent. It sloped downward almost immediately, and soon Brand found himself sliding—as he had before, from the higher levels above.

Salome gave a soft gasp, wrapped her bare legs around his waist, and clasped his shoulders from behind. Once again, Brand did his best to think holy thoughts.

The shaft ended suddenly, flinging them onto harsh, abrasive stone. Charlotte landed first, catching herself expertly and hopping to bleed off the momentum. Salome clung to Brand's back like a sack of potatoes, forcing him to graze his heels across the floor until he skidded to a halt. He was, once again, immensely thankful for the corduroys.

Salome slid off his back and stood, somehow graceful even in a sack-cloth wrap. She dusted herself off, managing to preserve a strange nobility.

Brand shot her a pettish glare and pulled himself upright, brushing off the worst of his scrapes.

They were in a kind of sump room. The floor was rough stone, slightly concave, sloped toward a wide steel drain large enough to carry off a man. Water stains darkened the concrete around it. Rust smeared the walls. A deep discomfort stirred in Brand—he didn't like the idea of the room flooding and sweeping them into the abyss below.

Lifting his eyes from the drain, he saw concrete tunnels running off in every direction. Above them was an endless shaft of darkness, lined with steel pipes that disappeared into the gloom.

To the right, on a raised ledge, sat a small bed, a mug, some papers, and a collection of random objects—stones, a steel bar. It hit Brand then, with a pang: this was Charlotte's home.

Salome walked over, placed her hands on her hips, and shook her head at the meager sleeping arrangement.

Brand moved quickly, trying to distract Charlotte before her feelings could be hurt. "Hey, Charlotte?" he said, staring into the drain.

"Yeah?" she replied.

"Where does this thing lead?" He nodded at the hole.

She stepped up beside him and looked down. "I'm not sure. I think it carries waste water out to the ocean. It hasn't been used since I've been here. But then, nothing here really works anymore. Most of the original residents died, and the palace... well, most of it has fallen into disuse."

"I'm surprised the High Queen doesn't just leave," Brand said.

"She *can't!*" Charlotte's face twisted with sudden fury, forcing Brand to take a step back.

"Sorry," she muttered. "*She's* taken everything from me. We're just her playthings here."

Brand looked at her, trying to think of something smart to say. Suddenly, her eyes widened in alarm, and she gasped. Then Brand felt something heavy connect with the back of his head. A streak of white-hot lightning burst through his mind. A second later, his legs failed him and he felt the floor rise up to meet him.

Opening his eyes, he found himself lying paralyzed on his side, near the drain—observing a sort of half-view of the room before him. He stared on through the red haze which began to run across his vision, unable to move.

A few seconds later, Salome brought her face close to his and looked into his eyes. Her face was twisted into a mask of hellish malice—a living embodiment of hate, all the more terrible because of her awful beauty. Her violet eyes were stormy wells of insanity.

Charlotte stood nearby, frozen in shock.

Salome began to speak, her voice carrying to Brand as if over a vast gulf.

"You disgrace me. You belittle me, Brand. You promised to protect Dimi—now look at her! You chose that redhead *slut* over *me!* All these false promises building up, Brand."

She let out an unhinged cackle.

"You think I didn't hear your whole knight-in-shining-armor speech to this... this *wretched thing*?" She gestured toward Charlotte.

"Your voices echoed *loudly.* Always the charming words and the pretty smile... Where's your easy laugh *now?* Where was your gallantry when Dimi's face was taken? Or when I was *hurting? Where?!*"

Her voice cracked like shivering glass on the last word.

"You're crazy," Brand mumbled weakly.

She gathered control of herself.

"I won't kill you. No, *I want you to suffer.* I will keep you alive —crippled, but alive—and when you've suffered as much as *I have*, I will toss you into the drain to be delivered, living, into the black depths below!" Her voice escalated into a high-pitched scream.

Once again, she attempted self-restraint and calmed her voice.

"But first, let me take care of your latest lady friend."

She turned on Charlotte and raised the steel bar.

Brand struggled to raise himself from the ground, but despite all the willpower he could muster, his body would not move. Charlotte stepped back with a small cry and raised her arms in defense. Brand gazed on as if in a nightmare, forced to watch the scene playing out in front of him—unable to do a thing to change its outcome.

He watched in horror as Salome swung the steel bar with all her lithe strength at Charlotte. She struck Charlotte hard on the forearm, breaking it with a loud crack. The girl cried out in pain, and her arm fell limp to her side. The second swing connected with the top of Charlotte's head, sending the girl down with a sob.

Salome struck Charlotte over and over, blocking Brand's vision with her own back—but he could hear the sounds. After this, Salome straightened and stepped aside, allowing Brand a clear view of Charlotte's pitiful form—bloodied, battered, and lifeless.

Brand would have cried out—wept even—but his body wasn't working. As he struggled to rise once more, Salome turned in his direction, looming above him with an evil, blood-spattered smile on her beautiful lips.

"I have waited a long time for this, you arrogant boy," she said.

She raised the bar with all the intention of breaking one of Brand's legs.

A flicker of movement behind Salome. The sound of bare feet slapping on the stone. Salome's eyes widened and she spun around, seeking the source of the sound. With a prickling horror greater than that of seeing Charlotte fall, Brand saw Charlotte rise once again.

Now she stood before Salome, somehow seeming taller than before. Her head hung slackly and her face was covered by her long, dark hair. Salome screamed and lashed out with the steel bar, but this time it hit Charlotte's head with a resounding *clank*, instead of the soft padded crunch from before. The steel bar was jarred from Salome's grip and sent flying across the room.

Salome edged away from Charlotte until her back was directly in front of Brand's vision. He could see the rise and fall of her chest as she breathed.

"What... what are you??" she cried at the approaching girl.

Charlotte's head snapped up and she smiled, sporting large black mandibles.

"I am Charlotte, *the High Queen!*"

Her eyes went black and seemed to suck backwards into her skull, leaving two pitch-black bores. Her small frame erupted in a tangle of black limbs and spiked tails—to Brand, it looked like a giant black scorpion exploding out of a tight, human-textured paper bag.

Salome's scream rang out in a single high-pitched note, abruptly cut short as her virile frame was torn in seven directions at once, exploding into a fog of red mist before being drawn into Charlotte's expanding black mandibles in one great breath.

Brand finally fainted.

A steady rocking motion brought Brand to. He was so dazed and confused that for a moment he forgot recent events. His first impression was that he was lying in the back of a rocking wagon or tied to the back of a horse, and wondered if he were on one of the wagons of the Zanonnites—still traveling through the forests of the *Darkwood Runs.*

He turned his head, stretching his aching neck from side to side. As he looked to his left, he saw a black, shiny surface—and beyond, a long, smooth, black limb. It reminded him of a strange nightmare he'd just had. He chuckled to himself and wiped a hand across a sweaty temple.

He went stiff.

It wasn't a nightmare! Everything rushed back to him and he began to scream.

The motion stopped and two long, black arms with clawed hands grasped him, lifting him around to face the front of the creature that had been carrying him. He realized he had been slung across its back.

He looked into a face of pure nightmare. Horrid, dark, insectile eyes stared at him, their countless facets gleaming with inhuman hunger. A hairy, black, half-human, half-insect face with slavering mandibles framed by grotesque human lips loomed before him. The creature's thorax was large and shiny, sprouting many long, chitinous limbs of various shapes and sizes. Behind, a massive flickering scorpion tail hovered in threatening motion.

Brand gasped—wanting to look away but unable to, instead finding himself locked in morbid fascination. The creature split its face in what he took to be a smile.

Charlotte spoke in a high but husky voice, the human words

somehow making it through her gnashing mandibles.

"Ah, *Brand*, where are your kind words now? Am I not beautiful? Wherefore has your gallantry fled? Now you gaze in horrified disgust at poor Charlotte. Was your love only *skin deep?*"

Brand idly realized that this term would forever have a whole new meaning for him.

Charlotte continued in her rasping voice.

"You humans are all the same. And the men are the worst of all. Damned *men!* Damned wizards!" She gnashed and spat in wrath with an almost human emotion that Brand did not fail to catch.

"Perhaps Salome was right to scorn you. Well, soon we shall reach my chambers and it shall all be over. I will put this fresh *meat*, this fresh *soul,* to good use."

She clicked her mandibles dismissively, indicating the conversation was over, and made to swing Brand back onto her back. Brand only had a few seconds before his fate was sealed, and in this time he stared at her hideous face, his future balancing on the thread of a needle.

Now, in moments of extreme, horrific, shock-ridden peril, the human mind will do one of two things: either it will shut down, forcing a state of complete catatonia, or it will rise to the challenge, going into super-active survival overdrive. Luckily for Brand, his mind did the latter—engaging all one-hundred-percent of its mental capacity for self-preservation. His consciousness was suddenly flooded with a crystalline clarity of perception, and his mind raced at the speed of light, searching frantically for a solution that would change his fate in an instant.

Looking into that horrid face, one thing stood out as incongruent with the rest—one thing was out of place—there was makeup on that grotesque visage. *Charlotte was wearing makeup!*
To Brand's immature, boyish mind this translated to: s*he may be a monstrosity, a demented queen of limitless power, ruling in a*

demonic, terror-ridden underworld—but, she was still a girl.

Brand said, "Your eyeliner is really beautiful."

Ridiculous, of course. The chances were one in a million that such a gambit would succeed. *But it did.*

Charlotte froze, ceasing in her motion of placing him on her back. Her black eyes stared into his with sudden suspicion and, Brand noted, a hint of guarded pain—as if she expected at any moment a cruel remark or a sign of his true disgust.

Brand kept focus and gave her his most winning smile.

Charlotte stared for a moment longer, then roared.

"You *lie!* You think I'm *disgusting!* Like all you human men do! I should... I should kill you right now, before you can dig your hooks into me!"

Her mandibles clashed inches from his face, but he knew his survival depended on remaining still—so he forced himself to confront the torrent of alien hate unflinching. And more, he forced himself to continue to smile.

"No," he said as she stopped her gnashing. "Indeed, I see you take time to care for your complexion."

She paused, staring into his eyes through her many facets. It was hard to read emotion in those reflective black lenses—but not impossible. It was there.

"Maybe I'll let you live a little longer," she said dismissively, then swung him onto her back and continued moving.

Brand breathed out in silent relief. Once his nerves had settled, he took a moment to orient himself.

All was dark, but from the myriad specks of silver light pockmarking the black canvas below, he could tell he was high up in the palace—some open space overlooking the nighted city from a great height.

Peering over the shiny black edges of his transport, he saw marble steps. Golden lanterns burned at regular intervals on both sides, and everything appeared in much better repair than the lower levels he'd grown used to. From other glimpses, he deduced he was being carried up a long, open staircase toward a high tower that loomed above the entire city.

Charlotte began to grumble to herself in that high-pitched, husky tone, and Brand realized she was not entirely sane—which made his position even more precarious.

"Damned world. *Damned wizard.* Tricked poor Charlotte. Gave her a bad world. *Useless world.* Nothing grows, nothing tastes good. Flesh is stale. Needs to be kept fresh. *Eat the boy?* Should eat the boy, before he turns stale and gray like the rest. But his green eyes. Beautiful eyes—*maybe I'll keep the eyes.*"

She went on in a barely audible mutter, mostly obscured by the louder clicking of her mandibles.

Brand grew more uneasy with every word and decided to interrupt. "How did we get here so quickly?"

"I can move where I want in an instant here. This is my world," she said, a note of cold dignity in her voice.

Brand waited for her to continue, but she didn't. He feared asking the obvious question—why they were walking somewhere now instead of teleporting directly—and instead asked another. "How did you come by this world?"

This evoked a great cascade of wracking shakes and gnashing clicks, bouncing Brand around uncomfortably. After a moment she said, "Out there." She waved a great, lean black appendage toward the sky. "Damned Thurean! Oh, if Thurean would step foot within my realm—how he would suffer. His death would take a thousand years. *He tricked me!* We made a deal. It was a *bad* deal. Look at this place." She waved another long limb.

"Thurean was a wizard?" Brand prodded, tentative.

A choked growl. A pause. Then, "Yes."

"And you can't leave?"

"No! Damned Thurean took me from my home world. Said if I served him, he would grant me a world of my own—where I am the strongest ____." (she uttered a term unpronounceable and incomparable to the human tongue, likely referring to Charlotte's own species). "I served that human. That *man*. For hundreds of years. And now this! I *am* the strongest ____ (unpronounceable word) ... indeed, I'm the *only* ____ (again, the unpronounceable word) here! *A choice joke*."

Brand didn't know the word she kept using, but he asked, "Can't you just make this place bright and beautiful again?"

"I *could*... but, I don't feel like it right now."

Definitely a woman, Brand thought.

"Well, couldn't you at least summon a great banquet of food?"

"What? And become like the gray husks of men down below? I tried it once. Like eating clay. I felt my body weaken instantly. No. Life is the one thing I cannot create here. Nothing sustains. Only fresh life from outside. *Fresh flesh, fresh souls*."

A great gurgling sound came from the thorax beneath Brand, and he realized with horror that Charlotte must be hungry—his life truly tottered on the brink of destruction.

An awkward silence passed before Charlotte spoke again. "No one has ever talked with me before. Perhaps we can talk a little *before...*"

Brand's mouth became suddenly dry. "*Before what?*" he croaked.

"Never mind. Never mind, *green eyes*." Charlotte produced a strange tittering, clicking sound, which Brand realized was laughter.

"So that's a *'no'* then?" said Brand.

"A *'no'* to what?" replied Charlotte, drawn in by the mystery of his words.

"Well, kill me if you must, but I was hoping for... at least *one* date." (If Brand had any scruples about playing on the emotions of a deranged, female alien monstrosity, they were outweighed by his concern for self-preservation.)

Charlotte stopped walking. A long silence. Then—"Nobody has asked me for a date before."

"So is that a '*yes*'?" said Brand.

"I'll have to think it over. One cannot just rush into such things blindly."

She continued walking, but Brand thought to sense her smiling on the other side of that shiny thorax.

"So the birds that spoke to Gilfingle were *your* doing?"

That same tittering, clicking sound. "Ingenious, wasn't it?"

Brand considered all the poor pilgrims she had lured in over who knows how many centuries. "Indeed."

"Thurean thought I would starve in here. Thought nothing could come out. I cannot come out—but my mind can breach the walls, just enough to reach those dull-witted feathery little things—"

"*Birds?*" ventured Brand.

"*Yes, birds.* The ____ (unpronounceable word) can do things even Thurean didn't know about.

"Funny how I'm now sustained by those little feathery creatures I always thought so useless during my time on Earth. Useless—because one would have to eat a thousand of them to feel satiated, yet they flit by too quickly to chase.

"But..."

She reached back and waggled a claw in front of Brand's face. "Not so useless in the end, were they? Mindless creatures are much easier to control. Not like you devious *humans.*"

"And what of this horrid green-red light here, can you not change it?"

"Ahhh, *disagreeable,* isn't it?" She laughed again. "A psychological ploy I devised to set the mood for my fresh playthings."

"It definitely worked on me."

"It did?! *Good.*" Charlotte seemed pleased, and Brand noted a hint of pride in her voice. "And the girl with the chain? Did that pull some heartstrings?" That tittering laugh again.

Brand found himself strangely nettled at this casual talk of toying with his emotions. "Ingenious once again," he said dryly.

Charlotte didn't notice his displeasure. After a time, she paused and said, "I am done with my walk."

With a whirl of exploding colors, like the reflection of shattered glass, Brand suddenly found himself standing in a grand, well-lit chamber—something like a king and queen's private salon. Rich gilded rugs decorated the floor, and golden-red banners hung at regular intervals along the walls. Beneath the banners were pedestals, each displaying a different treasure or work of alien art. The walls were polished marble, carved with fresco reliefs in a strange geometry.

He was carried into another room, this one centered on a long banquet table fit for royalty. The domed ceiling soared above, painted in exquisite detail with a landscape of Charlotte's home world—creatures like her shown in various triumphant poses.

The great black arms lowered Brand to the floor. Looking up, he realized just how massive Charlotte truly was—a towering black tangle of claws and mandibles, far taller than the giants below. She bent to meet him face to face, her reflective, many-faceted eyes inspecting him for the slightest flicker of revulsion.

With an act of facial control that would have put a world-class mime to shame, Brand pushed down his terror and maintained a smile. And as he did, he couldn't help but notice the massive scorpion tail swaying high above, poised to strike.

"I accept," she said.

"Oh..." said Brand, thrown off for a second. "*The date?*—why, that's wonderful!"

"I must prepare the meal. Go, seat yourself at the table."

"Anywhere?"

"At the far end. That way you won't be tempted to steal any of *my* food." She gave him a sly look.

Brand decided this was possibly a form of flirting among the _____ (unpronounceable word)—one likely loaded with implications well beyond his comprehension. He tried an inventive response.

"Watch out, I might just eat *your* share too!"

Charlotte giggled through her mandibles and wagged a hooked black finger at him.

"No you won't, you little hungry boy. I'm gonna eat *my* serve, then *your* serve—then *you!*"

Brand hoped this too was mere rhetorical flirting and forced an engaging smile until she turned away. Then he turned and walked, pale-faced and on shaky legs, toward the table.

Charlotte noticed. She stomped over, the ceiling lanterns catching the gleam of her polished thorax. She placed two clawed appendages on her hips and glared at him in a most womanly fashion.

"This won't do." She brushed her claws against the chair at the table's end. It fluttered into a million motes of carbon. She snapped her claws, and a wooden high-seat the size of a tall carriage appeared in its place.

She placed Brand in the high seat as if he were a toddler and slammed down the barrier to hold him in. He looked out across the plateau of wood that was his high-seat dining plate, feeling quite small and helpless—but worst of all, unmanly. He noticed a great arched window to his right, which provided a good view of the darkened city below.

"Okay, we can't be eating the dust and the chalk—we need our nutrients. Let me go find something suitable." With a black flutter of exploding dimensions, she was gone.

Brand was looking around and wondering just what he was going to do next when a voice called to him from outside the window.

"*Psssst!*"

Brand shot a startled glance in the voice's direction.

"Is she gone?" came Berengar's voice in a barely audible whisper.

"*Berengar!* Yes, she's gone!" said Brand, a sudden swell of hope.

"Good..." Berengar's head poked through the window as he prepared to climb in.

"Wait!" Brand yelled out, causing Berengar to duck back.

Charlotte had appeared beside Brand's high seat, holding a completely naked and unconscious Pathar in one hooked appendage, a similarly naked and unconscious Gilfingle in another, and a squirming, crying Ms. Taloulie in a third.

At least Ms. Taloulie had had the decency to wrap some old gauze around her barrel-bellied, buxom form.

Charlotte looked quizzically at Brand.

"Wait," Brand repeated with a chuckle. "We... uh... must have proper utensils. This is a special occasion, after all."

Charlotte shrugged oddly with her many limbs. "As you wish. Personally, I find such things... cumbersome—such is not the way of the _____ (unpronounceable word). But, if it will make *you* happy..." She flicked a claw, and a full set of exquisite, gilded china populated the long table, with an entire place setting before Brand on his high-seat.

Charlotte placed the sobbing Ms. Taloulie on the large dining plate in front of Brand. Upon contact with the cold plate, Ms. Taloulie squealed and looked up.

She saw Brand and cried out, "*Brand!!!*"

Charlotte went deadly still and pressed Ms. Taloulie down into the table under a heavy hooked appendage. "Are you... *personal* with this female?!" she hissed.

"A mere acquaintance only. She's ahh... not my type..." said Brand with a careless shake of his head—*Charlotte was clearly the jealous type.*

Charlotte glared suspiciously for a moment, then picked Ms. Taloulie back up and instead placed the nude, unconscious Pathar down on Brand's plate. She walked to her place at the other end of the table and set Ms. Taloulie and Gilfingle on a large silver platter.

Charlotte sat down with surprising grace and then addressed Brand. "Is everything to your satisfaction, Brand?" Her mandibles gnashed and began to drool above the unconscious Gilfingle and the cowering, half-fainting Ms. Taloulie.

"Ah, *one more thing*—I cannot eat my food raw. It will... give me indigestion," Brand said in haste.

"*How so?* Raw food is good for the stomach," said Charlotte.

Brand could tell she was becoming vexed by the short, sharp spasms her mandibles executed—she was *really* hungry.

"I... have an... eating disorder! Which weakens my... uh, digestive constitution. I must have my meat cooked," he fumbled out in a rush.

Charlotte sighed through her mandibles and stood back up. "*Males!* Now I know what my mother was talking about..." She flicked her claws, and Ms. Taloulie and poor Gilfingle were instantly bound in ropes that grew from the platter like vines.

"Let me go find that disgusting buffoon Kurlyle; he should have finished cooking the pastries by now." She vanished in a puff of tinkling dimensional shards.

Brand thought of poor Balin and Fonicia and shook his head, then called out, "*Now, Ber!* We don't have long!"

The athletic form of Berengar flowed lithely through the arched window and leapt across the gap to the table. After this he jumped from the table to the feeding tray of Brand's high-seat and ran in his direction. The Outlander was completely naked and didn't care a whit about covering himself.

Brand was too overwhelmed with relief to notice Berengar's nudity—damn, it was good to have the great oaf around again. He forced himself not to get all teary.

A second later he saw Alucard, riding on the Outlander's back, wearing a messy turban of gauze and carrying that accursed spellbook again.

"*Alucard?* What are you doing here?! This is no place for children, and didn't I tell you to leave that cursed tome behind?!"

Seeing Alucard made him think of something else—his random floating spells hadn't been occurring here!—A bleak boon indeed.

"That book is our ticket out," said Berengar, tearing Brand out of the high-seat and then throwing Pathar over one shoulder. "Let us waste no time. Alucard, you have been practicing that damnable spell, haven't you? Are you ready yet?"

"Stand all together, then I will begin," said the froggy creature with a grin.

"Quick then, let us gather on the table. I will free Gilfingle and Ms. Taloulie," said Berengar, holding up a large shard of sharp glass like a dagger.

They dashed to the edge of the eating tray and leapt onto the table. Berengar set Pathar and Alucard down and then darted off. Alucard turned to Brand and gave him a hug. Letting go, he opened the spellbook to a page covered in an inordinately complex pattern of shifting symbols.

Brand managed to wake Pathar by slapping him on the cheeks. The old man sat up, coughing hoarsely. By now Berengar had reached the other end of the table and was sawing away at Ms.

Taloulie and Gilfingle's bonds. A second later he was cursing and disentangling himself from an effusive Ms. Taloulie and slapping Gilfingle on the face.

"Ahhhh!" cried Gilfingle as he came to. "Where am I? I had the most *terrible* dream. Thron was there, and he was eaten by a most terrible giant boy."

"It was no dream," said Berengar, his steely eyes glaring down at the old Zanonnite.

"*What?!*" cried Gilfingle in fresh alarm.

"*Quickly!* To your feet!" Berengar yanked Gilfingle up and started dragging him and Ms. Taloulie toward Brand and the others.

"Oh, Brand! Pathar! Alucard!" cried Gilfingle when they were halfway across the table. "So good to see you! Where are we? Did we not make it to Paradise? *This table sure is large.*" He hesitated, tugging his hand from Berengar's grip. "What of Ms. Martinae?"

"Fell into a pot of leek stew," said Berengar with a snarl of impatience.

Gilfingle looked crestfallen, old and tired—even more so in his stark nakedness. "Balin and Fonicia?"

"Roasted in a wood-fire oven," replied Brand, sadly.

"Oh." Gilfingle looked as though he was about to break down. "And young, beautiful Salome?"

Brand just shook his head.

"Oh dear. Not her too. Not the young ones. What of Dimi and Muls?" No one had an answer. Gilfingle began to wail, overcome with heartache and grief. "What is this place? This is not paradise! This is a *hell!*"

"Mourn later, Gilfingle. We must save ourselves now," said Berengar, his blue eyes burning fiercely.

"To where? And what for? *Everyone is gone.* My charges are forsaken. This is not correct. *Not correct!*" He fell down and began to shake with mingled wrath and grief.

Berengar picked him up and began carrying him toward Brand and the others. "Are you ready, Alucard?" he called out anxiously.

"One moment, please," said Alucard in that calm voice of his.

For a moment, it seemed things might actually work out—then Charlotte appeared.

"That damned idiot burned the food—as always," Charlotte muttered. Then she froze mid-sentence, staring in stunned confusion at her empty dining tray. She held two bits of blackened, charred pastry in her clawed hands—the remains of Balin and Fonicia.

Charlotte began to shake and vibrate with rage. "Brand?!" she roared. "*Brand?!* What is the meaning of this?!"

Her reflective, many-faceted eyes caught sight of the group gathered at the other end of the table. "*Brand?!* Get away from him, you vile little nasties! Don't you *dare* interrupt our first date!"

At that, the last remnants of her control crumbled. She screeched like a gargantuan hissing cockroach and leaped from the far end of the table in one great, pantherish bound. Rising from her pounce, she loomed above them—a black kraken rising out of the ocean to attack a seaport—only the "seaport" was a gigantic hardwood table, set with expensive tableware.

Gilfingle stood and shook his fist at her, raving incomprehensibly.

Brand observed the ludicrous image of the old man—frail in his nakedness, wild white hair flying in a hedgehog mane—standing tall and firm against the force of a she-titan from hell. It was surreal. The losses of his Zanonnites had been too much for Gilfingle's sanity, and the old man no longer perceived his own danger.

"Stand down, *fiend!* You have taken too much from us! *Where is the equity?!* The *balance* must be restored!" he roared with all the fervor of an ancient, righteous bishop.

Charlotte scuttled close and stabbed at him with her great, flexible tail. Berengar cried out and, with a great leap, landed on the edge of her tail, pushing it slightly off its mark. He began stabbing at it with his piece of glass like a butcher with a dull knife.

Charlotte whipped her tail in annoyance, flicking Berengar high into the air. He came down heavily atop a coral-decorated china tea set, shattering the pouring pot. The impact knocked the wind from him, and now he struggled weakly among the shards.

Charlotte was too irate to even consider using her powers on these small, obstreperous subjects. She struck again at the indolent Gilfingle, her tail darting forth like a cobra. But at the last second, Ms. Taloulie—loyal to the end—barreled in from the right, carrying a wash-tub-sized steel sugar bowl like a two-handed shield.

The tip of Charlotte's tail pierced the sugar bowl, and the force of the impact sent Ms. Taloulie flying into a painted clay vase full of daisies, shattering it. Charlotte tore the sugar server loose from her tail spike and dashed it to the floor.

"Third time's a charm," she said in a venomous whisper through her clicking mandibles.

Brand went to run to Gilfingle's aid—then stopped himself. *Why are we all throwing our lives away for this old man?* he thought. No. He must save himself and his friends before this fool got them all killed.

In Brand's moment of hesitation, Charlotte's tail struck again—a black blur of motion. Pathar, with an inhuman speed brought on by seeing his master in danger, launched himself off the ground and intercepted the blow, knocking Gilfingle out of its path.

With a sickening tearing sound, the spike of her tail impaled the old Zanonnite, spraying red gore from his narrow back. Pathar screamed once, then went limp. Charlotte casually flicked him to the side, where he lay completely still.

Gilfingle's horror-stricken gaze followed his faithful servant's body all the way to the floor. At this, something invisible broke inside him—a change long in the making came to fruition. His haunted yet defiant gaze rose from the corpse of his dear friend and turned, slowly, upward to the sky.

"*Zanon!!!*" he screamed—a voice so loud, so reverberant, it stunned everyone present to silence. None could believe such power had come from that frail old man. "If you truly love your servant, *aid me now!!!*"

Charlotte's tail darted forth.

With a speed Brand had never imagined the old man capable of, Gilfingle spun to face her, snatched up a salad fork the size of a halberd, and leapt high above the strike.

Charlotte's momentum carried her forward, her weight stumbling her toward the table's edge. Still airborne, Gilfingle spun and, with a two-handed thrust, stabbed the fork into Charlotte's left eye matrix.

Charlotte recoiled with a hiss of pain.

"Ahhhhhhh, old man! You have *injured* me!"

"Ready!" said Alucard, sounding quiet in comparison to the chaos.

Berengar was still crawling out from the broken pot shards. Ms. Taloulie was unconscious among the vase fragments. Gilfingle stood proud at the edge of the table, facing off against Charlotte without an ounce of hesitation.

"They won't make it!" said Brand to Alucard.

Alucard sighed loudly, as if all this were an inconvenience. "I guess I'll just have to extend the spell's zone of effect," he said, and began chanting a series of power-laden syllables that cracked and warped the air around his little blue head.

"What do you mean by that?"

Alucard was now mid-incantation and could not stop for fear of worse consequences.

Charlotte lashed out at Gilfingle with twenty appendages of rending death.

Gilfingle leapt from the table with a dessert knife to meet her in the air.

Alucard completed the final syllables of the spell known as *Geandbryll's Handy Enchantment Inside-Outer*.

A white flash.

Blackness.

Chapter 12
"Magic is in the 'air.'"

Cil sat on an empty stall in the bright morning sun, swinging her legs back and forth over the ledge of the countertop while eating a flavored frost-cone made by one of the local vendors—an ingenious snack made possible only by the cold climate here.

It had been a whole night since Brand and the others had gone, and she had spent the time procuring snacks and drinks and new clothing for herself in her usual style, all with Alucard's bullions.

Some of the locals weren't half bad, though all refused to believe that something magical was afoot in their solid town of "normalcy." It was an interesting reversal of the superstitious masses found in every other place Cil had been, including her own village—but hey, those superstitions had kept them alive, *hadn't they?*

"By Selefay," she muttered to herself, "I hope these lug-brains are doing all right." She thought of Brand and fidgeted awkwardly, a slight frown creasing her delicate features, her green eyes distant and stormy.

A sudden flash by the fountain caught her attention. She jumped to her feet and ran over to investigate.

***

Brand hit the dusty ground of the plaza and bounced to his feet, still feeling the sense of immediate peril—though he didn't know where he was.

Then the bright yellow light of his native sun struck him, and he cried out in relief.

To his right, Berengar stood up from a crouch, Gilfingle tucked under one arm like a child, and—in a feat of inhuman strength—

had Ms. Taloulie slung over his opposite shoulder like a five-stack of grain.

To his left stood Alucard, unruffled and unconcerned.

A hiss brought Brand about, and he turned to see Charlotte. The irate Queen was still out for vengeance, and now she was coming directly for him.

"Don't you dare duck out on me, *Brand!* Brand, come back here!" she cried, bounding toward him. She was still large in comparison to him—though not so large as before. Now she was about ten feet tall to his six, but her rending fangs and scorpion tail still made her a dire adversary.

Berengar dashed past Brand at a full sprint, and Brand turned and ran after the Outlander, trying desperately to catch up.
As he ran, he glanced at the marble wall on his left and realized with horror that it was the base of the fountain in the center of the plaza—*they were still tiny!*
He risked a glance over his shoulder and saw Charlotte hot on his heels. He also saw Alucard step aside like a bullfighter, letting the maddened alien creature-Queen race past. She ignored the small froggy man completely—*she had eyes only for Brand.*
He wasn't entirely sure what she had planned for him, but he didn't care to find out.

***

Cil reached the fountain, and hearing a series of strange squeaking noises, started circling it at a quick trot. Then, as she rounded the marble structure, she saw a sight that would have been hysterical—if not for the imminent danger to her friends:

There was a six-inch-tall Brand kicking up dust, coughing, and running like mad, next to a similarly sized Berengar carrying a tiny Gilfingle and Ms. Taloulie as he went.

All were completely naked, except for Brand, who still wore his stout pair of pink-and-purple striped corduroys.

Behind them ran a small black scorpion-like creature, which Cil instantly disliked. She frowned and stomped on the creature with her steel-cap shoe—crushing it into a flat mass of black chitin and green goo.

Thus ended the reign of High Queen Charlotte I.

***

Brand inspected the crushed remains of Charlotte with a grimace and a number of contrasting emotions. He felt an odd sympathy for the creature—demon, devil, alien—or whatever it was. Sure, she was a horrid thing that had caused much suffering—yet she too had been fooled by a man, taken from her home world and left in that rigged dimension. She knew no better, and even if she did, what should she have done? He shook his head sadly, then was distracted by Gilfingle, who had just come to with a shout.

"Ahhhhh!" cried the old man as he leapt to his feet. He took on a defiant stance, possibly still thinking he was mid-battle with Charlotte, but then he saw Charlotte's crushed corpse and relaxed.

He looked at Brand, Berengar, and Ms. Taloulie. Then, with an anguished look, he said, "This is all that is left of us? Only six of the once joyous and lively troop? I have failed. I am no Corrective, no guide, no true *Zanonnite!*" Tears streamed down his wrinkled cheeks as he spoke. He looked older and frailer than ever.

Brand, regardless of his beliefs, decided on a whim to support the old man in his moment of need. He thought for a moment—then the right words came to him.

Placing a hand on Gilfingle's shoulder, he said,

"Grand Corrective, *yes*—fourteen staunch Zanonnites were lost, and this is a *terrible* thing. But... did you consider that today, through our actions under your guidance, we ended the reign of a true monster? Saved the lives of hundreds, possibly *thousands,* of future pilgrims?

"Is that not a balanced trade? Fourteen lives for a thousand?

"Perhaps Zanon truly guided your hand after all..."

Gilfingle froze while his wracked mind attempted to evaluate Brand's words. He inspected Brand with blue eyes, sparkling with a trickle of hope, though it was clear he was not fully convinced. "You are a good man, Brand. These are kind words. But is it *really so?* I am not so sure. Too much evil, too much suffering has come about for it to be *truly* holy work."

"Well, yes, I do..." Brand began, but he was interrupted by a sudden rushing feeling and a whirl of motion. The world around them strained, blurred, and seemed to shrink—in actual fact the world hadn't shrunk; it was they who had grown. All the remaining survivors had returned to their normal size.

Alucard was the first to speak. "With the death of that insect, it seems the enchantments binding us to her realm have, at last, dissolved entirely."

He began inspecting his own small body. "Though perhaps, if all things were equal, I might have grown large along with you all... ahhh, a vain hope."

Wam!

"Ouch!" Brand cried, reeling back from Cil's slap.

You bloody fool!" Cil raged. "Do you know how worried I was —" She paused mid-sentence and gave an embarrassed flick of her eyes. "Not that I care what happens to *you, beanstalk!"*

Brand rubbed his head and scowled. "You didn't have to hit me!"

Cil suddenly blushed profusely and averted her eyes.

"What is it?" said Brand, confused.

"You're all, you know... no clothes."

She was right. Brand looked down in alarm. Well, he still had on the colorful corduroys, but his feet and chest were bare. *Still, it wasn't cause for such blushing as that.*

A small crowd began to gather around them, and a hushed chorus of gasps and muttering broke out.

"They act as if they've come to see a show, Ber. What's this about?"
Brand turned to the Outlander with an easy grin on his face, which quickly melted as he looked down. His eyes bulged.
"Damnit, Ber!"

He looked back up to Berengar's face and was met with a leering grin, and a burning gaze. The blond giant let out a deep, rumbling chuckle.

"Gross, man," said Brand angrily as he looked away.

Cil had her back to them and refused to look in Berengar's direction.

Until now, Ms. Taloulie had been too concerned with covering herself to notice the commotion; however *now* she became aware of the gathering crowd, and looked over at them. Seeing Berengar, she let out a great sigh and collapsed into a dead faint.

Gilfingle became cross, and an ounce of his old Grand Corrective demeanor came back to him. "Get this man some clothes! He's destroying the equilibrium of the womenfolk."

A loud cracking noise reverberated from the fountain, interrupting the comical scene and riveting the attention of all. Brand and Berengar pushed their way through the small crowd to investigate.

The miniature palace in the basin was no longer glowing, and now a great black crack began to form. With a zap, it exploded into a puff of dust. A strange popping, sucking noise erupted from the air, followed by a tearing sound. A sphere of dimensional shards exploded outward, leaving behind a black hole where the palace had been. Then, the crumbling realm of Charlotte began disgorging five hundred years of accumulated foreign particles.

A torrent of human corpses in various states of decay, maim, and digestion poured out in a wave, filling the plaza in minutes and then pushing out along the avenues. Brand thought he saw the gray-fleshed corpse of the blond-haired youth who had chased him as a giant, as it tumbled away down a side street.

Locals and travelers alike began to scream and wail at the sight, and all were forced to cling to buildings and solid structures to avoid being washed away in the flood.

The tidal wave of corpses continued ever onward and outward—flowing beyond the streets and avenues to pour in a great flood over the edge of the bluff on all sides. A few locals caught in the tide were sent screaming over the edge to fall to their deaths amid a torrent of falling corpses, finally landing in a great heap upon the floor of the Sunken Tundra one thousand feet below.

Presently, Brand was hanging from a tall stone flagpole like a sailor, Alucard perched on his shoulder. He watched with anxiety as the flow of corpses finally slowed to a stop.

Looking over the remaining carpet of corpses, Brand saw Ms. Taloulie and Berengar across from him on the roof of a square stone structure with a sign labeling it as a winery. That man really needed to get some clothes on. Nearby, on another roof, he spotted Cil and Gilfingle. Good, they were safe.

Brand heard a small tearing sound, then felt the pressure of his tight pants ease up. A moment later he distinctly felt the cool mountain breeze on his private parts—the trusty purple-pink striped corduroys had finally given out.

Brand was left high on the flagpole—completely naked. "Why now?!" he cried out.

The unconcerned voice of Alucard came from his back. "It was likely *'Geandbryll's Handy Enchantment Inside-Outer.'*"

Brand scowled and climbed down the flagpole. Then, covering

himself with Alucard's spellbook, he picked his way over the corpses to the town-master's hall. Therein he found a pair of black trousers, a set of boots, a black and white coat with a crazy star-shaped collar, and a gray blouse. Ignoring the plaintive cries of the grimy clerk, he dressed and headed for the door.

Now outside once more, he surveyed the catastrophe before him —it would take some time before the townsfolk and visiting pilgrims came out of their state of shock. Then he saw Gilfingle standing nearby and instantly knew the old man was not well. Gilfingle was hunched slightly forward and his hands were clenching and unclenching, as if grasping at something unseen. His face was impassive, his blue eyes once bright were now cold and hard.

Brand approached and assayed a greeting. The old man said nothing in response. Looking closely, Brand could see that the old man's cheek was twitching oddly, and his body began to shake in an eerie fashion.

It seemed that this final horror had shattered whatever stability the old man had had left. The visible sight of so many pilgrims' corpses had finally tilted Gilfingle over the edge.

Brand spoke to him hurriedly. "Gilfingle? *Gilfingle? Grand Corrective?!* Are you okay, man?"

Gilfingle muttered, "All these poor souls. All these who were tricked into treachery by that vile spawn of hell!"

"I know, but the trap is destroyed now—she is dead too."

"It is not enough! *Not enough!* Where is the *equity!?* No. No! The balance must be restored! *The balance must be restored!!!" he punctuated each word with cold, fanatical deliberation.*

It was at this inopportune moment that the grimy clerk decided to totter out of the town-master's hall in order to reprimand Brand. Then, seeing the mass of bodies littering the ground, he went into a sort of dumb shock and stared wide-eyed out across the square.

Instantly he became the focus of Gilfingle's ire. The old man's bearing changed and he straightened to his full height like an old caterpillar. He even seemed taller, broader. He turned and walked with ominous strides toward the grimy clerk, his eyes burning like pits of blue hellfire.

Brand went to intervene, wanting to avoid trouble with the town constables, but Berengar held him back.

"Nay lad, this is justice."

The fat clerk looked uncomprehendingly at Gilfingle as he approached. Gilfingle grabbed the man by the collar in a vicious grip and drew him upwards to peer into his face.

The fat man snapped out of his confusion and became instantly hostile. "How dare you lay hands on me? I shall call the constables!" He then looked down, noticing Gilfingle's nakedness for the first time. "What is this? Some sort of sick ritual?"

Gilfingle ignored the man's complaints. "You have allowed uncountable pilgrims to be slaughtered in a nightmare so unthinkable that its very concept would turn your hair white and your skin gray—had *you* been the one to experience it!!!" Gilfingle said with deadly control.

"I already told you. I do not believe in such *nonsense.*"

"Yet, time after time you let them touch that—that *cursed thing!*" He stabbed a bony finger in the direction of the fountain.

"As I said, I assumed they tossed themselves off the cliff or something."

"*You lie.* You came each time to claim their possessions!" He spat out a mouthful of excess saliva, then continued, "You are worse than that—*that demon!* I should end your fool's life right now!" He raised a vicious, narrow fist.

"*Wait!*" said the town clerk, realizing the old man meant business—and lacking faith in his own guards. "What do you want? I'll do whatever you want!"

"Give me a *sword*. A *good* sword. A *large* sword."

"What are you going to do with it?"

"Get me the sword."

"Okay, but the largest one I have will be twenty gold bullions." Then, seeing Gilfingle's uncompromising stare: "But it's a fortune —"

Wham! Gilfingle slammed the man's head against a marble column.

"*Ouch! Okay!*" the clerk gulped in terror.

After this, Gilfingle led the fat man off into the town-master's hall like a whipped hound.

Brand and the others had watched the scene play out in amazement.

After an awkward moment of hesitation, Ms. Taloulie followed after Gilfingle at a brisk trot, covering herself with her hands as she went.

"Well," said Berengar. "The old man's still got a good heart in him. If it were me I would have chopped off the clerk's head."

Brand was distracted from the conversation as he saw two figures approaching. At first he didn't recognize them for their horrid faces, but as they neared, he realized who they were. "Muls! Dimi! *You're alive?!*"

They came furtively forward, afraid the others would sicken at the sight of their faces—they were indeed dreadful.

Brand tried not to show his disgust and said, "I'm glad you made it!—but, *how?*"

Dimi spoke hesitantly. "Thank you, Brand. *The monsters*... They thought we..." She looked at Muls with a fondness that hadn't been there before. "The monsters thought we were 'the queen's servants' because of our horrid faces, and feared to touch us..." She shuddered. "Oh but it was a terrible place."

Muls interjected sullenly, "They killed Thron."

Dimi squeezed his hand and looked at him, her grotesque face cracking into what might be a comforting smile.

Brand observed a certain tightness to their lips, a paleness to their faces. They had been through much—but they had *survived. They were harder.*

"What of the others? Gilfingle? *Salome?*" said Dimi.

Brand sighed. "Gilfingle and Ms. Taloulie are in the town-master's hall... That is all."

Dimi began to weep. "Oh Salome. Dear sister... Tell me, Brand, was it bad?"

Brand paled, recalling the image of Salome's form exploding before him into a cloud of red vapor before being sucked into Charlotte's maw. "She died a brave and painless death, protecting someone she loved," he said.

Dimi continued to weep but seemed a little reassured. "Thanks, Brand. That's something. We shall go to find the Grand Corrective."

Brand nodded, and off they went.

Brand, Cil, and Berengar located the bundle of their gear Cil had made from Salome's sarong and rearmed themselves. After this they purchased water and a week's rations for the four of them. This took them, in all, about twenty minutes, and now they were ready to continue their journey.

Brand was brought around by a call from Gilfingle. *"Hoy, Brand!"*

Brand and the others turned to gaze with awe at the new and much-changed Gilfingle.

The old man was not the Gilfingle of old. He now wore a pair of straight-legged gray leather trousers tucked into solid black boots. He had torn the sleeves off a heavy flaxen shirt and wore it like a vest, displaying a set of dangerous, wiry arms—goose-skinned and blue from the cold.

He had cut off his beard and whiskers, revealing pettishly downturned lips and a harsh, pointy chin, which gave his face a brutal, pinched look. He had tied his gray mane into a loose ponytail and drawn a greasy black bandana over the top.

His eyes were cold blue chips of lapis lazuli, and strapped to his back was an enormous single-bladed sword of curious craftsmanship. It had an ornate hilt of red leather, a spiky bronze guard, and strange markings etched into the flat of the blade.

"*Grand Corrective?*" Brand stuttered, somewhat taken aback by the hard look in the old man's eyes.

"No longer, good Brand." His voice was calm, certain, but with a harsh, steely note to it. "I no longer deserve that title. No, I have come to realize that Zanon intends a different path for me. There are those who can successfully guide Zanon's children to balance and tranquility, and there are others who are meant to scourge this world of the evil things which threaten that balance. *This* is what *I* was meant for. Henceforth, I am Gilfingle *the Equalizer.*"

Gilfingle stared broodingly to the south, as if already perceiving an evil presence in need of retribution. He made a quick, cutting gesture with his right hand and called out, "Shield-maiden Taloulie? *Quickly now!*"

"Coming!" Ms. Taloulie bounded forth from the town-master's hall, carrying a large rolled-up chart. She was wearing a makeshift kilt, re-tailored from a heavy woolen cloak. On her chest she wore a shirt of chain mail over a light woolen blouse. She had a wooden and steel buckler strapped to her right arm and a small round helm nestled on the crown of her large head. At her waist hung an axe, a longsword, and a crossbow. She pulled up short and placed the chart into Gilfingle's waiting hand.

"Thank you," Gilfingle said, turning back to Brand and unrolling the chart. "You aided me in my pilgrimage. I shall return the favor."

He motioned for Brand to look at the map.

"I located this among the great cache of treasures left behind by pilgrims. It's a more complete version of the old sketch you hold. Here—this is the town we're in, labeled 'Shie'Naru.'

"If you go this way"—he traced a jagged line running west of their current location—"this is the precipice you see. It stretches west like a great rampart against the Sunken Tundra.

"Follow it westward for two days' march, and you'll see another bluff, just like the one we're on now. This is the location of your artifact."

Brand pulled out his rough map. It was true—superimposed over each other, the charts lined up. Gilfingle's new map filled in all the missing gaps and included recent updates, such as the unnatural badlands to the east, and the safe roads currently used by Outlanders.

Brand forbore mentioning that, had they originally followed the Trade Road west, Twithik, Jamus, and Blakcab would still be alive —and Dimi and Muls wouldn't have lost their faces.

Then again, Brand wouldn't have joined them inside Zanon's Paradise if Salome hadn't lost her wits from the horrors she endured on the trail. *And so,* Alucard wouldn't have come with a spellbook to get Brand out.

And thus, all the Zanonnites would have perished in Charlotte's realm *after all.*

Therefore, in taking the more dangerous trail, Gilfingle had indeed saved more lives in the end.

Brand became confused, going back and forth in his mind over the logic of it.

"See, it is as I said," concluded Gilfingle. "Follow the cliffs west until you reach the next citadel of stone; there you will find what you seek."

"Thank you, Gilfingle," said Brand. "I appreciate it."

Gilfingle nodded curtly, again looking toward the southern skyline with an expression of grim brooding. "Now I must go. There is much wrong in the world in need of restitution."

He looked over his shoulder. "Shield-maiden Taloulie? Where are your charges?"

At that moment, Muls and Dimi came out of the town-master's hall. Each had wrapped their heads in a dark-red scarf so that only their eyes showed. They wore long-sleeved flaxen shirts and baggy flaxen pants, tucked into tightly wound sandals. Each wore a bandolier of knives across their chests and had a curved sword across their backs. They had leather belts hosting pouches and a number of other small weapons.

"We are here, Equalizer!" Dimi cried out as they pulled up behind Gilfingle and Ms. Taloulie.

Gilfingle introduced them with a hand gesture. "Friends, meet the *Veiled Redeemers*." He indicated Dimi and Muls, who shuffled embarrassedly on their feet. "Now," he said, turning his cold gaze southward once more, "*we go*." He began walking.

Ms. Taloulie nodded meekly and moved to follow him, clearly embarrassed by her new outfit.

Berengar grabbed her arm and held her still. "You wear it well. I have seen kings wear their armor less nobly than you. Do not be ashamed, *Shield-maiden Taloulie*."

Ms. Taloulie flushed and answered quickly. "Thank you, Berengar, for... everything."

Berengar grabbed her, pulled her close, and kissed her passionately on the lips until she was gasping for air. Gilfingle, turning to see why she had not followed, observed the affair without emotion, his face impassive.

"Oh... oh... oh," Ms. Taloulie gasped. "You *really* must stop." But she was smiling broadly. "Thanks, Berengar. I needed that. Goodbye."

"Good luck," he grunted, with a grin that flashed his pointy canines.

Ms. Taloulie nodded, then trotted nervously after Gilfingle, the Veiled Redeemers close at her heels.

"Berengar!" cried Cil. "You are terrible!"

"What? *She needed a kiss!... Ow!"*—Cil had boxed his ears.

Brand found himself laughing—despite all that they had been through. Berengar had a way with people like that. They watched the dwindling forms of Gilfingle and Ms. Taloulie, and the *Veiled Redeemers* as they started across the natural stone bridge. Berengar spoke first. "Did you see how he leapt at that fiend's tail? And the fell blow he dealt to its eye? Such a blow as even I cannot lay claim to..." Berengar's eyes narrowed, and he made a protective sign to the sky.

Brand knew what was coming next.

"Perhaps Zanon's spirit really did grace him with strength?" Berengar continued, scratching his chin as he glanced at Brand with wild eyes.

"Perhaps..." said Brand. He was more critical. "Or perhaps it was just the fact that Gilfingle believed it so thoroughly himself."

"Surely not!" Berengar said with a scowl. "After all you have seen, you still doubt?"

"I admit there is much I do not yet understand, but surely not *gods,*" said Brand with a nervous chuckle. Then, recovering his stubbornness, "I believe in *science,* and surely magic and all such things have a logical explanation."

"Indeed, for magic *is* science," announced Alucard, profoundly.

"Oh?" said Brand with a frown. "Care to explain?"

"It is self-evident. It would be like trying to extrapolate the statement, 'You are stupid,' by saying, 'It means that you are stupid.'"

Brand waved his hand in irritation. "You make no sense."

Alucard shrugged. "If you know, you know."

Brand straightened and looked at Alucard, his green eyes narrowing. "Well then, *Wizard,* if you know all about this stuff, how does magic work?"

Alucard replied without hesitation, clearly quoting something he had read:

"In order to alter the natural laws of this universe, one must think outside the box—literally, outside the laws of this universe. A task impossible for a mind which is itself subject to those same laws—or is it?

One solution to such a problem would be to:

1. Achieve a viewpoint that exists outside of this universe, independent from, and not subject to its laws—which can then observe the fundamental secrets of such laws from without.

2. Develop a method of communication with such a viewpoint.

All of this was mere theoretical conjecture—that is, until first contact was made with the Lantern Lights."

Brand stared blankly for a moment, then hid his lack of understanding with a jibe. "And you simply memorized all of this from your little *book*, hey?"

Alucard bristled. "And if so, *what then?*"

"Well," said Brand, chuckling at Alucard's display of sass, "tell me then, in your own words, how *does* a spell work?"

"Based on what I have read, it seems that everything in this universe is fundamentally a vibration. Thus a spell is an exact pattern of vibrations, which equate to, alter, or oppose a particular fundamental factor of this universe—or that of another universe. There may also be worlds based entirely on concept, which would have no vibrations at all. But in such places, spells would likely be redundant in any case."

"*Huh,*" said Brand thoughtfully. "So they are a sort of scientific code to *'cheat'* nature?"

"You could say that."

"And what are the Lantern Lights?"

"Thus far, I have not come across more than casual references to them. But I gather they have something to do with isolating the precise vibrations needed to form spells."

"All interesting," said Brand, casting a doubtful glance at Alucard, "still, I sense a fallacy somewhere. Surely such things aren't as simple as you suggest?"

Alucard did not bother to argue. Instead, he gave his peculiar, subtle shrug.

Cil was grinning and said, "He's outwitted you, Brand."

Berengar looked uncomfortable, then growled stubbornly, "It's not wise to trust magic... but it saved us back there, and I trust *Alucard*. I thought Brand was the smartest person I knew, but now I see I was wrong." He said it with all the frankness that made up his lighthearted, honest self.

"You guys can't be serious?!" Brand said. Then, tossing his arms in the air, he gave up and said, "Let's go."

They began heading down the main avenue toward the edge of town, stepping delicately across the bed of corpses.

After a moment, Brand said, "Say, you've been awful quiet this morning, Cil."

A slight smile lit Cil's face. She looked away and pretended to be cross. "That's because *you,* beanstalk, are doing enough talking for the lot of us! Also, nobody thanked me for looking after the gear, or thought to ask how I was doing after having to spend a whole night in one of those squalid taverns!"

"*By Makmellah!* While we were clinging to life, fighting giant demons in an unknown hell, you were worrying about the quality of your bedsheets!"

Cil shook her fist at him. "They were *dirty*! And they had *bugs*!"

Brand laughed out loud and asked, "What money did you use to pay for all that?—I noticed you have new clothes as well."

Cil became suddenly sweet. "Oh... I may have borrowed a little from Alucard's pouch—I didn't spend all that much!"

"It's ok. I forgive you," said Alucard placidly.

Cil thought of something else she had found in Alucard's pouch too, which made her lips twitch with mirth, but she didn't tell Brand about this.

"Hmmm. Spending others' money, hey?" said Brand.

"Okay, I'll let the insult slide this time," said Cil, all smiles.

"Yeah, yeah," said Brand.

They reached the stone bridge and started back across it. The magnificent view of the Sunken Tundra stretched out on both sides, but this time Brand took care to walk in the center of the walkway. A few minutes later, they reached the mainland and began heading west, following the great precipice.

Brand suddenly paused. "Cil, are you sure you want to come west with us? The main road there heads directly south to Keel. That would be the fastest way to get a boat back to your village."

Cil hesitated awkwardly, then said, "It's ok, I can head south with you guys once you get your artifact—after that you'll need to travel to Keel to secure transport back to Revilis Ko'hur anyway."

Brand shrugged, then looked at Alucard with narrowed eyes. "I never did get to find out where you got those bullions from?"

"From the box in the Zanonnites' wagon," Alucard replied, sauntering casually along at Brand's side, his webbed feet making small smacking sounds as he rocked back and forth in his curious strutting gait. *Zero guilt. All swag.*

"What? Are you a little Waggler now, that you would steel from the Zanonnites' community box?—Money collected from donations to fund the good of the Zanonnites? And didn't think to offer any of it back to Gilfingle as he left?"

"In a word... Yes."

"Yes *what*?" Brand said, now confused himself.

"It is as you said. I took the bullions from the community chest, meant to fund the good of the Zanonnites, and did not think to offer it back to Gilfingle."

Brand scowled. "But Al, that was their *community* treasure!"

Alucard shrugged. "They left the treasure behind when the heat sloths came, thus it belonged to nobody. After this fact, I found it. Therefore, it belongs to me. I fail to see how the disrelated fact of it originally being Gilfingle's treasure somehow connects to this other disrelated fact of giving Gilfingle some of *my* treasure?"

"The critter's got a point, Brand," chuckled Berengar. "Finders keepers in the Outlands."

"Don't encourage him! Also, don't call him 'critter.'" Brand snapped, then seeing he wasn't winning the argument, hunched his shoulders and walked on in silence—*being a parent was hard work.*

The sky was bright and clear in these parts, the air frigid and thin. To the north, beyond the great precipice, stretched the Sunken Tundra: a panorama of endless black dirt, pockmarked by frozen muddy lakes and occasional patches of thick dry grass, running forever northward before finally merging with the snowcapped range that marked the boundary of the Borderlands. To the south ran a forest of tall, dark trees. The trees were mixed in type, size, and color, but all were of a healthier, cleaner nature than those of the *Darkwood Runs.* Between the forest and the precipice ran a narrow strip of stone, almost like a path that traced the edge of the cliff.

The companions followed the narrow path west for two days, sleeping in small temporary shelters and using windbreaks with fires that Berengar set up—without which they would have likely frozen to death.

At around noon on the third day, under a sky of thick gray

clouds, they rounded a granite outcrop and another great bluff came into view. It stood alone, a few hundred feet out from the mainland, rising above the lowlands like a great floating island. The megalithic structure could be seen dominating the entire bluff, a structure of marble or crystal built with odd angles and alien architecture.

"There it is!" said Brand excitedly.

They picked up their pace and ran until they were standing directly across from it. However, something was amiss—there was no stone arch connecting the bluff to the mainland.

Berengar squinted at the sheer granite cliffs, shaking his head, then kicked a bit of rubble over the edge. "It's crumbled. But by Zom, God of Thunder, what did this? Based on these fragments, it looks as if it was blasted into a million pieces."

"A spell," said Alucard.

"How do you know that?" asked Brand, giving Alucard a critical look.

"Just a hunch, I suppose."

"Great," said Brand, flicking his head back to stare at the sky in frustration, his arms akimbo.

"Even I, with a full set of mountaineering gear, could not scale that bluff," said Berengar with a perplexed shake of his head.

Brand turned to Cil. "Any ideas?"

Cil shrugged. "Beats me."

Brand looked with some misgiving toward Alucard. The little knave had been quite resourceful lately.

"Alucard?"

The small froggy creature looked up impassively. His once bright-blue eyes were now dark blue with an iris of fiery gold containing black diamond-shaped pupils. "I must admit that certain expedients have been forming in my mind."

A pause. Then a toothy grin split his round, rubbery head.

Brand inspected his friend—or child, or whatever he was—
silently for a moment. Alucard's skin was a light blue these days,
and he had grown a small orange ridge in the middle of his head
that expanded into a rubbery dorsal fin running down his back.

"Yes?" said Brand.

"The flying spell," replied Alucard.

"You mean the one that left me floating randomly until it was
removed by being sucked into a demonic, nightmare realm?"

"Technically it was only held in abeyance in Charlotte's realm...
it was really *'Geandbryll's Handy Enchantment Inside-Outer'* that
got rid of it."

"*Great.* I feel *so* much better," replied Brand.

"I have practiced my pronunciation since then."

Brand still hesitated, crossing his arms and looking toward the
treeline. As he watched, a furry groundhog-like creature, as big as
a dog and with swollen, chubby cheeks, crawled out of the ground
and began tearing up an old log to access the grubs inside.

Brand rubbed his chin thoughtfully as an idea formed in his
mind. He turned back to Alucard.

"Say, Alucard... do you see yon giant, furry rodent?"

Alucard followed his gaze. "I do."

"*Don't you dare,*" said Cil crossly.

Two minutes later, the groundhog looked up in sudden alarm as
Alucard finished the final syllable of the spell. There was a sucking
magnetism of shifting energy and warping space. The groundhog
froze, its eyes wide and perplexed. All of its fur stood on end. It
knew something had changed, but it did not know *what.*

Tentatively, it hopped here and there, testing its limbs. Then,
wondrously, it leapt forth, kicking and paddling its legs as if
swimming in water—only it was swimming in the air. It landed ten
feet above the ground on the branch of a dead tree. It squeaked
with pleasure, and Brand swore it smiled, its buck teeth showing

between chubby cheeks.

"Oh, how adorable!" Cil cried.

"I'll take that as a successful experiment," said Alucard proudly.

"It does seem to be doing well," said Brand.

The furry critter poised in a tight crouch, then sprang skyward, soaring higher and higher until it paddled through the air above the trees.

Seemingly out of nowhere, a great leather-winged beast appeared, with an angular head and large talons. It shot toward the groundhog like an arrow and snatched it out of the air. The furry creature let out one great squeak and was carried out of sight.

"Let us try another route to the bluff," said Brand dryly.

"We shall take... additional precautions," said Alucard shortly.

Cil cried out in alarm and smacked Brand on the back of the head. "Oh, the *poor* thing! This is all your fault!"

"*Ouch!* Hey! I didn't know!"

"So," said Alucard, "I can only cast the spell on one person at a time. Specifically, who shall I cast the spell on?"

Brand looked to Berengar.

"Not I," said the blond giant, displaying his palms.

They looked at Cil.

"What, am I to be the next 'successful' test?" she said, with great sarcasm.

After much bickering, all decided to draw straws. Whoever drew the shortest straw would be first to bear the spell's effect.

Berengar began making the straws from some dead grass and meticulously measured their lengths. As he did this, Brand leaned over and whispered something to Alucard, who nodded impassively. While Brand was distracted talking to Alucard, Berengar took a moment to whisper something into Cil's ear. Cil nodded and grinned.

Berengar clapped his hands together. "Okay, I'm ready. Cil shall hold the straws. Brand, you go first."

Cil gripped the straws in her hand and held them before Brand. He chose the middle one and tugged. The straw was short. Cil expected Brand to disagree with her methods, but he didn't.

Instead, he cried out, "No! How could my luck be so dreadful!?" He looked forlornly toward his companions.

Cil and Berengar stood with their faces carefully controlled.

"Better luck next time, aye, Brand?" said Berengar with a compassionate pat on the back. "Well, it's settled. Cast the spell."

Brand let out a sad sigh. "Well, if it must be so... for my friends, I shall risk even *my life*. Alucard, please, do the deed." He held up his arms in resignation.

Alucard practiced once in his head, then recited the power-laden syllables aloud with great force and deft elocution. That same strange sucking feeling as before—the natural laws of space, time, and energy protesting their unnatural alteration. *Zap.*

Berengar and Cil stared at Brand expectantly. Brand stared back, face inscrutable, then lowered his arms.

"Well?" said Cil impatiently. "Can you fly?"

Berengar grinned. "Well, Brand? What does it feel like? Does it feel like when we were gliding—yeow! *Brand, you dirty dog!"*

Berengar had lurched forward into the air in his excitement...

Chapter 13
"The Living Light."

The Children of Light, so kind and wise, now became as gods in man's eyes.
They aided, guided, and lead,
They came to live and talk with men.
Worshipped by all on hallowed ground, With trysts of words and vows profound.
But from earthly pleasures did creep,
A sickness born of vanity, deep
The Children of Light, once clean and bright,
Now marred by hatred, wrought with strife
They raged long, and cracked the earth,
Man's vows were false, of little worth
Within their wrath, they lost their sight
No more the wise, the Children of Light
Slowly, over lengthening time,
Diminished, waned, the Children's might
Now still unknown, the Children's plight,
Those left alone in endless night
"The Lament of the Children of Light."—Peasants' folklore poem

***

Twenty minutes had passed since Alucard had cast the spell on Berengar.
Presently, the companions were floating through the thin air across the great gap between the bluff and the mainland. A thousand feet

below, the Sunken Tundra stretched out in misty silence.

Berengar bobbed along like a laden tinker's wagon, with Cil strapped to his left side, steel rod out and ready, and Brand strapped to his right side with his crossbow. Alucard rode on his shoulders with the spellbook open.

"That was a dirty trick," grumbled Berengar. "If I didn't enjoy flying so much, I'd have knocked your teeth out."
"Come now, Ber, you know you're the only one strong enough to carry the rest. It was the only option," replied Brand with a wry chuckle.

"Yeah, yeah, just keep those flying lizards off our backs," Berengar replied stonily.

Berengar was referring to the eagle-sized, leathery creatures nesting in great numbers along the cliff face. They flitted here and there, inspecting the group from a distance.

"You hear that?" Berengar bellowed, addressing the creatures anxiously. "Stay away unless you want to feel the taste of *cold steel!*"

Though Berengar didn't know it, his last command was completely unnecessary. Not even starvation could induce the reptiles in question to approach that strange, many-armed, many-eyed creature that floated in a sickly, awkward fashion through their territory and polluted the airways with its noisome chattering.

Berengar fumbled his way through the unusual mechanics of flying by incantation. It was something that had no set instructions and would have to be learned slowly, through much practice. Perhaps a master wizard, after years of study, could soar like a bird of prey through the sky—but Berengar merely floated along like a lopsided jellyfish, which slowly rotated in circles and constantly drifted off course.

There were sudden rises and dips when Berengar failed to estimate wind currents, eliciting ignoble screams from the entire group—including Berengar himself. There were startling bursts of speed when Berengar became excited, followed by jerking halts as he lost his train of thought.

Eventually, a heavily perspiring and nervously exhausted group of companions touched down on the bluff.

"Well. That went well," said Alucard without a trace of sarcasm.

Berengar kissed and hugged the ground. "I never want to leave you again."

"If I wasn't so hungry, I would have thrown up," said Cil.

Brand ran a shaky hand through his golden hair. "At least we're here."

They decided now was as good a time as any for lunch. They could eat and calm their nerves at the same time. As they ate, the clouds began to shift, causing occasional shafts of golden light to pierce the otherwise gray and dreary landscape, before being shut out again a few minutes later.

"Say, would you look at that cathedral, or whatever it is?" mumbled Brand around a mouthful of cheese.

"Aye, it's one of the finest structures I've seen. And that's saying something after touring the Vizier's Palace in Devirien'Su."

"Where *haven't* you been?" said Brand derisively.

"I hadn't been here until today," said Berengar frankly. "Now let's finish up and retrieve this damnable artifact we came for."

The companions approached the awesome structure that loomed before them, a great work of the mysterious Ancients, seemingly carved from a gigantic column of opaque quartz. Precise patterns had been carved into the quartz and then inlaid with another type of crystal—*photonic crystals*—and it gleamed and twinkled before them. Then, as a fleeting shaft of light fell upon the structure, the companions watched in awe as the carven patterns seemed to catch the light and channel it along their grooves. Within seconds, the entire structure was illuminated in a blazing glow. The sight was so dazzling as to almost overwhelm the senses.

All but Alucard gasped.

"..." Berengar rubbed the tears from his eyes and then looked again. "There isn't a word to describe this beauty," he said in awe. "I shall need to get some of this crystal for my next piece."

Cil merely nodded dumbly in reply, her green eyes alive with wonder.

Brand was speechless too, and as he let his eyes linger on a particular section of glowing swirls for too long, he got the strange feeling that it was drawing him toward it—not his body, but his mind. He had a fleeting sense of misgiving, then it was gone.

Barring the entrance to the great hall was a gigantic set of double doors, carved of white marble and hung under an elaborately carved arch of purple crystal. Across the gap between the double doors was a withered piece of parchment, ostensibly sealing the great doors shut.

The party stepped close to the doors and inspected the tattered paper. It looked as if it had once held a circular pattern of symbols, like those in Alucard's spellbook, but no longer. The years had withered away the fiber of the parchment, and now it hung faded and limp, barely attached to the door. If it had once held forceful symbols, they had long since wriggled free and escaped into the cosmos.

Brand nervously raised a hand, then looked at the others questioningly.

"I detect no forceful sigils. It is safe," said Alucard in his strange, clipped tone.

Brand reached out and tore loose the parchment. Nothing happened. He pushed at one of the doors, expecting to need Berengar's help, but he didn't. Instead, it swung open as smoothly as a well-oiled tavern door. Brand pushed the other one next, and now both doors swung slowly inward, one a little ahead of the other.

As they stepped out of the midday glare, their eyes adjusted to the inner dusk, and the shadowy outlines of the hall, and its strange devices began to materialize before them.

The place was an enormous, cathedral-like hall with a wide raised pillar at its far end, and beyond that, a gallery. The vaulted chamber was over seven hundred feet long and about two hundred feet wide. Three hundred feet above, its vaulted ceiling hosted innumerable reliefs of carved patterns. Likewise, the walls were carved with intricate angles and designs that combined with the ceiling's reliefs to form a single coherent structure.

The three companions moved further into the dim hall, their footsteps echoing loudly in the silence, making them feel strangely self-conscious.

So ancient and solemn, so grand and majestic was the place that for a moment the companions were frozen in breathless silence. They watched as light and wind swept inward through the open doors, enlivening a space that had been held so long in silent stillness. Then something amazing happened. A low humming sound began—like the quiet, beautiful chanting of a monastic choir. Brand looked around sharply for the source, then realized in awe that it was vibrating from the material of the structure itself. "It is the wind, blowing in and flowing through the patterns," said Alucard.

Words failed the companions as they observed the effect for a time. Then, they turned their attention back to the strange outlines they had seen from the entrance. Great cylindrical tubes of opaque glass were positioned at regular intervals along the walls of the hall. Each tube had a thick metallic cable attached to its head. The cables ran along the floor, eventually converging on and attaching to the central raised pillar. The body of the pillar was dotted with hundreds of metallic sockets and their dangling cables. On the pillar's platform above rested a clump of shadowy objects, indistinguishable at this distance.

Suddenly, the place's initial impression of beauty was replaced by an indefinable aspect of the sinister. Though none of the companions understood the purpose of the cylindrical tubes, they somehow sensed something horribly unnatural about them.

Perhaps it was because the entire setup brought to mind the image of a great black spider sitting at the center of its web, each strand connecting to a cocoon of stored nutrients.

The hairs at the base of Brand's neck prickled, and he hesitated, almost stopping. However, not wishing to look like a coward in front of Cil, he walked on—straight-backed and stiff-legged.

They made their way across the room, tentatively avoiding the thick snake-like cables as they went. The vaulted hall was so massive in its dimensions that, for a time, it felt like they were not making any progress at all. However, after what seemed an eternity, the dazed companions reached the pillar and saw it was of polished white stone.

A steep staircase of the same white stone spiraled about the pillar, giving access to the platform some fifteen feet above. The companions made their way up with Brand and Cil in the lead while Berengar followed behind, his wide eyes darting in all directions, his great sword shifting about in quick, jumpy movements.

Brand reached the top of the stairs and gaped for a stunned moment before gasping out, "Look!"

There it was, positioned atop a circular metallic pedestal at the back of the platform...

The cylindrical artifact from the chart—the object of their quest, and the payment to purchase his mother's freedom.

Brand's immediate urge was to rush over and grab it, stuff it into his pouch and dash from the cathedral—but prudence forced him to stop and inspect more of the strange system first.

There were a series of what looked like workbenches, each with buttons, knobs, and levers, as well as strange reflective sheets of glass he had never seen before.

All was dark and quiet. Nothing had been touched for a very long time.

Alucard strolled over to one of the benches, scratched his chin, inspected an ancient symbol, reached up with one stubby frog finger, and pressed a button.

"Halt!" Brand, Cil, and Berengar all yelled in sudden alarm.

A whiz and a whirl. A gentle humming from all the benches. A second later, all the buttons lit up with a strange blue light from beneath, and all the sheets of glass were illuminated in the same manner—displaying moving pictures and streams of symbols, the language of the Ancients.

Nothing else happened.

Alucard turned to look at them questioningly, as if their excitement was the most ridiculous thing in the world.

"Well," said Brand, with a practiced casual yet debonair gesture, "seems like this place had us all in a funk for nothing. Ho there, Al! What did those moving symbols say?"

"'Power saver mode off,'" replied Alucard, his face impassive.

"Humph... and that is supposed to mean something to me?" said Brand, scratching his chin where a wispy patch of blond stubble now grew.

"Recall the 'stored lightning' we spoke about?"

"Not in... all its aspects. However, I'm sure I grasp the gist of it overall."

"The Ancients called it 'power' or 'energy.' I believe it flows from the cylinder in your sketch and causes these machines to work."

"Fascinating. And what of these images?"

"It appears these devices have the ability to convert written commands into concepts, via an intermediate step of imagery impression. Certainly a far better medium than words."

"Indeed. However, some of these other images seem odd, even peculiar and, dare I say it—*perverse,*" Brand said as he frowned down at the screen before him.

"*How so?* They seem ordinary enough to me." Alucard waddled over.

"Not so. Take... for instance, this sequence of images."

Alucard strained on tiptoes to peer over the edge of the bench at the screen. "That is a recording of various mammals carrying out their reproductive cycles."

"Yes, quite so. I realize that now—but to what purpose?" said Brand dubiously.

"I believe the Ancients practiced bio-mutation and gene modification. Such recordings would be a necessity."

"Your words, frankly speaking, are beyond me. Still though, one wouldn't want to be caught 'working' hard at this job late at night. People would surely talk."

Alucard shrugged, not getting the point, and padded over to another screen. "I wonder who or what they were using this system to communicate with?" he finally said, his eyes tracing one of the cables over to the cylindrical vats lining the walls.

"Who knows? Perhaps 'gods?'" joked Brand with a glib smile as he paced over to the power cell. He rapped his knuckles on it. "Hello! Do you hear me, gods?"

"Do not speak of the gods with flippancy," said Berengar, shaking his head and looking around.

"Gods or no," interrupted Alucard, "I would... advise caution."

"It was just a joke, Al," said Brand, forcing a laugh and leaning against the cylinder.

It popped loose from its socket with a click.

A beep sounded out from the screens. A second later, screens, buttons, and everything else went dark. The whirring stopped. Once again, they stood in dusky silence.

Nothing.

Brand smiled and shrugged. "See? No harm done. Well, let me just put that back in..."

Before Brand could move an inch, his mind was hit by a psychic cacophony so cogent, so crushing and terrifyingly forceful in its magnitude, that he was instantly overwhelmed to the point of mental breakdown.

Cil screamed and fell to the floor face-down, shaking and tearing at her hair with both hands.

Alucard toppled backward like a toad gone cross-eyed and began to moan quietly on the floor between two of the devices.

Berengar roared like a speared lion and tumbled from the staircase to the floor fifteen feet below. He landed on his back and began thrashing terribly—his great muscles straining in steely knots, his great sword flapping uselessly back and forth on the stone tiles.

Brand went to his knees, clutching at his hair as a great presence —a permeation of pain, grief, and vitreous hate—impinged on his mind like the smothering consciousness of god. It compacted Brand's self-awareness down to the eye of a needle, while it grew to infinite proportions, surrounding him and pressing in on all sides, as large as the universe itself.

It threw an ever-flowing cascade of mental impressions at him, overwhelming his perceptions. A stream of happenings, portrayed in a series of ultra-realistic visions, hit his mind's eye. It was like dreaming vividly, or like being forced to watch one of those screens on the benches, ultra close-up and with every perception engaged—not just vision—so that he was living it himself.

He saw the Ancients working in this hall, ten or twenty at a time, manipulating the devices—pressing the screens and buttons. They wore long robes of various colors, extremely ornate and extravagant, and were adorned with other trinkets and gadgets unknown to Brand. Some wore spectacles, others fantastic hats.

Regardless of their magnificent adornments, they didn't appear noble or kind. They had the faces of men who are intelligent, excited, and somewhat self-absorbed. Also, there was a greedy fervor about them, and their eyes flashed with a calculating hunger behind their spectacles—lending them the appearance of fancy-dressed insects.

The men fed their mechanisms with power, and the carved pattern on the ceiling began to glow and expand into an intricate design that made Brand's mind reel—like the sensation he felt when looking at that sunlit swirl approaching the structure—only magnified a thousand times over. A moment later, a small light appeared in the center of the great pattern on the ceiling. A tiny, glowing globe. Like a miniature sun, gently bobbing. Then more came. A second later there were hundreds, and they began to flow down the walls in crystal grooves toward the cylindrical tubes...

The same sequence, but in other halls of similar design, with other groups of elaborately dressed men and women—flick, flick, flick...

Vaguely, amongst the swirling chaos of visions, the phrase *"until first contact was made with the Lantern Lights,"* came to Brand's tortured mind...

A miniature sun now hovered above the bottom half of a cylindrical tube, the tube's upper half still raised and not connected. The globe cheerfully bobbed in the midst of that glass prison with an innocence that wrenched at Brand's heart. The entire inside surface of the glass tube was painted like a mirror.

The upper half of the tube lowered, creating a perfect seal with the lower—completely covering the light within...

More of the same scene repeated—flick, flick, flick—a thousand times in a hundred halls...

The robed men were at the controls again...

Then he was inside the glass. He saw himself as the glowing globe—a vision from its viewpoint. He stared into an endless reflection of light—a reflection of himself—on all sides, no matter which direction he looked. It confused him. It looked like his home, but different.

For a human, it would be like being trapped in a tiny room with painted scenery on all the walls, fake windows to a nonexistent seashore—all a paper-thin parody of space and freedom. This is how Brand felt watching it from the view of the light creature.

Brand saw him—*it*—try to move away from this false place of light, but it could not. The walls struck him—*it*—with painful energy. He—*it*—threw all its might and energy—its light—against that fake realm of light. It only reflected back, washing over him—*it*—burning and confusing, exhausting it.

He forgot he was not the creature, and was lost for a time pushing harder and harder against the mirror, his mind burning and aching in a manner completely indescribable in human terms, but to which there was no upper limit. It seemed to continue in an ever-compounding loop of reflected force, searing his soul...

More of the same visions, multiplied a thousandfold over a thousand years, until Brand felt his mind begin to clank apart...

More visions from the creature's view. He now felt endlessly fatigued, his mind blank and sullen, only a sleeping shadow of his former self—it had been beaten into submission. Pestering images began to hit his mind, somehow arriving from the glass tube all around him. Requests for information and instructions.

He recalled how he had seen this world before being trapped in the tube. He had seen it in its essence—infinite lines of vibrations. Similar to himself. Similar to his own world. A world of endless light. He directed his attention toward the pestering requests, and sullenly began to answer them...

Then more of the same—flick, flick, flick...

On and on it went, pouring into Brand's mind until he felt he would explode—thousands of years of learning, tinkering, and torture...

The hall was now dark and empty, yet he—the creatures— remained. The creatures and their pain...

The force eased up and Brand was himself again. He realized that the creature's pain had not dissipated over time. Trapped inside those tubes, it had only festered, multiplied, and ripened into a terrible storm. Only the powerful electric currents had held the psychic energy in check—and he, fool that he was, had released it. Now the storm weighed in on him once more, and he felt he was about to fly apart on an atomic level. He couldn't even pass out— passing out would have been a luxury.

Right when he believed he would go truly insane, something changed. A small effort, like a tiny light amidst the raging abyss— a guiding presence—and it was on his side.

It pushed back against the storm. It was Brand and *it* against the world.

Brand started receiving another idea, separate from the main torrent being pushed at him, injected into the flow—a tiny effort, as if coming from another direction. He understood the concept immediately:

Smash the glass! it said.

This orienting purpose, along with the help in his corner, enabled Brand to stand.

He staggered drunkenly toward the edge of the platform. Cil, Alucard, and Berengar were catatonic now, lying about like dead people. Brand tottered down the steps and then stumbled over the edge, landing heavily next to Berengar.

Another wave of mental anguish dropped him to his knees. Then once again, that small light in his corner. His only ally, pushing, pushing at his side.

He stood up with a red-faced roar, the veins on his neck and forehead swollen and throbbing with the effort. He staggered past Berengar's still form toward the closest cylindrical tube. It was like walking against a wave at the shore break—only a wave of psychic horror.

On and on, the images flowed into him, attempting to drown him out and crush him. Tears streamed down his face, and his breath came in gasps.

His vision narrowed, blackness pushing in from all sides so that he was barely aware of his surroundings. He was tired. So tired.

As if appearing out of thin air, suddenly the glass tube was before him.

He fumbled for the short sword at his belt, grasping at the hilt like a man who had just done a sixteen-hour day of hard labor. He managed to draw the sword. It felt so heavy. Brand struggled with the weight of the blade like a lanky puppet.

With an indescribably heroic effort, he swung the sword with all his might.

Crash! Only a slight crack appeared. The glass was thick and tough—made to withstand any experiment. Brand felt like curling into a ball and weeping. The tiny light in his corner propped him up. He gathered his strength. He swung again.

Crash!

A larger crack.

And again.

Crash!

A skull-sized portion of the tough glass detached and fell inward. A blinding beam of light—like the sun's glare, but magnified a hundredfold—shot out into the dusky hall, melting away the tip of Brand's short sword and missing his head by an inch.

The shaft of light was so thick as it radiated in a straight line from the crack that Brand could not see through it. It beamed across the hall and fell on its opposite tube.

The outer glass of the tubes was not reflective, so the beam of light did not bounce off. Instead, it bored through—melting the thick glass away in a shower of sparks and flow of molten silicon.

The beam of light thickened and intensified as it was joined by a beam radiating in the opposite direction, coming from this new tube. Then, all of a sudden, the light vanished.

The psychic storm eased ever so slightly. However, to Brand, it felt momentous.

It was enough.

He staggered to the next nearest cylinder. It was still a struggle, but it was easier, and he still had his mental ally—his guiding *Lantern Light*. Which is exactly what it was, he realized. One of the Lantern Lights was helping him.

He smashed away at the cylinder with his mutilated short sword, this time ducking away on the final blow.

Crash! Another beam of light instantly projected outward. Again, it struck the opposite tube across the hall, melting away an exit route for *its* companion. Almost immediately, the first light vanished, followed a split second later by the opposing beam released by the action of the first.

Something shifted in the air—a change of sentiment among the Lantern Lights. Perhaps they realized what was occurring. The pressure on Brand's mind lessened dramatically.

Though the psychic pressure was still terrible enough to make one unaccustomed to it want to shred away their own flesh and pluck out their eyeballs with knitting needles, to Brand it was a breath of fresh air.

He looked over to where Berengar lay. The Outlander, being of unnatural constitution and fortitude, was the first to stir. The tanned giant began to shake side to side, as if wrestling an invisible serpent, and began growling like a savage beast. It was a terrible sight to behold in itself, despite Brand's other concerns.

Brand called out in the most commanding voice he could muster, "Ber! Ber!... *Ber!!!*"

Berengar's head flicked toward Brand with a look of such concentrated fury that Brand stumbled backward, for a second forgetting his task. Berengar's blue eyes were like two pieces of flint and showed no recognition—only stark, animalistic madness. Then a flicker of humanity appeared upon seeing Brand's face.

Brand tried again, pushing through a wave of nausea. "Ber! Smash the tubes! *Smash the glass cylinders!*"

He hoped it was enough—he couldn't spend more time on Berengar. Moving to the next closest cylinder, Brand raised his short sword like a man in a daze. Then suddenly, he recalled the crossbow at his belt. Of course!

He hadn't even recalled its existence until now. He drew it forth and aimed a shot that would direct any resultant beams of light toward the wall or another tube. He fired. *Crack!*

The bolt embedded in the glass and spider-web cracks began radiating outward. The bolt was incinerated and a thin beam of light shot forth. In a flash, it was gone. Dusky silence returned. Much easier than the short sword. Brand shakily took aim again and repeated the process.

"One hundred and ninety-five to go..." he muttered with a weak smile.

He continued on like an automaton. Raise the crossbow, aim, take a breath, fire and repeat. His own personal Lantern Light pushed him on, lending him the strength to continue. Another fifteen more cylinders were shattered and their inhabitants freed.

The psychic pressure dropped more and more with each one.

Berengar leapt up without warning like an angry lion. His eyes were wild and half-blind to the world around him.

Brand cried out again. "Smash the cylinders, Ber! *Beware the light!*"

Berengar didn't answer. He hunched his great shoulders and snatched up his sword. He staggered three feet to his right and began swinging at the empty air. Then he stumbled into the stone staircase leading up to the platform. Bouncing off it, he unleashed a desperate flurry of blows upon the steps. The strikes were so swift and fierce that, in seconds, he had carved up a tiny section of the staircase. Below lay a small pile of stone dust and rubble.

Brand shuddered at the thought of facing a truly desperate Berengar in battle.

The Outlander swayed drunkenly to and fro, then flicked back his hair like a lion brandishing its mane. His eyes flitted suspiciously around the room before locking onto a great cable before him on the floor.

"*Die, foul serpent!*" he screamed, and leapt at it with a great overhead slash.

The sword stroke sheared clean through the metallic cable and bit deep into the stone below. Instantly, Berengar let out a violent shout as his whole body was rocked by a convulsion and dashed three feet back.

The captured lightning, thought Brand. *His sword must have conducted the vestiges of stagnant energy in the cable.*

The jolt of pain—being more natural, more physical—seemed to shake loose the cobwebs of madness from the giant. His hearty vitality and natural endurance surged, and he exploded from his back onto his feet in a single motion.

"Ber! Smash the glass cylinders! *Beware the light!*" Brand reiterated.

The giant still didn't answer or look at Brand, but he hunched his shoulders, gripped his sword, and nodded grimly. Then, with a terrible battle cry, he charged the nearest cylinder.

He fell upon it with a swift slash that carved a broad gash across the glass. A second later, a section of the cylinder crumbled inward. The blinding light burned forth—so close it singed the hair off his knuckles and blistered the skin.

Berengar let out a hoarse shout of alarm and danced back. But it seemed like he didn't get the point, because he charged the next cylinder and repeated the process in the same reckless manner— this time roasting the hairs off his right shoulder. He cried out again, rubbing the burn. After that, he was more careful.

Like a gusty typhoon, he swept through the hall, slamming and smashing the vats with an efficiency Brand couldn't match, barely avoiding the beams of deadly light as they burst forth.

Brand continued his own work while keeping an eye out for stray beams from Berengar's strikes. Other than that, he didn't recall the details of the next twenty minutes. All he knew was that it was a nightmare trek through a living hell of mental and physical exhaustion, where he pushed every last tendon, every synaptic circuit, to its limits.

Presently, Brand staggered numbly toward the last untouched cylinder, focusing on it like a light at the end of a tunnel. He didn't consciously know why he'd left this one for last—it just hadn't seemed as urgent as the rest. Now the mental anguish was gone and only bone-splitting physical tiredness remained.

Berengar stepped up and joined him on his right. They staggered on, side by side—the Wolf and the Lion. They would finish the task together.

They reached the cylinder and crouched low, ready to avoid the light's projected path. Each held a blade in a limp hand. They began to swing upward, awkwardly and laboriously, from their crouching positions.

Crack. Crack. Crack. Crack!

A section of the cylinder shattered and crumbled inward. They waited, expecting a blazing beam. It didn't come. Instead, a soft golden light emanated from the crack, growing brighter and brighter by the second.

Brand and Berengar watched as if in a dream, stuck in frozen rapture.

Slowly, gently, a head-sized ball of light bobbed out of the riven glass and stopped to hover before Brand. Then a consciousness reached out and touched his mind. It was like a clean, warm breeze —full of love and comfort.

Before he knew it, Brand found himself weeping once more— but this time, weeping with relief. "You... helped me?" he said. "*Why?*"

The ball of light bobbed up and down, then began circling Brand's head like an affectionate animal, its buoyant motion carrying a clear expression of joy. It circled three times. Then, with a wink, it was gone.

Berengar was weeping now too and gasped out between sobs, "Why, I've never seen a sight so beautiful."

"Oh, you big softy," said Brand, chuckling and wiping tears from his eyes. "I really don't know what just happened... Oh! *Cil and Alucard!*"

"I'd forgotten them!" said Berengar.

Though bone-tired, they jogged back across the hall to the raised platform. As they approached the steps, they heard the quiet whimpering of a girl. They bounded up the stairs and found Cil crying softly in a wretched huddle.

Brand knew what to do—this was when he needed to be a good man and comfort her. He approached from the right, angled in, and gallantly put a tender arm around her shoulder.

She hunched her strong shoulders and let loose a right hook that sent him flying over the edge of the platform.

He landed heavily on his back and looked up dazedly from the ground.

A second later, Berengar's grinning face appeared over the edge of the platform and sent down a rumble of mirth.

Brand crawled weakly back up the stairs.

Cil had stopped crying and was looking around now. "Oh, what a terrible nightmare I've just had. It's good to see your faces again." Then, looking at Brand, she added, "I mean, anything's better than... whatever *that* was."

"Yeah? Well, you didn't have to hit me!" said Brand with a growl.

"Oh, and *who* decided to fool around with the artifact?" she shot back, readying her right for another blow.

"Easy all, Al is starting to stir," said Berengar.

They turned their attention to the little blue fish man, stretched out on his back like a drunk toad. He sat up and blinked his great round eyes slowly. "There are some things one just cannot *unsee*," he said.

Cil shuddered at the recollection. "Oh, it was *horrible!* I don't want to think about it. But... why did it stop? I mean, the vile men and the balls of light..." She stopped, as if realizing she sounded crazy. "Wait, what did *you* guys see?"

"We saw it too," said Brand with a grimace.

"But what you *didn't see* was what happened at the end," said Berengar with a proud grin.

"What do you mean?" said Cil, a weary frown creasing her small, delicate brow.

"Brand saved us."

"Huh?"

Brand waved his hand and smiled smugly. "Oh, it was nothing."

Then more soberly, "No really. It was mainly the Lantern Light. Berengar, don't you recall?"

Berengar stared blankly at Brand.

"You know, it was helping us push back against the horror the whole time—the little light thingy—you know?"

More blank faces.

Brand held up his arms in irritation. "You know, the one we freed at the end, Berengar... Help me out here."

"One of them *aided you?*" Berengar rushed over and raised Brand into the air. "Brand is *god-touched!* He is chosen! Loved by the gods!"

Cil rolled her eyes. "Don't make his head any bigger."

"Put me down, you idiot!" cried Brand.

Berengar put him down, clapped his hands onto Brand's shoulders, and stared intently into his eyes. "Tell me you don't believe in gods after *that*, Brand?!"

"What's this all about?" interrupted Cil.

"You should've seen it, wench! We were smashing the—"

"*First off!*" Cil jumped to her feet, ready to clout Berengar. "*Never* call me that again!"

Berengar stared at her uncomprehendingly, and it was Brand's turn to chuckle as Cil thoroughly educated the tanned giant.

After this, Brand filled Alucard and Cil in on the whole thing.

"Wow, *beautiful,*" Cil said in awe. She looked intently at Brand for a moment, then suddenly blushing, she looked away. "Don't let your head get too big, alright?"

"He's god-touched," repeated Berengar adamantly.

"This surely fills in the gaps in one's knowledge," added Alucard.

Brand didn't know about gods, god-touched, or any of this stuff. But he was very, very *tired.* He laid back on the hard stone platform and fell into a deep, dreamless slumber.

Berengar and Cil must have fallen asleep soon after, for when Brand awoke, there they were next to him on the stone platform. Cil was huddled in a delicate ball like a cat, her head resting ever so slightly against his shoulder. Brand was hit with a range of emotions, the foremost being one of astonishment. Then, with a secret smile of joy, he sat up and looked around.

Berengar was sprawled on his back, snoring loudly with his legs dangling over the edge of the platform. This was very unusual for the giant, who was normally first to rise and last to sleep.

The fact that the giant was sleeping so deeply spoke volumes about how much effort he had exerted in resisting the psychic storm. Unlike Brand, he had had no Lantern Light to aid him— another testament to the giant's great fortitude. Brand shook his head in wonder, rubbed his eyes, and stood up.

Alucard was already awake, tinkering with various papers and notes while referring to the wizard's tome, which he had opened on a nearby bench.

"Alucard?" said Brand sternly. "What have you been up to?"

"Oh, nothing very much," replied the two-foot-high creature.

A certain subtle quirk in the creature's voice made Brand instantly suspicious. "What do you mean by *very much*?"

"I believe that is evident in the definition of the words."

Brand spoke emphatically. "Since the precise moment I and the others fell asleep, enumerate exactly, in sequence, all of the actions you took until now."

Alucard's voice took on a peculiar, plaintive tone. "This is an impossibility."

"How so?"

"Technically, you fell asleep, and then Cil, and then, sometime later, Berengar. Thus, there is no *precise* moment for your command to attach to."

"Well then, since *I* fell asleep!" Brand said with paternal wrath

—Alucard's recent behavior was making him increasingly cross.

Alucard let out a long sigh. "I am *bored* with the topic. Can we not speak of something more *interesting?*"

"Alucard, I command you. *Tell me!*"

"Oh, would you stop that racket?" groaned Cil, sitting up and rubbing her eyes. "Damn, *I'm thirsty.* Brand, pass me your waterskin, will you? Mine's out."

"How long have I been out?" said Berengar, flicking his eyes open and climbing to his feet. "Damnable hells, I'm thirsty too!"

Brand stared daggers at Alucard. "This isn't over." He tossed the waterskin to Cil and stood up. "Where is the cylinder?" he said suddenly, looking around for it.

"It rolled over the edge when you were first hit by the pervasion of psychic vibrations. I collected it for you and dutifully placed it back on the platform. At this precise minute, it sits there, by the stairs." He smiled broadly and pointed.

"That is all very well but—wait, how many hours was I asleep?"

"Hmmm?" Alucard scratched at a nonexistent chin hair, a mannerism he had picked up by copying Brand. "It's hard to say— I was not paying much attention." Then, seeing Brand's eyebrows raising, quickly added, "Approximately twenty-eight hours, thirteen minutes, and twenty-five seconds, give or take a few mili-seconds."

"*Twenty-eight hours!?* Cil, did you leave me any of that water?"

Cil grinned impishly and dangled the empty sack in front of her.

Brand stood and began to pace in agitation. *"I too am now thirsty!"*

Brand licked his lips, which now seemed suddenly parched. "Let us go indeed! Alucard? Help me retrieve any crossbow bolts on the way out.

"Yes, father." Alucard stowed the spellbook and his notes in his pouch, threw it over his back like a sack of potatoes, and waddled off to his task.

Brand gave him one last suspicious glare, then picked up his gear and got to work.

They made their way across the hall swiftly, only stopping to collect Brand's bolts—only five of which were still in good condition.

Ten minutes later, they made it back to the main entrance of the structure. The double doors were in the same condition as they had left them when they had entered. The companions once again stepped through those gigantic double doors—out from that sterile place of ancient horror, out into the clean mountain air and the glaring light of an afternoon sun.

The view was beautiful and refreshing after being in that ancient dusty hall, but none of them took the time to enjoy it. For, gazing out across the great chasm between them and the mainland, they all knew how they would have to cross it.

Alucard was the only one who seemed pleased.

Chapter 14

"The Southbound Journey."

I have discovered that when dealing with the somewhat banal dimensions of "X," "Y," and "Z," one can reach entirely new locations, worlds, planes—whatever term you prefer—by traveling a certain distance along a single isolated vector, irrespective of the other two. Planar travel is not a new concept, but this particular method presents an intriguing and novel formula.

This method is achieved by applying an anchoring syllable to two of the three natural dimensions and an untethering syllable to the remaining one you wish to traverse. For instance, if you stabilize Y and X while untethering Z, a remarkable series of hospitable worlds can be accessed. How?—Simply walk. Just be sure to mark your coordinates—if, that is, you ever wish to return home. X and Y operate similarly: choose a direction and proceed. However, I strongly caution against a downward jaunt along the Y vector without exhaustive preparation.

People often ask how I acquired my mercurial arm. I won't delve into the details of that here. Suffice it to say, the popular fable of demons inhabiting a hyperbolic "underworld" is alarmingly close to the truth of things. Should you choose to open the way—even for just a peek—be sure to have your most trusted cantrips at the ready. For, even if you have no intention of going down, you may find something coming *up*.

—Comments on Dimensions: "X," "Y," "Z." Arch Mage Tacharris Tiris'liarno

***

After another stomach-wrenching journey across the chasm, Cil and Brand were presently "catching their breath" and settling their nerves.

"Oh, come now, you white-livered swines! My flying this time was much improved! I was *made* to fly!"

"Is that the cause for all those upward bursts and downward spirals?! We even frightened away the cliff beasts," retorted Cil, her face still green.

"If *faster* is your gauge of success, then yes, you have improved," complained Brand, wiping the sweat from his forehead.

Berengar argued the point stubbornly until Brand got tired and changed the subject to that of their journey.

And so they turned their backs on the still, lifeless panorama of the Sunken Tundra and set their gaze upon the cold forest to the south, with its endless sea of dead trees, thick with thorns and underbrush—the Western Foothills.

Brand argued that they should head back and take the more, well-traveled road south, but Berengar demurred, cursing about weak-boned City-Dwellers and insisting that a direct trek south would save them vital time—didn't Brand care about his mother? At that, Brand was forced to agree—how could he argue with that? And so southward they went, into the wilderness once more.

They spent three days trekking through a forest of tall, bony trees, many dead and dried out. The floor of the forest was filled with a sea of crackling shrubbery and sharp brambles, so that they had to struggle constantly to make progress, often using their swords to cut a path before them. Most of their journey was downhill, but there were no outcrops or open views of valleys below, no breathtaking vistas—only an endless sea of bony trees, oppressive in its sameness.

In the end, Berengar gave up on tracking the land's physical features and guided them solely by the position of the pale sun, using it to keep them on a bearing due south.

Around mid-afternoon on the third day, Berengar announced that the altitude had dropped significantly, based on temperature and humidity, and that he felt they must be nearing the southern border of the Western Foothills.

Presently, the companions found the ground leveling quickly beneath their feet. Then, fighting their way through a final wall of dead brush, they came upon a clearing—green and spacious compared to the dry tangle of tightly packed trees and brush they had grown used to.

On the opposite side of the clearing was a great archway formed by the spreading branches of two gigantic oaks.

"Wow, how *beautiful*," whispered Cil quietly.

"Now that's more like it!" said Brand. "And look yonder beyond those oaks—it seems green and spacious."

"One does wonder... if there is no heavy brush, will the supply of succulent rodents dwindle?" said Alucard, a note of disappointment in his voice.

Brand and Cil made faces at him, and then Brand spoke excitedly. "Forget that, Al. Let us find some goats, sheep, or cattle —or perhaps some of those *deers* I've heard so much about."

"I smell strange scents on the wind," said Berengar.

"You said the same thing about the last forest, and it was fine, apart from those queer birds. This isn't the *Darkwood Runs*. In fact, I wouldn't be surprised if we're running alongside that highway to the south to Keel. We'll likely meet up with it soon, I shouldn't wonder."

"I have traversed over two hundred individual and unique landscapes in my travels, yet I know not a terrain like that which lies before us," said Berengar, sniffing the air.

Brand rolled his eyes, well used to the Outlander's exaggerations. "Two hundred unique... really, Ber..."

Berengar flicked back his great mane, glared around, then sniffed again. Staring intently at the forest ahead, he drew his great sword and spoke: "Small fish-man, dwarf-frog-friend, son of Brand, do you ride on your father's shoulders for the present. My sword arm needs freedom."

"Stop calling him those things, Berengar!" said Cil, one dark-red eyebrow arched in anger.

Brand gave Berengar a dirty look and kneeled down for Alucard.

"As you wish, Uncle Ber," said Alucard, taking no offense at the Outlander's words. He put away his book and padded over to Brand. "It's okay—I can walk on my own now. There is no obstructing brush."

"Well, let us see what lies ahead," said Brand, loosening his hand-crossbow and winding back a shot. He swaggered forth with the crossbow carelessly resting on his shoulder, like some kind of medieval gunslinger, hoping to cut a dashing figure in front of Cil.

In fact, he had had no mirror to see what he really looked like. His coat was completely scratched up, tattered, and stained with mud and dirt. Likewise, his tight black trousers showed patches of skin on the backs of his thighs where he'd torn them—slipping down a jagged ledge in the dark two days earlier. His boots were muddy and chipped. His hair was stained with dirt so it was more brown than blond, and was so full of twigs and leaves it looked like the tangled coiffure of a druidic nature god. His face was terribly lacerated from his encounter with a large Stay-a-while vine, and the wispy beard trailing down his delicate chin struggled to stay connected to his face. Additionally, his odor was not entirely agreeable.

Ignorant of all of the above, he rocked forward through the archway on his boots with all the swagger of a drunken pirate.

Cil, in fact—both to Brand's irritation and benefit—wasn't looking at him in any case.

Brand, growing peevish at being ignored, began noticing how haggard Cil looked and decided it might be helpful if he let her know, so she'd have the chance to fix herself up. "Wow, Cil, you really look like you've gone through a rough few days. Definitely, some fresh water will do wonders for your face and hair. We shall stop at the very next creek and—"

He didn't get to finish his sentence, for Cil had boxed him in the ear.

"*What?*" he said with an innocent grin.

Cil shoved past him and stalked ahead with the dynamic economy of a wildcat. She had drawn her steel staff and was dutifully looking out for any dangers that might or might not exist in this beautiful yet unknown woodland.

Berengar held his sword at the ready and walked on Brand's right, keeping that side covered. Alucard walked behind and in the center of the others, where he could be protected and potentially cast a spell of some use. That is, once he had learned one.

This was, in fact, the tactical fighting formation they had trained in while traveling with the Zanonnites. Brand had to be in the middle because both Cil and Berengar needed room to swing. Brand, however, could still fire his crossbow or stab effectively with his daggers, despite the limited freedom of motion.

As they walked beneath the arch of oak trees, the air became warm and heavy with the musk of decaying vegetation and stagnant water. Here the trees were healthy, large, and spaced far apart. Great oaks sat at regular intervals, their branches sprawled selfishly above large swaths of turf, and kingly dawn redwoods stood in prominent positions, hundreds of feet tall, their many branches reaching out in all directions.

These and other great trees took up enormous swaths of space, leaving the areas beneath their sprawling canopies shadowy and free of other flora. Here and there, shafts of sunlight poured through gaps in the foliage, dappling the turf below with golden light. The ground itself was a luxurious, springy loam, covered in a thin layer of fine grass that was easily torn and kicked up.

Due to the spacing of the trees and the level ground, Brand and the others were granted a view of far scenery. Up ahead, they saw pools of still water, like a series of large puddles filling depressions in the land. Brand likened it in his head to a highly colorful swamp. Instead of dark and dreary, it was green and bright. The air was moist, and everything was covered in a fine, bright-green moss.

To their right were the crumbled remains of a black marble portico, its roof long since collapsed and only half its support pillars remaining. The heavy floor tiles were still in good condition, however, and the floor of the portico now appeared as a random, lonely deck set amongst the background of ancient trees.

Brand stumbled and his boot toe gouged the delicate sward, uncovering a handful of writhing pink worms. Cil cried out in disgust and leaped away. Brand quickly withdrew his boot, and the worms glared angrily at him, each from a single, evil eye at the tip of its head. Brand scowled in disgust, grabbed a nearby log, and dashed it on top of the worms, leaving them mashed and torn.

"That will bring us ill luck," said Berengar, shaking his head.

Brand shrugged. "I didn't like the way they glared at me... Alucard! *Get away from that!*"

"*Alucard!*" Cil cried in shock.

Alucard had squatted down by the crushed worms and had begun snapping them up like a frog. He straightened at Brand's command. "Not very filling. Yet still, *quite nutritious.*"

Berengar let out a rumbling chuckle. "The kid's got the right way of it. He's learning to survive in the Outlands, taking after Uncle Ber!"

"Enough of that. You'll eat only proper food from now on," Brand snapped with a shudder.

Ahead, a paved walkway of black granite flagstones could be

seen, and they decided to follow it. The ancient pathway wound its way around a great dawn redwood and then beneath an ancient mossy archway of solid jade. Now, graceful willow trees drooped around pools of water on either side of the path, and as they walked by these pools, they could see the grass still growing under the water, signaling that the depressions were not always full. For this reason, they were also not stagnant or foul-smelling.

Here and there among the trees and pools were moss-covered platforms of marble. Some had the remains of walls tumbling about them, while others seemed to have always been solitary platforms. Overall, the impression was one of looking across an ancient parkland—intentionally landscaped with water features and beautifully nurtured trees, now overgrown with moss and partially submerged by flooding.

Strolling beyond another pair of great oaks which stretched across their path, they found themselves walking beside a medium-sized lake. The lake looked man-made, and beside it was a beautiful marble platform, projecting slightly out over the water. Five large steps gave access to the platform from the landside, and there seemed to be another set of steps leading down into the water on the lake side. On the platform were a number of constructs—rotating pedestals, jade-handled pull-bars, and a number of different levers of varying lengths and materials.

Alucard was instantly interested. "I feel a strange affinity for those things. I must look. I must see."

"Must we tamper with everything ancient and likely disastrous?" Berengar hesitated.

"I feel I must do something with these devices, Brand. It feels... *right.*"

Brand scratched his chin, considering how best to answer. The devices did resemble those within the place where they found Alucard's egg—he had never told Alucard the details of his birthplace. How did one explain to a teenager that he was a genetically engineered slave, specifically designed to operate a set of underground water management devices?

"Well, son. There's a thing called déjà vu."

"I have read something of this—a word I found in one of the view screens in the... well, never mind."

"In the *what*?" said Brand crossly.

"A slip of the tongue."

"You turned the screens back on in that hall, didn't you?"

"Not in every respect."

"What does that mean?"

"At this stage, it is a moot point." Then Alucard looked back at the levers and switches on the platform, his face taking on an avid eagerness the likes of which Brand had never seen before. "I must know more about these devices. I must... I must... *work* them... we must *maintain the flows*!" He leapt up the steps to the platform and began tinkering with a binnacle-like device.

"Get him away from that thing, Brand!" called out Berengar.

"That's enough," said Brand, dashing over and scooping Alucard up under one arm before quickly retreating from the platform. Alucard kicked his little webbed feet and roared like a naughty child. This sudden display of strong emotion was startling, and Brand decided it would be best to remove him from the locale of the water devices as quickly as possible.

Twenty minutes later, when they were far out of sight of the devices, Brand set Alucard down and looked him over.

Alucard's little smooth face, big mouth, and bulging blue eyes were the picturesque example of *morose*. "I'm fine now," he said with a sniff. The word *hangdog* could never do justice to the sulky expression on the little creature's face at that moment. He fumbled his blue thumbs, with their bulbous ends, round and round. "I just wanted to see how they *worked*. Perhaps we could..."

"No!" said Brand, cutting him short. He took Alucard by the hand, and the companions continued onward through the parkland, following the ancient path.

Over the next few hours, Alucard's complaints and suggestions became fewer and more subtle, but he had clearly been mesmerized by the water-control devices. Brand made sure to hold his hand the entire time and didn't give him the opportunity to slip away. *It must be his programming kicking in*, Brand thought. They would have to keep an eye on him for some days.

As Brand mulled this over, he noticed that a large swath of land to their right was completely flooded with about two feet of water, and he could see it ringing the trunks of the willow trees, oaks, and redwoods in that direction. A few sections of tiled marble flooring were submerged here and there, and the remains of crumbling marble structures could be seen projecting out of the water in the distance. As they walked alongside the flooded zone, it seemed to get deeper and deeper the farther south they went. Likely, the land in that section was a large basin.

Now, a great lake stretched out to their right. A hundred feet out, the domed top of a marble gazebo could be seen jutting above the water's surface, and beyond it, the tops of a colonnaded walkway. Far out in the center of the lake was a gigantic statue of a man wielding a book and a scythe. Only the upper half of the statue showed above the water, but they could see it was carved from a single pillar of white opal, which refracted the afternoon sun into a kaleidoscope of scintillating glimmers.

"*By Lyier!*" swore Berengar. "A sculpture to blind the ages with its beauty. One to make the stars fall weeping from their eyries and pour forth their living-salamander cores." He paused and took a step toward the water as if contemplating swimming over to inspect the statue.

"Easy there, Ber. You're starting to sound like Alucard now. Let us move on from this place—it seems to be making us all giddy in the head."

"For once, I agree with Beanstalk," said Cil with a grimace.

"This place... it brings an undefinable nostalgia—the sad nobility of one's mightiest efforts, long since failed and decayed." Berengar brooded with misty eyes.

"That is the precise reality of the ruins before us," said Alucard impassively. Then, with controlled excitement, "However, if someone were to operate those devices back there—I only volunteer myself because I am qualified for the task—I feel this section of the park could be most easily drained."

Berengar gave Alucard a piercing glare. "Is what you say true?"

Out of the corner of his eye, Brand thought he saw the waver of a flat, pale face looking at him from the still water of the flooded lake. He jerked his head quickly to the right, but it was gone. With goosebumps on his arms and neck, he took Berengar by the wrist and led him along the path until the statue and the flooded lake were out of sight.

The forest grew denser and less landscaped after a while, but remained lush and fertile. The trees were still covered in green moss but now boasted an increasing number of vines and mossy beards.

The paved walkway finally came to an end and they found themselves following a dirt trail that continued south.

The flooded morass continued to their right and became more and more stagnant as they traveled south, the smell of decomposing plant matter thickening with every step.

Presently, Brand noticed a shadowy mound up ahead, emerging like an untidy hillock from the stagnant water. As they got closer, he saw the mound to be a sprawling pile of large, green rectangular blocks, half submerged in the swamp. The blocks were covered in a thick bed of moss and straggling vines. They looked like giant jade coffins, but were far too big for a man. Each was at least seven feet high, seven feet wide, and over fifteen feet long. There must have been about twenty of them dumped in that messy pile, as if a giant wagon had upended and left them where they lay. Behind the tumble of blocks was a titanic shadowy mass, barely visible through the murky surface of the water. Only two long, metallic antennae projecting above the green water hinted at the nature of the submerged object.

"What devil's work is this?" said Berengar, eyeing the blocks through slit eyes.

One of the blocks had been dragged slightly out from the pile and cracked open at one end. The green slab that had sealed one end of the container now lay flat before its open mouth. The ropes used to draw the block out of the water still draped loosely about the container, but they were attached to nothing, their opposite ends frayed and stained with a dark substance. The group approached the rectangle cautiously, edging around to see into its dusky interior from a distance, fearing something might still be inside. However, when they looked in from a distance, it was empty of all but a strange pile of detritus.

The earth in front of the container was badly torn up, and the confused prints of horse, man, and something else could be seen scattered about. The third set of prints were unrecognizable—five large wide-spread toes, like a human hand, but infinitely larger. Each of the toes seen in the spoor were lean and about a foot long. A rusty mat of dried blood covered the patch of ground before the container, filling many of the deeper hoof prints with thick coagulated scabs.

"It's like the remains of a battle, but with no corpses," growled Berengar uneasily. He then traced the prints carefully and began working his way through the event out loud.

"Here I see the hoof prints of four horses and eight to ten men.

The prints arrive from the south, are light, and of regular width apart—unhurried, unstrained. Here they mill about the edge of the mound, likely tying off these ropes. There, you can see the drag marks and discolored patch of tile where this one had rested prior to being moved. Here, the horses' prints are deeper, but steady and regular, clearly dragging a heavy weight—the block.

Here, the men mill about the mouth of the container, back and forth. Then something happened. Perhaps this front slab was opened—I do not know—but now the footsteps change. They are frantic, gouging the soft earth and darting in all directions in broad heavy strides. The horses do the same, turning the earth in their haste—yet they were still tied to the container. Then, the ground is scuffed and torn up by something even greater. Two horses break free and flee to the south. See these threads? Snapped under strain. But the other two... the hoof prints deepen, then are drawn toward the inside of the vault."

Berengar squatted down, took a pinch of the brown dried blood, and touched it to his tongue. Cil and Brand winced in disgust.

"Horse blood," Berengar declared triumphantly. He stood and continued. "The men flee in all directions. Then later, a monstrous spoor trails off after the human prints. And what a spoor it is! Never have I seen such a print, even among the demons of the *Darkwood Runs*, nor those of the Borderlands."

The big man shook his head in wonder and muttered fretful words under his breath.

Inspecting the inside of the container more closely, they saw that it was empty save for a few scattered mounds of a white, gelatinous substance, now too splattered in dried horse blood.

Berengar scooped up a sample on a single thick finger and sniffed it. "I don't know what this is, but I'm a dwarf if it's organic. It has the smell of the Ancients about. Also, I'll be damned if this vault is stone. I thought it jade at first, but it's something *else.*"

Alucard walked over to the side of the container and strained on his tiptoes to look at something.

"What's that?!" snapped Brand in agitation—the horrific scene described by Berengar had unnerved him.

"It's a label," replied Alucard.

"What does it say?" Brand asked as he crowded in close. "More of these damnable ancient symbols..."

"It says," Alucard began in his emotionless, clipped tone:

"63% Hircine Magnus. 2% Octopus (for regenerative cells). 28% Homo sapiens. 7% Demon—from Thrim Rift, 2000 yards dimensional vector Y, southward progression (for systemic coordination and non-antagonistic inter-gene adaptation). Growth enzyme B362."

"That sounds... absolutely dire," croaked Brand, an uneasy feeling overtaking him.

"You understood that?" inquired Alucard.

"No, not in all its aspects... You?"

"I have read nothing of these things."

"I understand two things," said Berengar, staring intensely into Brand's eyes, "and they are: '*demon*' and '*vile sorcery.*'"

"I heard demon, but where did it mention sorcery?" replied Brand, attempting a stroke of tremulous humor.

Berengar waved an arm in a dismissive gesture. "How can you have a demon without sorcery?!"

"Shall we open another to find out what was inside?" Alucard volunteered blandly.

"Nay, let us begone from these wicked hell coffins," said Berengar urgently, the blond hairs on his arms standing up like porcupine bristles.

The companions continued south through the ancient forest, sticking to the road, and the rest of the afternoon passed without incident. Presently, the sun began to set behind the western treetops, sending shafts of orange glare through the canopy of luscious green and casting shadows across the forest floor.

Berengar called a halt.

"What?..." Brand began.

Berengar held up a finger for silence and glared around, peering into the growing darkness among the foliage. After a time, he shook his head in irritation and whispered, "Something is nearby. Earlier, I sensed something watching us. Just now, I heard something yonder." He pointed to a location deep among the trees to the right of the road.

"I don't see or hear anything," whispered Brand.

"Me neither," said Cil with a shiver.

Alucard was asleep on Brand's shoulder, taking a nap.

"I thought I saw a flash of white just now," grumbled Berengar. "I'm of a mind to hunt down this skulking shadow that watches us but never shows its face. Better to face a foe head-on than let him come to you."

"Are you mad? In this dusk, and after what we saw back at the container?"

"Perhaps," said Berengar. Then he stared at Brand with burning blue eyes for a moment, as if considering whether to divulge his thoughts. But, he only shook his head and said, "Let us continue a bit more. I'd like to find a secure place for the night."

"Sounds good. I'm sleepy," grumbled Cil, yawning like a cat.

"I think my feet are going to fall off," complained Brand.

Berengar didn't bother chiding them. He was busy surveying the forest.

"Let's go," he finally said.

"Okay," said Brand, now too watching the tree line anxiously.

They continued on for a time, and the forest grew darker with every mile. Then Brand saw it—the flash of light reflecting off shiny white skin among the trees to his right. He halted Berengar with a touch on the arm, and they stopped to glare into the shadows. As they watched, a pale naked figure danced silently across the gap between two large trees in the distance. It paused halfway, turned its head directly at them, started, let out a soft gasp, and then disappeared behind the next tree.

"What was that?" said Brand.

"A naked man," said Berengar with a sullen frown.

After an awkward silence, Berengar urged them on and they didn't see the figure again.

As the dusk of night closed in all around them, they stumbled upon a large hollow tree beside the road. They chose this for their campsite and, covering the entrance with a number of dried logs, they went to sleep, huddled together like a pack of raccoons.

The night passed without incident.

At some ungodly hour in the morning, Brand awoke stiffly with Alucard curled up in his arms and Cil's foot in his mouth. He coughed once, gasped, and turned his head in the other direction. He came face to face with Berengar's purple silk loincloth. At this, he cried out hoarsely, tossed Alucard, who landed on Cil, and rolled out of the hollow, dislodging the improvised barrier and sending the dry logs tumbling in all directions. He dry-retched for a moment and then rolled onto his back, sucking in the fresh air.

"What was that all about?" Cil moaned sleepily. Then, "Oh, come here, little sweetie. Sleep with Aunty Cil now."

"Brand. What have you done?" came Alucard's flat voice, slightly strained. A muffled struggle. Then silence.

Berengar let out a low, menacing chuckle and Brand turned to see him grinning from the darkness of the hollow. Brand shuddered, then rolled onto his side and went back to sleep.

Something touched Brand's hand, and the nature of that touch brought him instantly awake. His eyes flicked open. Right above him, eclipsing the morning light, was a shadowed face.

The face was deathly pale, almost translucent, and terribly emaciated. Two great, round eyes bulged from sunken sockets. They were light blue and full of veins. The lips were thin, almost nonexistent and hung slightly open, displaying two or three teeth and a lot of gum.

Brand screamed. The face screamed. Brand screamed again and rolled away, scrambling to his feet—"*heat sloth,*" he immediately thought. But instead of rushing him, the thing withdrew quickly and dashed off into the trees, its thin, naked haunches reflecting the morning light.

Berengar erupted from the hollow after it and gave chase with his sword. Brand dashed after Berengar. A few seconds later, Cil and Alucard drowsily staggered out of the hollow and followed behind.

By the time Brand and the others arrived, Berengar had caught the wretched creature and was questioning it.

"What are you doing following us you wretched little skulk? Trying to slit our throats while we sleep? I should spit you like a pig right now."

Brand heard this as he rounded a large oak. Then he saw what was occurring. The "creature" was in fact a deathly thin old man— completely naked and malnourished to the extreme. Berengar had him by one arm, dangling him like a string puppet a foot above the ground. The old man's eyes were squeezed tightly shut and his face was creased with worry. He was terrified.

"Oh, leave him be, Berengar. Can't you see he's starving and harmless?" said Brand, suddenly cross.

"Why didn't he approach normally, then? Instead of skulking about like a leper." Berengar suddenly shied back, holding the man away from his face at arms length. "You don't suppose he *is* a leper, do you?"

Brand danced backward and covered his mouth, suddenly wary. "You make a good point. We'll have to quarantine you, Ber."

"Really?" Berengar looked at Brand in utter dismay.

"No, you big fool. He's just starving."

"Oh, you and your silver tongue, Brand!" sneered Berengar. Then his eyes widened. "Brand! *Behind you!"*

"Yeah, right. As if I'd fall for that trick," Brand said with an easy laugh.

Berengar dropped the old man and whipped out his sword in a flash. Then Cil screamed—somewhere off to Brand's right. Brand shot a glance behind him, suddenly uneasy. Then, as he watched, a great carpet of mud and vines lying flat on the soft earth suddenly heaved upward. Whatever it was, it had been camouflaged in a shallow depression in the swarth. Now it rose up, towering above Brand, nearly ten feet tall, a great avalanche of dirt and sticks rolling off its back and tumbling to the earth.

Its substance shimmered as it refracted the light and then resolved into solid colors. Before, the beast had blended perfectly with the forest floor. Now, it was a sickly pale pink, with splashes of gray and brown, where ratty patches of unhealthy fur clung to its flesh, except around its neck where it grew a thick gray mane. Brand's first impression was that of a gigantic, half-shaven bear. But as it turned its head toward him, its sleepy eyes rolled open

and he found himself staring into the face of a man—broad and
deformed, but unmistakably the face of a human.

Chapter 15

"The Chimera."

The great pink face stared into Brand's own with cynical, light-brown eyes, and the youth went completely still—devoid, for the moment, of all faculties but sight.

The creature breathed out heavily, filling the space between them with its warm, fetid scent. Its half-bear, half-man nose twisted this way and that, sniffing the air. Its gray lips rolled back in a terrifying wolf's grin—yet manlike enough to add an element of sinister cruelty entirely absent from the animal kingdom.

The thing reeked of rancid sweat, mixed with the stench of a dog's kennel and the sickly undertones of decomposing flesh.

Brand heard the snapping of wood and numbly looked down. Its four great paws—like horribly elongated human hands with long, bony fingers—clenched the ground, tearing up the earth and snapping a stray branch as if it were no more than a twig.

"Breakfast has been served, and in bed no less," it said in harsh, guttural tones.

With a terrible sound—half-animal snarl, half the cry of a man — the large head snapped forward like a dog chomping at a lizard.

"Move!" cried Berengar.

The golden giant sent Brand flying with a blow of his shoulder and caught the snapping jaws on the crossguard of his sword. Though he blocked the attack, the sheer force sent Berengar tumbling fifteen feet backward along the forest floor, where he lay, momentarily dazed.

The creature lunged to finish him off, but Brand staggered to his feet and fired a crossbow bolt into the beast's neck.

It cried out like a man, then turned to glare at Brand with a concentrated vindictiveness so potent it made his soul wobble loose from his spine.

Brand danced behind a large pine on jelly legs, pressed his back against it, and drew a heavy throwing knife.

"Okay," he thought. "This is it. This is what we trained for. *A single, killing thrust.*"

He planned out the sequence in his head. He would wait until the beast was almost upon him, spin out from behind the tree, and with a single cast, send his dagger speeding through the monster's right eye and into its brain, killing it instantly. It would fall at his feet, and Cil would congratulate him with smiles and praises.

Brand smiled to himself.

He heard the crunch of leaves as the beast neared the tree. Then he spun from behind it, swinging his heavy dagger in a wide arc to build momentum.

The horrible face was right there.

He cast the dagger. It flew straight and true—*into the beast's left eye.*

The beast paused abruptly in its advance. The dagger dangled grotesquely from its eye.

Good, thought Brand in that fleeting instant. *All is as planned. It should drop to the ground... any second now...*

Its great mouth opened wide and let loose a scream of pain, fantastic in its horror and enormity. Great globules of saliva expelled in a rush of breath, covering Brand in a blanket of viscous goo.

An instant later, quick as a striking serpent, the monster clutched Brand across the chest with one terrible hand and began slamming him back and forth against the earth like a dog worrying a rabbit.

Had the sward not been formed of such soft earth, Brand would have died then and there from broken ribs, neck, and spine—but this was not the case.

Then, luckily for Brand, the monster—filled with a human cruelty—did something a true bear never would have done. Instead of tearing him in twain and devouring him instantly, it casually tossed him aside, sending his limp form tumbling across the glade like a rag doll.

It wanted to play with its food.

It knew they couldn't outrun it. *So, what was the hurry?*

The thing let out a low chuckle of fiendish mirth.

Brand was left dazed and half-conscious, his shoulder dislocated from the pummeling. He rolled onto his hands and knees and began to dry heave.

Cil's scream cut through the fog of pain and nausea. It caught his attention, and he blinked at her stupidly through a blur of swimming colors.

She had climbed a tree and was pointing frantically at something near him. His ears were ringing. He tasted blood.

He followed her gesture to a gigantic dead tree with a hollowed-out end.

Galvanized by the sudden crunch of leaves behind him, Brand launched into a burst of motion he hadn't previously thought himself capable of. In one motion, he threw himself off the ground and dove headfirst into the darkness of the hollow tree.

Gigantic, angry laughter boomed at his back.

His dislocated shoulder hampered his movements, and he landed awkwardly on his side in a pile of leaves, further winding himself.

Behind him came the sound of splintering wood and the creature's frustrated grunts. He forced himself upright and looked toward the entrance of the hollow tree.

The great face filled the entire gap, glaring in at him like an angry cat—its mouth wide, needle-like teeth dripping with saliva.

He supposed that such a creature might very well be the real-life source of the fabled manticore in peasant folklore.

His train of thought ended abruptly as a long, bony hand reached in, claws raking at him, trying to drag him out. He backed up as far as he could, but the hollow wasn't very deep.

The beast glared in again. It could almost reach him, and he had nowhere left to retreat. From the look of glee on its horrid face, it knew it would have him soon.

It began rending and tearing at the dead tree, breaking off huge chunks with its great strength—closing the distance between it and Brand.

A voice came out of the darkness beside Brand. *"Hello, father."*

Brand almost jumped out of the hollow. Only the chimera obscuring the entrance stopped this instant reaction. He peered into the darkness beside him. *"Alucard?"*

"Who else?"

"What the devil are you doing here? You scared me!"

"I thought it wise to take refuge, given the circumstances."

"Yes, quite so, you are right. Don't you have a spell or something to blast this demon?"

"I only know one spell—and I think you'd agree our adversary is dangerous enough without the added faculty of *'flight.'*"

"Can't you learn another spell? A fireball or something fancy, you know, like what's in the stories?"

"Not while maintaining the spell of flight. I've tried. The symbols are forceful—they wriggle and writhe in the mind, unnatural to our world. They escape me. Just one spell makes my brain quiver and my eyeballs want to suck inward and liquefy. Two is *far* worse."

"Humph... doesn't sound very... well, *healthy.*"

"Brand, shouldn't you be focusing right now? I fear your concussion is causing you to become *distracted.*"

"Well, that may be..."

But Brand didn't get to finish his sentence. The beast, having chipped away enough of the tree, reached in with a great, splotchy arm and grabbed onto Brand's ankle.

Brand screamed—a long, effeminate howl—as he was ignominiously dragged from the dead tree.

Once again, he found himself on his back, face-to-face with that monstrosity. It glared down at him and smiled cavernously, rivulets of saliva dripping onto his face.

The great head blocked out the sun as it came closer. "The end is near, little rabbit. *Prepare to die,*" it purred.

Brand looked past the face, attempting to gain a final glimpse of the sky.

A tiny figure appeared above the creature, high in the air. An illusory phenomenon, he thought—*death dreams.*

But the figure rapidly increased in size.

It wasn't getting larger. *It was getting closer.*

The shape came into focus, resolving into the tense form of Berengar—muscles bulging across his chest and shoulders, sword held *point-down.*

The Outlander collided with the monster like a *thunderbolt.*

Ten inches of blue steel burst from its mouth above Brand, showering him in its foul blood.

Berengar had climbed a tree and leapt from it, coming down on the monster from a great height. The momentous blow had driven his sword clean through the creature's brain.

Now he stood on its head, legs braced wide, both hands still gripping the hilt.

The beast gagged horribly, the sword preventing the natural motion of its jaws. It let out a terrible choked wail, its brain quivering with pain and rage inside its skull so that the skin on its head twitched and stretched.

But for all this—*it did not die*.

Instead, it went into a berserk frenzy—tearing at Berengar, trying to rip the Outlander loose from its scalp. Berengar was scratched and grazed by its bony hands but held on tight, weathering the blows.

At that moment, Cil came out of nowhere at a full sprint, leapt like a cat into the air, and delivered a terrific spinning blow to the creature's good eye with her iron staff.

The monster roared and tried to bat her away, giving Berengar a moment's respite. Now both its eyes were closed, and it fought on with blind ferocity.

The devil's dance continued for a tense thirty seconds, with Cil pestering it each time it blindly reached for Berengar.

Presently, the beast began to roll onto its back like a wild animal, trying to crush the tenacious barbarian. Over and over it rolled, grinding Berengar into the earth—shaking him, jerking him, slamming and gouging.

In that terrible struggle, Berengar was out of sight half the time, only to reemerge again from underneath the beast—each time more bruised and battered than before.

On and on it went.

The manhandling Berengar endured was appalling. Yet he hung on stubbornly, like a bulldog, never letting go of his sword.

Eventually, the creature's movements began to slow—its thrashing had only worsened the wound. Its limbs twitched spasmodically, and its efforts grew less coordinated. Its hind legs collapsed, and it began to pant heavily.

With an inhuman effort, Berengar tore the sword loose in an upward sweep, severing a large portion of the monster's brain. It let out a final, spasmodic gasp and fell forward in a heap, its brain bulging out and its face hanging open in two disconnected pieces.

For the fourth time that day, Brand found himself looking into that grotesque face. *"It gets worse every time,"* he thought as he lay there, trying to catch his breath.

Berengar staggered down from atop the creature and collapsed heavily next to Brand.

The Outlander was gasping for air. Huge, bleeding grazes from the monster's talons crisscrossed his chest. The skin on his shoulders and back was raw—scraped by sticks and rocks when the creature crushed him into the ground. He was covered in dirt and blood, and his lips were half-mashed to pieces.

Yet, they split open in a grin.

"*A single, killing thrust,*" he panted.

"*Oh, come on!*" Brand snapped—then burst out laughing.

Cil flopped down beside them, cross-legged.

"Why are you two idiots laughing? That thing almost killed both of you!"

Brand aimed a weak kick her. She batted his foot aside and began laughing with them—*after all, she too was an Outlander.*

"Oh Brand, your arm! It's all wrong."

"Likely dislocated," Berengar wheezed. "I'll fix it in a sec."

Alucard appeared. ""I find myself *overjoyed* at seeing the faces of my companions—alive, and once more cheery and content." He smiled pleasantly.

"*Thanks,*" Brand muttered, his voice heavy with sarcasm. "You know, you *really* need to learn another spell."

"I considered attempting '*The Extremely Final Effulgence of Droswald the Unutterable*'... but, I thought further research prudent."

Brand blinked, then spoke quickly, "Sound thinking!"

Berengar rose. "Come, wolf. Let's fix that shoulder."

"It's fine... *Yeow!*"

"And now we're ready to fight again," Berengar grunted. "Who else *dares* face us?"

His eyes were bruised and half-closed, but still wild. He wiped at them continuously with a bloodied arm, trying to clear his vision as he scanned the woods for more foes.

"You're bleeding all over!" Cil said, examining him. "Let's clean you up."

She led him to a nearby pool, washed his wounds, and dressed them with strips torn from Brand's tattered coat.

Berengar drank deep from the pool, then smacked his lips.

"A good fight gets the blood pumping... but it's nothing to carving a sculpture."

He collapsed into unconsciousness.

"You rest too," Cil said to Brand, with uncharacteristic softness in her voice. "I'll keep watch."

"Thanks." Brand said, eyeing her askance. *Since when had she been so caring?*

He tried for a bit, but couldn't sleep. Instead, he lay there staring up at the green canopy above, aching from his injuries— occasionally casting sidelong glances at Cil, who sat in awkward silence nearby, gripping her staff and making a show of keeping a lookout.

An hour passed and Berengar rose, grumbling, "Sleep in the day is for babies and fat City-Dwellers. Let's go."

No one demurred.

They moved on, following the dirt road south.

Near dusk, they came upon a large wooden structure nestled among the trees. It was two stories high, made of rough-hewn boards, with a lean-to stable on the side. A flat, low porch stretched across the entire front of the building. The windows were covered with netting instead of glass, and the single door hung ajar.

Behind the structure stretched a dank swamp, as far as the eye could see.

A sign out front read: *The Safe Haven Inn.*

Brand squinted. "You think it's still operating?"

"Let's find out. I'm thirsty," Berengar rasped.

"It's filthy," Cil said.

"I'm hungry," added Alucard.

"Two and two," Brand declared. "I'm with Cil." He leered at her expressively, showing her that they had something in common for once.

"*Ew.* Never mind. Let's go check it out."

Brand rolled his eyes.

The porch's floorboards creaked ominously underfoot. Cil opened the door with a push of her staff.

Surprisingly, inside was a well-lit dining room. A long dining table. A bar. All made of ancient dark wood, well-cleaned and cared for.

Behind the bar stood a massive man, face still hidden in shadow.

"If you're coming in, *come in!* If not, *get out!* You're letting the bugs in," boomed a deep, harsh voice.

"Well, it's not haunted," said Brand bluffly. He flicked a serpent's glance around the doorframe to make sure no trap was intended, then walked in.

Berengar nodded approvingly, then stumbled over to the table and sat down. "Bartender! *Wine!*"

The bartender did not answer at once. Brand raised a curious eyebrow at this but shrugged and sat at the table beside Berengar.

Cil cautiously tagged along, sniffing the air and wincing at the stale smell of the place. She took a seat on Brand's left.

Alucard seemed completely unbothered by either smells or atmospheric moods, and he hopped up to stand on the chair between Brand and Cil, his small grey cloak billowing out as he thrust his little hands on the tabletop.

Berengar became annoyed. *"Bartender?! Wine!"*

The bartender leaned forward from the shadows, revealing a massive mane of coarse black hair, a beard to match, rugged features, and dark eyes that showed too much white. Resting two massive, hairy forearms on the counter, he glared across at Berengar like an angry bull.

"You didn't say what kind of wine, *friend.* How do you expect me to serve you without telling me what you want?"

Berengar glared back, his temper rising.

Brand interrupted with a judicial hand. "Forgive us, friend. It has been a long journey. Pray, tell us, what do you have on the menu?" The bartender was clearly an irascible fellow. Best not to incur his displeasure—*who knew what he would put in the food?* Brand thought to himself.

The bartender turned his hostile glare toward Brand. After a pause and a sigh of annoyance, he spoke.

"Why, the best of *Baltanian Bitter,* of course. What else?"

Brand blinked.

Berengar turned his head to glare at the barkeep. *"No wine?!"*

Brand interceded again. "Great! A round of Baltanian Bitter it is!"

The barkeep seemed distracted, staring complacently at one of the windows across the room, as if looking for something. He mumbled something under his breath, cast a final challenging glare at Berengar, and returned to pulling the ale.

Brand had to speak soothingly to calm Berengar down, but the barkeep seemed to have already forgotten the matter.

The big man then came around the counter, carrying four tankards, two in each massive hand. His body was the huge and heavy type, with a thick layer of skin and fat, but well-distributed and underpinned with the hard muscle of a forest-dweller. He was a head taller than Berengar and slightly wider. He looked like he'd felled the trees to build the inn with his bare hands.

The giant began placing the tankards down with disinterest—then he saw Cil. When he got a good look at her, his expression shifted, and he ventured a smile that was almost amiable.

"Well folks, y'all enjoy my best ale today. And where do *you* hail from, missy?"

"Clankerage," Cil said shortly.

"Never heard of it. But I'm sure it's a fine town, if one goes by the judge of you."

"It *is* a fine town."

"Well then, what brings you folks here to my fine establishment?" He now addressed the whole group.

Brand and Berengar watched the exchange with irritation and suspicion.

Brand said, "Well, we were traveling these parts this past week, but only this morning we encountered some strange doings on the road and felt it might be better to sleep indoors tonight."

The barkeep became suddenly still, then asked, "Strange doings? Which direction did you come from?"

"North, on the road."

"Ah, *north.* And what *strange* doings did you see?"

"A terrible monstrosity. But have no fear—this has been dealt with by yours truly... oh! and my loyal companions."

Berengar and Cil grumbled and jibed at this. Brand waved away their comments with an airy gesture.

"But there is still a queer old man out there who watched us from the woods. I cannot imagine what his intentions were."

The barkeep cursed darkly, and his eyes stared towards the window, "Old man, you say? *Dog bite him!* He's a pestilence on my land. Drives away the damn customers, he does."

He paced over to the counter, reached down, and came up with a longbow of massive proportion.

"I should end him now." He seemed consumed by the subject. Still cursing, he stepped quickly to a window. For a time he stared fixedly out into the forest with a maniacal intensity that was terrible to behold. After this, he peeked out the door and nocked an arrow.

Brand edged slightly off his seat and drew a dagger, ready to take cover in case he turned on them.

Without looking at them, the barkeep went on. "What did he say? He's a lying scoundrel, he is. I've lost more bullions... *bad for business... slinking and skulking... lying...*" He muttered on in disjointed fashion.

"He didn't say anything," said Brand, eager to calm down the maddened forest dweller.

The barkeep looked sharply over his shoulder at Brand. "*Truly?*"

"I speak truth," said Brand with an easy gesture.

"Unusual," grumbled the barkeep, somewhat mollified. He gave a final suspicious glare out the door, then returned the bow to its place behind the counter. After this, he came back to the table with some of his previous amiability restored.

"I take it you all will be staying the night?" He looked at Cil thoughtfully and stroked his great beard as he waited for a reply. Cil directed a challenging glare back, but the barkeep seemed not to notice.

Berengar glared at the man like an angry lion ready to defend its cubs.

Alucard stared on unblinking, observing everything impassively.

Brand fidgeted awkwardly and asked, "You currently have *other* guests patronizing your fine establishment?"

"They just checked out this morning," answered the barkeep with a wry smile.

"Indeed? Odd that we did not encounter them on the road."

"They went *south*."

"South, you say? Well, thank you for your hospitality, but you haven't spoken prices. I fear we are somewhat destitute from our long voyage."

Berengar eyed the tankards in sudden agitation. "In my land, starving travelers are not refused drink or food."

The barkeep's expression was unreadable. He seemed about to speak, but before he could, Alucard interrupted.

"Money is not a problem. Whatever the bill is, consider it paid."

Brand, Cil, and Berengar glared furiously at the small creature. Brand nudged him and whispered something in his ear.

"Oh," Alucard mouthed in response.

Brand put on his best smile and addressed the barkeep. "Excuse my young friend here. He is only a child and knows not the ways of the world. I've told him not to agree on a bargain before a price is set."

"The fee is nominal at *The Safe Haven Inn*. Our primary concern is the safety of our customers. These are strange times. Unknown things occur in the dim fastnesses of these ancient woods.

Had the old oaks a tongue for words—who knows what strange tales they'd tell of the things they've seen." He fondled his beard, a faraway look crossing his face. After a moment, he seemed to return to them.

"Consider the ale on the house—and dinner. I'll take a peck on the cheek from the lass, and that will be payment enough." He grinned ghoulishly.

Cil jumped to her feet and slammed her tankard on the table. *"Like hell!"*

The barkeep chuckled. "A spitfire, eh? Easy, easy, just a jest is all, *bright eyes. Just a jest.*" He spoke the last words ever so softly and continued to eye Cil in a manner not to Brand's liking. Coming to a decision, he said, "Dinner will be two silver bullions for the lot of you."

"A fair sum," said Brand, and then quickly consulted Alucard. "You have this much?"

"Have not a fear," Alucard replied.

Brand turned back to the barkeep and made a positive gesture. "Please, barkeep, bring us the best *The Safe Haven Inn* has to offer."

"Coming right up," said the barkeep.

He walked toward a doorway at the back of the room, pausing for a moment on the threshold. His right leg twitched awkwardly before he continued on and disappeared from view.

"An eerie fellow if I ever saw one," whispered Brand.

"I like him not. He has the dour face of a brooding Knel and the madness of a Kascheek mountain hermit," grumbled Berengar.

"His ale is sound, though," said Brand, emptying his tankard and inspecting its insides. "I seem to feel no ill effects."

"Me neither," said Berengar. "It is fine ale, to be sure."

"I'm not staying the night," said Cil with a shiver. "No matter how good his ale is." She took another long draft.

All three agreed they would drink and dine, but would not stay the night. If necessary, they would find another hollow tree in the forest.

Brand had been too distracted to notice that Alucard, too, was drinking a tankard of ale. It was as large as his head, and he had to use both hands to lift it.

Now noticing the act, Brand cried out, "*Alucard!* Put that down! You're too young to be drinking!" and snatched the tankard away.

Inspecting it, he took wrathful note that it was already three-quarters empty. He looked up and studied Alucard critically. Then, after a pause, he asked, "You seem to hold your drink well. Do you... feel any unusual sensations?"

"It feels like drinking water, except it has a fine and robust savor which I find most refreshing."

"Hmmm... strange," said Brand, scratching his straggly beard. "You've never drunk before? I would've thought—given your small stature and all..."

He stood up and pointed. "Here—walk a straight line along this floorboard."

Alucard did so without a shake, wobble, or visible tremor. Brand was impressed and put him through a series of similar exercises. Nothing unusual.

"Perhaps it's how the ancients made him? You saw how he ate the whole hamster leg—*bone and all,*" added Berengar.

Brand frowned. "I'll let it slide for now... but Al, tell me if you feel anything strange."

"Yes, Father."

They conversed for a time about their travels and their future plans. The barkeep returned with a platter bearing a steaming roast laid on a bed of baked root vegetables, seasoned with strong, unfamiliar herbs.

Berengar instantly took control of the roast and began carving off great sections with his dagger, serving it up to the others. At first, it seemed a polite gesture, and both Brand and Cil were favorably impressed. Yet Berengar's strategy soon became clear— he had carved off smaller portions for them so he could retain the body of the roast for himself. He lifted it in two hands and tore in with gusto, unconcerned by the looks of reproach Brand and Cil directed his way. The barkeep returned to the shadowed area behind the counter and watched them tuck in with an expression of grim pleasure.

The flavor of the food lived up to its presentation, though it had an odd tang to the meat, a faint bitter aftertaste, possibly from one of the unfamiliar herbs.

Berengar became instantly suspicious. "Ho, barkeep?! What meat is this?"

The barkeep seemed irritated and stopped grinning to glare at the blond Outlander. "Wild boar."

"What herbs? There's a certain bitterness that is not to my liking."

The barkeep became hostile and stalked aggressively around the counter to stand over Berengar, glaring down at the Outlander.

Berengar frowned and slowly craned his neck to stare up at the barkeep. The two were motionless for a long moment, confronting each other with grim faces, so still as to be carved from granite—two primordial savages, each primitive, wild, and fierce in his own way.

The barkeep broke the silence, speaking with offensive deliberation. "By your look, you're the experienced woodsman in the group. The girl is from a fishing village, and the boy has the soft look of a City-Dweller about him. They trusted *you* to look after them. Yet I look at you all, and I see bruised, battered, beaten, unkempt and malnourished folk. Where are *your supplies?* Where is the food *you* should have provided for them? And yet *you* come here to judge *my* meal?"

Berengar's face went from incredulous to one of boiling wrath. Now, he looked as if he were about to strike the man.

Brand attempted to calm him with a touch on the forearm and a raised hand. "Easy there, Ber... Barkeep, we are sorry. We want no trouble. Blood need not be spilt over the personal preference of taste."

"I want this boar to apologize. He *should have* provided better for you. He has no right to complain about *my* cooking."

"Now, now, be reasonable," said Brand. "Surely you're taking this too far..." Brand suddenly lost his train of thought. *What had he been going to say?* He attempted to recall it, feeling it was something important. *For the life of him, he couldn't remember.*

Brand noticed that Cil had her head on the table and seemed to be sleeping. His arms felt suddenly heavy, and the room began to spin. Round and round. Round and round. Through a fog, he saw Berengar kick back his chair in sudden animation.

"The food is drugged!" Berengar roared.

The only response from the barkeep was a low, murderous chuckle, like the growl of a waking bear.

Berengar stumbled drunkenly to his feet and struck the barkeep heavily on the nose. "*Son of a whore!*"

The barkeep reeled back from the blow, then roared, his face a mask of wrath. He lunged forth, blood streaming from his broken nose, and clutched Berengar by the throat with two great hairy hands. His black eyes bored into Berengar's own and he began to squeeze. Berengar's strength began to fail and he fell back against the table, unable to resist the murderous barkeep.

Brand's sight became dim and tunnel-visioned. The last thing he saw before darkness overcame him was the indistinct form of Berengar snatching his dagger—still red with the blood of the roast —and with the last of his strength, driving it deep into the ogre's gut. It had been an imperfect blow, not a single, killing thrust. The giant forced Berengar to the floor behind the table, still clutching the Outlander's throat in that terrible grip.

Brand awoke in a puddle of his own saliva, his face pressed against the hardwood tabletop. He sat up and looked around in a daze. The lantern had burned out in the night, but shafts of morning light shone through the two windows, illuminating the dim drinking room. Cil was still asleep on his left but was beginning to stir. On his right, Berengar was struggling to his feet with great effort.

What had happened? Brand's thoughts were scattered, jumbled and unclear. He recalled that he should be alarmed about something. Then something caught his attention. The food and the serving tray were spattered in blood in a most ghastly fashion. The tray had long since overflowed, and now small red streams ran across the tabletop to splatter upon the floorboards below. The pool of blood in the tray rippled with a regular disturbance. And then he heard it—a quiet, rhythmic drip. Drip. Drip.

He looked up—*and almost fell off his chair.*

The barkeep stared down at him from the ceiling, pinned there by something embedded in his midriff. His arms and legs dangled limply around a face so contorted with pain and rage it scarcely looked human. His eyes bulged wide, as if he had died in the throes of a terrible paroxysm of wrath. His hands were frozen into great, clenching claws.

Berengar, now upright and leaning heavily on the table, noticed Brand's horrified gaze and looked upward. "*What the devil?*" he muttered.

"Oh good. You're awake," Alucard's voice said. It was quiet, almost a whisper.

Brand turned quickly toward Alucard. The small creature stood in a rigid posture of concentration, looking up at the dangling barkeep without blinking. He looked haggard and exhausted, like a dehydrated frog. Rivulets of sweat ran down his rubbery blue scalp and his hands and legs were trembling.

"Al! What's going on?" Brand asked.

"The barkeep did not die from Berengar's strike. I deemed he was still a threat. So, I placed him on the ceiling, where you see him now. He struggled for many hours. Only recently did he become still. His vitality was... indefatigable. Even now, I retain him there out of caution."

"But, if you cast the flying spell on him, why didn't he simply fly back down?"

"That is because I didn't cast it on *him*. I cast it on Berengar's dagger."

"Genius! Wait... you can do that?"

"Apparently so."

"But... it only lasts for, what, forty minutes or so? Yet I see the morning light streaming in yonder window."

"I recast the spell—*As many times as was necessary.*"

"Oh, is there no limit?"

"Brand?"

"Yes?"

"Can I release the spell now? I am *very tired.*"

"Oh... yes, you poor little fellow. *Yes!*"

Berengar's fierce blue eyes glowed with pride as he regarded Alucard. "Aye, lad. My arm is ready. We will take it from here."

Alucard sent the knife—lodged in the barkeep's sternum—across the ceiling and into the far wall, where the body collided with a thud. He released the spell. The body slid down the wall, leaving a thick streak of blood upon the planks in its wake.

Alucard collapsed in sheer exhaustion. His small head lolled back against the chair and he went completely still. His unblinking eyes gave the unnerving appearance of death. Brand let out a sob of alarm and clutched Alucard's limp frame to his chest, inspecting his little blue face.

Berengar rushed over in a panic and placed his fingers before Alucard's mouth. He let out a sigh of relief. "He is breathing. He is just asleep."

Such was Alucard's mental exhaustion that he had fallen into a dead faint with eyes wide open. Brand tenderly closed them and held him while he slept.

Cil, having just woken up, looked around perplexed. "What happened?"

Brand filled her in.

She glanced over at the barkeep's corpse. "Take that, *dog of hell!*" she said, then spat on the floor.

The companions moved to another table and took a moment to gather their wits and let Alucard rest.

Then, to a scene already grotesque and peculiar, a further element of the ludicrous was added.

A pale, haggard face appeared in the window—the old man who had stalked them in the forest. His eyes bulged at the sight of the crumpled barkeep, and he peered in with eager concern before disappearing from the window. Seconds later, the door began to open in tiny increments. The face appeared, peering through the slit. The companions didn't move. The door creaked open further, revealing the thin, naked form of the old man. Only now, at this distance, could they see how emaciated he really was. He was sheer bones and tendons, and his skin was so pale as to seem translucent.

Slowly, furtively, he slunk through the doorway. He paused awkwardly and stared at the companions. They stared back, making no sudden movements. Then, seeing the bloody corpse anew, the old man made a sound, deep within his throat— somewhere between a gulp and a sob. Then, creeping forward like a pale rodent, he flicked a single anxious glance at the companions and made his way to the body. He stood over it, hands clenching and unclenching in jerky spasms. Tears formed in his eyes, falling in great heavy droplets to stain the floorboards at his feet.

Brand and the others watched in silence.

Now he made a guttural croaking sound, as if trying to activate vocal cords long out of use. Dry, wheezing noises issued forth. He looked pleadingly toward Brand, then tried again. Finally, words issued forth from his toothless mouth in a hoarse whisper. "He... he is dead." He pointed at the barkeep with a long, bony finger.

"Yes. What is your relation to this man?" said Brand with growing nausea. "Did he do this to you?" Brand indicated the old man's body.

The old man didn't respond. He simply stood there, staring at the corpse, shaking his head.

"Well, whatever he was to him, he's dead now," said Berengar grimly.

They probed and prodded the man for an explanation, but he would speak no more.

The three companions left the old man standing above the barkeep like a pale, disembodied soul staring down at its own corpse.

Pale-faced now, they strode past the sign that read: *The Safe Haven Inn* and continued down the road.

The companions traveled south for a day, and spent a wakeful night by the side of the road. At the dark hour of midnight they saw the glow of a great blaze, far back down the road—the burning of a large wooden structure...

The next day, the forest quickly gave way to open steppes and soft rolling hills stretching as far as the eye could see. To the south, between a gap in the hills, glimpses of blue appeared on the horizon. Brand realized with a swell of exhilaration that what he was seeing was the familiar color of the Trade Sea. They were finally on their way home. *"Not long now, Mother,"* he told himself. *"Soon we will be reunited and I'll take you some place safe. We will certainly have the bullions for it—that is, if the Mad King keeps his word..."*

Brand found himself suddenly uneasy and took a moment to

examine his feelings. Freeing his mother was, of course, something of vital importance, but becoming extremely wealthy—once the pinnacle of his aspirations—now seemed somewhat tawdry. The magnitude and scope of the outside world, the troubles of mankind at large, and the dire possibilities hinted at in that ancient crystal hall—all these things made his prior ambitions seem narrow-minded. Even selfish. He resolved to return and free his mother, but after that... *what then?*

They continued on, now passing by tilled fields, worked by men and women with rugged square faces. They sported star-shaped hats like great red flowers, and wore skin-tight suits of green fabric. They seemed friendly enough, but when Brand attempted polite conversation, they brandished hoes and rakes, then fled in fear. Frustrated, Brand gave up his attempts and they moved on.

Around noon, they reached the crest of a large grassy hillock and found themselves looking down upon a shallow valley of windswept grass. A cool breeze with the scent of the sea blew back Brand's hair, and for a moment he gloried in the smell and feel of it. Cil and Berengar experienced it too, and now a mood of excitement overcame the party.

Smiling cheerfully, they looked down upon a small, peaceful-looking settlement nestled in the meadowlands at the base of the valley. Across from the village, out on the grassy plain, stood four white columns, evenly spaced to form a square. The columns were impossibly tall and continued upward into the blue sky until they grew indistinct to sight.

They descended into the valley and, after an hour, reached the settlement. They ate a brief lunch provided by the generous folk of this small town. Then, learning that Keel was only a few hours' march beyond the next hill, they decided to head on.

With a backdrop of purple-red fire spilling across the western horizon and shadows stretching long across the plains, the companions reached the port town of Keel.

Chapter 16
"Keel."

In the year 1451 (Skir Calendar), a group of adventurous City-Dwellers from Revilis Ko'hur set sail in a flotilla of three small galleys to explore the western coastline. Though braver than most, their fear of the unknown wilderness kept them from spending their nights ashore. Instead, they spent each night at anchor in their galleys, and did land-excursions only during the hours of daylight.

After a week and a half of cautious progress, disaster struck. While navigating a promontory of granite cliffs, a treacherous current pulled their ships into the rocks, smashing them to splinters. Many lives were lost amid the chaos of crashing waves and shattered timber. Yet, a surprising number survived, finding themselves washed ashore in a narrow bay, hidden within the cliffs.

Ironically, the treacherous currents that spelled their disaster, saved their lives in the end; as, along with the sailors, it washed up a substantial quantity of cargo and ship wreckage which was then used for their survival.

Utilizing the "fortunately" delivered wreckage, the surviving members built a defensible camp at the mouth of the bay and surrounded it with wooden stockades. They lived within the walls of their camp for weeks, fearing to explore the plains beyond their defenses.

This was apparently prudent, for the plains turned out to be inhabited by a peculiar race of nomads: three-foot-tall humanoids with gray skin, bald heads, and fluffy tails. The nomads rode a form of mount which seemed to be of the same species as themselves but dull-witted, heavier of build, and which walked on all fours.

The nomads had previously enjoyed hunting small bands of

traveling humans; chasing them across the plains during the day or ambushing their camps at night. Thus, the nomads now thought of men as prey for their hunting games.

(How this was learned is worth noting: Early in the war against the nomads, one of their kind was captured and tortured by the men of the camp. Its strange babblings were recorded phonetically and, years later, after the war had ended, a traveling scholar was able to decipher the recordings, which stated the above.)

Thus, on the twenty-first day after the camp's construction, the survivors beheld a strange sight: fifty of the above-mentioned nomads, armed with small spears and wearing leather jerkins made from human skin, rode up to the stockade, chattering indignantly in their strange tongue—apparently upset that the humans hadn't ventured out to be hunted. A volley of arrows from the men in the stockade wiped out half their number. The surviving nomads, rather than fleeing, became even more indignant, motioning for the men to come forth. A second volley from behind the stockade finished the remainder.

This exact scene repeated daily. Each morning, a fresh band of nomads arrived to reenact the same bizarre confrontation. Though the warfare was not difficult, the sheer persistence of the nomads required constant vigilance. Every man and woman in the camp was pressed into service, whether crafting bows, gathering supplies, or standing watch. Survival demanded unity, and internal disputes were harshly punished.

Life in the camp settled into a grim routine. They survived by eating fish caught in the bay, berries foraged from nearby slopes, and, when desperate, the corpses of the fallen nomads. The beneficent current continued to deliver wood and detritus from the sea, which was put to good use in the construction of more structures and weapons. After a year, the nomads were extinct.

Around this time, another expedition fell victim to the

treacherous current of the cliffs. A second band of men and women, their ships and supplies washed ashore in the bay, were welcomed into the settlement. The stockade expanded, new structures were built, and the camp became a thriving village. It was named Keel in honor of the ships whose remains formed the foundation of its structures.

The people of Keel mastered the cliffs' deadly tide races and built signal towers to help guide incoming ships. They quarried the cliffs to construct a quay and began to explore the surrounding plains. The next set of ships that came were able to navigate the cliffs safely, and later returned to Revilis Ko'hur to report their findings. In the hundred years that followed, Keel became the major western outpost of civilization. This resulted in a number of unnamed fishing villages being established along the coastline between Keel and Revilis Ko'hur.

In the present, Keel is famed for its unique flair, its sea-themed dress code, and its traditional *ship-wreck style* architecture, which lends the town its distinctive aesthetic.

The Customs and Laws of Keel:

Keel has a unique set of social rules—a blend of City-Dweller pragmatism and Outlander ruggedness. While no formal law code exists, the town follows several unspoken principles:

Murder is forbidden. Intentional killing brings the wrath of the entire town, leading to swift execution—either by a thousand saber cuts, or by hanging the culprit over the far promenade; a meal for the sixty-foot water stalker. Accidental deaths in brawls, however, are generally forgiven.

Home turf has advantage. Defending one's home or own property carries social weight, and bystanders are more likely to offer their support. However, feuds, muggings, and duels in the street are common, and often treated as sport—provided no murder is involved. Ongoing rivalries between local parties can become a source of communal entertainment.

The town is sacred. Any act that threatens the town as a whole—such as arson—is punished as harshly as murder.

To outsiders, the actions of Keel's people can appear erratic. Yesterday's foe may be today's ally, and disputes often resolve as suddenly as they had begun. Yet, beneath this baffling veneer of apparent whimsy lies a complex code of conduct, understood on an instinctual level by the locals. New arrivals to Keel are likely to undergo a rude awakening. For, while death is unlikely, bruises and stolen possessions are almost guaranteed—a small price to pay for the exhilarating prospect of future revenge.

A Guide to Keel
By the Traveling Historian, Gesto Decampri

***

The first thing Brand noticed was the absence of a wall surrounding the town, suggesting that these parts were not prone to raids by bandits, forest demons, or other strange dangers. This was a comforting thought to Brand, who was weary of peril and rough living. He longed for comfort, fashionable dress, and good wine—perhaps even the polite company of civilized females. Such women as might appreciate his wit, style, and charms—unlike this barbaric Outlander girl. At this last thought, he flicked a glance at Cil, who had recently boxed his ears—for what, she only knows.

The town appeared to have no particular planned design. Wooden structures of all shapes and sizes sprawled outward from a central area in every direction. They followed the main street, which curved like a crescent through the town. As they walked, Brand observed the odd variety of buildings as they passed them. The structures ranged from small, flat-roofed shanty huts, to large three-story constructions that looked more like individual houses stacked atop one another than a single planned design. Some of the larger buildings were fortified with barbaric shields, spears, planks of wood, and sheets of tin, resembling individual pirate strongholds.

A nautical theme ran through the town's décor. Many huts and fortified buildings were adorned with anchors, heavy ropes, and often had wooden prow statues projecting from their facades. Large sections of the buildings seemed fashioned from salvaged ships. A range of smells assaulted their senses: ale and wine, worn leather, burning wood, stale sweat, and the stench of cesspools wafting from dingy alleyways—all mingled with the briny overtone of the sea, which somehow made everything else not so bad.

Brand grinned at the familiar scents. "Just like home," he muttered.

"You City-Dwellers never learned to keep yourselves clean," Berengar complained.

"I'd hardly call these folk City-Dwellers," replied Brand with a sneer. "They have no style. Just wait until we reach Revilis Ko'hur proper. I bet it's clean in there! With nobles, balls, gowns and all!"

Berengar remained unconvinced. "Not if it's anything like the king who rules it. He had more than a few screws loose."

"True, we certainly found out why he is called 'Ezeret the Mad King.' But he was at least *majestic,* what with his red silk robe and all?"

Cil took offense at Brand's earlier comment. "This place has more style than *you, you dirty sunflower!* Look at yourself for a change."

Brand rolled his eyes.

Cil had been to Keel before with her father, before she had been kidnapped, and knew something of its unique customs. She took a moment to fill Brand and Berengar in as they walked.

"My kind of place!" said Berengar after Cil had finished. He flashed his canines and added, "Let us find a tavern and get down to business."

"I agree wholeheartedly," said Brand with an easy grin.

"Yes, let us!" chimed in Alucard, "That substance *'ale'* was most agreeable. In all candor, I feel a certain urgency to consume more —especially since Brand didn't let me finish my last drink."

The others stopped walking and stared at the small blue creature.

"Why, you are still spicy about that *aren't you?!*" said Cil with a leer.

"I fear we have ourselves a drinker!" said Berengar.

The three companions fell into a hearty chortle which helped to wash away the horrors of the trail.

They had progressed further into town, and the street was crowded with swaggering buccaneers in flared leather boots, billowing silk shirts, and great colored sashes tied at their waists. Some wore tricorn hats; others, silk bandanas. All sported gold rings in their ears or noses, with more gold adorning their wrists and fingers. Hardy seafaring men, tanned and bearded, strode about in plain cotton blouses and breeches cut off at the knees. Sly rogues and brutish bruisers leered from alleyways, making catcalls at passing women.

The women of the town were of all colors, and their dress varied widely. Some dressed like their male counterparts—sailors, rogues, or buccaneers—while others adorned themselves like lascivious harlots in scanty dresses and garish jewelry. Some were indeed harlots, but others only copied such a style out of whimsical fancy.

The town was built around a single major street which flowed in from the north, arced through the center of town, where there was a great quay, and then continued out of the town, becoming another road that followed the coastline west. The arc of the main street was the heart of town, with major inns and shops on one side of the street, and the quay promenade and bustling docks on the other. Beyond the bustling docks lay the narrow bay, hidden between two rows of granite cliffs that jutted out into the ocean.

The main street was formed of hard-packed dirt and was illuminated by smoky oil lanterns, hanging precariously from wooden or iron posts stationed irregularly throughout the town. Many buildings also had their own lighting—iron lanterns hung on posts mounted to their ramshackle facades. Lusty-eyed women cooed at Brand and Berengar as they passed, and more than a few swaggering buccaneers dared whistle at Cil, though her venomous glare sent them swiftly away.

Every so often, one or more rogues would edge suggestively toward the party from an alleyway, but each time, a single look from Berengar would send them scurrying back into their crevices.

Alucard drew more than a few strange looks, and at one point they were approached by a bald man with a painted face who claimed to be an animal trader. He was dressed in a mantle of feathers, and the colorful plumage—along with his painted face— gave him the aspect of a decadent court eunuch. He fervently demanded that they let him purchase Alucard for his collection and wouldn't let up until Berengar sent him reeling with a swift buffet of his open palm. The man cupped his reddened cheek, directed a wounded gaze at Berengar, and then returned to his wagon, which was piled high with caged, screeching creatures of every description.

The companions reached the arc of Main Street and the center of town. Across the street, the quay promenade was filled with night revelers going about their affairs; the docks and bay beyond were silent and dim. To their right loomed a massive four-story building, illuminated by the smoky, yellow light of a large oil lantern posted by its door. The building's facade was formed of myriad ship parts —curved planks of wood, a quarter of a "poop deck," parts of masts, and a large carved ship's figurehead projecting boldly above the entrance. The figurehead depicted a bare-chested mermaid, three times life-size, her flowing red hair and outstretched arms giving the impression of amorous invitation. Hanging from the various parts of the facade were ropes, bits of net, and even a resting anchor by the door. A sign hung from a post beside the entrance, opposite the lantern, that read: *The Sea's Embrace.*

Berengar grinned up at the figurehead. "I like it already."

The door was slightly ajar, displaying a tantalizing slit of warm golden light. Entering *The Sea's Embrace*, they observed a large drinking room, designed like a ship's mess hall, with long tables spaced apart and running lengthwise across the room. At the right end was a staircase leading to a mezzanine floor above, where more patrons ate and reveled. The staircase then continued upward to higher floors.

Along the left side of the room ran a prominent bar. Behind it stood a burly, shaven-headed man sporting a black goatee and clad in a white apron. At the back of the room, below the mezzanine, was an open area for entertainment and events, surrounded by cozy private tables and cushion-laden recesses.

Just then, a spindle-legged rogue in colorful dress and a three-peaked hat tumbled over the mezzanine rail and came crashing down onto one of the rectangular dining tables. The table's legs gave way and man, table, and hat clattered to the floor in a messy heap.

The barkeep roared something from behind his counter, and a massive bulk dislodged itself from a shadowy nook in the wall to the left of the bar. A hulking bouncer with swollen cheeks, red braids, and a great red beard stepped into the light. He reached the rogue in three great strides and lifted him from the floor with one arm. With the other, he raised a gnarled wooden club.

The rogue cried out indignantly, unleashing a stream of high-pitched invectives to defend his case. The stony-faced bouncer clubbed him once, twice, three times. The rogue's head, with its three-peaked hat—now resembling a bedraggled bandana—hung slackly to the side. The bouncer carried the limp body to the doorway, tossed him casually into a pile of trash on the side of the street, and returned to his shadowy station by the bar.

The barkeep noticed the newcomers and hailed them over. "Ahh! Always good to see new faces in town," he said, then gestured at the broken table with a pained expression. "My apologies. A nasty business. But let me tell you, I am not without mercy. That was the fourth table D'artge has broken—and that's saying nothing of his attitude. Bah! I'd had enough. Will he live, you wonder?" He raised his hands in mock bewilderment. "*Who knows?* His life is now in the hands of great Selefay, god of the sea and bounty. Such things happen *all the time.*" His eyes widened theatrically and he made a gesture as if to renounce all responsibility for the act.

A second later he squinted conspiratorially and growled in a low, dangerous voice, "Damned dog's-son ruin my tables, will ye?!"

After this, he brightened and waved a dismissive hand. "Well, what can I do for you travelers?"

As they approached the counter, the barkeep appeared to notice their tattered clothing and unkempt condition. With a scowl of distaste, he moved to summon his bouncer once more.

Brand quickly intervened. "Halt your ire! Call off your juggernaut. Have no fear! We are neither penniless vagabonds nor questionable deviants. We are, in fact, a special delegation from the king himself, just now returning from a quest, so great in its scope, that it would tax your very sanity merely to conceive of it."

The barkeep hesitated, eyeing Brand with uncertainty, his hand paused mid-gesture toward the bouncer.

"And yes, we can pay our keep," Brand continued, producing

Alucard's pouch and dropping it dramatically on the bench. The effect was less than perfect. For the pouch, being jam-packed with Alucard's oddities, bulged awkwardly and emitted various questionable sounds. Still, somewhere in there, could be heard the clinking of bullions.

The barkeep inspected the pouch dubiously. "Hmmm. I *do* have rooms available, should you be able to afford them—which I somehow doubt... Also, how long will you be staying? I am chary of shady clients who drift from inn to inn on a daily basis."

"What's the daily room and board for three chambers? I should think that we will be here for a few days at least... When does the next ship sail to Revilis Ko'hur?"

"The ships sail infrequently," the barkeep said complacently. He then directed a brooding, bushy-browed frown at Alucard. "And what of your... pack animal? Can it not retire to the town stables? I, quite frankly, fear for my expensive rugs."

Brand answered smoothly, "Do not be alarmed by his appearance. He is our companion, and what you see is the result of a most dreadful alchemical accident."

The barkeep hesitated further, scratching his black goatee.

Cil shoved Brand aside, reached across the counter, and grabbed a fistful of the barkeep's beard. She spoke through clenched teeth, her voice deadly calm. "Listen up. I've endured unthinkable conditions these past months. I've been inconvenienced, starved, mentally abused, and beset by abominations. I haven't bathed in weeks. I'm tired, and my feet hurt..."

The bouncer moved purposefully toward them, but Cil directed a single glance in his direction. Whatever the look conveyed, it froze the man mid-step and sent him retreating back to his station. Even Brand and Berengar, though only on the periphery of its vector, went pale and straightened their backs.

The barkeep listened with rapt attention.

Cil continued, "If you don't give me a room and a hot bath immediately, I'll hang you from the mezzanine rail using his—" she pointed at Berengar—"loincloth as a noose."

"And that's only the first thing I'll do. After that, I'll—"

The barkeep waved a trembling hand. "Please! I have heard more than I wish to hear. Two floors up, first room on the right. A hot water tub is on its way. Your friends' rooms will be arranged shortly."

"Good." Cil released his goatee. "Brand will arrange the payment." So saying, she stalked off and up the stairs without a backward glance.

The barkeep rubbed his aching chin and directed a dark glare after her. "The wildest she-fiend untamed. By Selefay, I believe she's torn a few patches of my beard out by the roots! Well, since we've come this far, I'd at least like to be paid for harboring this hellcat. Pay me four days board in advance. Two gold bullions for the lot of you!"

"What?" raged Brand. "An outrageous sum!"

"Pay up or get out! I don't want to do it, but I'll drag that demon out of here, even if I have to round up all the bruisers in Keel to do so. Nobody freeloads off *The Sea's Embrace*, nor its owner— which is to say, *me!* Igan Crood!"

Brand sighed. He was tired of tension, tired of foraged meals, tired of feeling unclean and bedraggled. He needed a bath, a fresh outfit, and a nap. He agreed wholeheartedly with Cil, perhaps too wholeheartedly—him being a man and all—but hell, he needed a haircut and his nails were a dreadful mess.

Reaching into Alucard's pouch, Brand felt past an assortment of odds and ends, some of which confounded his senses, and finally pulled out two heavy coins. He paid them over.

Igan seemed honestly surprised and genuinely pleased. His entire demeanor changed, becoming suddenly bluff and affable.

"Well, now that you're a paying customer, all is changed! Please, make yourselves at home in my fine establishment. What's mine is yours. The past is the past, and already I've forgotten any nasty details of our initial engagement. They float from the mind like so many bits of salt on the sea breeze." He made a gracious gesture and indicated the stairs. "Let's get you settled."

He led them upstairs, past the mezzanine level and into a long hallway with doors on either side. As they passed the first room on the right, they heard the splashing of water and Cil's muffled voice singing a childish rhyme. Brand chuckled. The singing stopped abruptly, replaced by a suspicious silence. They moved on.

Berengar was given a room two doors down on the right, and Brand and Alucard were to share the room at the end of the hall.

Igan Crood, with palms clasped together, delivered a final address: "Now then, there are loose, comfortable clothes provided in each room. However, if your tastes require something more fashionable or particular, I'd recommend *Tinsel's Tailors*, a few doors down." He leaned in conspiratorially. "Be sure to tell him who sent you, so he gives me the credits. None of us have all we want in this life, do we? Ah, we must do what we can to get that extra edge." He performed a self-deprecating shrug.

He looked down at Brand's boots, noticing a toe sticking out of the right one. "Ah... you'll be wanting some new boots. I'd recommend Harful the Cobbler. You'll find him three-quarters around the bend on Main Street—that's the street we're on now. Just walk to the right and you'll find him. But look at me, talking your heads off. Get some rest. I'll assist you with everything else in the morning. Ah, right—I'll send up some washtubs shortly." With that, Igan paced off down the hallway.

"What do you make of him?" Brand asked.

Berengar shrugged. "I've seen his kind all over. As long as we pay him, he'll be all smiles and servility."

"I was thinking the same. Say, Alucard, what in the devil do you have in this pouch of yours?"

Alucard snatched it back hastily. "Oh, just some *bric-a-brac* I have collected along the way."

Brand narrowed his eyes and inspected the little creature. He could easily overpower Alucard and find out, but the thought of forcing him to reveal the contents of his private pouch just seemed wrong. Brand shrugged. "At least tell us how many bullions you have, so we know how long we can afford to stay here."

Alucard became obstinate. "This is my personal treasure. I worked for it. *The matter is clear.* I have most generously offered to cover your expenses for now."

Brand grew indignant. "*What?!*" He dived at Alucard with hands outstretched. Alucard darted behind Berengar, who announced he would hold Brand back until he settled down.

After a few minutes, Brand realized how ridiculous he must look —his skinny figure covered in tattered scraps, his hair a mess— wrestling ineffectually against what seemed an immovable mountain of rock.

"Okay, okay! I'm good," he said, relaxing and slumping his shoulders.

Berengar released him and stood back, grinning. "Promise you'll let him do as he wishes with his own effects."

Brand glared up at Berengar with a hangdog expression. "I promise. I'm tired. I'm going to bed."

He walked into the room, flopped onto the bed—still wearing his ragged clothes—and soon fell into a black, dreamless sleep.

Brand awoke to the friendly rays of first light streaming through the window beside his bed. He sat up and looked around. The room, though not luxuriously furnished, had all the basic necessities: a single large bed, a couch in front of a second window (where Alucard had slept), a wardrobe, a rug in the center, and a side room with a latrine that drained out into the alley beside the inn.

"Morning, father," said Alucard, sitting up on his couch and throwing away his dirty gray cloak, which he had used as a blanket.

Alucard seemed refreshed, though Brand could never tell how much the little creature actually slept.

"Morning, Al."

Brand got up and collected the buckets of soapy water Igan had left outside the door the night before. The water was cool, but the temperature in Keel was warm and he didn't mind. He washed himself thoroughly and showed Alucard how to do the same.

The complimentary outfit Igan had provided consisted of airy white cotton trousers, a matching long-sleeved blouse, and leather loafers of the kind worn on small boats. Brand dressed quickly and went downstairs with Alucard.

He found Cil and Berengar eating breakfast on the mezzanine floor. They sat at a window-side table overlooking the eastern backstreets of Keel. Cil had cleaned herself up and somehow styled the issued clothes into her typical look by tearing off the sleeves and cutting the pants short at the knees. Her face was clean, her green eyes bright, and her dark-red hair shone in the sunlight.

She looked Brand up and down with a subtle, mocking smile, then went back to her food.

"What's that supposed to mean?" Brand asked crossly.

Cil just looked at him archly and shook her head.

Brand sighed and sat down, pointedly turning his attention to Berengar. The giant looked much refreshed; his bruises were already fading, and his scabs peeling off. Either his wounds had been mostly superficial or the giant was an unnaturally fast healer —most likely the latter.

Berengar was also clean, wearing the white outfit and looking like a bodybuilder on holiday. The collar hung loose, displaying a tanned, powerful chest, and the sleeves were rolled up, revealing bronzed, muscular forearms. He directed a brotherly grin at Brand. "Good to see you're up, wolf-pup."

"Thanks, Ber. How do I get some of what you're eating?"

"Igan will come around shortly."

"Great. I could eat a horse."

"And what of you, Alucard? Don't tell me you've been fooling around with more of that wizard's magic?" Berengar asked affectionately. He clearly thought much of the little blue creature, but his cultural revulsion for magic was not easily dismissed.

"I have been practicing daily, but I find my mind can still only retain one spell. I am currently attempting to recite a new spell in my head without losing track of the flying spell. Once I can do this, I will pick a second one and learn it in full."

Berengar let out a sort of growl, like an anxious bear, and shook his big blond head.

Brand arched an eyebrow at Alucard. "Make sure to get my approval before choosing the spell."

"This idea was abundantly clear from our last conversation."

"We spoke of this before?"

"When you were asking for my aid in the hollow, while beset by: '63% *Hircine Magnus*. 2% octopus (regenerative cells). 28% *Homo sapiens*. 7% demon—from Thrim Rift, 2000 yards dimensional vector Y, southward progression (for systemic coordination and non-antagonistic inter-gene adaptation). Growth enzyme B362.'"

Brand bristled. "I was *distracted* at the time."

Alucard shrugged his little shoulders with a certain negligence. "By 'distracted' you mean 'decisively chastised by the *63% Hircine Magnus. 2% octopus (regenerative cells). 28% Homo sapiens. 7% demon—from Thrim Rift, 2000 yards dimensional vector Y, southward progression (for systemic coordination and non-antagonistic inter-gene adaptation). Growth enzyme B362. "'*

"Yes, you don't have to rub it in! Also, why can't you just say 'the monster'?"

"*Monster* is somewhat of an imprecise term. Such vagueness can cause untold mishaps." Alucard waggled a little blue finger at Brand.

Brand growled and craned his neck to look around. "Where *is* that damned innkeeper?"

There he was, coming up the stairs to the mezzanine.

A moment later, Igan stomped over to their table on heavy legs. "Good morning," he said cheerily. "What'll it be?"

"I'll take what they're having, and a light, fruity morning wine," Brand replied, making an intricate gesture with one cupped hand.

Igan blinked, looking perplexed for a moment, then nodded. "Certainly. And for your... unfortunate companion?" He eyed Alucard askance.

"I can place my own order. I do not see why not, since I am the one paying!" Alucard replied.

Brand and the others exchanged looks of amazement. The little creature was developing a surprising amount of sass lately.

"You tell him, Al!" said Cil, her green eyes sparkling.

Igan stammered, "Ah... ah... ah... yes, certainly. My apologies, good sir."

"I'll take what my father is having."

This further confused Igan, but Brand hastily indicated for him to double the order, saying simply that it was a long story. The barkeep stomped off, shaking his head and directing a single worried glance in their direction.

The food was of high quality, and Brand thoroughly enjoyed himself, though the wine was clearly taken up a year before its full maturity. Also, Igan would certainly need some clarification on what constituted a morning vintage. Overall, however, Brand was favorably impressed.

After breakfast, all decided they would explore the nearby shops to get some basic necessities. For Brand, this meant a barber and a tailor. Cil wanted to pick up specific supplies, and Alucard asked to go along with her. A certain exaggerated casualness on Cil and Alucard's part triggered Brand's suspicions. But, seeing as *hair* was a sore spot for Alucard, he figured it was better not to rub it in by taking him along to the barber's.

Berengar wanted to check out the docks, so the party split into three, each going their own way with a cheerful wave. Brand swaggered down Main Street in a good mood. He hadn't felt this clean or well-rested in weeks. The weather was fine, and a comfortable sea breeze rustled his loose cotton clothes.

Five stores down, he spied a wooden sign with the words: *Cuts Like a Cutlass* painted on one side and *Franthric Carter Barber Shop* on the other.

Brand moseyed on in.

The first thing he noticed was a row of chairs laid out in front of mirrors along the wall—some occupied, some empty. The second thing he noticed was himself in one of the mirrors.

He hadn't realized how bad things were until now. His blond hair and beard were overgrown, ragged, and stained. In his loose cotton outfit, he looked like a shipwreck survivor after a year on an isolated rock—either that, or a religious prophet.

A rotund, pale-faced man with a stylish black mustache, a double chin, and a greasy black comb-over ushered Brand into a seat.

"What'll it be, sir? Care to browse our trademark styles?" The man handed Brand a booklet filled with detailed sketches of various hairdos.

What a novel idea—they should institute this in the barbershops of Drifts End, thought Brand.

He chose a style depicted on a young, fashionable grandee. The cut gave his hair a definite arrangement and style—slightly shorter around the sides and back, with the front and top combed back in a wave. Additionally, it was thoroughly cleaned, oiled, and scented, leaving it shiny and refined.

He paid the barber for a job well done, using some of the pocket money Alucard had given him. How it galled to be on his own son's financial leash! Then, unable to bear his clothing any longer, he borrowed a pair of scissors from the barber and made a few adjustments of his own. He clipped and folded the hems of his pants so they were tighter and fashionably short, resting just above his bare ankles. After a few other tweaks, he walked out of the shop looking like a young noble on a harbor cruise.

His next stop was the tailor Igan Crood had recommended. Upon entering, Brand found himself negotiating a sea of clothes, packed tightly onto hanging racks. The colors and styles on the racks were uncountable.

Behind this chaotic ocean of fabric stood a short, somber man in his later years. He wore a crisp gray outfit, had a clean-shaven head, and sported a large, eccentric beard of fifteen distinct loops. On one eye, he wore a monocle mounted on a fixture that allowed him to add layers of magnification as needed. The man clicked his tongue and eyed Brand up and down with obvious distaste.

"Your tailoring is definitely substandard," he said curtly.

Brand grinned awkwardly and shrugged. "The original cut was even worse."

The old man stepped close, quickly made a few exact adjustments, and deftly sewed the hems in place with jerky yet precise motions. Brand somehow felt as though he'd just been soundly chastised.

The tailor stepped back, critically eyeing his work. "Not ideal, but it will have to do. Fixing bad work already done is all the more difficult."

"Yes... I see that now," said Brand, somewhat chagrinned.

"Now, how can I help you? And before we start—are you sure you can *afford* my services?" The tailor continued to inspect Brand with a candor that Brand found almost insulting.

Brand made an airy gesture. "Money is not an issue. I need evening clothes of the latest fashion and the highest quality. Some charming accessories to accompany the outfit would certainly do no harm. After that, I'll need a travel outfit: dark leathers, sturdy yet comfortable, and an inconspicuous cloak. Yet all should be well-fitted and fashionable in cut."

The man raised an eyebrow. "Such things are easily within my capabilities... Hmph. Money is no concern, you say? Well, in that case, I shall begin showing you some sample selections at once. As for the travel outfit, it will need to be completely custom made. However, I currently have no engaging projects." He sighed and threw up his hands dramatically. "*The life of a tailor!* I will take your measurements today and, provided I am not interrupted, it shall be ready within four days."

"I am amenable to this," said Brand.

"Good. Oh, and my name is Hardfy Tinsel. Pleased to make your acquaintance." He held out a steady hand.

Brand took it. "The name's Brand. The pleasure is all mine."

Tinsel nodded. "Now, about your evening wear..."

Tinsel brought forth a variety of dashing outfits and accessories, each to be scrutinized under Brand's fastidious gaze. Three hours later, Brand left the store with a neatly packaged bundle.

His next stop was the cobbler. The process there was similar to his visit with the tailor, and he left with a pair of dashing, black, high boots and another pair of dark, soft leather ones, for travel. By the time he arrived back at *The Sea's Embrace*, it was a little after noon. He found Berengar and the others finishing their lunch at the same table as breakfast.

Berengar hailed him. "*Ho, Brand!* What took you so long? You shop like a woman."

Cil scowled. "Please, don't group *him* with us."

Brand ignored their comments and called for the innkeeper to bring him some food, along with a warm afternoon wine. He also gave precise instructions as to what an *afternoon* wine was. After this, he took his effects to his room and laid them out neatly for the evening.

When he returned to the table, his food and wine had arrived, and he tucked into both with gusto. Brand decided Igan's choice of wine had slightly improved, but still fell short of excellence.

Once his initial hunger was sated, he sat back in his chair and held his glass up to the light, inspecting the gleaming rays through its contents. All was right with the world. "So." He addressed Cil and Berengar magnanimously, "What did you guys get up to this morning, my dear friends?"

Cil scowled and rolled her eyes.

"I got my sword and dagger honed..." said Berengar with a shrug. "Then, I got a new loincloth for when I find these rags too restrictive." He indicated the white cotton outfit. "And," now his eyes gleamed, "I did find a quality chisel and hammer for my next sculpting project... Oh, and here. I got you a new shortsword, since your last was melted by the gods of light." He handed Brand a shortsword in a dark leather scabbard.

"By my daggers, thanks, Ber!" Brand picked up the new sword and buckled it on. "And Cil? What of you and Alucard? No more spellbooks, I hope."

"You can't buy spellbooks at a store, silly." Cil replied, then she looked down, embarrassed. "I got some useful clothes. You know, for... travel and... combat—just in case it's needed." Then she looked mischievous again and said, "As for Alucard, ask him yourself."

Brand smiled complacently as he listened, then suddenly frowned. "So, what did *you* get, Alucard?"

"Oh, just some *doodads*. Nothing really important."

Brand frowned and gave it up—there was no convincing Alucard when he got like this.

The afternoon passed in ease, with Brand lounging about the mezzanine floor, playing cards supplied by Igan and occasionally practicing on Jamus' wooden flute. Brand knew he couldn't leave until passage was available to Revilis Ko'hur—so until then, he would relax and *recoup his strength*.

Cil came and went but mostly reclined like a red-haired cat on one of the couches at the back of the mezzanine, surreptitiously watching Brand as he played and occasionally calling out insults when he made a mistake.

Alucard tried his hand at cards but never quite grasped the point. Berengar played with Brand for a while, until a string of losses caused him to stalk growling out of the inn.

Brand retired to his room before dinner to ready himself for a grand evening of revelry. He was certain this outfit would dazzle any female with its splendor—even the irascible Cil. At lunch, he had requested a private mirror be placed in his room, and presently, he paced back and forth in front of it, trying out various poses and expressions until he could pull them off with casual ease. Making them seem natural—or even accidental.

With one critical eyebrow raised, he brushed back his hair and gave his outfit a final inspection. He wore flaring black boots with silver trim, tight black trousers with a single silver stripe running up the outer seam of each leg, accentuating their length. Around his waist was a black leather belt with a solid silver buckle in the shape of a wolf's head, jaws open in a ferocious roar. His white shirt was of finely woven silk, bleached to perfection, with gemstone buttons that sparkled in myriad colors when he shifted his position.

His black coat hung with rakish swagger on his lean frame and was cut in the style of a pirate prince. It boasted an intricate collar, silver trim, and white stripes down the double-breasted front. A fanciful clasp of emeralds, woven into the pattern of a leaf, adorned his left breast, matching his green eyes. The coat hung casually open, and his hand-crossbow and short sword were slung from his belt. Hidden within the coat were his throwing knives, mounted in accessible positions.

Satisfied with his appearance, Brand positioned his hair to its most advantageous angle and headed downstairs.

Brand walked with a slow rocking gait down the stairs to the mezzanine level, his expression one of affected indifference. He glanced around. The others weren't present. He went sulkily to their lucky table to wait.

A few catcalls from women lounging on the couches incited him to stand back up, walk over, and lean casually against the mezzanine rail and put on a show of *noble brooding*.

Some surly, rugged rogues now jeered at him.

"Who's this fop?"

"He thinks he's at a fancy ball."

And other comments of a more unprintable kind were made.

Brand ignored them with studied indifference, striding about in search of further opportunities to show off his outfit. When Berengar and Cil didn't show, he decided to see what was occurring downstairs—where was Alucard anyway? Was he in Cil's room??

The ground level was filled with patrons of all kinds and colors —mostly a high-class clientele, due to Igan's lofty prices. At the back of the room played a peculiar band. The band was formed of

an extremely thin man wearing a short-sleeved robe which he had
left hanging open, displaying nothing beneath but a breechclout.
He was stomping the ground with bare feet while thrumming a
three-stringed instrument made from a snapped-off oar. Behind
him sat an extremely fat man, playing a fantastical instrument
made from a single large metallic barrel, with many arms, pipes,
and levers. He played by blowing into a mouthpiece, while
pressing down various levers and stomping on a set of foot pedals.

Brand tore his eyes from the band and, looking back to the
dining area, noticed a group of dark-skinned buccaneers lounging
at one of the long tables, playing a card game unfamiliar to Brand.
He decided they must be from the southern continent. Of all the
inn's denizens, these men were the most rakish and swaggeringly
dressed.

One of the buccaneers noticed Brand's inspection and looked up.
He was a handsome youth, around Brand's age, with straight
features, dark skin, and deep blue eyes. The two exchanged looks,
inspecting each other's stylish outfits with mutual admiration. An
instant connection was formed, though whether it was one of
camaraderie or competition yet remained to be seen.

The young man wore a navy-colored buccaneer's outfit, tailored
to precision, with flashy flaring boots and a stylish blue three-
pointed hat adorned with a white feather. His waist was girded with
a white silk sash, and large gold earrings dangled from his ears. He
was sitting at the head of the table and seemed to be the leader of
the group.

"Hoy, fair-skinned brother!" he called out in a unique, sing-song
accent. "I like your style. You dress like my own kin." His voice
was rich and melodious.

He leaped to his feet with the agile grace of an athlete and held
out a hand. He was about five feet eight inches, three inches
shorter than Brand.

Brand eyed the outstretched hand suspiciously, then took it. The young man pulled him into a warrior's embrace and executed a series of intricate hand gestures and finger clicks. Brand, familiar with similar patterns among the rogues of Drift's End, did his best to keep up, though the sequence was foreign to him.

"By Yundra, Dri, and Umi! You talk the talk."

Brand smiled and shrugged with false modesty. "What can I say?"

The youth raised a hand and grinned. "Ha! Indeed. You seem to talk the talk and look the look, but can you walk the walk?"

"Huh?"

The youth clapped his hands and the buccaneers leaped to their feet, surrounding Brand in a circle. They all grinned as one, their clean white teeth flashing in the lantern light.

The dark-skinned youth wore a rapier on his right side, and it now danced into his hand as if it had a life of its own.

"Draw your sword, white brother of mine, and we shall see if you can walk the walk!"

Without waiting, he lunged at Brand with a wild thrust, laughing brightly as he did so.

Brand danced back, drawing his shortsword in time to parry the lightning-fast slash. He crouched low under another lunge drawing a dagger in his offhand. He slashed at the man's midriff. The leader bridged, throwing his legs back while leaning forward with his arms flung wide, evading the blade's path by a hair's breadth.

Brand reversed his dagger with lightning speed and instinctively thrust at the man's neck.

The pirate laughed, dropped his arm, and caught the dagger with the hilt of his rapier. He then kicked at Brand's groin. Brand cried out but, anticipating such a move from his street-fighting days, rotated slightly and caught the blow on his inner thigh. He pretended to fall over a table in dismay, and the pirate danced forward to slap him with the flat of his blade.

Igan Crood roared from behind his counter, "No bloodshed in here!"

But as his bouncer approached, seven sets of sullen eyes glanced his way and the man decided it was best not to interfere.

Brand, understanding Igan's warning and realizing the pirate wasn't fighting to kill, adjusted his tactics accordingly. He snatched a tankard from the table and flung its contents at the youth's face. The pirate ducked—right into the flat of Brand's short sword as he swept it up along the side of the youth's head.

The youth yelped and staggered back, holding his reddening cheek, genuinely surprised. Then, grinning like a blue-eyed panther, he began to laugh.

"My white brother *walks the walk!*"

A cheer went up from the dark-skinned buccaneers surrounding Brand and, to his surprise, the fight stopped as quickly as it had started—or so he thought.

The leader, still flashing his perfect white teeth, held out his hand to Brand. "My name is Talin. Talin of Meran. And you are my brother, just as I knew it from our first locking of eyes. Tell me, what is your name?"

Brand grinned wryly, recalling the kick to his groin, but extended his hand. "The name is Brand, *if you must know*... Is this how you commonly introduce yoursel—"

Talin clasped his hand, pulled him in close, and slapped him hard with a solid open-handed left. Brand's ears rang from the blow, and he completely lost his temper.

That's it! he thought.

Snatching up a dagger, Brand deftly hurled it at Talin's ear, aiming to slice free a dangling bangle. Talin adjusted his head just in time; the throwing knife severed a lock of curly hair before embedding itself in a wooden pillar. Talin swore, pressing a hand to his hair. His blue eyes flashed with anger, and he leaped at Brand.

The fight re-ignited to the whoops and cheers of Talin's rogues. Talin launched himself at Brand with a lightning-fast flurry of saber strikes. Brand parried desperately with his short sword and dagger, attempting to shift to close range. With a spinning twist that closed the distance, Brand slipped a dagger thrust through Talin's guard, but the pirate drew a dagger of his own and deflected the attack.

Back and forth the two danced in a whirlwind of glinting blades. Brand managed to slash free a section of cuff from Talin's right sleeve. Talin swore as only a sailor can. He retaliated with a wicked sweeping slash, severing the napkin-like frill from the front of Brand's expensive shirt. Brand screamed like a woman in disbelieving wrath.

The focus of the fight shifted. Now, instead of targeting each other, the two rogues began to target each other's apparel.

Brand executed a downward slash, which Talin parried, only for Brand to reverse his dagger and stab upward, impaling Talin's fancy hat. With a flick of his wrist, Brand sent the hat spinning into the air above Talin's rogues.

Talin roared and retaliated with a blinding-fast stroke. Brand barely turned sideways in time to avoid it, but this was precisely what Talin had anticipated. The real intent of his attack became clear as the blow sheared free an entire row of gleaming buttons from Brand's coat.

Brand's face turned purple, his vision swimming with a rage so cogent it nearly drove him unconscious. He launched a series of rapid cuts, slicing away ten tiny corners of cloth from various parts of Talin's outfit, forcing Talin back against a mezzanine support pillar. Seizing the moment, Brand dropped his short sword, drew a second dagger, and flung both at once in a double-handed toss.

The daggers pinned Talin by the armpits of his coat to the pillar behind him. Talin's rogues erupted into laughter at the sight of their leader bested in such a comical manner. Talin's face darkened and he roared in fury, jerking himself free. Whether due to a flaw in the coat's stitching or perhaps the many slashes it had already endured, the entire backside of the coat tore away, leaving it pinned to the pillar.

Talin was now fuming, his white undershirt exposed where the body of his coat had been torn away. He flew at Brand like an angry poltergeist, the two blue coat sleeves still on his arms looking like disjointed, floating limbs against the pale shirt beneath.

At the back of the room, the strange two-man band struck up a rakish waltz—built around the devil's fifth—as Talin stalked after Brand, stabbing with his "floating" arms. Brand retreated, trying to parry the relentless attacks, but the buccaneer was implacable.

During a particularly vicious exchange, Brand lost his footing and was forced to block a heavy blow while flat-footed. The force of the strike sent him spinning, and he sprawled, catching himself with the tips of his fingers on a nearby table, doing a sort of acrobatic full-body stretch.

Seizing the opportunity, Talin slashed a great "X" across the back of Brand's coat. Hearing the sinister tearing of his prized garment, Brand roared and slammed the table with both fists. Rising like a she-serpent from the table, he prepared to deliver a retribution worthy of the offense.

A mocking laugh cut through the din, instantly distracting both combatants from their textile feud. As they looked to the door, a group of men crowded into the inn and arrayed themselves in a stand-off.

Brand and Talin were both a spectacle of rags and tags. Their once expensive coats were a tangled mass of shredded ribbon, and their undershirts were nicked with a thousand plucking cuts. Shattered clasps and pieces of bent jewelry hung in disarray about their bedraggled forms.

The leader of the newcomers swaggered forth. His coat was of golden silk, heavily embroidered with gold and silver thread across breast and sleeves. His pants were of the blackest silk, his boots polished and flaring. Rings, bracelets, and chains of gold bedecked his fingers, wrists, neck, and ears.

Despite the extravagance of his outfit, it was poorly tailored and this, in combination with his pudgy frame and overlarge teeth, made the entire ensemble look absurd and ridiculous—a beaver dressing himself in expensive but ill-fitting castle draperies.

The man spoke. "Well, aren't you two the most colorful pair of wharf-rats I've ever seen. Is this the latest fashion among the squalid quarters of Keel, then?"

Igan took offense to the remark, and a red glare shone in his dark eyes.

Brand and Talin stiffened at these crass and unnecessary comments and turned to face the insulting newcomer, their body language suggestive of a shift in factions. Their own disagreements would have to wait—here was a common enemy.

"And who might you be?" Brand sneered. "You, who is bedecked like the fetish hut of a sub-man pygmy I encountered in the Varus'Dorae badlands?"

The man took two steps back in shocked affront and grasped the hilt of his saber. His eyes narrowed.

"*The words of a wretched peasant!* Look at your bedraggled apparel—your very presence mocks the dignity and style of all Keel."

Brand looked down at his tattered garments and winced.

Talin shouldered his way in front of Brand, baring his own tattered breast to the man. "What did you say? You upstart, goat-toothed, potbellied, false-guru, pedophile, rantalion, goblinoid bibelot-looking son of a she-goat?!"

Talin continued, "I know you, Thedmir—for a rat too. Take your band of cheap sellouts back to the gold merchants' guild and suckle at the feet of those warrior women you serve.

"Women who'll let you lick the soles of their boots, *but never anything else!*

"You make the same mistake all weak men do—hoping that if you grovel long enough, they'll throw you a crumb of lovin'.

"*Bah!* The false hope of chaste little boys!"

Talin burst into coarse, offensive laughter at his own jokes.

Thedmir froze, his face going red with wrath. He bellowed something unintelligible in a voice hoarse with emotion. He regained control of himself and a wicked grin spread across his face. "Bring forth *Killer.*"

One of his men at the rear cried out a signal, and Thedmir's group parted. A great shadow loomed in the open door, and a massive figure squeezed into the golden light of the inn's lanterns.

Brand and Talin gaped in shock and instinctively stepped back a pace. Talin's companions, Igan, and the rest of the inn's patrons tensed in alarm.

The being that now stood before them was as tall as Berengar but far broader. Where Berengar's physique was a monument to primeval strength and heroism, this man—or creature—was a grotesque mass of brute animalistic lust.

He wore only a badly cut vest of fur on his chest and a bearskin kilt around his waist. His feet were shod in high-strung sandals of dark leather. His immense arms were scarred and hairy, and ended in massive, claw-like hands that clenched and unclenched spasmodically. His calves bulged like hempen sacks tightly packed with giant walnuts.

His face was a ruin of scars, and his black, beady eyes glared at

Brand over a calloused pug nose. Where Berengar's presence inspired admiration, Killer's evoked primal dread.

Thedmir smirked triumphantly and cheers erupted from his men. "*Killer! Killer! Killer!*"

The two parties faced off for a moment in tense silence. On one side, Brand, Talin, and Talin's seven rogues. On the other, Thedmir, his motley swarm of twenty cutthroats, and the towering monstrosity called Killer.

Killer's black, porcine eyes continued to bore into Brand's own. *Why do they always single out ME?* Brand wondered in dismay.

A strange, animal-like moan issued from deep within Killer's throat and his lips parted, releasing a spill of saliva onto the floor. Brand and Talin blanched, gripping their swords tightly, their knuckles straining white.

The silence was suddenly broken by an incongruous sound—a hearty sailor's chant, sung in an off-key but cheerful voice.

Another bulk pushed its way into the inn, moving through the crowd of Thedmir's men. It was Berengar, swaying and singing as he went, clearly intoxicated. He must have started drinking earlier in the afternoon, during his jaunt along the quay.

Berengar seemed oblivious to the tense standoff, treating Thedmir's men as mere shadows to be brushed aside on his way to the bar. In his right hand he still clenched a limp, empty wineskin. He paused between the two factions and stared dumbly at Brand for a moment before giggling at some private joke.

He made an indescribable gesture at Brand's clothing and began to stagger toward the bar. But, as he passed the looming form of Killer, an instinct surfaced in Berengar's inebriated mind. He suddenly turned his head to the left and a cry of alarm escaped his lips. "*Tschaaa!*"

Without hesitation, he sent Killer sprawling with a vicious, sledgehammer left. Berengar stared for a second in confusion. "My apologies, stranger. I thought you a wild beast that had made its way into the tavern."

Killer got back up.

As if Berengar's punch had been a signal, both sides erupted into motion, charging into a chaotic clash.

It was Brand, Talin, and Talin's rogues against Thedmir and his twenty cutthroats—Berengar had his own problems.

The fighting was brutal but mostly non-lethal—pommels, flat blades, clubs, and fists flew.

Thedmir's men might have carried the day due to sheer numbers, but Thedmir's own malice proved his undoing. He attempted a lethal thrust at Brand's exposed back—a move that would have transfixed the blond youth and brought about certain death.

Brand turned to see the steel coming his way. He arched his back in fear, flinching in a most unmanly fashion. Yet Igan took offense at such malicious swordplay and, roaring with indignation, stepped in to strike down the blade with a blow of his heavy, knotted truncheon.

In an instant, he became a contestant in the fight and his bouncer was compelled to follow. The innkeeper waded into the fray, dealing out vigorous blows with brawny arms and a gleeful expression on his pale face.

Then, as if on cue, the entire crowd of the inn's patrons rose from their seats, transforming from passive spectators into active combatants. They took Brand's side without hesitation, sweeping down upon Thedmir and his men with chaotic fervor. All manner of improvised weapons came into play—tankards, stools, varnished fingernails, and even a wooden sandal.

Thedmir and his men were soundly thrashed, broken, and driven fleeing from the inn. The fight continued outside, and the fleeing combatants were chased in small groups through the streets, to eventually be caught, beaten, and robbed of their bullions, jewelry, and anything else of value.

Such was the way of Keel.

Chapter 17
"Bullions."

"Gold, though sought by many, is but a lifeless metal—its weight burdens the hand, and serves no true need."
—Quote by Baron Amun Intuliguo,
Local noble and self-acclaimed philanthropist of Revilis Ko'hur

As altered to form the motto of the Wagglers' of Drifts End:
"Gold, though sought by many, is but a lifeless metal (until put into use for oneself)—Its weight burdens the *other person's* hand, and serves *them* no true need."
Apparently coined by the Wagglers after finding the original framed upon his study wall during their famous ransacking of his estate.

***

Berengar, Brand, and Talin reentered the Sea's Embrace, laughing uproariously and staggering from limps that hadn't been there an hour ago. Behind them came Talin's seven rogues in similar fashion, their once-dapper outfits now equally ruined.

Igan Crood hadn't followed the fight beyond the threshold of his inn—he had to protect his possessions—but he greeted Brand and the others heartily with a round of ale on the house in celebration of their successful brawl.

"Showed them lousy snobs, didn't we, lads?" he said cheerfully, grinning with a gap in his teeth that hadn't been there before. "Thedmir and his kind stay at the *Golden Hornet Inn,* and I'll not let them think they can come and give us what for in my own place. That spot is a ripoff anyhow, but today we showed them who's the better inn, didn't we, lads?!"

"Yessir!" replied Talin heartily.

Brand and Talin's previous dispute was now forgotten, and they sat together around a rectangular dining table on the first floor of the inn. Berengar and Talin's seven sailors filled the rest of the table's seats.

"A messy business," said Brand in plaintive tones. "Much better had it been a clean robbery, but apparently such course brawling is popular here."

Talin laughed and cried out, "Hark how he talks like a haughty noble! What think you of this, my lusty rogues?"

The others laughed and began the beginnings of a chant in their sing-song voices. Talin held up a hand, and his voice cut out like a whip. "Peace. There will be time for a song later." The others stopped at once but kept grinning.

"First, let us talk. Brand, as you can see, I am the leader of this band of merry rogues," he said, indicating the others. "I would know more about you—whose rakish dress impresses, who speaks with a silver tongue, and who yet holds his own with the king of the throne." He raised his hands, indicating himself.

Brand shrugged, pleased with the compliments. *I wish Cil could hear this!* he thought. "I'm from Revilis Ko'hur. Born and raised in the outer quarter known as Drift's End."

"Ahah! Revilis Ko'hur! We anchored in that port once or twice. A fine city, as far as places go these days—but the locals don't fight fair."

Brand took exception. "And they do where you come from? I've seen naught but barbarism since leaving Drift's End."

Talin laughed merrily. "Easy there, Brand. It's true, is it not?"

"Right it is," interjected Berengar, "Brand's the only honorable one among the dogs. And the king's as nuts as a squirrel... without a nut." At this he grinned drunkenly, proud of his own wit.

Talin flashed his teeth at the golden giant. "And you are?"

"Berengar, of the Borderlands."

Talin's handsome face brightened. "From the *Borderlands,* you say?"

"Aye. And before you start: Yes, it's fierce. Yes, monsters. Endless fields of ice—*yes*. We're savage barbarians, sure, who cares... Good. Now we can get on with the drinking." Berengar grinned and took a large draft from his tankard.

"But what of the *women?*" said Talin, an avid gleam in his eye.

Berengar paused mid-drink, one steely eye glinting over the rim. Then he grinned mysteriously. "*Aye*. Fierce as plunging into a frozen lake. Gusty as a pounding hurricane. Tumultuous as riding the northern sea... As avid as—"

"Please. I've heard more than I care to hear," Brand interrupted. Talin was bobbing up and down in his chair like an excited rooster. Brand eyed him with distaste. "Get a hold of yourself, man."

"And why should I? I'm young, handsome, athletic, and a bachelor. The world is ripe for the plundering!"

Brand rolled his eyes. Perhaps growing up in a brothel had dulled his taste for female glamor—or perhaps it was just his nature. Either way, he couldn't abide such desperation.

Talin's mind had already moved on. "Now, this brings me to something I've been meaning to ask. Brand, you say you're from Revilis Ko'hur. Am I wrong to assume you wish to return there?"

Brand squinted slyly. "Why do you ask?"

Talin raised his hands in mock innocence. "Hear me out. I'd like to make you a deal."

"Please, outline the terms. I promise no action until the terms are laid out, of course."

"Certainly. But first, let me introduce you to my trusted

companions. If you're to work with me, then you're my brother, and if you're my brother, my merry rogues are your brothers too. Such is the way of Meran."

Talin pointed out each rogue in turn. "There's 'Tiny,' my first mate." Tall, handsome, and dark-skinned, he was a mirror of Berengar in physique, clad in royal purple.

"Next is 'Aberdash'—steersman." Rangy, with the long thews of a runner, and an aquiline face. Forest green coat.

He indicated a squat, broad man in brown. "'Fara'—good with all things mechanical."

"'Dogbatti'—master of the whip," said Talin, nodding to a caramel-skinned man in a slim black coat.

"Then there's 'Jabari Runewrit'—bard and poet." Lean, handsome, solemn. A coat of deep blue.

Talin grinned as he pointed to a brooding giant. "Unleke Mountain Fist, bare-knuckle champ of the fo'c'sle." He wore only a lavender silk sleeveless shirt.

"And last, but never least, 'Stervy the Nutcracker'—who uses his 'good leg' with vim and vigor."

Laughter erupted, including from Stervy himself—a misshapen little man with a dark walnut peg leg and a bright yellow coat.

"Pleased to meet you all," said Brand, raising his tankard.

"Likewise," mumbled Berengar, dozing.

"Good. Now that we're all brothers and lusty rogues together, let me tell you our situation:

"A month and ten days ago, we pulled into port and docked our girl, the majestic *Slippery Stefania.* Paid the dockmaster his fare and staggered over to the tavern—land swaying underfoot—intent on refreshing ourselves. Halfway through the night, Stervy, who'd drawn the short straw and gotten quartermaster duty, stumbles in, sailing-wet and screaming: *'Bloody trickery!'*"

Talin suddenly paused and stared up at the stairs, momentarily struck dumb. He gulped and then said, "By Imra, the Great Cat! What is *that*?!"

Brand followed his gaze. First, he saw Cil and wondered at the quality of Talin's perturbation, finding himself shoving down a stroke of sudden jealousy. Cil certainly looked handsome in her eccentric fighting outfit: a new pair of iron-toed shoes, brown breeches, a green loose blouse with the sleeves torn off, and a great red silk ribbon wrapped around her waist and tied off in a large bow at her back. Her arms and hands were wrapped in fighter's cloth, and she carried her short steel staff. Surely, she was attractive, but her looks certainly didn't call for Talin's intent glare —the man was a rabid dog—*or did they!?* This last thought inexplicably sent a wave of panic up Brand's spine.

Then, shifting his gaze slightly downward, he saw what had truly caught the buccaneer's attention. There, presently reaching the bottom of the staircase, was Alucard. Upon his head was a high-quality wig, seemingly woven of a woman's glossy black hair, braided into many thick strands that jangled around Alucard's grinning face as he swaggered toward the table on his bowed legs. Into the braids were woven innumerable colored beads and precious gems, including more than one diamond, which glistened frostily in the yellow light of the inn's lanterns. Around his waist was tied a small but intricate jeweled girdle of bleached sharkskin leather. The girdle supported a long dagger in a sheath, which was long enough to be a short sword for the diminutive Alucard.

Stervy, who was closest to the staircase, craned his neck to see what the others were staring at. Catching a glimpse of Alucard's approaching face, he kicked back his chair, let out a hoarse wail, and hobbled rapidly from the inn.

"Oh, hey, Alucard," said Brand warmly as the creature approached the table.

"Hi father."

Talin and his remaining rogues stared in hushed silence. Slowly, words found their way to Talin's lips. "Do my eyes deceive me? Its like a cross between a freshwater carp and a pygmy headhunter!"

"Easy there," said Brand hotly. "This is Alucard, *my charge*."

Talin looked around at his men and made a gesture as if to ask, *have I drunk too much or do you see with your eyes the same as me?* The others nodded earnestly, and Talin grunted in relief.

After a moment, Brand said, "What is up with Stervy? I understand Alucard is unusual, but surely..."

"Well, if you saw what took Stervy's original leg, you'd understand..."

"Indeed," Brand said somewhat complacently, still nettled at their attitude toward Alucard. To change the subject, he waved for Cil and the froggy creature to pull up a pair of seats.

"Forget his looks, my friends. This is merely the result of an alchemical accident. He's a companion, along with the rest of us."

Talin got over his shock and his usual humor returned to him. Shaking his head, he burst out in a hearty chortle. "Our adventure in these northern seas gets stranger by the day! How's that, my rogues? He's one of *us* now. And see what he did to poor Stervy?!" At that, the rest of his rogues went into hysterics.

Brand sighed, then noticing Alucard's hairpiece once again, he said crossly, "In the name of my mother, *what is that*, Al?!"

"Hair," beamed Alucard proudly. "Cil braided it for me."

Brand reached out and felt it, then drew back in alarm. "It feels... *real*." Then, noticing a slight perfume he had not smelled in some weeks, "What is this? *Lilac.* Who?... it smells like... *Salome!*" Brand jumped to his feet and shook his fist at Alucard. "Are you mad? You *did* cut her hair off that night. You almost got me killed for that!"

Cil chuckled cruelly in the background.

"Let's not jump to conclusions, father. There were other, more definite factors at work that occasioned her madness... and your resultant trip to Zanon's paradise," replied Alucard in his calm voice.

"It *was* a definite factor!" Brand raged.

"Let us not talk of Salome anymore. I am bored with the subject," said Alucard blandly. "Besides, we have more immediate concerns to address."

Brand stuttered, his face a picture of wrath, and then said, "What —what pressing concerns?"

"Our gold supply has been completely exhausted. Thus, I advise we immediately take up employment so we can pay our lodging, which is due in two days. Not to mention transport back to Revilis Ko'hur."

Brand struggled for words. "You spent *all* our funds? On this— this gaudy, glamour-ridden coiffure of a deceased woman's stolen hair?!"

"In a word: yes."

"I'm gonna rip that thing off your head and sell it *right now!*"

Cil, Berengar, and all the buccaneers burst into hearty chuckle, further stoking Brand's ire.

Talin held up a hand, admonishing Brand. "Now, now, brother, don't throw shade on this tiny brother's swag. His braids are as rakish an accessory as I have seen on any man of worth. Let me get him a hat and coat like my brothers wear, and he shall be as one of us!"

"I agree with Talin!" said Cil with a gusty laugh. "Besides, I spent *hours* braiding that thing. Don't you *dare* tamper with my work!" She raised an eyebrow and glared at him threateningly.

Brand made an inarticulate sound—the beginnings of a cry of wrath—but then caught himself and relaxed, deciding that if it came to it he'd steal the wig later on. He realized something else had also annoyed him—*How dare they assume to tell him how to raise his child?!*

Talin distracted him from his brooding with a raised finger. "Aren't you going to introduce me to the lady?"

Cil directed her most engaging smile at Talin and said, "Take notes, Brand."

"Ah, yes of course." Brand's etiquette training from his time with the Zanonnites kicked in, and he correctly introduced Talin to Cil. "Lady Cil, I would like to introduce Talin of Meran to you. Talin, meet Lady Cil."

"Much better, Brand," Cil said with an impish clap of delight. Then, to Talin, "Pleased to meet you."

Some of Talin's rogues were clearly enchanted by this green-eyed, red-haired wonder, but Cil paid them no heed beyond the initial introductions.

Berengar was now resting his head, face-down on the table. He seemed to have fallen asleep, one hand still gripping his mug and the other, his dagger hilt.

Brand brought Cil and Alucard up to date.

Talin continued on, "Now, where was I? Oh yes! Stervy comes in panting like a bordello girl and as wet as one too, and yelling, 'Bloody trickery!' So I leap up from my game, grab him by the shoulders and I says, 'If it's an emergency, then speak up, you dirty dog! Aren't you meant to be watching the ship? What's gotten into you?'

"He says, 'Cap'n, the ship was boarded by a party of great big blond-haired Outlanders! So I start cracking their nuts likes I always do... but Cap'n...'

"Stervy gave me a look as if all he knew as solid and real in the world was confounded and turned upside down upon his head. He looked so confused and miserable that my anger was aroused and my heart reached out to him in sudden compassion.

"'But what, good Stervy?!' says I.

"'I cracked their nuts, Cap'n... but, Cap'n, their *nuts didn't crack!* The next thing I know, I'm tossed overboard and struggling through the surge towards the quay, the sound of their scornful laughter echoing out above my head.'

"At this news of this poor treatment of our good Stervy, red rage flashed into my heart and, likewise, the hearts of my rogues. All jumped up from the game table, sober-faced and stony-eyed. 'Nobody tosses Stervy overboard!' says I. My brothers concurred, and so we all took to the streets, ignoring the solicitations of the innkeeper regarding our bill. We made our way to where the *Slippery Stefania* had been docked, ready to deal out the sea's justice. But, when we arrived, we saw her unmoored and pulling away from the quay. We watched, speechless, as our dear girl and her cargo of plunder faded into the dusk of night.

"We waited for the robbers' return to Keel, with the smoldering vengeance of a slighted eunuch, but they didn't return that day. Nor the next, nor the next. The days turned into weeks as we swilled away our gold in a roistering of deep depression—you see, the *Slippery Stefania* is like a part of us. Without her, we was lost. Much of this period of grief I have forgotten, like a bad dream upon waking.

"Then, finally, one morning, as I strode bleary-eyed and hungover from my dockside den, with the day's first drink in on my tongue, I saw her—swinging into the pier—the *Slippery Stefania.*

"Quickly, I roused the lads, and we readied ourselves for a fight —to the death if necessary. We vowed we wouldn't let our Stefania out of our sights again. We took position behind some crates by the mooring pin and waited.

"The ship was secured, and the gangplank cast down. Fearing delay, we bounded up the gangplank with swords in hand, expecting a bloody and doubtful fight—but never expecting what awaited us."

"The ship's crew were not men. Not men, no. Men we could have dealt with. We found ourselves confronted by the fiercest, hard-bitten band of she-bears you ever saw. Armed and armored to the teeth, with hair of liquid gold and eyes like the northern glaciers. They shouted taunts and such, which we couldn't understand for their accent. Nor could I have listened even had I understood their words, for at that moment, I had fallen in love, with all the force of my romantic young heart. There, on the poop deck, looking down at me with an expression of scornful disgust, stood the captain, golden-haired queen, hard as Devirien Steel.

"That was the last thing I recalled of the incident, since at that second, the blow of a mailed fist knocked me senseless. I'm told that, while I lay there unconscious—no doubt dreaming of my newfound love—my lusty rogues were soundly chastised by this group of haughty shield-maidens, before being driven down the gangplank and onto the pier, conquered, ravaged and dispirited.

Upon waking from my slumber the next day, I went into action planning my revenge. No longer would we swill away the days. We were not worthy of such females! We had not prepared, and we had paid the price. I kicked my rogues into action, putting a curfew on carousing and instituting a strict daily training routine. Later, I learned that the she-captain's name was Kris—Kris of Valr." He stopped for a second and shook Berengar awake. "Outlander, you know of this place?"

Berengar swayed upright in his chair, gave Talin a red-eyed glare and said, "Sure." He then went back to drowsing.

Talin seemed not to care and went on, "I further learned that this same band occasionally visits Keel, to spend their plunder on feminine pleasures and dainties, such as the exclusive spa."

"Wait," said Cil, "what ship did they use prior to stealing yours to visit Keel?"

Talin waved a hand dismissively. "Who cares? You're missing the point—we need to get our *Stefania* back!"

Cil took on a stubborn expression, and Talin quickly corrected himself. "Perhaps they previously ventured on land, or perhaps they lost their own ship to another band of rogues."

Cil accepted this but wasn't done. "Wait, one more thing."

"Yes?"

"There's a *spa*?"

"Yes, indeed. A facility also owned by that cretin Thedmir. He gives the warrior-women special access and hopes to ingratiate himself with them. The fool."

"Okay, cut to the chase," said Brand impatiently.

Talin grinned. "Well, I couldn't help but overhear your friend here, Alucard, mentioning a voyage to Revilis Ko'hur."

Brand winced; he hated his plans getting out and about. "Yes. And what of it?"

"Well, here's the deal. The warrior women are twelve in number, and me and my rogues make eight. With your four, we could match them one for one.

"Help us teach this overstepping band of she-bandits a lesson, and we will give you free passage back to Revilis Ko'hur—that is, after I take a moment to repay Kris in the most *intimate* of ways." At this, the handsome youth's face took on an almost sinister expression of contemplative glee.

Cil shivered. "Ew, gross."

Talin laughed throatily and continued, giving a summary of the plan. "The barbarianesses could arrive any time in the next week or two, based on their prior habit, and this time *we shall be ready*."

Talin laid out a tactical plan for all to follow, each member having their part to play. Then he went into particular detail regarding one of the more dangerous women. "One woman in particular, a shield-maiden who goes by the name of Gilgamina

Neerstar, needs special consideration. Her size is prodigious. Her fierce valor, beyond reproach. Her beauty, megalithic. At each of her bare-handed blows, she fells a single common man."

Brand and Cil both pointed eagerly to the sleeping figure of Berengar.

Talin nodded. "Good. It will likely be a close match, but he looks to be a sound fighter."

Hands were clasped in a warrior's grip, and the covenant was fixed by oaths—all except for Berengar, who slept away the minutes, unaware of his future task, or perhaps…plight.

Talin stretched and yawned. "Good. Now that that's settled, it's our curfew. We can't miss our morning training session. Be seeing you around—oh, and by the way, Brand, be sure to clean yourself up. You look ridiculous."

Brand scowled, then, remembering his lack of gold, leaned forward eagerly. "So, Talin, before you go... since we're in this together, would you be able to lend me a few bullions so that I can..."

Talin raised a hand and cut him off. "I'm sorry, Brand. I really would like to, but I'm afraid I am as broke as you are." He made a show of examining his own tattered garments. "I blanch to consider what I may end up wearing on the morrow myself. If you will recall, we have had no ship with which to make excursions—or *incursions* with for some time. We are now living on the mere *vapors* of long gone treasures."

Brand cursed and shook his fist after him. "Cheap bastard. What happened to all that talk of 'brothers' and 'lusty rogues'?!"

Cil chuckled. "Brand, you look like an angry yellow-crested rooster in those tattered undergarments. Whatever happened to your clothes?"

Brand scowled. "It's a long story." He waved a hand dismissively and took a large draft from his tankard.

"I'm glad to see you made new friends, Father," said Alucard.

"*You!* If you had not been so extravagant, I'd be able to replace my outfit."

Alucard shrugged slightly, negating responsibility. "What happened to the not inconsiderable stock of bullions I gave you to use?"

"Oh, so it's *my* fault?" Brand growled.

"It is clearly not *mine*," said the small frog-man, his weighty braids clicking and jingling with their gemstones.

Brand staggered off to the gaming table and, introducing a set of cards he had taken from the Cave of Ator Periconias, played a number of successful hands while Cil stayed at the table to look after Berengar.

Alucard watched Brand excitedly from beside the gaming table, eventually questioning why Brand had put a certain card up his sleeve instead of back into the deck. The other gamers—a pair of heavy-set adventurers and the third, Igan's bouncer—swelled with rage and threatened to throw Brand off the quay on a charge of cheating. With some quick talking, and by the act of returning 29 of the 30 silver bullions he had won, Brand managed to convince them that the card was a keepsake and assuage their wrath.

Brand, in his current state of dishevelment, found himself the clown of the inn and gained no more attention from any of the womenfolk present. Eventually, a sad and dejected Brand tottered up to his room and passed out on his bed.

Stirring awake around mid-morning, Brand dressed once again in the loose white cotton outfit, paired with his worn boating loafers. It reeked of poverty, but he wore it in as stylish a manner as possible, leaving the top of his blouse unbuttoned and affecting an airy, carefree swagger.

He joined Cil and Alucard on the mezzanine for breakfast, and they discussed how they would earn money for another four days room and board. They needed two golden bullions for the lot of them. Cil still had five silver bullions left, which was exactly what she needed for her share of the cost. She, unlike the boys, had been organized and prepared enough to at least save that much. Thus, she didn't need to work and, refusing Brand's requests to work with him for the greater good of the group, stated that she would be busy relaxing at the inn or enjoying the bathing pools in the nearby bay.

Alucard had spent his coin down to a bullion on that headpiece and agreed to team up with Brand in earning their share of the board. Today, the fish-creature wore a rice-paper lantern he had found in the alley next to the *Sea's Embrace*, claiming that the wig was for special occasions only. Cil said that Berengar had risen early and gone out in search of labor work at the docks— apparently, Brand noted with a sort of perverse pleasure, the golden giant had wasted away his money too.

Finishing their late breakfast, which had dragged out into a lunch, Brand and Alucard parted company with Cil and headed over to the quay-side promenade across the street. Talin and his rogues were just at this minute leaving a vendor, each with a roasted sausage on a kebab. Brand noticed with a keen eye that Talin was once again fitted out in a beautiful blue outfit with a matching hat and coat.

"Good morning, brother!" said Talin with a grin.

"Morning, Talin." Brand eyed his outfit curiously. "Nice outfit— strange that—I thought you bereft of all funds?"
Talin raised a hand, just like the night before. "Ah, I know what you must be thinking. Brand, this was my last set of clothing." He made a show of patting his pockets down again. "Nope, nothing left over after paying for this one measly meal—the first in days." He shook his head in mock pity. "I'll let you know as soon as I have something extra. Gotta be going now, we have our training

session!" He turned and headed off in haste down the street, shouting back over his shoulder, "Maybe try the docks for some work? Good luck, Brand!"

Brand turned toward the pier and sullenly observed the packs of sweaty, shirtless laborers loading and unloading the few ships in port.

Alucard made polite conversation. "There seems plenty of room for employment at the docks."

Brand grimaced and approached a foreman. "What are the terms of employment?"

The sturdy foreman eyed Brand's lean frame without enthusiasm. Then, seeing Alucard, his eyes brightened with interest. "Hey there, little fella! Do you want a snack?"

"Sure," said Alucard.

The man nearly jumped.

Brand redirected his attention. "Sir, terms of employment?"

The man shook himself, then said sternly to Brand, "Two copper an hour. But we won't put up with any *slackness* on the job."

Brand walked away in disgust.

"What's wrong?" said Alucard.

"Two copper bullions an hour, *to slave away like that*?"

"I'm sure there's some way to make money using *magic*."

"Don't you *dare!* You may bring the whole town down upon us! Magic isn't a normal thing, you know? Nobody even believes in it where I come from!"

"That sounds like great profit potential."

"I *absolutely forbid it!*"

"So, the dockyard?"

"By no means! Let me think, will you?" Brand swaggered casually over to a nearby stall, where a particularly delicious-looking array of packed ice confections had caught his eye.

The swarthy store manager noticed Brand's interest and spoke up. "You like what you see, aye? The most refreshing treat in Keel. The perfect snack on such a sweltering day as this."

Brand licked his lips, which now seemed suddenly parched. "How much are they?"

"Five copper each."

"Five copper? That's nearly a tenth of what I need for room and board at the *Sea's Embrace—an extravagant sum!*"

"Aye, I agree. It is an *extravagant* treat. The ice must be preserved and imported from the northern wastes. Only the most *worthy* and *noble* citizens can afford such a *luxury.*"

Brand paid over the single silver coin he had left.

The man wrapped up two of the treats in paper, giving one to Brand and one to Alucard. Finding a comfortable bench near the water, Brand sat down, motioned Alucard over, and began nibbling at his confection.

Alucard climbed onto the bench beside him, ate his own icy treat in a single gulp—paper wrapper and all—and then said, "Now we need ten silver instead of nine."

"Don't be such a *killjoy,*" said Brand, taking his time to enjoy his own treat. "Ahh, this is *exactly* what I needed to think clearly! See," he gestured toward the brawny, tanned men working along the dock, "this is why laborers stay laborers. They are too busy rushing to and fro, hither thither, in all manner of helter-skelter to ever sit down and figure out a better way to earn a living."

"Go on?" said Alucard, his naturally conniving mind taking an instant interest.

"My dear friend, I have just this second come up with a plan that will make us far more money, with far less effort."

"Yeah?"

"Yes. Do you recall the first night we arrived in Keel and saw that exotic animal trader? Let me explain..."

Fifteen minutes later, after searching the alley behind the *Sea's*

Embrace, Brand and Alucard had what they needed: a wooden crate, an old raggedy blanket, and a tattered rope. Choosing a conspicuous spot on the quay promenade, Brand upended the crate and put the ragged blanket around himself like a cloak. The rope he tied around Alucard's neck like a collar, and told him to squat like a toad, resting his hands on the ground as well as his feet.

Brand opened his empty pouch and placed it before them on the ground. Then, standing on the crate, he cried out in a brassy voice, "*Come one, come all!* See the gigantic talking frog! *Free to view!* Five copper bullions to ask it a *question!*"

Business was brisk, and by late afternoon Brand and Alucard had accumulated over twenty-five silver bullions in various denominations. Brand was now busy counting his money. A shadow loomed behind, and he turned in sudden alarm.

A grotesquely made-up face. The rustle of many-colored feathers crowding in on him.

The exotic animal trader.

He must have been in a dead run, for he hit Brand with a belly thrust of enormous velocity, sending the leaner youth flying off the crate to land sprawling on the hard-packed dirt some yards away.

"*This* is my territory! How *dare* you cut into my beat!" the animal trader roared, his fat double chin wobbling beneath his face of clownish makeup. His gold bangles jingled and jangled on large, fleshy ears as he spoke. His great belly quivered with agitation, and his flabby breast, waxed clean of hair, heaved grotesquely beneath the flimsy strap of his purple silk toga.

Brand tried to gather himself, rolling over to his hands and knees. Another shadow.

He looked up to see the animal trader charging again, great flabby arms outstretched.

Brand roared an insult and rose to meet him—then froze in the act of drawing his daggers. He wasn't allowed to deliver lethal blows in Keel! In that moment of hesitation, the man caught him off guard in a mighty bear hug, lifted him up, and began to worry at his left nipple with his bare teeth like a wild animal.

He was shorter than Brand, but far heavier. Brand struggled, arms pinned to his sides, completely unable to extricate himself from this unexpected horror—this quivering slab of padded muscle, like a sleekly-fat, oiled seal.

Brand screamed, a high-pitched feminine cry of dismay. The man forced him to the ground and fell on top of him, pressing Brand's lean frame into the dirt beneath. It looked like a walrus wrestling with a gazelle. The man's shaven chest smothered Brand's face. Brand turned his head to the side in search of air.

There was Alucard, squatting nearby and cheering him on. "You can do it, Father! I have faith in you! *A single, killing thrust!*"

"It's *not allowed!* Damn you, Al, help me!"

"Try to take over *my* spot, will you? Exotic animals is *my* niche! We don't take kindly to newcomers pushing us out of what's ours here in Keel, boy! Hehe, taste my sweat! You like that, do you? *Ha!*" The animal handler seemed to get a perverse pleasure from molesting Brand—in addition to beating him down.

Brand opened his eyes wide and strained his neck in search of anything that would help. There—was that Berengar?

Yes, it *was* Berengar, walking past, shirtless and wearing only a loincloth. His muscles slick with sweat and bronzed by the sun. He carried a ship's replacement anchor over one great shoulder and had a group of women fawning after him with chilled sacks of wine in their hands. He grinned down at Brand as he swaggered by.

"Help, you great oaf!" gasped Brand.

"This is good training for you. Give it to him, Wolf!"

He swaggered off, the females following close behind.

"Ber? Berrrrrrr!!" Brand wailed.

An hour later, a bedraggled, scratched-up, and oily Brand

hobbled back to the *Sea's Embrace*. He reeked of odd animal smells, and his mouth was salty with the fat trader's sweat.

Alucard walked beside him in a cheerful swagger. "Well, that was a productive day, at least," said the small blue creature.

Brand let out a long, piteous groan. "How so? That damned animal trader shamed me in the worst way, ruined my last good set of casual clothing, and worse—confiscated *all* the bullions we made today!"

"Well, he gave *me* a delicious biscuit, at least."

"You idiot, that was a *dog* biscuit."

"I stand by my previous statement."

Brand made a limp gesture, too tired to argue. Alucard continued, "Well, the good news is we have at least two more days to figure out the ten silver bullions."

Ignoring Alucard's comments, Brand slipped through the lobby of the inn, up the stairs, and into bed. *The only good news is that Cil didn't see what happened today,* he thought. *That would have been beyond dishonor.*

That night, instead of staying in bed, Brand sat at the small table in his room, brooding over what the animal trader had done to him. Around eight o'clock, Brand's vindictive streak failed him, and he passed out, still sitting upright at the desk. Alucard, finding Brand there when he awoke, laid some pillows on the floor next to the chair and managed to drag him onto them without waking him.

Brand slept until twilight. Donning the old raggedy cloak from the previous day, he slipped out into the night without a word to Alucard, Cil, or Berengar. He blended into the crowds of Keel like a shadow, and none of his friends saw him for the rest of the evening...

Chapter 18

"A fair exchange is no robbery."

To Kris, My Steely Snow Blossom:

I shall not lose the hour we met—Your eyes,
cold blue as oceans fret
Where frost and flame together gleam;
and steel-wrought light outburns a dream
Across the seas I've dared to roam,
from starlit isles to tempest foam
In search of one whose soul would dare,
to chase the wind, to laugh, to share
The revel bold, the thieving art—
the storm-born creed that binds the heart
Now ever near your flame I steer,
as twin-blades drawn, or oars held near
And in your absence falls the night...
Though tell me true... was it my height?
Penned by Jabari Runewrit, at the behest of Captain Talin

***

The next morning, Brand came down to breakfast. He had washed the white cotton outfit as best he could, but the dirt scuffs from the animal trader's assault still showed faintly across the fabric.

Ignoring Cil's and Berengar's suspicious gazes, he asked breezily, "Now, how are my dear friends today? A wonderful day in Keel, isn't it? The water is clean and blue, the food is great—if you can afford it, of course—but who needs gold and luxuries when you have friends, right?"

Cil scowled. "You're acting weird."

"Me? I'm *fantastic!* How about you, Cil? Your hair is quite red and beautiful today." He beamed at her.

"No, you're definitely acting weird."

"If happy is weird, then yes, I am weird! Haha! Well, my friends, excuse me, I wish to walk the promenade. Toodle-oo."

Brand swaggered downstairs and out into the street. Cil and Berengar watched him go with frowns of concern.

"*What is up with him?*" said Cil.

Berengar growled, "Bah. Perhaps the shellacking he got yesterday affected his wits. He's been funny ever since... but usually he would stew on such a thing, not be so gay and happy."

"Oh, he stewed *indeed,*" said Alucard. "Two nights ago, he sat awake at the table until dawn, his face a mask of displeasure. Then, he slept on the floor throughout the day and went out in the evening. I don't know what he did then."

"And now he's chirpy today?" said Berengar, scratching his golden beard. "Say, if he goes out again tonight, why don't we three follow him and see what he's been doing?"

"Sure," said Alucard.

Cil leaned forward, suddenly excited. "That sounds like *fun!*"

"But we need to find a couple of old blankets for cloaks, and you, Alucard, need to ride under my cloak on my back. Brand is a wily one, and it won't be easy to trail him without him noticing."

"Deal," said Cil.

"Ok," said Alucard.

The three finished breakfast and went about their own affairs for the day. Tomorrow, they would need to pay another week's board. Cil had her money. Berengar would have enough by day's end. Alucard and Brand had nothing to show for their two days—but Alucard decided that if Brand wasn't worried, he wouldn't worry either.

That evening, Brand returned for dinner and then, claiming he was tired, went up to his room. Berengar and the others went outside and wrapped themselves in their dirty old blankets. Alucard was on Berengar's back as planned, his small face peering over the Outlander's shoulder from within his cloak.

Cil watched the front entrance of the inn while Berengar went into the alley around back. After a few minutes, the yellow square of light from Brand's window flickered, then vanished. A gentle creak. Movement in the dark of Brand's room. The window raised. A flitter of silvery moonlight caught a cloak of dirty gray wool—Brand, climbing down the side of the building like a great gray rat.

Berengar moved back down the alley and imitated the call of a nighthawk—the signal for Cil to join him. Then, fearing he would lose the trail, he poked his head back around the corner just in time to see Brand slinking off toward the mouth of another alley.

Berengar started to follow, then froze. Ahead, Brand had stopped suddenly and scanned the alley behind him. He looked back and forth, then up toward the rooftops, before moving on.

Cil had heard the signal and arrived. She squirmed in close and peered around the corner. Her voice, the mere whisper of an evening breeze, reached Berengar's ears. "What's happened?"

"There." He indicated Brand slipping into the farther alleyway. "Stay on me."

Thus it was that Berengar, Cil, and Alucard trailed Brand through the network of back alleys that made up the inner works of Keel. Ducking projections from crooked buildings, avoiding tangles of sailors' ropes strewn across the ground, squeezing through tight crevices where the alley had nearly vanished entirely, and occasionally stepping over drunken revelers or scandalous lovers.

Presently, Brand reached his destination: a peculiarly empty street in a fairly nice part of Keel's eastern district. A few commuters dotted the long stretch, moving in small, quiet groups. They seemed to be locals—not adventurers, sailors, or revelers. A quiet neighborhood street.

One side was lined with houses, slightly better built than most in Keel but still in the same crooked style. The other was bordered by a long stone wall, eight or nine feet high, running the length of the street before falling away into more buildings. Likely the remains of some failed effort to build an organized district.

Berengar, Cil, and Alucard pressed themselves against the shadows of their alley and peeked out. Cil's delicate face beneath Berengar's, and above them both, Alucard's round blue face peeking from the Outlander's hood. They looked like three mice stacked atop one another in the dark.

Brand approached a spot in the wall and leaned casually against it, glancing around. Every time he looked in their direction, the three faces ducked back.

It quickly became clear he was waiting.

His moment came. When the street was empty, Brand scaled the stone wall with catlike ease.

Berengar grunted in approval. "We've been outside cities so long, I've never seen Brand in his element."

"I didn't realize he had *any* useful skills," Cil replied, her lip curling impishly—though a strange glow in her eye hinted at something more.

Now atop the wall, Brand disappeared for a moment, then reappeared, struggling with a bulky object. They could barely make it out—a dark blotch against the stars. He moved around up there, fiddling.

They waited. And waited. Eventually, they grew drowsy. Nothing more moved atop the wall. The night stretched on.

Locals occasionally passed. Each time, Cil and Berengar lowered their faces and pretended to be urchins huddled in the alley. They were ignored.

Around an hour past midnight, by the moon's angle, Berengar tapped Cil lightly on the shoulder. Someone familiar was approaching.

The animal trader—oiled feathers and all. Earrings, bangles, and baubles clinked as he waddled up the street. Two hired bruisers followed, likely escorting him home. His belt pouch swayed, heavy with bullions.

He stopped at the house directly across from Brand's perch. The guards waited as he unlocked a series of heavy bolts. Then he paid them off and waddled inside. The sound of bolts clanking into place echoed down the street.

"The lad must have stalked the man to his house two nights back," Berengar murmured in awe.

"Creepy," said Cil.

Berengar shrugged.

Again they waited.

They were not disappointed. Around two a.m., Brand climbed down the wall, trailing a line of heavy rope. Ignoring the locked door, he located a small projection just above and to the right of the frame and secured the rope to it with a complicated knot.

Then he returned to the top of the wall.

His silhouette reappeared, straining with a larger, more solid object. He pushed it over the far side—a heavy shape vanished from view. The rope snapped taut.

A crunch. Then a rending groan.

The projection Brand had anchored the rope to stretched... then tore free. The entire structural beam ripped loose and dragged across the street. Part of the facade gave way. The wall around the door sagged, then collapsed. The door fell flat.

Brand's keen eye had spotted the weakness in the haphazard construction—like a missing piece in a puzzle—and used it to devastating effect.

A muffled cry from inside the house. Brand's form ducked low on top of the wall. A few seconds later, the animal trader came squealing forth from the gaping hole where his doorway had been. He carried a small dog, which he clung to and squeezed in his perturbation. His shiny round form glistened nakedly in the moonlight. The dog became agitated by the squeezing and bit him so that he dropped it, cursing, and let it run back into the house.

The animal trader dumbly considered the destroyed facade. Then, following the path of destruction, he spied the tangled mass of rope at the foot of the wall. He tottered over to investigate, still in a state of perplexed shock.

As he approached, the shadowy form of Brand rose up—a dark bulk clutched in his arms. The light of a nearby lantern caught it. A bulky sack of potatoes.

Brand tossed the sack down. Then jumped.

The animal trader looked up just in time. His head disappeared into the sack—he didn't even have time to wail. He staggered from the impact. Then Brand landed with both feet on top of the sack, kicking down as hard as he could. The trader's body crumpled like a slaughtered ox.

Brand rose from the heap and dusted himself off. The animal trader was clean unconscious.

Brand darted into the house. Seconds later, the alarmed barking of the small dog rang out. A few more seconds, and Brand emerged again, carrying a heavy purse. He clipped it to his belt. Then, seeing the street still empty, he paused. Almost as an afterthought, he stripped the unconscious man of all his jewelry. Tucking these into the now-bulging pouch, he gently cupped the man's cheek in the palm of his hand—a simple gesture, yet peculiarly sinister given the circumstances. Then, like a gray shadow, he vanished over the wall.

Cil whistled in disbelief. "Gods, let me not get on Brand's bad side."

Berengar grinned like a lion. "I like a good brooder! Besides, in Keel, an equal trade is no *crime*." He chuckled and clapped her on the shoulder. "When it comes to vengeance, the boy's a constructive genius."

Cil grunted and smiled wistfully.

"I am proud of you, Father," said Alucard, raising a small green-blue fist into the night air. "We shall eat some more of the icy *luxuries* tomorrow!"

The next day, Berengar and Cil found Brand lounging on a silk-covered divan on the mezzanine with Alucard. Strewn about the surrounding tables were a pack of cards, a stack of empty mugs and plates, and a range of iced confections. Alucard's elastic belly was swollen like a fat toad's. Brand looked slightly bloated and now wore an immaculate outfit of black silk, filigreed in silver at all the right places. His shirt was unbuttoned at the top, and a matching black-and-silver coat hung over the chair beside him.

Later that day, when it came time to pay another four days' board, Brand was there. Right on time.

Brand spent the next week in luxury—lounging through the day, swilling away the early evenings at the gaming table with Talin and his crew. Nothing untoward occurred, apart from the occasional visit from the suspicious animal trader. Each time, Igan would signal Brand to hide and explain to the man that the poor youth had been holed up for days, suffering from a severe case of dysentery. And each time, the trader would scan the room as if hoping to catch a glimpse, until Igan had him escorted out by the bouncer. Furious and foaming, the man would hiss and spit insults as he was frog-marched out of the inn.

Brand was even kind enough to start covering Cil's expenses once her silver ran out—and he did so with a magnanimous largeness that irked her no end.

Berengar, meanwhile, was happy to work away the hours in the sun to earn his keep.

Finally, the day they'd been waiting for came.

Brand and the others were eating breakfast on the mezzanine when Stervy charged into the inn asking for them. Igan pointed him up, and the one-legged man hobbled up the stairs in a huff.

"The *Slippery Stefania!*" barked the panting Stervy. "She's been spied rounding the granite cliffs to the north of the bay. She'll be docking in an hour, assuming they ride the tides right."

Brand jumped to his feet, his demeanor shifting instantly. "*Fantastic!* Finally, me and Berengar can return to Revilis Ko'hur, where my mother awaits." A pause. Concern flickered across his youthful face. "She *better* be okay."

"Aye, she better," said Berengar, with a fierce curse and a brooding glare eastward.

Brand nodded, that vindictive streak flashing green in his eyes.

Cil nodded too—quietly, less enthusiastically.

Brand looked at her. "What's the matter?"

"Nothing." Cil shrugged. "Let me pack my stuff too." She walked toward the stairs.

Alucard clapped his hands. "Good! Out of this town so I can use magi—"

Brand raised a fist and shook it at him.

Stervy didn't catch the word, but eyed the creature suspiciously —he'd never truly gotten over his fear of the small blue man. "Aye, aye," he muttered. "Now get your gear. There may not be time to return for it if things get out of hand."

"Out of hand?" said Berengar. "Who are we fighting?"

"Just wait and see. You've yet to witness a *real* brawl in Keel. Who knows how this one'll go, or whether the locals'll choose sides. The place'll be a damn riot!" He grinned.

"You say that like it's a *good* thing," said Brand.

Stervy just chuckled. "Go on, get yer gear!" He hobbled back down the stairs and out the door.

Brand cast a troubled glance after Cil as she disappeared up the stairs, then turned to Berengar.

"What's up with *her*? She's been acting weird all week."

"Well, lad. You haven't exactly paid her much attention."

"Why? Because it's a *bad idea* to do so, that's why—less clouts to the head that way."

"Yeah, well. Did you think to ask her what she'll do next, now that we're heading back to Revilis Ko'hur? It's not like you *invited* her to come along or anything."

"Why *wouldn't* she be welcome?—I just thought she'd want to... you know, go back to her village?"

Berengar shrugged. "You never know until you *ask*."

Brand scratched his chin, thought for a moment, then said, "Okay, I'll talk to her."

They fetched their gear, gave a final farewell to Igan and the bouncer—who waved them off with a few embarrassing tears (likely more for the lost coin than anything sentimental)—and headed toward the quay.

At the planned ambush site—a narrow stretch of quay hemmed in by crates and half-collapsed tackle sheds—they met Talin and his seven rogues and reviewed the plan.

The hour arrived.

The *Slippery Stefania* pulled into the pier and anchored. Mooring lines secured. Gangplank thrown down.

A great sailing chant echoed across the harbor—sublime altos in haunting harmony. The voices of many powerful women rising in unison. Brand couldn't make out the words—the northern accent was thick—but he thought he heard something about fjords and ice-cold currents. The chant continued as the unseen crew prepared to disembark.

Brand hadn't known what to expect, but even if he had, it wouldn't have helped.

Down the plank marched twelve of the fiercest-looking women he had ever seen. Still chanting. The rhythm lent a dynamic charge to their already commanding presence. A ripple of hushed exclamations escaped the lips of all the men. Only Alucard and Cil remained unaffected.

Each woman was tall and well-made—athletic yet unmistakably feminine. Straight, symmetrical features. Soft pink lips. Eyes glacier blue, or blue-gray with amber flecks. Hair golden, styled in intricate braids. Each wore a blue steel armor-plated loin guard, matching breast cups, and a long white-furred mantle lined in blue silk. High-strung sandals. Their bare thighs, bellies, and arms dazzled Talin's men into near stupefaction.

Brand wasn't distracted by their bodies—he'd grown up around nudity. But he *was* distracted by the looming possibility of hand-to-hand annihilation. Cil showed only a grim petulance. Alucard simply stared, uncomprehending.

Berengar wasn't drooling either.

Berengar wasn't drooling because he was *terrified.*

He had slept through Talin's entire briefing. And was just now realizing exactly who they were up against.

"*They* are who we're fighting?" he hissed in sudden alarm.

Talin looked at him, confused. "Yes, big man, did you not hear the plan?"

Berengar glared at Talin, eyes wide. "If I had, I wouldn't be here right now! Those are Borderlands shield-maidens of the *third tier!* *Twelve* of them! We would barely have a chance in hand-to-hand combat—if they bring their weapons ashore... we haven't a chance..."

Talin and the others stared blankly, doubt creeping in.

Brand, suddenly nervous, cleared his throat. "Ber, we've got to try. This is our ticket back to Revilis Ko'hur. *My mother...*"

"Damnit, I *know* it!" Berengar began to curse furiously under his breath. Then, seeing they were out of time, consigned his soul to Mackmellah and readied himself for the rush.

The women had reached the pier and were walking toward the ambush site. Thankfully, they'd left their shields and war weapons aboard—likely aware of Keel's rules, and confident in their hand-to-hand abilities.

"Well, there's hope," Berengar muttered.

As the raiders huddled behind crates, observing the oncoming force, Talin assigned each man a target.

One woman stood apart. A primeval titaness. Matron of chaos. She-warden of the elder abyss. The colossus of feminine perfection. She stood eight feet tall and weighed well over four hundred pounds. The stones of the pier groaned under her step. But she wasn't fat—no. She was sleekly muscular, round in all the right places—perfectly proportioned, just two or three times the size of the others, who were themselves far from ordinary.

"There she is, Ber—that's your opponent. *Gilgamina Neerstar.* You got this! Just an *opportunity* for *training, right?*" Brand grinned wickedly.

"*What in the chaos of creation?...*" Berengar whispered. But there was no more time.

With yips and cries, Talin's men sprang from hiding and swarmed the titanic females from all sides. As Brand rushed out, his eyes locked on a figure at the rear—smaller than the rest, yet impossible to miss. This must be Kris of Valr.

Not by size, but by presence did she dominate. She was the leader—not a titaness like Gilgamina, but a goddess who dictated the world's creation.

Time slowed. Their gazes met like frozen statues among the

charging crowds. Her lips moved, and he thought he saw her mouth the words: *Such green eyes. Such golden hair.* The intensity in her gaze overwhelmed him. He stumbled back.

"Quit gawking, beanstalk! You're making me sick!" Cil's voice snapped him back to reality.

A second later, Kris's voice cracked through the chaos like a whip. "Girls, bring me that *boy!* I have chosen a new *toy!*"

Brand felt electrified. That possessive hunger in her voice... where had he felt this before? A flash of Salome's face, merged grotesquely with Queen Charlotte's mandibles, passed through his mind. He shivered, brushing it aside. Focus.

Someone must have tipped off the townsfolk. The promenade and main street were suddenly lined with hundreds of spectators, cheering and clapping with each clash. There was Thedmir and his crew—though Brand knew they wouldn't interfere. The sentiment in the air was clear: this rakish contest of pirates' valor versus the northern shield-maidens would not be interrupted.

Atop a pile of crates near the *Sea's Embrace*, the kooky band had begun to play—a rebellious sea shanty on violin and drum. Igan joined in with a massive pair of cymbals, crashing them in time with the tune.

The song spoke of wild adventure, plunder, and forgotten treasure—and it freed Talin's men from fear. Brand felt his own confidence returning. The brawl had begun.

"Change of plan, lads!" Talin shouted. "Protect Brother Brand at all costs—he needs to make the ship!"

The two parties collided. Never before had Keel witnessed such a melee—fierce men battling their female counterparts in a tide that surged and rolled like a stormy sea.

Brand dashed atop a row of stacked crates, looking for an opening. Two women slammed the crates below. He somersaulted over them, clutching his purse and travel pack. Two of Talin's men leapt onto the women to restrain them. A second later, they were the ones pinned beneath the shield-maidens—back and forth it went, somewhere between wrestling and lovemaking.

Two more women darted for Brand at Kris's command, but Tiny and Unleke intercepted. Stervy tried to block a third, but she knocked him clean off the pier with a casual buffet. A splash followed his cry.

Brand dashed behind the woman and shoved her over the edge to follow after Stervy. Another scream, another splash.

To his left, he saw Gilgamina Neerstar hoist Berengar over her head, spin him once, then hurl him through the ceiling of a storage shed. The golden barbarian vanished among the splintering boards as Gilgamina waded in after him. That was the last Brand saw of Berengar that day.

A gap in the line. A path to the ship.

Brand darted for it, Alucard clinging to his back, braids jingling in all directions. The roars of wrestling echoed around him.

Suddenly, cold blue eyes blocked his path.

Kris of Valr.

Talin swooped in from the left. "I got this one, brother! She's *mine! Yippee!*"

The buccaneer charged with joy—and met her rising fist.

Talin dropped like a sack of wet flour, eyes rolled back, a cherubic smile on his lips. He landed at her feet. A folded scrap of paper fluttered down beside him. Brand thought he glimpsed a few lines of poetry on it. He blinked, then looked up.

Kris stepped between him and the ship. "You're *mine,* boy."

"Like *hell* you overgrown hussy!" came a venomous voice from behind.

A flash of red shot past—Cil. She spun in, swinging her staff with acrobatic precision. Kris leaned back, dodging, then countered with a crushing blow. Cil ducked, launched into a butterfly kick that nearly caught Kris on the chin. Kris caught her shoe in a gauntleted hand and tugged. Cil curled, rolled, and landed on all fours.

Kris's leg whipped upward—a full split—then descended like a falling axe. But Cil was gone. Rolling aside, she darted in with a feint. Kris braced to dodge. Cil paused mid-thrust, reversed, and cracked her staff against Kris's shin.

Kris howled, head snapping forward—right into Cil's brutal uppercut.

The barbarianess flew backward, unconscious, landing atop the already-out Talin.

A cry rose from the women at seeing their captain fall.

Brand didn't wait.

He, Cil, and Alucard sprinted for the ship.

Just as they reached the gangplank, a horrific shape lunged from a crate and tackled Brand, tearing at his bag and pouch.

The animal trader!

Brand cried out, scrambled up, and engaged in a tug-of-war with the man.

Cil had already reached the plank. "Leave it, Brand! *Look out!*"

Two women were charging down the pier. Faces like wrathful goddesses.

Brand let go and bounded up the gangplank. He and Cil hauled it aboard and loosed the mooring lines. The ship began drifting free —and Brand froze.

"What's the matter with you?" Cil snapped.

"I have no idea what to do!"

"What? You've *never* handled a ship before?"

"No, of course not! I grew up in Drift's End. We couldn't *afford* a ship!"

Cil cursed under her breath about impractical men and dashed across the deck, freeing lines and adjusting sails. Wind caught the canvas. She stationed Brand at the wheel and showed him where to hold the tiller, then sprinted to winch up the anchor.

Moments later, the *Slippery Stefania* slipped away from the pier and out into the narrow bay.

Brand and Cil observed the fighting continue from their position at the rail of the *Slippery Stefania*.

Cil was making an obvious effort not to look at him, and he finally realized she was annoyed. Tremulously, he reached out and touched her shoulder, bracing for a swift buffet.

"Hey," he said.

"What do you want now, ugly?" she grumbled.

Brand swallowed. "I'd be honored if you came with us to Revilis Ko'hur—I mean... unless... you know, you don't *want* to."

Cil didn't look at him, but her body seemed to relax. "Sure," she said.

"Huh? *That's all?*"

"What else did you want to hear?" said Cil, suddenly flustered.

"Well... don't you want to go back to your family?"

"I mean—they'll be there when I come back, you know? By the sounds of it, *your* mother may not."

Brand sobered. "Yeah, right. Well, I appreciate the help. I didn't think you'd want to come."

"No, *I do!* I mean—well—it's not like I have anything better to do... so."

"Well that's flattering."

Cil laughed. "Don't be so nettled, beanstalk! *Hey!* Look at Jabari facing off against that lean maiden! *Give her one, Jabari!*"

Brand chuckled too, and together they watched the fight play out ashore, cheering and placing bets all the way.

As night wore on, the fighters from both factions grew exhausted. Refusing to yield, they broke into pairs to settle individual scores. Those without a partner sat glumly on the pier, or wandered across Main Street to find an inn—and what went on in those one-on-one overnight contests of stamina shall not be written in this account.

In the morning, Brand and Cil maneuvered the ship around to the northern edge of the bay, where they were to collect the rest of the crew. The men were late, and Brand had plenty of time to brood over the loss of his purse and travel bag.

Finally, the crew began to trickle into sight, arriving in ones and twos. All walked with a strange, limping gait, as if struggling to remain upright. Bruised, battered, and worse for wear, they carried in their eyes the proud light of clear and manly victory.

Cil and Brand helped the wrecked men aboard, where they flopped to the deck like panting fish.

"Christ," said Talin. "Kris gave me a run for my gold—but I *conquered* her prowess in the end."

Cil laughed scornfully. "What do you mean? You were out in one blow. *I* knocked her out!"

Talin grinned lasciviously. "That was only the *beginning* of the battle. When we awoke later in the evening, tangled together on that pier... *that's* when the *real* fight began."

Cil grimaced and looked away from the glare in his eyes. "Men are *disgusting.*"

Talin chuckled. "I tell you, Runewrit, your poem served me when I needed it most. Gave me the unfair advantage to turn the tide—I owe you one."

Runewrit frowned, wearing the sadly noble expression of a forlorn lover. "A lute. I want a lute. The lute of a Devirien noble."

"Done."

Berengar appeared last, torn up like a man mauled by a beast. He had tears and lacerations across his skin, massive splinters from the storage shed protruding from his ribs, and claw-like gouges across his back. His upper thighs were bruised purple, and his loincloth hung in shreds. He hobbled aboard but grinned broadly at the sight of Brand.

"By my mother, Berengar, you look worse than after fighting that chimera."

"Hah! That thing was only seven percent demon. Gilgamina is all *one-hundred!*"

Brand stared at him, uneasy. There was something in Berengar's eyes that unsettled him. "And what of Gilgamina?"

Berengar chuckled. "Aye, I met her in battle. Went toe-to-toe with her on even ground. For a time, she had the upper hand, and I fought for my life against the *surge* of her *tumultuous* passion. But once I learned her *rhythm*, I rode the current until her *vigor* was spent. After that, I reached the *heart* of the matter and showed her the full *measure* of my valor... Eventually, I *penetrated* her defenses..."

"And then?" asked Alucard, eyes wide with innocent curiosity.

"And then... I *plundered* her *booty*." The big man grinned through split lips and tried a wink, which failed due to the swelling around his eye.

"*Disgusting!*" said Cil, covering her ears.

"*Enough!* I've heard too much already," said Brand, holding up a hand.

At that, Berengar, Talin, and the rest of their lusty rogues burst into a chorus of laughter that echoed across the water and through the narrow bay.

Chapter 19
"Revilis Ko'hur."

The City of Revilis Ko'hur was re-settled approximately 1,520 years ago—only a few months after what is now referred to as *The Great Calamity.* What the calamity truly was, remains largely unknown. However, there is evidence of some kind of societal upheaval, with large sections of mankind mysteriously vanishing.

Unfortunately, much of the information now available has been pieced together from the folklore of the superstitious peasants of Drifts End—a source I personally blanch at, in terms of accuracy and credibility. Yet, since there is often a shred of truth in ancient fables, I am compelled to at least document it, and will detail it as such in this brief study.

Facts I have personally gathered about the city:

Revilis Ko'hur is located on a strip of level grasslands between the sandy beaches of the Trade Sea, to the south, and a ridge of cliffs to the north. These cliffs form a small valley, which then levels out once more into grassy plains, and beyond that, forested foothills.

The city is circular in design and surrounded by a magnificent wall of polished white stone or crystal (no scholar alive today has been able to discern its makeup with certainty). The wall is estimated to be well over 150 feet high and entirely unscalable due to its pristine smoothness.

Beyond the wall rise cryptic towers of strange design, reaching even higher into the sky. They appear to be made of the same white substance, adorned with various metals that glint in the sun, and shimmer in the moonlight. The towers vary wildly in shape: some fluted, others flat, and some of a geometry so alien as to defy description. Their number and function remain matters of conjecture.

Aside from the gigantic double gates, which must have served as the city's main entrance in ages past, there are several gatehouses that could allow entry. All are either sealed tight or guarded by loyal, taciturn sentries. From questioning these guards, I gleaned that Ezeret, the "Mad King" (why he earned this title, no one will say) and his nobles may use the towers as living and operational quarters. Further inquiry, however, was met with hostility and threats of capital punishment, and I was forced to desist.

Information gathered from folklore:

Before the Great Calamity, the local stock of people now inhabiting Revilis Ko'hur were more numerous, scattered across the surrounding coastal regions and inland areas. Within the city lived a more advanced race—elite scholars and fabled wizards commonly referred to as *The Ancients.*

In the months following the calamity, rural folk noted nothing unusual. The initial disaster seemed to affect only the Ancients and their cities, leaving peasant communities untouched.

Gradually, however, strange things began to emerge from the north. "Creatures" of unknown origin and hideous aspect preyed on man, woman, and child. Humanity was slowly driven southward. Whether these creatures were released as a side effect of the Great Calamity, or had always existed—their threat formerly held in check by Ancient science—is unknown.

(*Creatures!? Wizards? Obviously, the far-flung tales of peasant superstition!*)

A particular village, fleeing a large-scale attack, was driven to the shores of the Trade Sea. There, they stumbled upon the grand city of Revilis Ko'hur. Its ramparts were empty. Its gatehouses, silent.

This first group was more fortunate than those who came after— they claimed the city and shut the gates behind them, declaring it full.

The next wave of refugees arrived only to find the gates closed. With no shelter, they huddled against the outer wall, hoping for mercy. Receiving none—but also not immediately devoured by the so-called "creatures"—they built rough shelters, fished the Trade Sea, and waited.

Monsters seldom approached. There was still plenty of prey to the north. And so the outer encampment grew. Word spread of the new "outer settlement," and soon a steady flow of refugees began to arrive.

The camp became a village, filling the small valley north of the city. The city-dwellers held sway, possessing a wealth of goods and supplies found within the walls. Trade began: fish, game, and food for tools, clothing, and weapons. A king was appointed by the nobles. A strange, semi-coherent society emerged.

The inner city remained Revilis Ko'hur. The outer settlement came to be known as Drifts End. In time, "Revilis Ko'hur" became a loose term, used to describe both.

Due to the lingering fear of attacks, properties closest to the city wall became the most coveted. The privileged pressed near the gates, while the poor spread across the outskirts. Eventually, the entire valley filled with makeshift structures.

Through trade, the people of Drifts End amassed enough weapons and manpower to repel further creature attacks. After many years, the attacks ceased altogether. Emboldened, some began to settle in nearby plains and hills—but never far from the sight of the great white wall.

(*Varying theories exist regarding the disappearance of the fabled "creatures." Some say Lyier, god of the plains, blasted them with golden lightning. Others say they turned on one another, dwindling themselves. Perhaps—as I believe—they were never there at all.*)

Further facts about Revilis Ko'hur and Drifts End:

Today, Drifts End is a sprawling city in its own right. Ramshackle wooden buildings, stacked one atop another over fifteen centuries, cling to the steep valley and beyond. From a distance, it resembles a great spill of debris flowing down the mountain—especially in contrast to the perfect symmetry of Revilis Ko'hur's walls.

The people of Drifts End are known for their greed and obsession with status. They are avid gamblers and spend much of their time in drink and games of chance.

By contrast, the nobles within the walled city are believed to be gracious, cultured, and versed in the arts. They wear the finest silks and adorn themselves in gems. However, this cannot be confirmed. They never leave the walls.

Sadly, most city-dwellers today—whether from Revilis Ko'hur or Devirien'Su—do not dare venture beyond the security of their walled societies. I have yet to visit the cities of the southern continent, but I suspect the situation there is much the same. Thus, recent accounts of the northern wilds are increasingly rare.

Reliable knowledge of the past is either lost or hidden away in forgotten bastions deep within the Outlands. Therefore, I believe it is necessary for someone of a hard-eyed, practical temperament— such as myself—to take the steps required to uncover the truth. It is my purpose to dispel the cobwebs of superstition and myth that still shroud the minds of men.

To that end, I am planning an expedition into the unknown north in the coming weeks.

I look forward to providing my readers—in my very next writing—a full report and accounting of what occurred 1,520 years ago.

A Brief Study on the City of Revilis Ko'hur By Ak'Mirage — Scholar, Philosopher, and Historian of the Common People of Devirien'Su

This manuscript, written shortly before Ak'Mirage embarked on a research expedition, was left in the care of the Drifts End library twenty-one years ago. To date, no report of his return has been published.] — Drifts End Librarian

***

The *"Slippery Stefania"* followed the coastline east; manned by Talin and his hearty crew of rogues, and backed by a strong, steady wind that sent the ship plowing through the swell.

Brand had entirely lost track of their progress, and spent his time curled up in the throes of seasickness, until the rocking of the ship finally put him to sleep each night. Sleep was no mercy, however, for his dreams were filled with hazy visions—one in particular came more often than others: the image of Salome's wicked face grinning down at him, only to be torn into motes of shredded flesh by Queen Charlotte. Regularly, he thought he heard the sounds of Alucard chanting the verses of odd spells over and over.

Finally, the torturous journey came to an end, and Brand was pulled, shaking, from his cabin to walk the top deck on swaying legs. Looking out across the bay, he realized now that they were in the placid harbor of Revilis Ko'hur. There shone the gigantic white walls, and beyond, the ramshackle city that was so familiar to Brand—Drifts End. He was really home. *Thank the Lantern Lights,* he thought.

Talin dropped anchor and broke out a keg of wine and enough food stores for the whole party, then called Brand, Cil, and Berengar to join him on the poop deck for the purpose of discussing their next move. Brand ate little, still suffering from his sickness, and though the bay was calm and the ship still, he yet seemed to continuously rock to and fro.

Talin spoke up. "So, my brothers and sister, I say we slip ashore in small boats under the cover of dark and scale the wall with *grapples!* After this, we slay this *Mad King,* rescue Brand's mother, and grab as much loot as each can carry before once again taking to the sea!"

Brand declined, saying "I appreciate the enthusiasm, Talin, but I had something *somewhat* different in mind."

Talin was taken aback. "What? Hoy, Tiny! How many times have we successfully carried out such a plan?"

"Many a time, Cap'n."

"Right. So, is this not the tried-and-true method used by raiders since the beginning of time? Why should it have lasted so long if it doesn't work?"

"It's not that, Talin," said Brand, with a wry smile at his friend's enthusiasm.

"What then? *The grapples?* Marvelous tools. Why doubt them? Statistically, they exist because they're workable implements! Why call them into question now?"

"Talin, even if we could scale the walls—which I doubt, because they're over one hundred and fifty feet high and smooth as polished glass—the guards would be alerted and waiting for us atop."

"So it *is* the grapples." Talin frowned.

"It's *not* the grapples. Behind those walls is an entire city of men loyal to Ezeret. Of the many towers, we don't know which the king uses, nor which my mother resides in. A small group would be more effective, since we mustn't be seen at all. And there's a better way to get over those walls than grapples."

Talin's eyes grew wide with disbelief. "Better than the

grapples?" He turned to Runewrit. "*Truly?*"

The lean-faced man shrugged back at his captain and shook his head uncertainly.

"We have a way over the wall, but it will only carry us four. I can't go into details, but you must take my word on this."

At once, Cil and Berengar divined Brand's intentions, and Alucard's blue-green face brightened with excitement.

Talin growled deep in his throat like a spurned tiger. "Damnit, Brand, you think to have all the fun and leave us sitting out here like beached sharks while you die a *glorious* death?"

Brand was taken aback in turn. "I *intend no death!* Why, this is not to be thought of. A long life lies ahead of me."

Talin's face took on a sly expression. "The plunder involved must be *greater* than you *wish* to share then! I see... Good one, Brand. But cut me in on this, will you?"

"*No,* what I have in mind is the safest and most workable way to rescue my mother and live."

Talin swore and began to pace back and forth. After a minute he sighed and looked down at Brand with arms akimbo. "We'll wait here for a day in case you need to make a getaway. And when you're looting that treasure, don't forget about your brother Talin, *okay?*"

"Deal."

Tiny and the others grinned and clapped.

"Hopefully there's a bloody fight as part of your getaway," said Unleke, a wicked grin splitting his dark face.

"Hopefully not. I intend a peaceful bout of poetry writing in this harbor," said Runewrit with a sorrowful stare across the bay.

The others began to chime in, arguing over their favored course of events.

Brand and his companions prepared their meager belongings and then waited out the rest of the day. Night came, and Fara prepared a dinghy to ferry the four companions to the shore.

Talin met Brand and the others at the rail to see them off, his seven merry rogues crowding around behind him.

"Brand, are you sure you don't *at least* want an escort to the wall?"

"We will be fine, Talin. No one knows we are coming."

"Alright." He turned away. "Come see me whether you need a hasty retreat or not. You owe me some of that loot!"

"What? After you pulled that stunt, holding out on me when I didn't even have a shirt on my back?"

Talin grinned without answering, waved him and the others farewell, and swaggered back to the captain's cabin.

Brand grinned too.

Tiny and the rest said their goodbyes, and Brand and his friends clambered down a rope ladder to the waiting dinghy Fara had prepared for them. Fara was already sitting passively at the oars, and once they had boarded, began rowing them to shore. They made landfall without incident and said their farewells to Fara. A moment later they were staggering up the sandy slope toward the lantern-lit structures of the tiny port.

"Ah, there's that familiar Drifts End stench. It's good to be home! Don't worry, Mother—not long now," said Brand with a bluff grin.

"I can't wait to meet Grandma!" said Alucard.

"I'm sure she will be fine, lads," Berengar said, giving them both a tense grin. The big man was clearly concerned.

Cil, to Brand's surprise, smiled at him compassionately—a gesture his mind would return to more than once as the evening progressed.

Brand led them to a dockside provisions store. He now wore his tailor-made black traveling outfit, but the others would need something to help them blend into the dark.

The four of them entered, with Alucard bringing up the rear. Brand found four black cloaks that suited his needs and approached the grizzled, gray-haired man behind the counter.

"How much for these four cloaks?"

"Depends how much you need them. Prices change regularly here in Drifts End."

"Oh, I found them comical and considered it a mere whim for a dinner dress-up. We're not that interested in them anyway. I'm sure there's a seller more in need of patronage somewhere nearby," Brand replied blandly, making motions to return the cloaks.

"Oh. Well, in that case..." stammered the old man, suddenly grinning. "Why, you should have said you were guests of a local! Taking that into consideration, I'd say a silver bullion each."

"Oh, never mind then. We can find some old rags by the docks. We were going to trash them anyhow."

"Oh, in that case, it would be silly to charge that much for them, since they will be destroyed anyway. Let me see—if I remove the goodwill surplus... the best I can do is five coppers each."

"Are you *sure*? I can always look around in the back alleys instead."

"No, for honored guests, please let me do this for you."

"Okay. *Good.*" Brand motioned for Berengar to pay the two silver bullions—the only two Berengar had left from his labors at the dockyards.

Berengar looked at Brand in sudden outrage. "*What?* I'm paying?"

Brand cut him short with a gesture. "Please, Ber, not in public."

Berengar grudgingly paid over the two silver.

Brand silently cursed the animal trader once again. Had the disgusting man not viciously bereaved him of his hard-earned coins—not once, but twice—Brand wouldn't be haggling with this golden-haired oaf over a pittance for these cheap cloaks right now.

Brand tossed one of the cloaks over Alucard before the owner could get a good look at him. He asked for a pair of scissors and made some adjustments, clipping the seams together with some pins to reduce the slack around the arms and waist, then stood back to inspect his work.

Alucard looked like a hooded little hunchback, his blue-green face rugged up in his cloak, and the store owner seemed much relieved when they finally left his shop.

Once outside, the others donned their cloaks and headed toward the great wall, radiant in the silvery rays of the moon. Stopping one hundred yards from the wall, they began circling eastward, making their way around to an unpopulated section. Unlike the north and west sections, the land to the south and east was mostly bare of human habitation.

Stopping in a clump of small Aleppo pines, Brand and the others secured their gear and prepared their flying setup. Brand climbed onto Berengar's front, wrapping his arms and legs around the larger man and holding on. Cil did the same on the Outlander's back. Brand began to curse quietly at his ignoble positioning, but a buffet from Cil quickly silenced his complaints. Alucard stood nearby in his little makeshift cloak, the spellbook open in his hands, looking every bit the part of a demented dwarfish frog-wizard.

He cast the spell of flying with an ease and facility that was impressive to behold. So familiar was the spell to him that he managed it quietly, with no more than a tiny blue shimmer to signal its coming into being. Even Berengar, who greatly feared sorcery, seemed proud and trusting of their small, skilled companion. Alucard's tiny round face, made even more blue by the flash of magic, beamed as if to say, *I was made for this. I am the master wizard!*

Instantly, Berengar felt his physical location shifting to the ebb and flow of his will, and he held his position still through the medium of thought. This was the third time Alucard had cast the spell on him, and the golden giant was finally starting to get a knack for its operation. Alucard climbed onto Cil's back and took position on her shoulders, clasping onto Berengar's hair like a set of reins.

The big man grinned. "Hold on tight. I'm not holding back this time!"

"What?!" Cil and Brand gasped in unison—Berengar hadn't mentioned this part at all...

Brand made to protest. "Ber, *hold on!* We need to—*taaaaaaaaaaaaalllllkkkk!!!"*

Whoosh! They were up and away into the sky, shot like an arrow from a Borderlands longbow into the black of night.

That evening, more than a few people in the port spoke in hushed whispers about the strange, ghostly wail they heard reverberating off the great wall and echoing out across the bay.

Upwards they soared, rushing toward that black, star-dotted

vastness. Up, always up, with the wind in their hair. Then suddenly, just when Brand was starting to think he might actually enjoy the journey, they came to a sudden, stomach-lurching, mid-air halt—as if they'd hit an invisible wall!

Brand and Cil rocked in their positions, straining not to be dislodged from Berengar's burly torso.

Now they hovered, high in the sky—possibly over three hundred feet—and on par with the tips of some of the towers of Revilis Ko'hur. Below them and slightly to the north was the great white wall, glistening brightly in the moonlight. Berengar was silent.

"Ber?" Brand croaked in terror.

He looked up at the Outlander. Berengar's face was set in an expression of sheer anxiety. Great rivulets of sweat ran down his angular forehead.

"Ber, what the *devil* is going on?" Brand asked.

"Brand, something *terrible* occurred to me."

"*What!?*"

"Well... you know, if this flying *thing* is controlled by my thoughts, what if I *accidentally... you know*... imagined that it stopped working, and then we all plummeted to the ground?"

"You great oaf! Stop *thinking* about it—"

Brand let out a squeal of dismay as they suddenly lurched downward ten feet, before halting to tread air once more. Cil wailed in fright and clung to Berengar like he was a life raft, almost knocking Brand out of his leg holds with her fidgeting.

"*Stop that*!" Brand cried at Cil, fighting for his grip.

"Don't worry," said Alucard, his voice the very pinnacle of calm collectedness. "The spell doesn't really work like that, Berengar. Yes, thought controls directional motion, but the spell cannot simply be canceled by its wielder's imagination. I have wrought the spatial-energy altering syllables around Berengar, and they are held firm in their anomaly for the duration of the spell."

"Ahhhh." Berengar let out a great sigh and relaxed. "Thank you, Al. That makes me feel a lot better."

"You're welcome."

Almost instantly, Berengar froze and looked tense again. "But *what if...* I, for instance, *accidentally* couldn't stop myself from *imagining* plummeting to the ground, and then it happened? I had a dream like that once."

"You damnable *fool!*" hissed Brand. "Stop thinking altogether and get going! The course is *that* way!" He pointed toward the city. "Look, follow my hand! *That* is the way we are going! *Go!*"

"It's fine, Berengar. What you said is not possible. Just try to focus on Brand's directions, and you'll be fine," chimed in Alucard cheerfully.

Brand managed to keep Berengar oriented and distracted enough to prevent further introspection, and thus-wise, they made their precarious progress toward the towers of Revilis Ko'hur.

A few minutes later, they were over the wall and floating high above the dark and silent streets of the city proper. Brand called for a halt, his face pale and sweaty. "*Al,* how much longer will the spell last?!"

"Another twenty minutes at least," said the small fish-man confidently.

"Okay, good. Now, let's try to divine the location of Ezeret's tower." He frowned down at the darkened city, a sense of unease growing quickly in the back of his mind. "Something's wrong here, Ber."

"Yes," answered the big man, frowning as he looked past Brand's upturned face at the city below. "It is *empty.*"

That's exactly what had been bothering Brand. *Where were the lights? Where were the people?* There was no evidence of occupation anywhere in sight. Just the lofty peaks of blacked-out towers all around, with ancient, dead devices resting in rusty, silent heaps atop their balconies. Strange metal shapes and objects littered empty streets, which seemed un-trafficked for centuries. It was like looking down upon a city of the damned.

Brand began to get the strange notion that the entire experience with Ezeret was a dream, a drugged hallucination.

The city of Revilis Ko'hur was not the stage of exclusive and grand balls, filled with the fair ladies and nobles of a prosperous and elite paradise. It was an uninhabited ruin, empty and desolate —a sad relic of a time before the Great Calamity.

All this time, Brand had thought about getting wealthy enough or distinguished enough to make his way into that society. He felt strangely disabused of a childhood dream or hope, and oddly disheartened at this fact—it had all been a mirage.

"*There,*" whispered Berengar, distracting Brand from his brooding and pointing toward the northern edge of the city.

Brand squinted, and then he saw what the Outlander's keen vision had detected: a single oval of light, shining from the window of a tower looming above the northern gatehouse.

Five minutes later, they were there, hovering near the tip of the tower in question, its architecture of spiraling steel and crystal defying the very principles of engineering.

"Should we enter from the top or bottom?" asked Brand.

"Top if we can. He won't expect that," grunted Berengar in a whisper.

"Okay."

Berengar started descending around the tower in a slow spiral.

About halfway down, they found the dark recess of an open window. Berengar took them through the arch, and they floated into the room like a silent, many-armed ghost. After this, Berengar touched down, and all four of them felt the comforting certainty of solid ground beneath their feet once more.

"*Phew!*" said Alucard, taking in a deep breath.

Brand, peering closely at the small figure, saw that Alucard was actually perspiring. "What's up with *you*?" he asked.

"I'm just glad we arrived in one piece. All that talk of Berengar accidentally dismissing the spell..."

"...But you said that wasn't possible."

"Technically... it *could* occur if one's willpower were strong enough."

"Don't tell me that!" Brand exclaimed in panic. "That's the *last* time we're flying!!!"

"It's fine, Brand. I have it under control," broke in Berengar bluffly. "I have mastered my fears. I shall carry us safely, wherever we set our minds to." he said, grinning and flexing his arms proudly.

Brand paced back and forth in agitation for a moment, then said, "Let us continue. Did anyone bring a torch?"

"Inventory was your job," Cil's voice came out of the dark to Brand's right.

"Since when?"

"Well, you procured us the cloaks, did you not?"

"Berengar *paid* for them."

"That's right, damnit. And you owe me two silver bullions," complained Berengar from somewhere in the shadows to Brand's left.

"Let us focus on the task at hand. Such biased and inaccurate carping grates on the nerves," replied Brand. Then, "Berengar, you've spent much time traveling by night, why don't *you* lead the way?"

"Right after you, *Brand*. *You* are the master thief, after all."

Brand grimaced and edged forward into the black corridor ahead of them. Almost instantly, he began to imagine unseen hazards, pitfalls, and myriad monsters lurking just ahead in the darkness. He paused, sweating with fear. Quickly, he drew his short sword and used it as a sounding rod, lightly tapping the walls, floor, and ceiling as he went, praying it would warn him of any dire conditions awaiting him.

Thus tapping, whispering, and cursing, the companions explored the floor of the tower they were on, straining their eyes against the velvety darkness in a vain attempt to develop some form of subhuman night vision — it didn't come.

After a sweaty forty-five minutes, Brand's tapping discerned what seemed to be the beginning of a flight of stairs. After a pause, he started down in the same careful manner, Brand in the lead.

Down and down they went, in complete blackness — not a glimpse of a lit room or doorway, just the endless steps underfoot and the quiet, echoing taps of Brand's blade ahead. All other senses seemed to wash out, lost in the repetitive sameness of their strange journey. Time seemed to slow down, and Brand began to lose track of how long they'd been in the tower, but feared speaking in case King Ezeret was near.

The walls and steps began to glow with a faint reflection of white light, its source somewhere around the corner and out of sight. Presently, the faint notes of a haunting song drifted up from below — a woman's voice, accompanied by the plucked notes of a lute.

Berengar put a finger to his lips, signaling silence, and motioned the others onward. Brand nodded, and they continued down the stairs, guided by the reflective illumination of the tiles and the ethereal notes of the melody. Another bend of the stairwell revealed a slit of white light below them, indicating the presence of a door, slightly ajar.

The music grew louder — if music it was — for it seemed merely a series of disjointed, sorrowful strokes, never quite finishing their chords nor progressing in any logical melody. It was also, Brand noted, strangely familiar. He began to wonder if he were really hearing it at all, or if it was just a figment of his imagination.

Slowly, hesitantly, the companions approached the slit of light and crowded around. Berengar and Brand carefully checked for traps around the doorframe but found nothing. The door seemed designed to slide sideways. Brand tried easing it open, but it wouldn't budge. Then his deft fingers found a sort of knob in the center of the panel. Not really knowing what it was, he pressed it in, and with a small whir, the door split in half, its two panels automatically retracting into the doorframe.

Brand gasped in dismay as dazzling white light flooded his senses. He tensed, expecting instant alarm and violent uproar. Nothing came. The nervous companions now stood awkwardly in the center of the wide-open doorway, looking into the brightly lit room like rats caught in the beam of a lantern.

The room was large and constructed of pristine white marble. The far wall was curved and continued around in a great circle. A large table, curved to match the shape of the room, stood near the wall ahead of them. At the head of the table sat the Mad King, seen in profile, his pale face set in an expression of placid ecstasy, his eyes closed and head cocked slightly to one side. He seemed not to have noticed the intrusion, and indeed seemed to be bobbing his head and humming along to the ghostly notes. After a second he paused and raised a soup spoon to his lips, sipping at it delicately. Standing to the right of the king was — Brand's mother! And she was the source of the tune. She was singing softly and plucking an expensive-looking lute.

"Mother!" Brand cried out involuntarily, stepping through the arched doorway. Berengar cursed and moved out to Brand's right, covering his back. Cil did likewise on Brand's left, and Alucard brought up the rear. Their formation was just as they had drilled in times past.

As they stepped through the doorway, the rest of the room was instantly brought into view. Looking behind them, they saw that the stairwell was merely a thin cylindrical spire at the center of the room, and that the room itself continued around it on all sides in a perfect circle. Couches and tables, laden with numerous decorative objects, were positioned around the outer wall, all curved to match the architecture of the tower. They now saw that the dining table was incredibly long, running in a curving arc at least halfway around the room. Brand's mother and Ezeret were the only occupants.

His mother cried out, "*Brand!*"

King Ezeret turned his head, examining them with a single pale-blue eye. His expression was mild, even amiable, and he seemed completely unperturbed by their incursion.

"*Oh?* More guests? Well, one cannot complain, though it is only by chance that I had extra food prepared—a stroke of *luck! Come,* take a seat." He waved them over.

Brand's mother looked haggard, the corners of her eyes pinched with nervous tension, but otherwise seemed unharmed. Looking at Brand, she brightened slightly and gave him a weary smile.

Brand inspected his mother intently, pacing across the room. "Has he harmed you?" He gestured fretfully toward Ezeret as he approached.

She graced him with a tired but indulging smile, as if to say: *is there a man alive that I cannot beguile, my son?* — but all she said aloud was, "No, I'm fine, my dear Brand. Ezeret has showed me proper hospitality. I'm glad you are alive. I thought you'd surely be dead, leaving the safety of the city and all."

King Ezeret viewed the affair with a look of quizzical disbelief. "You two... *know* each other?"

"Your Majesty, that's my mother. You held her for ransom, do you recall?"

"Oh? Is that right? Well, then this is a happy reunion and a time for celebration!" Ezeret clapped his hands with childlike glee. "We shall break out the castle's best wine. Sit! *Sit!* The soup is getting cold." He motioned for them to take seats.

"We are taking my mother and leaving," said Brand coldly.

Ezeret nodded thoughtfully. Then withdrew a strange copper rod with an orange crystal attached to it and rested it meaningfully on the table near Brand's mother's arm.

Brand eyed the rod for a moment, then said, "What is that?"

"Never mind, but please, take a seat."

"It is dangerous," said Alucard from behind Brand.

Ezeret looked up at Cil and Berengar, then began motioning with exaggerated movements of his hand. "Sit, *sit!*"

Berengar and Cil exchanged wary glances with Brand. Brand nodded tensely, eyeing the rod, and took a seat a few chairs down from the king. Cil and Berengar nervously followed suit.

"By my faith, you are a tense lot, aren't you? Why, I see you've made two more friends..." Then, craning his neck to get a look at Alucard, he paused. "What in Toth's name is a *Waterworks Technician* doing here?"

"He's a friend," said Brand.

The king's eyes widened with exaggerated emphasis, and his manner became conciliatory. "Each their own. Who am I of all people to judge?"

"You know of the waterworks?" asked Brand with interest, then cursed himself for his impulsive curiosity.

"Read of them only. Like so much of the wild and wondrous things out there—all at the tips of my fingers, but never directly *experienced.* Maddening. You get it? *Mad*-ending? *Ha!* Don't let it be said that I can't take a joke now!"

The others stared back in silence, unsure whether they should laugh or not. After a moment, Ezeret peeked at Brand with a sly, bright eye from the side of his pale face. "By the way, how is it that you made it past the guards? They are still well and alive, I trust?"

Brand considered for a moment, knowing his words might affect the livelihood of some hapless guard. "We came in from the top."

The king thought on this. "Hmm. Most visitors use the more usual route of the lower central arch..."

Not wanting to reveal their magical methods, Brand hastily added, "Indeed. We climbed."

"*Really?* Well, that at least explains the sweat. You all smell dreadful, by the way. Humph... I shall make a memorandum to have the windows above locked."

"Where is the rest of the city? The people? The nobles?" Brand asked, his curiosity once again getting the better of him.

"*No more questions!*—not until you try the soup."

Brand looked down at the tableware in front of him. It was exquisite porcelain, adorned with ancient designs. However, there was no soup. Looking further, he saw that all the serving trays, plates, bowls, and pots were completely empty — even the one the king had apparently been sipping from. He looked to his mother in surprise, and she gave him a pained smile in acknowledgment.

"Well?" said the king.

"Your Majesty, forgive me, but in all candor, there is nothing here to taste."

Ezeret frowned and scratched his chin. "Hmm. Could I have imagined it then?... Still, I read somewhere that that shouldn't make a difference. I guess I'll have to work that... Oh bother. Now the guests are here and the table is empty." He giggled, placing two fingers across his lips, hiding a smirk. "Oh my, this is embarrassing, isn't it!? *Awkward!*" His eyes flicked right to left in wide-eyed mirth. He suddenly looked at Brand's mother. "Wait... that means that all this *time*..." He raised a hand to cover his face, and burst into a paroxysm of silent laughter, his whole body shaking with the effort of it.

"Oh, forgive me. I had just pictured this dear guest of mine sitting here all this time, expected to dine with me—yet having no food—and forced to pretend at eating for fear of my reaction upon hearing the truth, no doubt.

"Oh my, oh my. What a *ludicrous* predicament! The *insane* things people will do to please their king."

Brand felt the hairs on the back of his neck begin to rise. Shooting a quick glance at Berengar and Cil, he saw they were both experiencing similar unease. Alucard, however, was unperturbed, and was busy trying on different pieces of tableware as hats, eventually settling on a blue-jade serving pot with a long handle and delicate designs depicting a flock of bluebirds in flight.

Brand turned back to Ezeret. "Very funny indeed, Your Majesty. Now, shall we give you this artifact and take our reward?"

"Yes. Let us go. My dear subjects, we have dillydallied enough for today." The king leapt to his feet with such suddenness that all present flinched back in alarm.

"Onward, to the *Chamber of Hope!*" He took Brand's mother gracefully by the elbow, the copper rod casually grasped in his opposite hand. He began escorting her toward the door, then paused to look back at Brand. "You have the power source, yes?"

"Yes, I have it right here. Pass my mother over and we shall part company..."

"Without you seeing the great show, the grand finale? *Never!* Tush tush, Brand, that would be such a waste. Come on then." He strode on light feet toward the door, his red silk robe fluttering about his ankles.

Brand hesitated. Letting the king control the situation was maddening—and likely fatal—but how did one control a lunatic who had his mother in his grasp? At any moment, the king could snap, and god knows what that rod would do to his mother. He groaned and, rising from his chair, followed after the king. Berengar and the others joined him, each scanning for an opportunity to end the king's life without endangering the lovely brown-haired woman at his side.

They followed the king down the winding stair until they reached the bottom floor of the tower, another well-lit round room of white marble. This room, filled with curved couches, must have once served as a parlor or lobby. At this moment, however, the couches were occupied by two parties of armed men.

Ten men in the king's red livery leapt to attention from the couches on the right side of the room. Each was outfitted in chainmail, carried a longsword at their belt, and a crossbow on their back. At the sight of Brand and his companions, crossbows were drawn and bolts winched into position.

On the left side of the room stood another party—one of motley appearance and dubious discipline. They rose slowly and stubbornly for the king, a band of seven of the most vicious Wagglers known to Brand from his days in Drift's End. All were clad in various types of leather armor, reinforced with bits of plate or chainmail. A single steel gauntlet here, a chain patch over a shoulder there — all the results of ramshackle, haphazard craftsmanship born in the worst parts of Drift's End. Each man was scarred and brutal in countenance, armed with daggers, shortswords, and likely other concealed tools of distress and mayhem.

This party was headed by a lean figure in a dapper suit of well-made black leather, complemented by a green cloak. At seeing Brand and his friends, the man's handsome face curled into a smirk, and he ran a gauntleted hand casually through his mop of glossy black curls. Glowing amber eyes glared confidently at Brand. It was Lain Locke.

Berengar cursed profusely. "I knew we should've taken our chances earlier. This was a trap all along! *Damnit.*"

"Trap?" said Ezeret, overhearing Berengar. "How so? This is merely my *entourage*. Did we not just enjoy a friendly dinner above?" He looked at one of his guards on the right side of the room. "The peasantry gets the most wild notions at times, do they not?"

"Yes... yer majesty. Quite so," answered the burly guard nervously.

"What is he doing here?" Brand stabbed a finger toward Lain.

"Oh? You disapprove? He has served me well. Think of it: *The Royal Guard*, the loyal and trusty execution arm of the king himself." He gestured grandly to the armored men on his right. "And then we have *The Serpent's Fang*!" He made a showman-like gesture toward Lain Locke and his men, as though unveiling a new invention. "The king's execution arm in the shadows—always watching, always ready to strike against conspirators. Grand idea isn't it?" His eyes became wide with excitement as he spoke.

Lain eyed Cil boldly and winked at her.

Brand turned to Cil with a flicker of inexplicable jealousy but took heart when he saw her glaring angrily back at his suave nemesis.

Lain noticed Brand's annoyance and smirked. "Hear that, Brand? We're not '*Drifts End Wagglers*' anymore. Now we work for the king himself. The Wagglers have come a long way, now that *I'm* in charge."

Brand growled, "Where's Teravan?"

Lain laughed. "Oh, that old sumptuous mothball with his rules and his 'no killing'? He expired worse than an old leather suit." Lain made a mocking motion of drawing his hand across his throat.

"*You bastard!*" Brand spat.

Brand's mother gasped, tears welling in her eyes.

Lain addressed her. "Don't worry, love. I'll take good care of you in Teravan's stead—*you* and that little red-haired flower *too.* There's enough Lain to go around." He smirked lasciviously.

Brand shivered at the thought. He had heard tales of what Lain did to the women he kept. *He was a sick man.* He'd been a sick boy too. Probably from his mother, she had been a lunatic. Passed away some years ago. The devils only knew what she had done to him as a child. "You're not well Lain," he said coldly.

"Now Brand, is that any way to talk to your *father figure*? I mean, with me replacing Teravan, I'll be the closest thing to a *dad* you'll have."

Berengar growled, his muscles tensing as though ready to pounce.

"Oh, Lain," said King Ezeret. "You are such a dreadful braggart. I'll not have you insulting my guests." He waggled a long pale finger at the rogue.

Lain inclined his head with a sardonic smile. "Yes, Your Majesty." His face was impassive, but a certain burning light in his eyes told Brand of the murderous designs he must be scheming up.

Ezeret turned a perceptive, pale-blue eye on Lain, raising a finger to his nose with a look of sly suspicion.

Perhaps the king had noticed Lain's intentions too, thought Brand. Then, looking around the room, he noticed that there were in fact three factions: the Royal Guards, Lain and his men, and

Brand and his companions. *Had the wily king set things up this way intentionally?*

The king went on, "That's better. I'll not have coarseness ruining my great moment of victory." Ezeret turned, one arm still hooked around Brand's mother, and addressed the room. "Look at the crowd we have here. My, my, aren't *I* the popular one?" He smiled cheekily and went on, "Well, I shall not disappoint my dear subjects. Now is not the time for individual feuds. Today, we make a change—a change the ancients fumbled, but which *I* shall not. *Onward to the Hall of Dreams!*"

Chapter 20
"The Codex of Proto-Cosmic Absolutes."

My dear Tacharris,
I know what you have obtained.
I beg you—do not use it. Do not even read it.
You saw what happened to Clamdival—and to all who existed in the recorded experience of his mind. Such is the result of meddling with what was never meant for the minds of men.

I know you believe you will be different. That you can contain its breadth. Do not be so arrogant as to ignore your limits. Many great men have fallen, shattered by their own self-assurance.

Again, I entreat you: do not read it. Do not even open it.

If not for your own sake, then for everyone else. For Kara. For Tris.

Your dearest friend and faithful pupil, Acherie
—Tattered vellum found in the tower of the Mad King

***

Cil whispered in Brand's ear, "I thought it was the Chamber of Hope?"

Brand shook his head and shrugged.

The king moved onward to the entrance and pressed a panel on the side of the broad doorway. The door flicked open, revealing a dark and desolate street beyond.

The king marched out like a victorious general, dragging Brand's mother along at his side. Brand and his companions, Lain and his men, and the royal guards followed behind, all watchful and wary of each other.

Brand repeated his question from earlier. "Your Majesty, where are all the people? The nobles, the citizens?"

The king tittered quietly, not looking back. "What a choice joke that is, Brand. Don't you see them? There, in the windows, watching with great anticipation at the procession of their brave king—watching and waiting to be *saved*." He waved a hand vaguely toward the towers and structures they were passing. Following the king's gestures, Brand saw only dark, silent cavities, gaping at them from all sides.

After a few more turns, the king located the structure he had in mind. A great, oddly-shaped cathedral. The strange structure loomed before them, its design instantly familiar even in the dim light. Berengar and Cil hissed, and a sinking feeling slithered like a serpent into Brand's stomach. He and his companions had seen such a structure before — on an island cliff towering above the Sunken Tundra.

The cathedral of psychic horrors, where otherworldly beings of light had been enslaved and tortured by their unscrupulous predecessors.

Sensing Brand and his companions' sudden tension, King Ezeret directed a tremulous grin at Brand, tugged his mother closer, and marched onward.

Now, the moonlight struck directly upon the cathedral. Its glimmering rays were captured and redirected into flowing channels of liquid silver, articulating alien patterns across its outer surfaces. The doors of this particular hall had been left wide open, and Brand could see that the silvery illumination was even greater within.

The faces of Ezeret's Royal Guard were pale and tense, clearly unnerved by the expedition. Even the hardened brutes of Lain's crew seemed uneasy. These were city-dwellers, after all, unacquainted with the terrors Brand had experienced in the Outlands. Brand smiled grimly. Somewhere along the line, the *strange* and *eerie* had become mere normalities to him. A bitter boon, but useful.

Ezeret led the crowd up the terraced steps and through the open doors of the cathedral. Inside, the refractive properties of the crystalline walls caused the silvery rays to be amplified many times over, bathing the vaulted hall in a brilliance brighter than the direct moonlight outside.

The room was a chillingly familiar sight. Along both walls were the cylindrical capsules, running the length of the four-hundred-foot chamber. The broad, patterned floor was scored with myriad ruts, housing heavy metallic cables which snaked from the capsules to a central console at the back of the hall.

One major difference struck them: the glass cylinders were all raised, their circular platforms empty. There were no Lantern Lights trapped in here! — A small comfort, and short-lived, for the entire setting made King Ezeret's intentions clear. They should have stopped him earlier in the tower when they had the chance.

To interrupt or attack the king at this juncture would mean certain death for Brand, his companions, and likely his mother as well. But... he found himself wondering, could that actually be the lesser evil? What unholy plans brewed in the unhinged mind of King Ezeret? Clearly something to do with the artifact and the Lantern Lights, but then what?

Ezeret turned to address the group, his voice resonating through the crystalline hall. "I know many of you think me mad. But what I do, I do for mankind. I alone have read the ancient scriptures and fragments that tell of our past and our *future*. The truth is that the ancients entangled themselves in something that unhinged their very reality, causing a selective but mass disappearance. I know not where they went, but clearly, they are not *here*.

"The question is not *what* happened, but *why* it happened. What problem drove them to such extremes? That, at least, they recorded before their vanishing." His voice took on a fervent urgency. "With their science, through their star charts, they predicted the nearing of a terrible ruination. A *real calamity.* Not the minuscule 'Great Calamity' we speak of, which only affected wizarding societies and their adherents, but a cosmic event that has the potential to wipe out life on Earth—a nearby supernova. One that is still yet to occur, at some point in the next hundred thousand years. In addition to the supernova, the planet itself is undergoing a super cooling. The fields of ice creep ever southward, swallowing more and more habitable land. Eventually, the world will be submerged in a true ice age, lasting millions of years—at least that's what the ancients predicted."

Ezeret's words hung in the air, his audience staring on with rapt attention. Even Brand and Berengar, who viewed him as an enemy, couldn't help but feel the ring of truth in his words. *Had the king's madness regressed, allowing a brief period of mental clarity to shine through?*

The king went on. "These things the ancients foresaw and sought to circumvent, with the help of the fabled *Lantern Lights.* According to the research notes I have read, they conceived of a tool. A manuscript of sufficient power to move all of mankind to another world. Such a manuscript was requested of the Lantern Lights—this much I know. For I have read the *First Absolute,* as transcribed in the notes of the great Tacharris Tiris'liarno himself. Upon reading it, I immediately saw things differently... I saw things how they *truly* were. That minuscule part of the full manuscript took something from me—perhaps my sanity—*but it gave me so much more!*"

A wild gleam entered his pale eyes. "Strange how so much is vague to me these days. Yet, this remains crystal clear. I *must* recover the rest of the manuscript!"

He raised an arm in a sweeping gesture toward the exit. "Out there, in these towers, my subjects watch with bated breath. Long have they awaited this moment."

The king suddenly peered around as if for something he had lost, his face a mask of confusion. "Now..." he said thoughtfully, as he began pacing back and forth, "where *was* I? I can't quite recall..."

It seemed the "remission*"* was short-lived.

Lain Locke cleared his throat, catching the king's attention. "The artifact, Your Majesty. The one you had Brand fetch."

Ezeret clapped his hands together. "Ah! *Correct!*" He looked to Brand expectantly. "Well, do you have it?"

"Aye." Brand drew it from his pouch and held it out for the king to inspect. The cylindrical metallic object glinted dully in the moonlight radiating from the ceiling. "A deal is a deal, Ezeret. Let my mother go."

Ezeret looked around, a perplexed expression crossing his pale face. Then, spotting Brand's mother to his left, sudden recognition flared in his blue eyes. "Ah, this lovely companion of mine is your mother? You should have said so! Yes, by all means. *Here!*" He released her and stood stock still, watching her go, his arms held awkwardly at his sides.

Brand, Berengar, and Cil held their breath as Brand's mother took a tremulous step away.

Ezeret screamed, the hand holding the copper rod shooting out like the striking head of a cobra. Brand, Berengar, and Cil all gasped, lurching forward in anticipation. Brand's mother cried out at the rod's touch... But, nothing happened.

The king cackled maniacally, slapping his thighs and wiping tears from his eyes. "Oh, you should have seen the looks on your faces. The rod is harmless! You are so *ridiculous.* I would never hurt someone so *dear* to me!"

Damnit, it was all a trick! We should have taken him in the tower when we had the chance! Thought Brand.

"Jerk," growled Cil.

Berengar almost lunged at the king then and there, crossbows or not, but Brand and Cil held him back. Brand's mother staggered to her son in consummate relief, and the two embraced.

"Oh, my beautiful boy!"

Brand winced, blushing, and disengaged himself from her arms. "Not now, Mother..." He turned to Ezeret. "A deal's a deal, Ezeret. We're leaving."

The king's voice gained an acrid, harsh edge. "Not so fast—guards, ensure nobody leaves during my performance. Besides, I am quite fond of your mother, Brand. Her voice has been... a source of calm and relaxation... Let us finish this business and then *discuss terms.*"

"*You treacherous dog!*" roared Berengar.

"*Damnit, Ezeret!*" cried Brand. "A deal is a deal!"

The Royal Guards tensed, their crossbows leveled at Brand and his companions.

To Brand's left, Lain let out a quiet, sinister chuckle. His men swaggered in place, cracking their knuckles and necks, eager for Brand's group to make a move. Brand cursed himself once again for not handling the king back in the tower when he had the chance.

Ezeret ascended the stairs to the console platform, moved to the short pedestal at the back of the platform, and inserted the power cell into its socket. The whirr and buzz of machinery filled the room, and the palpable tension of great amounts of electricity traveling along cables sent a shiver through the air.

The king laughed, this time gleefully, like a child. Lain watched him intently, his golden eyes glowing like a predator's in the silver light.

Brand had a number of mixed feelings at that moment, but the one which stood out most was that Lain was *far* worse than the king. "Ezeret!" he called out. "Don't trust that serpent!" He pointed to Lain. "He means you harm. You honored your bargain, so I give you this advice before I go."

The king, absorbed in his task, ignored him.

"You're *mad,* Brand," Lain sneered. "Why point the finger at me, when it's *you* who plotted his demise? *Royal Guards!* Watch this youth—he's as untrustworthy as a two-bullion harlot."

"Enough out of both of you," barked the chief of the guards, his brassy voice trembling slightly. "Stay where you are and watch yourselves. The king's orders." He motioned to his men with a shaky hand, and soon both Brand's and Lain's groups were covered by the sights of sturdy crossbows.

Lain laughed, holding his hands up innocently. "Here I am. No need to fret."

On the console platform, the king typed furiously on keys and buttons, consulting an old leather-bound journal at his side. The strange machines, with their glowing screens, were just as those in the northeastern version of this hall.

A click, then an intense whooshing, sucking feeling reverberated through the hall, as if space-time itself were stretching and groaning. Alarms beeped in excited bursts, and certain lights on the console platform began to flash. Then came a sight of such horrific and cosmic profundity that all present were struck dumb with stupefaction.

The carved channels in the ceiling began to glow brighter, flowing with an alien light, different from the mere silvery rays of the moon. The strange glow spread from the center of the ceiling pattern, branching into smaller connections and offshoots, overwriting the original pattern and amplifying its brilliance. The original design, formed naturally by the moonlight, was lost in a labyrinth of soul-tugging swirls and hooks.

Looking up at the vast, glowing pattern, Brand felt himself irresistibly drawn toward it, just as he had felt the fleeting, momentary tug when gazing on the hall in the Sunken Tundra for the first time. But this time, the pull was a thousandfold stronger.

"Don't look up," came the lilting voice of Ezeret, drifting from somewhere in front of Brand. His voice seemed vague and oddly distant, as though echoing across a great gulf. Now, Brand began to hear the strangled cries of his friends and the others present in the hall as they too beheld the great pattern above.

A small hand tugged at his sleeve. "Don't look that way, Brand," came Alucard's voice, soft but urgent, wrenching Brand's gaze from the glowing pattern.

King Ezeret's voice echoed again, disembodied and detached from reality, like a narrator recounting their plight. "The pattern creates an inverse traction. It delineates the weave and makeup of space-time itself, but in such a way as to create a pull on a sister dimension, an attraction that draws the Lantern Lights from their realm of bright energy to ours. Don't look too closely, for the wavelength created by the light resonates with the *soul*."

A sudden, indescribable sound came from one of the Royal Guards. Brand snapped his head to his right just in time to see a guard stagger, and then go deathly still, as his soul was torn screaming from his still-living flesh. The light instantly faded from the man's eyes, but his body remained upright. It began making tentative, jerking movements, walking stiffly this way and that without purpose — alive in form, but not in essence. Brand stared on in dumb horror as the mumbling, bumbling shell of a man tottered like an infant for three paces, then collapsed into a heap on the floor. The shivering form curled in on itself, whimpered, and finally went still.

The terror of this scene had an unexpected silver lining. The sheer spirit-rending horror fixed the attention of everyone in the room so thoroughly, it shielded them from the allure of the pattern above.

The brightness of the pattern now intensified further, drowning all else in shadow. All color was washed away, transforming the hall into a theater of stark blacks, whites, and grays.

"A case in point," came the cheery voice of the Mad King, his tone incongruous with the nightmare unfolding around him.

Then a new horror began. A distinct, sucking, zapping sound rippled through the room, accompanied by shifts in air pressure and bursts of energy that made Brand's ears pop. Resisting the pattern's pull, he forced his eyes to remain slightly averted, and saw in his peripherals a small orb of light flitting down a channel in the wall. A moment later it reached the waiting platform of one of the raised glass cylinders.

It was a miniature sun, radiant and alive, and Brand recognized it instantly. It was a Lantern Light.

The glowing orb hovered below the raised glass tube, trembling as if bound by an invisible force. Its restrained bobbing, its leashed vibration, stirred an inexplicable melancholy within Brand, and soon he found tears welling in his eyes.

A second orb followed, then another, each taking its place beneath a raised tube along the walls. Brand turned, his tear-blurred gaze taking in the scene. Hundreds of shimmering lights flitted down from the pattern above, routed through the crystalline walls like fireflies drawn by an unseen force. Each was captured and held in place beneath its respective tube.

Brand wanted to speak, to cry out, but his voice was heavy and choked with grief. The room became a forest of trembling lights, every platform now occupied by a pulsating sphere of pure energy. Then, one by one, the mirrored glass cylinders began to lower, entombing the Lantern Lights, cutting off their radiant glow.

The luminous pattern above winked out, plunging the room into darkness. Gloom settled heavily over the chamber. The afterimages of radiant Lantern Lights still darted across Brand's vision, casting purple spots wherever he looked.

Around him, choked gasps filled the silence. He heard curses, ragged breaths, and more than a few broken whimpers. The tragedy of the moment had affected not just Brand, but all who had borne witness.

King Ezeret's voice rang out in the darkness above, addressing the captured Lantern Lights as his hands moved deftly over the console buttons. The glowing blue screen before him faintly illuminated his pale face, his whisky-brown hair.

He spoke aloud while typing the keystrokes that would translate his words into concepts the Lantern Lights could comprehend:

"Lantern Lights, I have you in my control.

For many of you this is a new and unnerving experience.

I know you are alarmed.

Fear not.

Do as I say and I will release you to your own designs once again.

Our world is in danger.

I need one thing from you.

A tool.

Men that came before me obtained it from your kind once before.

They named it 'The Codex of Proto-Cosmic Absolutes.'

Search the matrix of your peoples' collective consciousness, as I know you can.

Recall the content of this book and deliver up its meaning to the console for translation.

I command thee and give thee freedom to reach enough to recover this knowledge.

If you hesitate...

I shall deliver a pang, a vibration — harsh and uncomfortable to your kind...

Do not resist...

Your energy will be reflected and amplified against you by the energy-charged mirror within your prisons..."

A palpable psychic aura filled the room — an aura of anger and dismay. Certain cylinders shook and seemed to vibrate internally, untold forces operating within their irresistible prisons.

"Do as I say, or things will only get worse...

I now deliver the first vibration..."

A charge of radiation shot down the metallic cables and into the cylinders, its passing generating an electromagnetic field that caused Brand's hair to raise on end.

A psychic wave of sorrow radiated throughout the room in response.

"You're hurting them, you bastard!" Brand cried, his face now wet with tears.

The Mad King went on, "Hurry now...

Time progresses swiftly...

I deliver a second and amplified impulse..."

A mental wail, a psychic scream, erupted throughout the room, shaking all present to their foundations.

A pause.

King Ezeret's voice: "A third..."

One of the receiving machines clicked into operation, pouring out a stream of text on his view-screen.

"Ah," said Ezeret, his face a rictus of bliss, his pale-blue eyes wide and staring. "*You have found it.*"

He let the stream of text finish generating on the view-screen, then pressed another set of commands into the console. A reel of ancient paper, covered in text, began spooling out from a slot in the side of the view-screen.

Ezeret waited, his lean frame held in a posture of angelic rapture. "It is done. Now I shall finish reading what I started so long ago!" His hands, claw-like in the silvery light, raised the scroll of paper in triumph. Then, a shadow loomed behind him.

Brand instinctively searched for Lain at his left. There were his men, in various postures of shaken perturbation—some clutching their heads in disbelief, others on their hands and knees trying to recover. But Lain was gone.

"Royal Guards!? *The king!*" Brand called out. But, looking to his right, he saw that the nine remaining guards were in far worse condition than the toughened, dark-souled rogues of Lain's personal pick. The Royal Guards were still digesting what had happened to their companion. They were panting and trembling. Two dropped their crossbows and tottered backward as another nudged the lifeless body of his comrade with a steel boot. Yet another turned and ran screaming from the hall.

All this Brand saw in a second before glancing back to the console platform.

"No!" he cried out—not truly caring for the king, but knowing that Lain would certainly be *far worse.*

Lain was now holding Ezeret from behind, his figure tall and powerful compared to the thin, delicate frame of the mad king. Berengar snatched his heavy dagger from its sheath and threw it. It passed within inches of Lain's head.

Brand drew a throwing knife from his coat and flicked it toward the traitor. He was a split-second slower than the Outlander, but his aim was truer; if Lain hadn't instinctively jerked his head to the left, Brand's knife would have impaled him through the mouth. As it was, the small blade skimmed past Lain's jaw and severed off his left ear.

Lain roared and yanked the king's head back violently. With his other hand, he tore a razor-sharp dagger across Ezeret's throat, severing jugulars, windpipe, and all between. A fountain of bright crimson sprayed through the air, its particles catching the moonlight and sparkling like miniature specks of powdered diamond—*but far more valuable.*

The blood rained down to settle upon the console view-screens and the tiled floor before the platform. It no longer dazzled with life and light, instead becoming still and dark, a mat of oily black liquid that spoke of death.

Lain snatched up the printed transcript and began reading. Almost instantly, his expression changed—his features stiffened, growing almost wooden, while his eyes burned brighter: amber witch-fire glowing in the dimness of the hall.

It was too late for the king, but now they had to stop Lain from reading that manuscript.

A silent shadow flickered at the edge of his vision. Brand looked up and saw Lain's men, sweeping toward the remaining Royale Guards.

Brand cried out, *"Lain has killed the king!"* Then he grabbed his mother by the arm and sent her reeling behind him.

The guards, shaken and uncertain, were slow to respond. Only two managed to raise and fire their crossbows before the fast-moving rogues reached them. A burly rogue went down, a Royale bolt jutting from his left eye, his body collapsing into stillness as a pool of crimson spread beneath his downturned face. A second rogue caught a bolt in a mailed forearm and rolled to the floor, tugging at it.

The six unharmed rogues continued their death-sprint toward the guards, vicious weapons at the ready.

Four of the eight Royale Guards panicked and ran for the door. The remaining four dropped their crossbows, drew longswords, and rushed to meet Lain's men.

The injured rogue grunted and tore the bolt free, then let out a vicious chortle, holding the bloody shaft up like a trophy. His laughter turned to panic as he caught the flash of Berengar's heavy

blade thundering toward his face. A split second later, there were
only six rogues left in the hall.

Now, the rogues beset the remaining guards like six panthers
attacking a herd of water buffalo. The guards were more heavily
armored, but the rogues' small, quick blades found every gap.

By the time Berengar reached them, two guards were already
down—one bleeding from a slit throat, the other with a knife
buried in his eye. Two rogues broke off and turned to face
Berengar, but the golden-haired giant hit them like a thunderclap,
his great sword carving silver crescents with each stroke.

His first blow sent the upper half of one rogue's head flying like
a tossed discus. The second avoided the same fate by throwing
himself backward with desperate speed.

Cil caught up to Berengar and landed a spinning blow to the
back of a rogue's head just as he withdrew his dagger from a dying
guard. The force of her strike sent blood streaming from the
rogue's ears and his spirit soaring free from his body.

Brand dashed past the skirmish, Alucard in tow, heading toward
the platform where Lain stood, still as a statue, his amber eyes fi
xed on the scroll. He was making strange noises — hisses and
sucking gasps deep in his throat.

"*Look out, Brand!*" cried his mother.

A black hulk stepped into view, blocking his path. Braak—the
most brutal fighter in all the Wagglers. He towered at six-foot-
seven and over three hundred eighty pounds. Leather armor
reinforced with chain covered his torso and thighs, and steel-plated
gauntlets protected his arms. His face was dark, brooding, scarred
from a hundred brawls. In his hands, two short swords looked like
mere daggers.

A glance to the right told Brand that Berengar and Cil were
occupied. The final Royal Guard had fallen. Berengar fought two
Wagglers, holding them back with powerful strokes. Cil went toe-

to-toe with another.

Brand was alone.

Braak raised both swords, grinning wickedly. "Your Life String has finally run out, *Brand.* I'll carve up your kidneys for dinner."

Brand gulped and raised his short sword and dagger. They looked pitiful compared to Braak's great hulk. *So this is where it ends?* He thought.

A quiet mutter sounded at his side. Alucard stepped forth, head level with Brand's belt, a small webbed hand pointing at Braak. Braak looked amused.

The muttering reached a crescendo and ended with a sucking sound—and that familiar warping of the air Brand would never grow used to.

Braak's amusement turned to horror as he was launched like a comet toward the cathedral's ceiling, four hundred feet above. A distant crunch and a splatter of red marked his end.

Brand turned to Alucard, stunned. "Alucard, did I tell you I *love you?*"

"Not often enough."

"Was that a *joke?* No time for *jokes!* Let's get to Lain!" He smiled and tugged Alucard onward.

But Alucard tugged back. "It's too late now, Father. Lain has already read too much. We must join Cil and Berengar, *or all is lost.*" Something in his tone froze Brand's breath.

Without hesitation, Brand grabbed him, pivoted, and dashed to their companions, who were finishing the last of the Wagglers.

Then he felt Alucard drag behind. Brand looked down. Alucard was thumbing through the wizard's spellbook.

"Al, we must hurry! You said we had to reach the others!"

"I know, Father—but I *must* do this too."

Brand scooped up the three-foot creature and ran. Alucard, cradled in his arms, flipped through the pages at an inhuman rate.

Moments later, they were all together, in formation. They didn't know what to expect—but they were ready.

Alucard began to chant. The syllables twisted the air. This time, the spell warped the minds of those *near* the caster, not just the wielder. But Alucard seemed undisturbed, focused, lips moving faster and faster until they blurred.

At that moment, the world around them vanished — not by Alucard's doing.

Despite all Brand, Cil, and Berengar had faced, their minds would have cracked then and there if not for the familiar mutterings of Alucard...

Chapter 21
"Lain Locke."

The state of the house was a complete mess--*even for Drift's End.*

I found the poor lad crying, covered in blood, in the bag room. His face had been gashed pretty badly. Found the mother in the next room, cutting herself up with a large shard of mirror glass. Her eyes were wild--real eerie-like. Never could get used to them lunatics' eyes.

I locked her up in the district brig until she calmed down--didn't know what else to do with her. Got the boy cleaned up.

I know they'll release her in a few days, and she'll go right back to that home. Nothing else can be done--kid's got no one else.

But mark my words: nothing good'll come of it.
Incident Report
Drifts End Constable J.C.

***

The vaulted hall was gone. Swept away like a folding canvas. In its place: infinity. An expanse of pure white. No time, no mass, no sound. Only Brand, Cil, Berengar, and Alucard remained, standing in formation like a stone in a river.

"What is this place?" Brand asked, shaken.

"Lain has removed the natural fundamentals of our world. At least for us—*here* and *now*. I do not know what happened *elsewhere*," Alucard replied calmly.

Brand opened his mouth, but something above caught his eye. A dark speck hovered high in the whiteness. It moved—or focused —or simply *was* closer.

It was Lain Locke. His hair hung loose in luxurious curls. His amber eyes were wide and blissful. His face, flawless. The scar was gone. The ear, restored. Gone was the leather armor. In its place, flowing robes of green and white silk, a golden mantle across his shoulders. His outfit glittered with jewels — diamonds, rubies, and emeralds most of all.

Lain addressed them. His voice was calm, haughty, but with a strange, tinny echo.

"I have done it, Brand. I am now a *god*."

"No matter what you read, Lain, you're not a god. You're *crazy* for reading that manuscript."

"Crazy? No. *Empowered, enlightened* certainly. But never *crazy*. For the first time, I see things as they *are*—not as they appear, Brand, but as they *are*." Lain raised a hand and looked into it. "Flowing vibrations. All malleable to my intentions."

"Sorcery of the most *vile* degree!" cried Berengar, his eyes wide and panicked, his mouth foaming from sheer agitation.

The iron rod shook in Cil's hands and she was perspiring heavily. Her face was pale and wan. Even the normally tough and resilient girl was greatly disturbed—and understandably so.

Brand himself would have fainted or gone insane already, had his peculiar survival mechanism not taken over, driving him to superhuman mental clarity—for the sole purpose of sheer self-preservation, of course.

"I can control everything now. The very fabric of space and matter is a mere plaything to my thoughts. Gone is other-causality," Lain continued, as if narrating a story to them. His voice seemed to come from all directions at once.

Some part of that ultra-survival intelligence in Brand told him to immediately take a shot at Lain's certainty.

"Well, we're still here, Lain, so obviously you're not as in control as you *think*."

Though Brand tried to sound confident, his voice cracked and rose an octave or two mid-delivery.

Lain paused, a look of shocked realization on his face. "Well," he said, attempting to dismiss the concept, "that is an *easy* fix. Now I shall think you away. *Begone.*" He waved a hand and stared at them intently for a moment. Nothing. "What is this stubborn defiance?! You are my subjects! Now, *obey* your god!"

But rage as he might, nothing happened.

Then, Lain turned the full intensity of his lambent eyes upon Alucard, as if only just noticing the creature's presence.

"Ah. *He* defies me with a spell."

"What's he talking about, Al?" Brand asked.

"I am maintaining a 'zone of causality' about us. But, please, think of something quickly, Father. The spell weaves and bucks under my influence. I do not know how long I can control it."

"Well, no matter," Lain continued, almost absentmindedly. "It seems I'll just have to resort to conventional methods—for now."

He glared at Brand.

"Let's see if you can keep up with me now, Brand. An *ear* for an *ear?* An *eye* for an *eye?* A *hand* for six *hands?*"

As he said the word *hands*, he held out his two hands, and each held a wicked curved knife. His limbs blurred, his arms multiplying. He now had *six* arms, all holding the same pair of curved daggers.

Lain cackled.

"Or should I say three *bodies* for three *bodies?*"

Mirror-perfect duplicates split from the original and floated on either side of him. Where there had been one Lain, now there were three. Each smirked and hurled taunts and curses at Brand and the others.

Another stroke of genius, born out of sheer desperation, came into Brand's mind.

"But which is the real one, *Lain?* What if *you* are just a copy now?"

Lain laughed—then suddenly frowned. The other two Lains seemed to consider the idea. They turned on each other and the original, each attempting to assert dominance.

The original Lain let out a wail of dismay—and instantly, an endless blanket of Lains filled the white space around them, blotting out the light. All vying for supremacy.

A chaos of voices blended into a buzzing, unintelligible audio vibration. Then, a single scream cracked through it like a whip.

The duplicates vanished. Once again, there was a single Lain — pale, shaken. He had almost lost control.

Brand cried out, "You're unstable, Lain! You can barely control yourself, let alone anything else!"

Lain stared back, his face folding and creasing with his madness.

"Why are you *always* against me, Brand? Don't you see Ezeret wasn't fit to rule? He denied the people of Drift's End the protection of the city proper. No one has lived inside those walls for *centuries!* The nobles died out long ago—if they ever existed! A privileged few held charge of this dead city, lording it over us! *I* will protect us *all*—from people like Ezeret, from monsters like *that* creature in your midst that has bewitched your minds, from the great ruination the King spoke of... I do this for *you*, Brand. For *you*."

"Is that what you told Teravan, before you drove your knife into his back?"

"Into his back? No, Brand. Teravan went for a little swim in a well."

Lain waved his hand.

The familiar figure of Teravan materialized, slouched in a wooden chair twenty paces away. Once a ruggedly handsome man in his late forties, now his gray eyes stared vacantly from a face bloated with long exposure to water. They were the eyes of the damned—opaque, glazed. His feet were bound in a single large lead boot filled with hardened plaster.

Brand blanched.

"Lain, *you bastard.*"

Lain laughed cruelly.

"Your naive tricks won't keep you alive this time, *Brand.* I will *end* this resistance. Then, I shall rule over the world as its one and true *god!*"

"Get ready," grumbled Berengar, sensing the shift.

Alucard spoke up, beads of sweat forming on his round, rubbery head.

"I maintain a five-foot spherical radius of space. Beyond this, the natural laws of our world do not apply."

"Stand in a triangle around Alucard. Protect him at all costs," said Berengar.

"You can't beat us, Lain. You're weak. You can't even control your own thoughts," said Brand, still goading.

Lain laughed.

"Your mental games won't work on me now, Brand. Already I feel my power stabilizing. Now... how about an audience?—to watch as I carve you and your friends *limb from limb.*"

He grinned and snapped his fingers.

Beside Teravan's corpse appeared Brand's mother, sitting in another wooden chair. She was alive, but unmoving, her eyes rolling sideways to observe her ghastly company. She whimpered, trembled, but couldn't move. Then she caught sight of Brand and locked eyes with him, tears beginning to form.

"Leave my mother out of this, dog!" Brand shouted, losing control.

"Easy now, Brand. I could atomize her with a thought. Be thankful I'm keeping her alive—*just a little bit longer.* Now... who else do you care about? *Ah, yes.*"

He snapped his fingers again.

Barthinol appeared beside her, red-faced and terrified, held in a chair by invisible bonds. He glared at Brand, his eyes screaming for answers. (Barthinol, was an innkeeper in Drift's End, who had looked out for Brand since his youth. The uncle or grandfather Brand never had.)

For Brand, it was a nightmare made flesh. *"Bartha!"*

Lain chuckled.

"Hmmm. A bit dull, isn't it? My victory deserves fanfare. Hmm... a string quartet should do. But oh my, we are missing a member. Who shall be on the cello?"

"I know..." He snapped his fingers.

The pale corpse of King Ezeret appeared beside Barthinol. His head hung lopsided, barely connected. His blue eyes were glassy. His mouth frozen in the blissful rictus of death. A great ragged gash split his throat, his robe soaked in blood down to the waist.

"There. Ladies and gentlemen—and frog-misfits—behold our honored musicians."

He gestured grandly to the grotesque quartet.

"Now!" he went on. "*The instruments.*"

He snapped his fingers again.

Teravan jerked upright, held by invisible strings. A viola appeared in his arms.

Brand's mother yelped as unseen forces forced a violin to her chest. The same with Barthinol.

Finally, a finely carved cello appeared in Ezeret's lap.

Brand had the fleeting, terrible thought that the Mad King would've appreciated the joke.

Lain continued, "The musicians are in place. The heretics stand defiant. He, of pure and just intention, shall strike down the villainous rebels with a single blow. The stage is set. *Let the show begin!*"

Lain closed his eyes, overcome with ecstasy. He raised his hands like a conductor and made a series of elaborate gestures.

Since when did the dog know musical theory? Brand wondered. *The dog must been studying...*

On cue, the quartet began to play — a piece that would be rediscovered two and a half eons later and become known as *La Tempesta di Mare*. It began with calm: violins trilling above the cello's sway. Then the viola joined in with haunting harmonies that warned of danger to come.

Lain floated fifty paces above them, eyes closed, humming along, arms slicing the air.

Then he opened his eyes.

"Now, how about some visuals?"

He flicked his hands to and fro, hither and thither.

Pillars of fire erupted, mile-high. Colors churned around them — a storm of particles, a kaleidoscope. They stood at the center of it, on a small white platform with the four companions and the ghoulish musicians.

Above them stood Lain, the master conductor of reality. Beyond the circle, chaos. All of it moving in rhythm with the music.

Lain held out his arms and laughed. Then, the next time Brand blinked, Lain was right before him, his arm lashing out with a dagger thrust aimed at Brand's heart.

Berengar parried the blow with his longsword. "Stay focused, wolf!"

As quickly as Lain had appeared, he vanished again.

Brand heard Cil grunt as she parried a strike that came instantly from her left. Then Berengar. Then Brand. Round and round it went. Lain appeared, slashed, stabbed, and withdrew again from the bubble of causality, only to reappear from another random angle.

Brand noted that Lain couldn't appear in more than one place while part of him was within the bubble. Still, the companions—especially Brand—were hard-pressed to avoid the attacks. Each strike came without warning, from some unpredicted direction, and gave them only an instant to react.

Now, as Lain struck again, Berengar's lightning reflexes lashed out and severed the rogue's hand from his arm. A fountain of blood sprayed across Brand's face. Lain screamed and yanked the stump from Alucard's zone of protection. Almost instantly, his arm was whole again, his clothing intact, unsullied.

He let out a demonic chuckle of triumph—and continued the assault.

Lain became a blur of motion, appearing and disappearing with such speed that Brand, Cil, and Berengar had no time to think. They fell into a reactive rhythm—a combat pattern born of sheer survival instinct, held together by their training as a trio.

Brand focused on defense. The rest of the world fell away. His vision tunneled. No thought now—only action.

The quartet began to play faster and faster, the piece evolving into a storm of sound, like rising winds over turbulent seas. Somewhere beyond the plateau, a strange and hellish drum began to thunder.

The violins screamed, pounding out jagged, irregular rhythms.

In an odd flash of clarity, Brand saw Ezeret's corpse playing feverishly on the cello. The pale hands flew across the instrument's neck, guided by Lain's unseen puppet strings. The glassy eyes stared into Brand's soul as the severed head bobbed to the tempo, mouth frozen in that madman's rictus.

The three companions parried, countered, dodged — a blur of motion, a knot of wildcats fighting back-to-back against an invisible attacker. Individual blows blurred together. Sweat drenched them. Their chests heaved. Their veins throbbed, bulged.

The music grew manic. The puppet musicians jerked in time to the frenzy. Brand's mother and Barthinol were barely conscious, locked in stupor — but they could not stop.

The storm raged on.

Alucard cried out, "I cannot hold the spell much longer!"

Brand, Cil, and Berengar couldn't respond. They were locked in the defense of their lives.

Lain laughed—tireless, relentless.

The music, the attacks, the chaos—all surged in mad harmony, rising to a sense-numbing crescendo.

Alucard staggered, faltered, almost dropped to his knees.

The bubble wavered, then shrank.

It was no longer large enough to contain all of them.

Lain saw it instantly. He stopped mid-assault and hovered above them—untouched, not even sweating.

With a cruel smile, he raised a finger and pointed at Berengar.

Berengar tensed.

"Go to *hell!*" cried Lain.

Brand reached toward his friend, instinct taking over, expecting a shout of agony or some fierce reaction from his friend—but Berengar didn't scream. There was not shout or roar. No explosion... He just stared at Brand for a second, perplexed...
Then he was gone.
Deleted from existence, like a dream upon waking...

Brand screamed, his mind caving inward.

Berengar had always been the constant. Since leaving Revilis Ko'hur, he had always been there—a constant source of stability. *And now he was gone.*

"Please, Father," Alucard said with a gasp. "I can't hold it any longer. You, Cil, and I will meet the same fate if you don't think of something."

Brand, roused by the sound of his charge's voice, clawed his way back from the brink of unconsciousness.

He looked around. His mother. Barthinol. Cil. Alucard. The corpses of Ezeret and Teravan.

Above, Lain hovered, his scowl frozen in mocking delight.

Brand had to act—*before everyone else met the same fate...*

A wisp of an idea came to him—faint, desperate, improbable.

He went for it.

Brand frowned thoughtfully and said, "Lain. Your power is *truly* dangerous."

"To everyone but *me*, yes! Did you not see what happened to your friend, Brand? That's what he gets for chopping off my arm. Each of your companions will go the same way. *One by one.* Then your mother. Then you."

Brand kept his tone calm, curious.

"But surely, Lain... could it really be true that *anything* is possible? *Anything* you imagine?"

Lain beamed. "Of course. Indeed it is!"

"So whatever you think really *becomes* real?... Aren't there limits?"

"No, Brand. There are *no* limits to my power—as you've seen!"

"But doesn't that make it dangerous for *you*, too?"

"You can't win this debate, Brand."

"No, really, Lain... didn't you *lose* control earlier?"

"So what? I took it back. Now I *am* the master of all."

"But what if you couldn't? Imagine that."

"Absurdities!" Lain flicked his head back and laughed, triumphant.

"But..." Brand pressed.

"But *what*? There's nothing you can do, Brand."

"But what if you accidentally imagined *imagining* yourself out of existence *forever*?"

Lain laughed again—louder than ever.

Then stopped.

His eyes widened. His face froze in a rictus of pure terror...

Then—he was gone.

A strange sucking pop, like a cork pulled from a wine bottle...

And just like that, reality settled around them.

They were back.

Back in the ruined hall at the center of the dead city of Revilis Ko'hur.

There lay King Ezeret's corpse. His mother. Barthinol. Teravan.

Everything else Lain had created—the quartet, the chairs, the instruments—gone.

Brand collapsed to the cold floor, utterly spent.

Cil and Alucard dropped beside him.

A profound melancholy washed over him, compounding the exhaustion.

From somewhere far off, a voice: "Brand!? *Brand?!*"

His mother's voice.

Another voice...

"Brand?! *Lad?!*"

Barthinol...

Then—darkness.

When Brand came to, the silvery moonlight had been replaced by the golden light of midday, glowing through the crystal ceiling.

His mother and Barthinol were there, dabbing his forehead with a wet cloth — god knows where they found it.

There, beside him, sat Cil. Dirt-faced, bloody, beaten. Loyal.

There, on his other side, Alucard, still cloaked in that oversized black robe.

He looked up at Brand with concern. "You're awake, Father. I was worried," he said.

Cil grunted and gave him a soft fist-punch to the shoulder. "I'm sorry, Brand..." she said, green eyes rimmed with tears.

"Berengar... he's *gone,*" said Brand.

Cil wiped a tear from her eye as it formed. "I know."

Alucard looked down at his small, chubby hands glumly. "It's... it's my *fault,* Brand. I... I couldn't hold the spell... It was my first time trying this one... I... I've been practicing retaining two spells since keel like you asked Brand... But...I... failed..."

"Don't say that, Al!" said Cil sternly. "You did your best."

"No... I... I had to *choose.* I had to *choose* one of you to go. Brand is my father... and... well, I didn't think he'd want *you* to go... So... My choice decided Berengar's death."

Such a display of emotion from Alucard, who until now had shown very little, was enough to pull Brand out of his own misery and care for his charge.

"No, Al. This was Lain's doing." Brand put an arm around Alucard and tried to put on a brave face for the stricken creature. "You did good Al. You did good."

In spite of his bluff sentiment, the rest of the day was a blur for Brand. He vaguely recalled his mother and Barthinol advising rest, the comforting words of Cil, and wandering through the empty streets of Revilis Ko'hur, back to Drifts End. Once they were outside the wall, Barthinol took them to his inn in Drifts End—Barthinol's Den.

These events happened around Brand as a vague dream—a dream in which he was merely a spectator. Mostly all he saw were repeating visions of Berengar's face, in all of its various altitudes and expressions, juxtaposed by the image of him fading into nothing. The memories of their adventures together played over and over in his mind, and his ears rang with haunting echoes of Berengar's cheerful laughter.

That evening, Brand, Cil, and Alucard sat at a table in Barthinol's Den. Brand was miserably drinking from a tankard of Barthinol's best liquor. Cil and Alucard sat across from him, silent and morose, not knowing how to comfort the blond-haired youth.

They had the whole den to themselves—Barthinol had emptied it out, and the rest of the usually-packed tables were quiet and patron-less.

Barthinol was tending to Brand's mother in a sleeping chamber at the back of the den—apparently the king had forced her to sing for long periods of time, at times for multiple days on end. Thankfully, he had done nothing else to her, and all she needed was some solid rest.

Brand, however, was suffering from a different kind of damage. His stomach churned with grief, and he dully wondered when the pain of his loss would go away. He stared blankly down into the golden liquor in his cup. Its colors swirled and glowed as they reflected the light of a nearby lantern. Strange—the glow seemed unusually bright. He squinted up suspiciously. Just a regular lantern.

He looked back into the liquor, intrigued. There! It was definitely brightening. The glare reflecting from his cup seemed almost to hurt his eyes now. Suddenly, he looked up. Directly above his head hovered a small, glowing ball of light—a miniature sun. A Lantern Light!

Somehow Brand knew at once that it wasn't just any Lantern Light—it was the very same one he had freed from the great hall above the Sunken Tundra. The only one that had not been driven mad. It bobbed cheerfully in front of his face, seemingly happy to see him. Now, it began a slow orbit around his head.

"Oh, it likes you, Brand!" said Cil, a small chuckle of pure joy bursting from her lips. She stared at the globe of light, her clear eyes filled with fascination.

The mere presence of the thing seemed to comfort Brand, and he found himself momentarily lifted from his melancholy. "Why, what are you doing here?"

A thought was impressed upon Brand's mind—a concept of himself, Cil, and Alucard removing the artifact from the great hall in Revilis Ko'hur; the Lantern Lights being freed from their prisons and winking out of existence—back to wherever they came from.

"Yes. Yes, that's right. We freed your friends."

The thing bobbed up and down and did a few more orbits around Brand's head. By the look on Cil's and Alucard's faces, the concepts had also reached their minds.

Another impression came to Brand: an image of himself, looking sad and morose.

"Yes. That's me," answered Brand with a wry smile.

"I think it's asking why you are sad, Brand," said Alucard.

Brand tried to think the thoughts back at the creature. "My friend. Berengar. He's dead." He said and thought.

The thing shook back and forth, as if disputing the fact.

"No, he's gone, you silly thing. I saw him vanish."

A series of complex concepts hit Brand's mind one after the other, but he failed to follow them.

"I don't understand," he said, looking at Cil and Alucard.

Cil shook her head, as confused as Brand.

Alucard suddenly grinned, his eyes bright. "Brand, it said that Berengar is not technically dead. By removing the natural laws of this world, Lain brought about a condition where whatever he thought became true."

"Yes. That's the *issue,* Alucard."

"Yes, but what exactly *did* he say to Berengar?"

Brand paused, a strange trickle of hope building in his stomach. "He said, 'Go to *hell.*'"

"Exactly," said Alucard.

"So, he sent him to hell? Isn't that the same as dying?"

"No," said Alucard, becoming even more didactic. "Hell is technically a proposed dimension, filled with dire creatures, such as demons and devils—I have seen snippets of information in my book—references to other places dubbed as 'hells' by *The Ancients*. But Lain didn't know anything about those. So the real question is: what was '*hell*' to Lain?"

"You lost me at dimension," said Brand.

"What I gathered from the Lantern Light just now was that, to Lain, hell was a concept he evolved based on the folklore he was given as a boy. Likely an exact and personalized concept that had no real-world duplicate. What the Lantern Light is saying is that, when Lain unlocked the laws of this world—with the Codex of Proto-Cosmic Absolutes—his thoughts became the ultimate causality. Existence, to comply with his uninformed command, was forced to create a new realm to fulfill his concept. Lain's own version of hell was materialized in the form of another unique dimension."

Brand looked back at the Lantern Light. "So, where *is* Berengar then?"

An image, a concept, a feeling—all at once—hit Brand like a dream.

A wild and desolate landscape stretched as far as the eye could see. Great, stark bluffs of red stone dotted an endless desert of coppery sand. Active volcanoes polluted the skylines in every direction. There, on a bluff three hundred feet above the desert below, stood a lone, barbaric figure. His bronzed chest muscles reflected the red light of a strange sun high above. In one hand, he held a huge gleaming greatsword.

Toward him, on the desert below, rushed a horde of misshapen creatures—some with three legs, some six, some twenty, others hopping on one. On and on, the mass surged like a carpet of insects, blackening the earth.

The man was grinning down at the approaching horde, his long hair billowing in the smoking-hot wind. It was Berengar, and he looked to be enjoying himself.

Brand leapt to his feet. "He's still *alive!*—But for how long? We must find him. He could be killed at any minute in a place like that!"

"Perhaps not so easily," said Alucard. "Who knows how time passes there, or how the laws of that realm work? It's quite possible that he will adapt to the realm, gaining unique faculties for his survival."

"This is great news!" cried Cil, leaping up and shaking Brand by the shirt. She then smiled awkwardly and released him, stepping back.

Brand smiled back at her and nodded, tears of joy filling his eyes. He turned back to the Lantern Light. "Thank you, friend. But how do I get to this place?"

A series of complicated concepts flashed through Brand's mind. He looked to Alucard, confused once again.

Alucard explained, "There are a series of spells we must locate. I must learn them. After that, we must learn the precise coordinates of any dimensions that closely mirror Lain's creation. After this, we must make an educated guess, bridge a hole, and 'hop' across. If we get it right we will still... well, *exist.*"

"*Huh,*" said Brand. "Well... I like not the sound of that. But, whatever it takes..." Brand turned to the Lantern Light. "One more question. I know you came to thank me for helping your friends this time... but you helped me before. Why did you help me? Why *me,* rather than Berengar or Cil?"

The small sun bobbed up and down, then projected another image into Brand's mind: A tall, lean man in black leather pants and a fashionable white blouse stood in a clearing, bright, sun-dappled forest stretching out in all directions. The man was surrounded by at least twenty Lantern Lights, bobbing and orbiting around him. He had unruly blond hair, bright-green eyes, and a great blond beard.

Another image followed, showing the same man in a great hall, similar to those Brand had encountered, but different. His face was lined and creased with worry as he stared down at a blue-lighted screen. He turned and hastily tore free the cylindrical power cell from its slot at the back of the platform. Two hundred Lantern Lights were set free.

Another similar scene played, and another, and another.

Brand was gobsmacked. He turned to Cil and Alucard. "You don't suppose..."

"The chances are..." said Alucard.

"Yes... I believe that must be your father, Brand," said Cil, her eyes bright. "He has been helping the Lantern Lights for a long time..."

"..." Brand found it hard to speak. Then, finding his voice he croaked, "How many of those terrible places exist out there?"

"Who knows," said Cil with a grimace.

"I wonder if there are more spell books left around in those places," said Alucard, his interest suddenly piqued.

"Now, now. Just because you saved the day doesn't mean you can go whole-hog on this spell business. Didn't you learn how dangerous these things are after seeing what happened to Ezeret, Lain, and The Ancients?"

Alucard shrugged. "That was *The Codex of Proto-Cosmic Absolutes*—the very delineation of the fundamental makeup of reality *itself!*—At least in *this* universe... I just want to learn a few more spells to help your father."

Brand frowned. "Well, I guess that would be fine. They have been uncommonly useful..."

"Thank you again, for everything, my friend."

The Lantern Light bobbed twice, as if in response, then winked out of existence.

After a long pause, Brand turned to Cil and Alucard, trying to act nonchalant. "I feel I owe it to Ber. He saved my life more times than I can count." He hunched his shoulders and looked away. "Alucard, would you mind helping me find Berengar? The journey will be dangerous, but... I can't do it without you."

"That's a given," came Alucard's voice from behind him.

"Thanks, Al."

"I'm coming too." said Cil.

"You, sure?" said Brand, his back still turned.

"Of course I am, you idiot beanstalk!" But her words lacked their usual bite.

Brand clenched his fists. A few tears splattered onto the floor before his feet, wetting the wooden planks. "*Cil?*"

"Yes, Brand?"

"Thanks."

"You're welcome, Brand."

Brand shoved down his emotions and looked up at the warm light of the lantern hanging above him with a smile. "Al?"

"Yes?"

"Would you start teaching me how to use *magic?*"

The End.

<h1 style="text-align:center">Epilogue</h1>

On Eighth Avenue, a short, squat man wearing a brown trench coat and fedora walked into the Times Square Diner.

The maître d' of the place looked down at the man with a frown. The man's trench coat covered his entire body and was a little too long, dragging on the ground slightly. He wore black leather gloves on his hands, though it wasn't cold out. His brown fedora was pulled low, covering much of his face. A pair of large black sunglasses obscured the rest, along with a black beard that looked too stiff—could it be fake?

"A table for one, good sir—a private booth, preferably," said the man. His voice was strangely clipped and bore a faint, odd accent.

Deciding the man was harmless, despite his strange dress, the waiter took him to a secluded booth as requested.

"Any drinks to start off, sir?" asked the waiter.

"Yes. A double shot of Jack."

The waiter looked at the clock on the wall. It was 11:00 a.m., and on a Tuesday, too. Well, he thought, each to their own. He walked away to get the man's drink.

The man pulled out a writing pad and pen, both seeming overlarge in his small, gloved hands.

He muttered to himself, "Where should I start? Should I tell of how I secretly watched my own birth, from a pocket of extra-dimensional space? And how I conceptually projected the name of one of my favorite anime characters into my father's mind, forcing him to choose it for my own name?—And how this slight temporal interference likely brought about the entire Queen Charlotte affair?"

He scratched at his chin—it was itchy from the fake beard. "No, not that. How about when I saved the world, with the spell *Fingalad's Pocket of Stable-Causality*?" He paused. "No. It would be bad taste to brag. I think I will start from the beginning of my father's adventure—shortly after he left Revilis Ko'hur for the first time. So long ago now—but then again, time is of no consequence these days. Yes, my dear father—his is the story I shall write."

The waiter dropped off his double shot of Jack, then hesitated, eyeing the short man shrewdly.

"Are you sure you're old enough?"

The short man's only answer was a strange series of alien syllables, hissed under his breath. A small ripple warped through the air, causing the bar clock to skip a beat. The waiter's face became emotionless, like that of a mannequin. He turned mechanically away and walked back to the bar.

The short man downed the double shot of Jack in one gulp, raised his pen, and began to write:

"The Living Light: From Gods to Ashes..."

FOR MORE FROM THIS AUTHOR

Thank you for reading *The Living Light: From Gods to Ashes*. If you enjoyed this book, more stories, worlds, and adventures await you.

Audiobook
Experience *The Living Light: From Gods to Ashes* in its full dramatic narration from Blackstone Publishing at:
www.downpour.com/the-living-light-from-god-s-to-ashes

More Books by Taliesin J. De Launey
Darkmaw: A Banquet of the Fairies — an eerie, dreamlike horror story set in rural Japan, blending folklore and surreal dread. Available now at: www.amazon.com *(search "Darkmaw A Banquet of the Fairies")*

Connect with the Author on Substack
Stay up to date with upcoming novels, short stories, and behind-the-scenes insights into the worlds I create:
https://alucardjdelauney.substack.com